Vengeance!

Aaron Michael
Nitterer

Penny Dread Tales
VOLUME IV

PERFIDIOUS AND PARANORMAL PUNKERY OF STEAM

Cover Art & Design
by
Kathryn S. Renta

Edited
by
Christopher Ficco

RuneWright, LLC Publishing
Aurora, Colorado

CONTENTS

Penny Dread Tales
VOLUME IV

PERFIDIOUS AND PARANORMAL
PUNKERY OF STEAM

FOREWORD

Christopher Ficco

When I put together the first *Penny Dread Tales*, I hadn't the slightest inkling there would be a fourth volume, and in as many years. They're time-consuming, with a fair amount of admin work and chasing down bits and pieces ... like bios and artwork and PayPal addresses and real mailing addresses. And then there's the reading of all the submissions and editing those that will be included. There's working with the artists to get the cover right (thanks to Laura Givens for cover #1 and Kathryn Renta for everything she's done with the remaining three current covers). There are lots of I's to be dotted and T's to be crossed.

If you ever met me, you would probably guess right away that I'm not what you would call an "admin" sort of guy. And yet, I've kept doing these anthologies, and the intention is to keep doing them each year, although I really do need to get better at making AnomalyCon as my due-date. Maybe next year.

So why? Why do I keep spending the hours I do putting these together when I could be writing? Well, some would shout out the guess, "For the money!" To which I would politely smile and oh-so-subtly shake my head. I sell copies, to be sure, but it's Taco Bell money after all the costs are factored in. Granted, I can eat a lot of Taco Bell, and I do, but that's beside the point.

I do these anthologies for two reasons, and two alone. The first is the excitement and satisfaction I get when I read emails from writers who were accepted, many of whom placed their first short story sales in a Penny Dread volume. The second is because I *love* the stories that have been included thus far. I enjoyed reading them, even editing them, such as I did. There are some great stories and some good stories. There are even a few that other editors would possibly turn their noses up at.

I have a different take on the editorial process. Some editors look for only those stories that are not only visceral but which follow today's concept of "the formula." In the same way I am not an "admin" guy, I'm even less of a "formula" guy. I don't like rules, and I abhor the cookie-cutter notion of fitting stories to industry-accepted molds.

The *Penny Dread Tales* series has been a platform for different kinds of writing. Some very different. But in each and every story I've found voice, distinct voice indicative of the writer who was kind enough to send me a story.

This year's batch of submissions was even more special. I had authors asking me if they could submit ... authors whom I respect a great deal. As my girlfriend can attest, I question my endeavors every day. The anthologies, the writing ... all of it ... I'm constantly wondering if I should even be in this business. The interest of these authors in *Penny Dread Tales* is a validation for me, a victory of sorts for someone who could use a few.

So it is with a great deal of honor and even more humility that I present to you *Penny Dread Tales Volume IV: Perfidious and Paranormal Punkery of Steam.* I consider myself truly fortunate to be the one who gets to share this collection of steampunk tales with you, and I hope you enjoy them all as much as I did.

— Christopher Ficco

DOWN ON VENGEANCE CREEK

Aaron Michael Ritchey

[signature]

You wake up, now, Jasp."

The voice shook me to the hurt, and Lord, did I hurt right then, every part of me, even my toenails. But the memories pained me worser than my body. Memories of what happened to my Lucinda and my kids, cryin' and shriekin' for me to hep. But I couldn't. I'd been tied down, shot up, cut upon, over and over.

I figured the flames of my house burnin' down would kill me, but it wuzn't so.

I found myseff lyin' on a wood table, splinters diggin' into my back. The memories made me cry. Then I got mad. I lurched forward, but chains snapped me back. I'd known chains when I worked cotton, as we all did, all us slaves.

Tears on my face, but a rage in my belly, I hollered, "You let me up now, so I can kill every last one of you!"

Low laughter, but not mean—understandin' wuz there in that laugh, understandin' of someone who knew what chains felt like.

"Thass what I need you to do, Jasp. Thass the spirit. But you iz gonna hurt. I'z sorry for that, but ain't nothin' I can do. You gots to have a clear head for what you gots to do."

I knew that voice. It wuz Daedalus, helluva name, but then in the West, we all got to choose our own names. Ain't no masters no more, to name us. Lincoln done set us free. But in the South, freedom didn't mean much. So we went out to Wyomin', that's where I took Lucinda, Martha, Mary, and Cassius, all out west.

To farm. To pan a lil' gold out of Vengeance Creek. To be free.

I opened my eyes to look at Daedalus sweatin' over me. I wuz in his blacksmith shack, and the fire made him glow like an angel. Horseshoes hung on the walls, along with farm tools, and every type of nail and hammer you could think of. Lot of things I couldn't name, but then Daedalus wuz the best blacksmith in the territory, if not the world. Everyone said so. Folks came from a hundred miles away to have him do work for 'em.

No light 'tween the boards, so it wuz night. How'd I survive the day? It wuz autumn headin' into winter, but I wuzn't cold. Nossir. If anythin', I wuz too hot. Sweat dribbled down my face.

I shook my bonds. "Daed, why'd you chain me up?"

"Found you three days ago, Jasp. You almost dead, all burned, and in terrible pain. But I fixed you up 'cause you have a mission."

Three days dead, like our Lord Jesus. I closed my eyes and lay back. Somethin' itched in my chest. Couldn't scratch, 'cause of the chains.

"What mission, Daed? What you talkin' about?"

"Billy Callow and his men, they need to die. And you gots to do it tonight. I knowed you ain't no fightin' man, but I hope you can find it in your heart to take the lives of them dogs. 'Cause they jus' dogs, needin' to be put down."

Billy Callow and his outlaws. They got wind I'd found gold. I did. A lil'. Only a lil'. 'Twuz enough for his men to come and see how much. They took what they could and beat me, killed my kids, cryin' and shriekin' Daddy, Daddy, Daddy. Over and over.

'Til they were quiet with death. My wife wept for what they did to her, weepin' 'til they silenced here. And set fire to my house. The flames of hell. Billy Callow, face like swamp wood, laughin' in his long duster and brand-new cowboy hat. Looked like a troll, but dressed like a dandy. Goddamn that Billy Callow and his gang, half-dozen of 'em.

Pain got worser, as did the itchin', all along the leff side of my body. "I can kill 'em, Daed, I got the stomach for it, but how can I? I'z all busted up."

Daedalus didn't answer that question, but kep on talkin'. "I had to chain you so I could work. Sorry, but you wuz thrashin' all around. I

4

needed you still. To fix you. Did all the work in my secret workshop, but brought you here just 'bout an hour ago."

Visions flashed in my head, of an underground place, walls of dirt, showin' muddy. Papers, drawings, notes and numbers, staked into the clay with twigs. Shelves stocked full of complicated machinery hung about. Bottles burbled in a web of glass and tubes next to a forge and anvil. Books lay piled all about. I didn't know Daedalus' history, but I reckoned it involved whole libraries, though he didn't talk like he wuz educated. Then again, maybe his education didn't involve words, only numbers. Most of what I remembered I couldn't explain, but above all, the pain came back to me, the hurt of being burnt alive and livin' through it.

Now in Daedalus' smithy, he rattled the chains and locks 'til I heard them clatter to the floor. I raised my arm, only my right. Couldn't move nothin' up and down the leff side of my body, not my arm, not my leg.

I went to scratch at the itch on my chest, but I didn't have skin there, nossir, only metal.

Shames me to say it, but I screamed and went crazy, 'til Daedalus caught my face. He bent down close, beard on his cheeks, no hair on his bald head. His eyes were red, and he had a hiss in his mouth. "Easy, Jasp, easy there. I changed you, made you into a killin' machine. You gonna die, but you already dead, so that shouldn't worry you none. Your family's in heaven, waitin' on you. Only gonna be 'bout fifteen minutes 'fore you see 'em again. Billy Callow and his men are in the saloon 'cross the street. You hear me, Jasp? You gonna have fifteen minutes to get 'em and every minute gonna hurt you worser 'cause the firebox iz gonna get hotter and hotter in you. I'll hep you sit up, so you can see what I done."

He hepped me sit. My leff leg wuz all gone, gone forever. Instead, I had metal pistons and an iron foot. My leff arm wuz also gone, gone forever, and instead I had a hatchet connected to more pistons. My whole leff side, metal. My tattered britches covered my bottom half. On my top half, I wore a leather harness. Revolvers hung down from leather thongs.

Brass staples pinched my skin to the metal all up and down my leff side, up my belly to my chin. My flesh wuz swelled up and red 'round crusted scabs where it was fixed to the iron.

More screams rose in my throat, but I kep 'em down. "What'd you do to me?" I asked in horror.

Daedalus shook his head, sadly. "I get ideas, Jasp, strange ideas. Sometimes I think they come from the Lord, sometimes from the Devil hisseff. When I found you still alive, even with half you burned away, well, I knew what I could do. I could make you the Lord's righteous sword here on Earth. You iz partly my engineerin', partly hoodoo-voodoo from old Africa. I put a steam engine in you, Jasp, and I gots to light it up. Then you gonna move like a locomotive. No time to practice. You gonna have to learn while you go. Fifteen minutes iz all you'll get."

I kinda knew what he had done, only kinda, but 'twuz enough. I'd seen trains and knew what the chugga, chugga of the engine did to the pistons. Made me shaky to think I might be more train than man. Then again, if I thought too much about what I wuz now, I'd go bread-crumb crazy. Better to keep my mind on my hate. I'd only have fifteen minutes to put them dogs down.

The saloon wuz jus' across the muddy street from Daedalus' smithy.

"Light me up, Daed. I getcha. Light me up and point me at 'em."

He brought a burnin' stick over from the forge, and dang me if I didn't watch him open a door in my belly below my ribs. He touched the firebrand to somethin' inside. I winced, but I had so many pains, one more didn't matter.

Daedalus talked steady. "The water tank iz already filled. Gotta wait a minute for the steam to build." The itch wuzn't nothin' compared to the fire startin' to glow in my belly. Yessir, that fire wuz gonna get hotter and burn me where I wuzn't metal.

He brought over two double-barrel scatter guns, sawed short. He put one in the harness on my back and stuck the other in my leff hand.

"Blow 'em to hell, Jasp. And God bless you doin' it."

I locked eyes with that blacksmith, the last friend I'd know on earth. "God bless you, Daed, for givin' me this chance at revenge." I swore I'd get Billy Callow, Bud Davidson, Dutch Stone, Ace Custer, and the other three outlaws ridin' in that gang.

For Daed, for Lucinda, for Martha, Mary and lil' Cassius.

The engine started. Smoke belched out of a copper chimney built into my leff shoulder. The pistons started to move, hissin' steam, gettin' more violent, until my leff arm swung the hatchet down and my leff leg kicked out. Daedalus pulled me off the table. "Go, now."

My leff foot struck the floor and my right foot raced to catch up to it. Where my leff foot went, my leff arm followed, hatchet hatchetin' down. I hopped metal foot to human foot, metal foot to human foot, and on out the door.

Mud wuz all frozen in swirls of hoof-and-foot prints. I wuz grateful for the cold 'cause the heat in my belly wuz firin' up.

Only gonna get worse.

I couldn't imagine what I looked like, half-man, half-steam machine, hatchet instead of a hand, smoke and steam blowin' off into the wind. Looked like a demon, sure, but inside I wuz all avengin' angel.

I lumbered across the street and I couldn't stop, my metal limbs wouldn't let me. I bashed right through the bat-wing doors of that no-name saloon. I'd only been in there once when I wuz told I had to do my drinkin' with my own kind. Kerosene lamps glowed smoky. The bottles behind the bar looked like rat poison, and Whitfield, the bartender, kept it all watered down from the creek out back. Rough pine tables and chairs littered the room. Brass spittoons lay about stained and tarnished to a dull. One wuz turned over, and brown ooze spilled out onto the sloppy floor. The room smelled like rank men, puke and piss. Only two ways out of that ramblin' shack, the front door and the back.

The place wuz packed full. Every eye fell on me. Some men I knew, some were strangers. For a space of time, no one moved, no one said a word. Fright had shocked 'em still.

Then the saloon exploded into a racket. Chairs scraped the floor, tables were turned over, screams of fear and cursin', lots of cursin'.

No time for me to look around no more, I wuz movin' like a train. First outlaw I saw, I went for. I brought up the scatter gun and unloaded both barrels into one of Billy Callow's men in his chair. Blew two bloody holes through his chest.

My pistonin' leff leg crushed his body and I hatcheted down another of Callow's men, didn't know his name. Then another. This one had tripped over the corpse of the outlaw I'd jus' murdered, fell against me, and I axed off his head.

I'd killed swine 'fore and chopped up chickens, but I never thought I'd find myself butcherin' men. It wuz gory work, but like Daedalus had said, these outlaws were jus' mad rabid dogs needin' to be put down.

Some folks stood with mouths flappin' open, some ran for the back door, others ducked behind tables, firin' guns at me. Cinders blowin' from my chimney got stuck in my eye, and I couldn't see a thing for a minute. Bullets pinged off the metal of my body, sparked, and some found flesh, but I didn't feel nothin' but the heat from the firebox in my belly, makin' my teeth chomp against the burnin' pain.

I didn't feel powerful, nossir. Seemed like the machine in me had a mind of its own, and I wuz along for the ride. Still, I felt desperate to do my bloody work 'fore the agony overwhelmed me. I blinked 'til my sight cleared. I saw Callow and the rest of his gang, behind a table, unloading their pistols on me.

I plucked a revolver off a thong on the harness across my chest and fired back. Missed. I thumbed back the trigger and fired again. My bullet whined off somethin', but not the men I wuz tryin' to kill. I'd heard of double-action revolvers, but unlucky for me, Daedalus didn't have none to give.

All my shots were bad. I wuz movin' too fast I couldn't steady myseff to aim. So I locomotived on at 'em, hatchet a blur. Callow and his outlaws fled from the turned-over tables where they'd been takin' cover.

A big mob jammed up the back door, bottle-necked it. The gang clawed at the crowd, trying to get through.

I called out, "Billy Callow, Dutch Stone, Ace Custer, Bud Davidson, I'z here for all you, to make you pay for what you done."

The four devils turned, and oh, I saw the wide-eyed rollin' fear on their faces, and I laughed at it. I wuz thrilled, halfway done with the work. But the pain, Lord, the pain in my belly wuz gettin' worser as the firebox got hotter. I reached back and grabbed the other scatter gun from the harness and charged toward them. I used one barrel on Dutch Stone, but only got him in the side. Nearer to Bud Davidson, I hopped off my right foot, came down on my leff, and smashed the hatchet into the outlaw's skull. Hook an ax to a train, and you can understand the force at work. The blade chopped through Davidson's skull so I could see his brain. I wanted another hack at him, to bury my hatchet in that squish, but I couldn't stop.

Jus' three leff now, Callow, Dutch and Ace.

They jumped aside, and I wuz pushed up against the regular men. I didn't want to kill nobody who wuzn't an outlaw, so I turned away and buried the hatchet into a big beam of wood. It stuck there. All the pistons seized up 'cause my leg and my arm were connected. With the hatchet stuck, my leff leg got stuck too.

The pistons squealed, but they couldn't move. The pain made me scream, the pain of the firebox burnin' and the rage of me failin'. Smoke bled into my eyes. Embers from the engine popped near my ears. I couldn't see. I couldn't move.

Ace Custer grabbed me, tore me off the wall, threw me down on the ground. I landed on my leff side. Lord, I felt the fire in my belly tumble— the hot coals shiftin' to burn new parts of my insides.

My pistonin' arm and leg didn't stop, they went and went, spinnin' me 'round like a turtle on its back bein' spun by mean kids. 'Round I went, the world spinnin' in circles. I dropped the scatter gun, revolvers came undone, and still I couldn't stop.

Billy Callow spit down at me. Brown tobacco juice dripped down his chin. His nervous laughter showed his relief. "Well damn me to hell. It's that spade we kilt. Ha, up and about, he's some kind of monster, but on the floor, he ain't nothin.' Looks like that genius, spade blacksmith across the street made hisseff a Frankenstein. Well, we'll kill this un first, then the blacksmith."

Panic shocked me. No, not Daed. I had to get back up. Jus' had to. In my spin, I managed to get my eyes workin'. All the regular folks had skedaddled, even Whitfield the bartender. Billy Callow stood over me with his big Colt in his hand. Ace Custer stood next to him, lookin' green and scared, and next to him, Dutch Stone, grippin' his bleedin' side.

A gunshot roared. Hit the floor by my head.

"You fellers grab him, keep him still, and I'll put a bullet in his brain," Callow said.

I can't rightly tell of the sorrow and fury I felt at that moment. Daedalus had done his job, but I had failed to do mine. I'd be killed. Callow, Dutch, Ace, would live and more good folks would die. Includin' my friend the blacksmith.

"Jesus hep me!" I shrieked.

Heaven didn't have no answer for that. The only sound wuz the men laughin'.

I'd heard them laugh 'fore, when I'd been tied up in my house as they shot my kids. As Ace Custer raped my wife.

I wuzn't tied down now. Only had a second 'fore they grabbed me. I skittered near a wall, and on my next turn, I moved the hatchet so it splintered the thin pine. Twuz enough to stop me for a second, enough for me to flip over to my right side. My leff arm and leg kep chuggin', but I wuzn't spinnin' no more. My right hand found the scatter gun. I brought it up, stuck the barrel in Ace Custer's crotch, and pulled the trigger. He screamed and fell back. I'd splattered his manhood across the saloon floor.

I planted my leff foot against the wall, and it kicked me away. My hatchet found Dutch Stone's leg. Chopped through it and he fell in front of me. I got up on my right knee, my leff foot kickin' and kickin'. The fire slid around in my belly, and I ground my teeth against the agony, the sheer agony of my belly full of flame. Hot and gettin' hotter.

Balanced on my right arm, I let my locomotive hatchet fall again and again on Dutch Stone, splinterin' his spine until I axed through his skull and leff him almost entirely cut in half.

I skipped forward and got on my feet again. Ace Custer wept. I still had one revolver on my harness. Up close so I couldn't miss, I silenced him.

The saloon wuz empty now, and I wuz the only thing movin' and makin' noise.

Callow had fled out the back door.

I couldn't think a single clear thought. I wuz jus' pain and blood, screamin' flesh and horrific steel. And pistons goin' and goin', drivin' me to finish the work, to kill Billy Callow.

Out the back door I went, into the cold, which for a moment, made the pain lessen. Nothin' out back but sagebrush plains and Vengeance Creek, a little trickle of a river, nothin' like the mighty Mississip' back where I'd come from. Hot steam ghosted around me from the pistons slidin' up and down.

Somethin' brushed my face, and I wuz awake enough to know it wuz snow, fallin' like cotton fluff from a gray midnight sky. The snow hissed when it struck the metal of my belly now heated to a glow. I smelled somethin' cookin'.

Had Whitfield started up his grillin'? No, I realized. Horror. Horror. Horror. It wuz me that wuz cookin'. My own skin turnin' to char, and my own juices sizzlin' down.

I didn't have long. My time wuz short, but I had one more to kill. One more.

Billy Callow stood in Vengeance Creek, a bucket of water in one hand and his Colt in the other. He taunted me. "Come on, spade, come on and I'll put out your goddamn fire and end your goddamn life one last time!"

I pistoned toward him. I tried to trigger back the revolver in my right hand with my thumb, but it went awkward in my fingers and I dropped it.

Frustrated, I hollered. Callow's bullets pinged off my metal, punched my shoulder, ricocheted off rocks behind.

I splashed into Vengeance Creek, and I knew I couldn't fall. Billy Callow's bucket wouldn't do shit against the hell-fire in my belly, but if I tumbled, the water would put out the steam engine, and I'd be done.

River rocks shifted under my feet and I tripped. Callow's bucket of water hit me, and it wuz heaven sent. It cooled me for a second, so I could right myseff and not go splashin' into the creek. Still goin', I struck

Billy Callow, not with my hatchet, but with my whole body. His revolver plunked into the river. I threw an arm around him and howled. The Lord gave me strength 'cause I could not have done it on my own.

I picked him up and carried him, twistin', thrashin', cookin' him like I wuz cookin'. I got 'cross that river, but I wuz blackin' out now, dyin' my last time. If I let go of him, he'd get away. I might get heaven and my family, but I couldn't leave with such unfinished business.

I couldn't let him get away, but I wuz done. What to do?

With my last strength, I got my right hand on the hatchet handle and pulled. I pulled my metal leff arm until the pistons bent. I bent them more to break 'em, so I could make a steel hook to hold Billy Callow against me. I made a chain, partly metal, partly muscle, so he couldn't get away. With my leff arm broke, my leff leg stopped kickin'. We both struck the dirt, with me on top of him. I clutched him to my breast in an awful embrace.

I smelled the stink of both of our flesh fryin'.

He wuz screamin' as the steam engine's firebox burned at a full roar.

His screams, louder and louder.

The fire, hotter and hotter.

Screams louder.

Fire, hotter.

I growled into his face. "Holler, you son of a bitch, holler so the Devil knows to come and getcha."

And he kept on squealin' 'til death claimed us both.

About the Author

Aaron Michael Ritchey's first novel, *The Never Prayer*, was published in March of 2012 to a fanfare of sparkling reviews including an almost win in the RMFW Gold contest. Since then he's been paid to write steampunk, cyberpunk, and sci-fi western short stories, and his story, "The Dirges of Percival Lewand" has been nominated for a Hugo award. His next novel, *Long Live the Suicide King*, is currently giving hope to the masses. Kirkus Reveiws calls it a "a compelling tale of teenage depression handled with humor and sensitivity." As a former story addict and television connoisseur, he lives in Colorado with his wife and two goddesses posing as his daughters.

The Curious Case of the Frozen Revenant

Gerry Huntman

Nick Smith heard the strange cacophonous sounds emanating from behind the hill, not far from where he had set camp. This was cattle country belonging to his parents, and no one should have been there, not within twenty miles. Not legally, anyhow.

He calmed his spooked horse and carefully climbed the hill, rifle in hand. His hands were trembling. While he'd shot rattlers, coyotes and rabbits, as well as his pa's steers when the need arose, he had never fired at a man. Never needed to. He was only fourteen years old, although tall for his age, and on the shy side. His short-cropped brown hair, green eyes, and fine facial lines, were more a testament to a townsman than a rancher's son.

As Nick crept around a large rock outcrop on the apex of Williams' Hill, he expected to see a fire or light from a camp. There was nothing. He was relieved and anxious at the same time. He returned to his camp, picked up his kerosene lantern, and re-entered the neighboring gully with his light source.

There wasn't any sign of activity. No sign of explosion, no burning embers.

He was more terrified than ever. He progressed into the thick, semi-arid underbrush of the narrow gully, and despite the sweltering night, felt a cold breeze caress his right cheek. He shone his light past a large, yellow-flowering saltbush, revealing a glistening flat surface. Nick's anxiety dissipated, replaced by curiosity. He approached the unusual formation.

It was a large block of ice, the size of a coffin. *In a gully in the rugged Gila Mountains of the Arizona Territory, in the middle of summer—in the middle of nowhere.*

He tilted his lantern toward one end of the block, expecting to find something in it, already gleaning a shadow that faintly resembled a human form. He gasped as he saw through the translucent ice a man's face with the appearance of slumber … beneath a well-worn Stetson hat. There was too much ice to make out the features of the man, but he sensed that this was a dude he wouldn't want to cross … when he was alive.

Nick nearly jumped out of his skin when a second set of explosive sounds echoed from near the top of the hill he had climbed down from only minutes before. Lights flooded the surroundings, centered from where the explosion originated.

He picked up his rifle and ran up the trail, leaving his lantern on the block of ice. There was enough light glaring from the top of the hill to illuminate his path, but too much to allow him to see what was distantly ahead. He was afraid again, but he was damned if he was going to let whatever was happening to continue on his family's ranch.

He climbed to the crest, rifle poised to shoot. Light glared from strange looking lamps fixed to a carriage three times the size of a stagecoach, constructed entirely of iron. A smoke stack jutted out of the top of the contraption, near its rear.

A door opened; a portly man in a tweed suit climbed out, wearing a gold monocle, and sporting mutton chop sideburns. He smiled when he saw Nick.

"Boy, by the look of your demeanor, I would venture to guess that you have found the block of ice. Am I correct?" His accent was thickly foreign to Nick's ears, guessing it was upper class English.

Before Nick could respond, another figure appeared at the iron carriage's door. A radiantly beautiful Chinese woman, wearing traditional silk clothing, although she wore flowing trousers rather than a dress. She had a determined look about her, and yet there were signs she had been recently crying.

"How … how did you get that carriage here? Only horses—"

"Boy," the woman said, with almost faultless English, her accent had a distinct English twang, just like the tweed man, "Sir Thomas asked you a question."

"S ... sure. The block's down a ways, easy to find ... It's got a body in it."

"We know," Sir Thomas replied, hurriedly grabbing a small chest and lantern from within a storage unit on the side of the carriage. "Come with us," he ordered.

With the aid of the lamp that didn't appear to use oil, they quickly traversed the gully trail. Sir Thomas was surprisingly spritely for a man of his weight and middling years.

"Is it too late?" the Chinese woman asked of the Englishman.

"I hope not, Princess. Jacob is hardy."

Jacob. Nick only heard of one man called Jacob, from the snippets of conversations between his parents, and talk in the two streets of Clifton. A shiver ran down his spine. *No, it can't be.*

Sir Thomas was the first to get to the block. "By George, as I hoped. Astounding. The water had enveloped him, froze instantaneously, but it did not freeze his body's cells. I think we can resuscitate him."

He swiftly opened his wooden chest, pulled out two bronze discs with handles on each, both of which had wires leading back into the chest. "My Princess," he said, "can you crack the ice without placing undue impact injury on Jacob's body?"

The woman touched the block, which had already lost ten percent of its volume to the warm night. "Yes, I can do it."

"Then proceed, Your Highness. I don't know how much time we have left before the ice actually harms his body."

She nodded and stepped back, crouching like a dancer. She raised her hands to head height, forming white-knuckled fists. She slowly, smoothly, changed her position, her facial expression tense with concentration. She raised her fists again like an animal ready to strike its prey, when suddenly she shrieked a high-pitched sound and struck both hands against the block. The ice explosively shattered, leaving the man's upper torso and head free, unharmed. She repeated the process, quicker this time, allowing his whole body to be released.

Sir Thomas stepped quickly in, tearing the man's jacket and shirt open, placing the twin discs on his bare chest. "Princess Hui-ying, can you do me a favor and trigger the switch in the chest for me?"

She plunged her hand in the box.

The man's body arched, as if he was in spasmodic pain. A small plume of smoke rose from his chest, with the smell of burned hair. Sir Thomas placed three fingers on the man's neck.

"Please try one more time, Princess, and pray to Quan Yin that it works, as there is only enough charge for one more attempt."

She pushed the plunger a second time, causing the man's body to jerk again.

This time Sir Thomas didn't have to check the man's pulse, as the figure lying in shattered ice gasped and coughed.

Hui-ying leapt to his side, hugging the man who already was shivering. "Jacob, you have returned."

The man called Jacob opened his eyes. He grimaced and peered to his left where his arm was resting loosely on the ice. He opened his hand, revealing a pear shaped blue sapphire, nearly the size of his palm.

* * *

Nick sat at a fold-out table next to the iron carriage. He had helped carry Jacob into the vehicle, amazed at the scientific equipment and bronze dials and gauges covering most of the walls. There was little room to move in the majority of the carriage—Sir Thomas slid a narrow bed out of a side panel, where Jacob was placed, and covered him with blankets.

Sir Thomas climbed out of the iron carriage and joined Nick and Hui-ying at the table, who were sipping green tea.

"He will recover quickly, just needs some rest. Some fancy medicine acquired from my scientific colleagues in Germany—and the speed of our intervention—worked in his favor."

Hui-ying turned her attention to Nick. "You must be confused," she said sympathetically.

"Uh, darn right. Everything. That dude, Jacob ... he isn't Jacob Chalmers, is he?"

Nick didn't expect the visitors' reaction of surprise.

"Remarkable," Sir Thomas said. "The Sacred Stones, they really are interconnected with our lives, aren't they."

"Truly," the princess confirmed. She sipped from her tea cup. "What is your name, boy?"

"Nick. Nick Smith."

"Nick, my name is Xian Hui-ying, and I am from China. My companion is Sir Thomas Page, and he is from London, England. You are correct in thinking that our third companion is Jacob Chalmers, who was formerly a gunslinger from the Arizona Territory. I presume we are in Arizona, near his home?"

"Ahh, yep. Don't know much 'bout him, but he definitely was a gunslinger. A bounty hunter I 'spose. Closest thing to home for him was Clifton—that's a copper mining town 'bout two days ride to the southeast from here. Only a few hundred live there, but it's the closest thing to a town anywhere near to this ranch. My dad owns the Triple C Ranch in these mountains, and we raise Texas Longhorn."

Sir Thomas sampled the green tea and sighed. "A delectable brew, my dear." He placed the cup ceremonially on the table. "Nicholas, you have been drawn into a rather extraordinary adventure, and given our appearance in Jacob's home territory, I do not believe we can discount a reason for us being in this specific location, meeting you. You may have a role to play in our quest. Aside from this most esoteric connection, we need your help to get about this part of the world. We are unfamiliar with Arizona until Jacob is fully recovered."

Nick scratched his head, guessing he got the gist of what Sir Thomas was saying. "What do you mean, 'adventure'?"

The pair opposite him exchanged glances, their serious dispositions softening.

Hui-ying said, "I am the youngest daughter of the Emperor of China. When I was born the Court's astrologers informed my father that I was the successor to the Guardian of the Five Sacred Stones, protector of this ancient artifact that is said to keep the Empire as one. Quan Yin, Goddess of Mercy, bestowed this gift to the Emperor of the time, thousands of years ago, a statue that depicted her in the lotus position, a hand held out with the five gemstones imbedded in her palm. They are: citrine that represents the element of Earth, white diamond for Metal, blue sapphire for Water, emerald for Wood, and ruby for Fire. These Stones, together, unify the people of China with the power of Quan Yin's blessing, as well as the symbolic significance of the five elements."

"The sapphire in Jacob's hand?" Nick asked.

"Yes," Hui-ying confirmed. "We now have three of the Sacred Stones. An old enemy of the Emperor's Court, The Society of Heaven and Earth, stole the gemstones three years ago, and I have been hunting them since."

"*We* have," Sir Thomas corrected.

"Yes, the three of us. We are now known in China as The Righteous and Harmonious Three."

Sir Thomas snickered. "A name that does not sound imposing in English, I am afraid, but it nevertheless has endearing qualities."

Nick asked, "How did you two buddy up with Miss Hui-yin?" He checked to see if his reference to the princess was appropriate, and felt relieved that there wasn't any noticeable response to his choice of words.

"A long story, old chum. All tied with the Sacred Stones."

"The princess followed tenuous paths of inquiry in her first year," Sir Thomas continued, "which finally took her to Prussia's capital, Berlin. I had … well, let me say I had an irreconcilable disagreement with Her Majesty's Government, and took solace with the science fraternity patronized by the House of Hohenzollern. While they are as stuffy as England, I was not caught up in … aah, another story.

"While demonstrating a new form of electric storage device that I invented to several Polish scientists in Berlin, there was a commotion down the Royal Palace's corridor. To my surprise, I found Princess Hui-ying in mortal combat with a visiting Chinese dignitary who I had previously only the briefest acquaintance. It was truly an amazing battle, defying my understanding of physics and human biology, and at its conclusion the princess won the day. The Palace Guard arrested her, but not before I gazed upon her countenance and knew that there was a greater tale to tell, and that she was, indubitably, in the right. At that moment, I did not see her palm a priceless citrine, cut in the shape of a pear.

"That night I stole into her cell and discovered why she was in Prussia. The dignitary was a member of The Society of Heaven and Earth, and was custodian of the Earth Element Stone. I don't know how—although I can guess—the princess was able to secretly retain the gem while being incarcerated. I helped her escape and I found myself again in need of a new safe haven. It did not take me long to join her in her quest, and to come to the realization that instead of finding a new place of refuge, I should bring my home along with me." He waved his hand at the iron carriage. "I call her the *Iron Queen*."

Hui-ying continued the story, "Through Sir Thomas' eminent scientific skills, we harnessed the gem's property to locate the next stone in the Great Harmonious Cycle—Earth generates Metal through Water through Wood through Fire, and which generates Earth. And so the cycle continues. Sir Thomas had already invented a device that allows people, and objects, to instantaneously transport from one place in the world to another, but it was fraught with danger without a sure indication of direction—a property which the Sacred Stones had, but they were restricted to just locating the next gem in the cycle."

"Excellently summarized," Sir Thomas said. "The device actually 'folds' space. I installed it in the *Iron Queen*, fitted with a navigation chamber that can hold one of the Sacred Stones. We appeared on this hill, having located the sapphire that was in Jacob's frozen hands."

"What about Jacob?" Nick asked. "How did he join your group?"

"Ah. Jacob. The citrine allowed the princess and I to almost instantly transport to where the second stone, the diamond, was located. The Society of Heaven and Earth have a strong following among some of the Chinese in Australia, and the *Iron Queen* appeared near a goldfield in a town called Ballarat in the Victorian Colony." The Englishman theatrically bowed to Hui-ying to complete the story.

"Once near a Sacred Stone," she said, "it is not difficult for me to locate it. I get a sense of where it is; a part of my training as Guardian. A terrible battle took place, as I underestimated how many followers of the Society were there. When I thought I was about to fail, Jacob appeared, to my rescue. He shot several of the Society followers down, which allowed me to win the day. We recovered the diamond." She hesitated, blushing slightly with a downward glance. "Jacob and I have since become … good friends. He was on a personal journey himself, and left America's shores to find solace. Instead, we have found each other."

They finished their tea, and Sir Thomas packed away the tables and chairs. He asked Nick to stand clear as he entered the driver's compartment of the *Iron Queen*. A rumbling emanated from the giant carriage, and it's sides unfolded in complicated patterns, expanding into glistening metal-roofed, canvas-walled tents on both sides, allowing ample room for beds and a table for repast.

Sir Thomas noticed Nick's look of incredulity. "An adjustment I made when we grew to three."

* * *

Jacob recovered quickly, as Sir Thomas predicted. Nick saw him walk slowly and carefully into the left annex where everyone was enjoying fine Chinese cuisine.

"And you didn't invite me?" Jacob asked. "Princess, your vegetables and noodles is my second favorite meal!"

"What's his first?" Nick asked.

"T-Bone," Sir Thomas and Hui-ying said in unison.

Hui-ying flew into Jacob's arms, who struggled to remain upright. "Woah, girl, I was frozen, remember?"

She whispered something in his ear, where Nick only picked up the words 'warming up'. He was no fool, he knew everything and anything about the world at fourteen, and it also made him feel a little 'warmed up'.

Sir Thomas introduced Nick to Jacob and quickly gave an account of the events since Nick had found the block of ice.

"I'll be darned," Jacob said bitterly. "Of all the places in the world where I could have appeared, I'm back in the Gilas. Of all the God-forsaken corners on this globe, why would the Emerald Stone be here?"

"More importantly," Sir Thomas added, "why does your personal past cross paths with the location of the Stone?"

Hui-ying served her noodle and vegetable dish to the gunslinger. "Quan Yin's Stones are powerful. I was taught this from the moment I entered the Shaolin Monastery for my education and training. I believe there are no coincidences where the Sacred Stones are concerned. There must be a reason why you appeared here."

Jacob ate ravenously, like a man who had been starved a week. When he nearly finished his second helping, Nick asked, "How did you get frozen?"

Jacob pulled a face like he had been bitten; he rubbed his stubble chin and sat back in his chair, leaning precariously on two of its legs. "I 'spose you know about our callin'. How much of the story 'bout the Stones have yer heard?"

"Australia," Nick said, excitedly.

"The Victorian Goldfields. Yeah. Seeking escape from my past and gettin' instant wealth—and instead found a different treasure." He gave Hui-ying a wink. "With the diamond placed in Sir Thomas' iron contraption, we winked into a bleak, cold land, which turned out to be Mongolia. And I reckoned the Gila Mountains was cold in winter! Hoowee! Compared to the first two stones, this leg of the adventure—my first, really—was tough. Real tough." He briefly touched his right arm. "I got hurt and it took a long time to heal. Thanks to Sir Thomas' smarts and some neighborly Mongolian tribesmen, we weathered the winter and found the varmints who had the sapphire. There was a big fight and it wasn't easy. The sapphire was kept on a pedestal in a cave network as big as a palace, and while Hui-ying was fightin' the leader, I grabbed the Stone and … well, next thing I remember is waking in the gully."

"I will finish the story," Sir Thomas said. "The pedestal was set with a clever trap that instantly froze Jacob. I observed, in that instant, our companion enveloped in water which froze, as opposed to his body being frozen in itself. Then, in the blink of an eye, the sapphire glinted through the translucency of the ice, and the block disappeared.

"We were so worried," Hui-ying said. "We couldn't be absolutely sure where he went."

"That is true," the inventor said, "however the balance of probabilities was that the Sacred Stone somehow, in some way, transported Jacob to where the emerald was located. Fortunately, since the sapphire was in Jacob's possession, we hastily retreated to the *Iron Queen* and transported with the aid of the Diamond Stone, to where it was located, including Jacob."

"Quick thinkin'," Jacob said, shaking his head in disbelief with his good fortune. "If you didn't act quickly I would've been a goner."

"Indeed."

Jacob was clearly eager to continue the conversation, but over time he was showing signs of weariness, and had to retire to bed. Nick saw him walk with Hui-ying to the other tent attached to the *Iron Queen*, finding himself sharing the remaining tent extension with Sir Thomas. A comfortable cot was set for him, and he fell asleep dreaming about murderous Chinese warriors in icy Mongolia.

* * *

Nick woke just before sun-up, finding Sir Thomas already packing things away.

"I better go now," the young teenager said, "'cause I gotta rustle up some cattle and get them back to the stockyards."

Sir Thomas stopped packing and sat on the second iron step leading into the carriage. "Nicholas, we would be grateful if you would come with us to Clifton. You know the place nearly as well as Jacob, and you are familiar with what has been going on over recent years. You might enjoy it as well."

Nick grew excited by the offer, but on reflection, his enthusiasm quickly deflated. "I wish I could, but I can't stay away from home for that long. It's two days ride to Clifton, and another two back, not to mention the time there, and back here rustling the cattle again."

"Ah, your decision is based on a false premise, Nicholas. You are assuming we are riding horses or driving the *Iron Queen* over rough terrain."

"What do you mean?"

"You will see, soon enough."

After quickly and efficiently packing the portable furniture into the iron carriage and folding the extensions back into the walls of the vehicle, Sir Thomas allowed Nick to sit with him in the driver's cabin. He started the engine by winding a small wheel and pressing a large button next to it. The *Iron Queen* vibrated with the running of its powerful steam engine.

"Nicholas, I will explain briefly how this invention of mine works. Are you interested in science?"

"I … I guess so."

"*Be so*, my boy. It is the way of the future. It will be only a matter of a handful of years when horses will no longer be used for transport, except in the less fortunate nations and principalities of this planet. Become a scientist.

"The *Iron Queen* is unique, a one-off. There is no vehicle like it in this world. There is a large water tank at its rear which, when converted to steam, provides the power to cause it to move and also run a number of other devices that generate electricity—which in turn operates devices that operate on this form of power. There is sufficient electricity generated to charge a number of batteries as well. However, there is another invention that is of particular interest. It extracts hydrogen gas from some of the water, which is the fuel to run the engines. Do you see what I have? I have a steam engine that virtually runs itself except for the need for water. I have a small furnace near the engine, which primes the engine if we find ourselves without hydrogen, but to this day, I have only had to use it once."

Nicholas was again left largely in the dark, but understood enough to know that the *Iron Queen* was a marvel. "Does that mean that we can travel very fast to Clifton?"

Sir Thomas laughed. "Oh, very fast indeed, but not in the way you think." Once he was certain that Jacob and Hui-ying were secured in the main compartment of the carriage, he pulled a lever on his control board.

"Nicholas, hydrogen is the lightest element known to mankind. It is, aside from its dangerous flammable properties, an astonishingly efficient material for balloon flight. If I change the configuration of my machine to producing more hydrogen, and less mechanical power, I can create a large volume of hydrogen."

The roof of the carriage unfolded, releasing a bright yellow Chinese silk membrane that rapidly expanded into the shape of a balloon of immense proportions, two hundred feet in diameter.

"You probably didn't see it, but there is a long hose that is drawing extra water from the stream where you set camp," he explained, "as it takes a great deal to fill this balloon. The *Iron Queen* is not light—although you would be surprised how much of her structure is constructed of aluminum, a very expensive and lightweight material indeed."

Nick stuck his head out of the cabin to see the colossal balloon expanding and rising above him. When it was half full, the carriage lurched but stayed put.

Sir Thomas patted his control panel. "She wants to rise, but I haven't released the anchors beneath the carriage. We don't want to career into a mountainside, or tree."

When the balloon was completely full and the water tank at capacity, Sir Thomas retracted the anchors and hose, and the *Iron Queen* swiftly rose.

"When we get to the right altitude, I will release enough gas to set us level. We can dump some water to rise again, if need be. The wind is mild, which is good, as I will now steer and power this air-ship with the aid of small windmill sails that are set to the rear of the carriage."

When the height of the air-ship was stabilized, and the sail-propellers were in operation, the converted carriage made short work of travelling above the Gila Ranges, and with Nick's assistance, toward the mining town of Clifton. After a few hours in the cabin, Nick passed through a door into the cramped main carriage area where Jacob and Hui-ying were seated. The gunslinger was cleaning his Smith and Wesson six-shooter.

"Glad you're comin' with us," Jacob said.

"Me too, sir. Do you think the Emerald Stone is in town?"

"Pretty sure, son. Can't see it being anywhere else. I remember there were a couple Chinese families there, running a few local businesses."

The young boy paused, appearing torn.

"Out with it, Nick. You want to ask me somethin'. I've had a dark past, and a lot of it happened in Clifton. Is that it?"

Nick's face turned red. "Yeah, I guess so. My pa called you a gunslinger. Does that make you a—"

"Bad man?" He laughed, although there was no humor in it. "Gunslingers come in all kinds of colors, although none of 'em hold much to the sanctity of human life. I 'spose I didn't, but I only went after bounties. Goin' overseas, and meeting Hui-ying, has changed everything for me. I'll never go back to being a bounty hunter."

"Why haven't you come back to Clifton before?"

"Long story, Nick. Let's just say the family of someone I killed in a gunfight ambushed me and wounded my arm—badly. My drawing arm wasn't good—permanently damaged, so I left, to think about my future ... what I wanted to do. That's why I took a steamer from San Francisco to the Victorian Goldfields."

By midafternoon the *Iron Queen* arrived at Clifton, with a small buzzing crowd quickly gathering at the field chosen for landing. Sir Thomas expertly steered the craft to the landing target, allowing the carriage to gently descend with the release of hydrogen gas from the balloon. Before the occupants could ready themselves to disembark the craft, internal winches and other clever machinery were already gathering the balloon skin into the roof compartment.

Nick noticed from one of the carriage windows that the crowd hushed when the *Iron Queen*'s cabin door opened. Sir Thomas was the first to alight, bowing to the cowboys, miners, prostitutes, craftsmen—forty in number.

Princess Hui-ying followed, triggering murmurs from the crowd.

Nick was next, causing more comments and an old-timer shouting, "What're yer doin' with these here strangers, Nick-boy?"

Before he could respond, Jacob descended the steps.

The crowd became dead quiet. A dog was heard barking in the distance. A slight breeze picked up small dust eddies from the field and nearby street.

Sir Thomas Page broke the uncomfortable silence. "Citizens of Clifton! We might seem an odd group, but we are merely visitors to your fine town! Can anyone help direct us to a hotel where we can stay?"

A matronly figure was about to answer when she was cut off by the crowd parting for a lone figure slowly approaching. He was an imposing figure, well over six feet tall, with long dark hair beneath a black leather hat. His unshaven face exuded arrogance, disdain. Twin Army Colts were loosely holstered at his hips.

"Jacob Chalmers. We thought we saw the last of you, you murderin' snake. Don't understand why you're here, since your draw's slow. Does it still have my slug in your arm?"

Jacob didn't flinch. "A lot's happened since then, Zeb. I'm here for other business, nothin' to do with you, or the Dudes. Leave it be." He moved away from his companions, making sure they weren't in the line of fire, and hovered his hand over his Smith and Wesson Model 3.

Zeb spat tobacco onto the dusty field. "You still owe us. My brother's rotting in the grave 'cause of you. You skedaddled last time, but it aint goin' to happen again. It finishes here."

Nick looked around in panic, but Sir Thomas placed his chubby hand on the boy's shoulder. "If Jacob can't back out, he can look after himself," the scientist whispered.

Hui-ying stood still, her muscles tensed. Her eyes darted about, looking for any other antagonists.

"I don't want to kill you," Jacob said to Zeb, who was now only twenty yards away. "If you back out, you'll live. Simple."

"Draw," Zeb snarled.

"Nope. If you move for your guns, I'll draw. Nothin' else."

A young tradesman shouted from the crowd, "I'd draw, Jacob. No-one's ever beat Zeb. He's the fastest in this here corner of Arizona Territory!"

Jacob stood statue-still. Waiting.

Zeb snarled again and went for his revolvers with fluid speed.

Jacob drew his gun like a lightning bolt and shot Zeb through the heart before the Dude even touched his Colts, sending him flying backwards. Lying on his back in the blood-pooling dirt, Zeb stared into the sun with only enough life in him to wonder how it was possible for a man to draw so fast.

Like everyone else, Nick didn't see Jacob draw. One moment his hand was hovering over his revolver, then next the gun was pointing where Zeb had been standing, smoking.

The crowd, which had grown to nearly one hundred, dispersed, not hiding their respect for Jacob's miraculous skills, and indicating zero sympathy for Zeb's demise. A few provided advice to the rest of the Clifton citizens to find safe hiding places, because the "lead's gonna start flyin'."

Hui-ying gathered her companions together. She said quickly, "I saw a few men running into the saloon over there. We should get indoors."

Jacob scanned the other end of town. "There's Hovey's Dance Hall. Anton won't like it, but we need it for our base."

Sir Thomas drove the *Iron Queen* to the dance hall, and the four adventurers entered the premises. The hall should have been full with revelers, but there were only a few hardened drinkers yakking at their table, and several men drunk and unconscious on the floor. The place was definitely a dance hall, complete with raised stage, but it was also clear it made most of its money from booze.

A man in a dusty suit, with a large wide-brimmed hat, walked onto the stage from behind one of its large, velvet curtains. "Jacob Chalmers. It's been a while, heh?"

Jacob took several steps forward. "Anton. I'm sorry to say your place might get shot up a bit in the next little while."

The man on the stage laughed uproariously. "It wouldn't be the first time, friend, and it won't be the last. I suppose I should be flattered that the infamous Jacob Chalmers chose my hall for refuge." He noticed the others who had enter his hall. "Ah, you have companions! Let me introduce myself—I am Anton Muzzonvich, owner of this establishment. Please, come on up stage and we can have a drink in my rooms."

"I'm not sure we'll have enough—" A gun shot sounded from outside and a window shattered inward.

Hui-ying grabbed Jacob's arm. "I will help defend, but I want to visit the Chinese community as soon as possible. After all, the Sacred Stone is why we are here."

Sir Thomas said to Nick, "I believe it is time for us to find a safe location in this establishment. Jacob and Princess will look after this … distraction."

The pair ran to the stage where Anton had already disappeared to a place of safety. Several windows crashed, and a side door smashed in.

Sir Thomas and Nick made themselves comfortable behind an upright piano, on stage.

Hui-ying was nowhere in sight. Jacob turned a small table over, facing the front and side entrances of the dance hall, revolver in hand.

"How can he draw so quickly?" Nick whispered.

"A bit of a story, Nicholas," Sir Thomas replied, keeping his voice low. "Jacob was seriously wounded in the arm, and it didn't heal properly. He did not talk much about it when we met him in Australia, and he still prefers not to speak of that time."

"That time? Sounds like he's fixed."

"Well, in a way. You may recall that he had been seriously injured in Mongolia. In fact, he lost most of the same arm that was previously shot."

"That's not possible, he's got two of them."

"Now he does. One of my areas of expertise is constructing clockwork automatons. It took a while, but I constructed an arm and hand for Jacob, in many ways superior to muscle and bone. It has a self-winding mechanism that allows him to operate his arm efficiently on a continuous basis, but if it needs to be worked hard, or some of its specialized functions are used, he has to supplement the spring-based energy by winding the mechanism."

Three scruffy men rushed into the hall through the side entrance, diving behind furniture, guns brandished.

One of the outlaws poked his head up to shoot and immediately caught one of Jacob's bullets between his eyes.

"Jeeesus!" one of the others cried.

Hui-ying dropped twenty feet from the rafters to the floor, right between the two remaining outlaws.

They scrambled to their feet, aiming their guns hesitantly toward her, worried they would get caught in crossfire.

The princess leapt high in the air and kicked both guns out of their hands simultaneously with each foot, breaking their hands in the process. One of the assailants was a big, strong man, and swung his good fist at her. Hui-ying easily dodged the punch by bending slightly backwards, and, falling to a kneeling position, returned a punch to his solar plexus. As slight as she appeared, the two hundred and sixty pound bear of a man was flung ten yards backwards from the blow, destroying a table, knocking him unconscious.

The remaining man ran for his life, but Hui-ying sprung into the air, somersaulting over him, blocking his way out. She fired three rapid punches to his face, kidney and stomach in the blink of an eye. The outlaw was maimed and unconscious before he hit the floor.

"Jacob!" came the distant sound of someone outside Hovey's Dance Hall.

"Dang it," Jacob muttered. He strode over to the door, keeping out of line of sight of anyone outside. "What is it, Ned!"

"Come out like a man, instead of hiding with your friends like some chicken-shit coward. Just you and me. If you don't, I'll fire Hovey's."

"What do you want to do?" Hui-ying asked.

"If we stay, my friend's business will be burned to the ground; if I go out alone they'll gun me down with a dozen men, maybe more. Ned is the last of the Lowry brothers, and he's the head of the Dudes. They were all murderin' scum, and there's no reasonin' with Ned—I killed his two brothers, and crippled their pa. He wants me real dead and buried."

"Then we must go out and remove the threat," the princess replied.

"My thoughts exactly."

"They will have the building covered from all sides, and there are no adjoining buildings," she summarized. "There's one large tree out front, near the *Iron Queen*, but we don't want to risk damaging her. This situation would appear to be not unlike our encounter with the Society in Ballarat. I say we do this fast, to catch them with as much surprise as possible."

"Agreed again," Jacob said, and kissed her passionately. "And that's why I love you."

She provided a small, but endearing smile, and then her stern, focused visage returned. "And I you, Jacob. Let us remove the threat now."

Nick had already emerged from behind the piano and saw Hui-ying disappear through the front door at a blurring speed. He rushed to a window to see what was happening outside.

Jacob followed the princess, diving behind a horse trough, followed by bullets kicking up the dirt of his trail. Hui-ying raced in a tight corner for the outer wall of Hovey's. Defying the laws of physics, she ran its entire height and, using her grasp of the guttering as a hold, back-flipped onto the roof. A shot zipped past her as she ran, appearing almost like she was floating in the air.

A few more shots few by her, but the outlaws failed to bring her down.

Jacob fired three shots at those who were targeting the princess. It kept the assailants low, except one, who was shot in the neck, gurgling and bleeding out.

Hui-ying had run out of roof, but she kept running. Gasps came from some of the men in the street as she moved in a curved trajectory in the air, legs pumping, without losing altitude. A shot rang out, and inexplicably, on seeing the bullet coming straight for her, she tumbled in the air and dodged it.

She landed behind four barrels being used as cover by several outlaws. In a split second they were down and out. Two men ran toward her to get a better line of fire and were cut down by Jacob—each bullet piercing their hearts.

Sir Thomas was next to Nick, watching the battle in front of Hovey's Dance Hall. "Jacob has great speed with his arm and hand," the scientist said, "but he is still tired from his ordeal with the ice. He had better be careful."

Jacob raced from his cover to join Hui-ying when a rifle shot hit his right arm, sending him spinning onto the dusty main street of Clifton.

Hui-ying let out a cry, too far away to intervene.

A tall, thick-set, heavily bearded man with a Rebel officer's style hat appeared from behind a general store corner thirty yards away, keeping his rifle trained at Jacob's still body.

"I got yer shootin' arm, Jacob; yer done fer." He stood still, next to the store, aiming at Jacob's body in a military rifleman's stance. "Get up so I can make it clean, man-to-man."

Dudes were running in from the other end of the street. Hui-ying back-flipped twice, using the momentum to somersault twenty feet into the air, landing among them.

Jacob slowly climbed to his feet, holding his right arm with his left hand, in pain. He was side on from Ned, seemingly to protect his wound.

"Turn to me, Jacob. Face me like a man."

Jacob's lower arm separated and dropped to the ground, revealing whirring gyros through its open end.

Ned raised an eyebrow in complete surprise.

Jacob twisted and dropped to his knees, aiming his steel stump at the outlaw.

The shot from Ned's rifle passed over Jacob's head, hitting Hovey's Dancing Hall.

A small cylinder of steel propelled from Jacob's stump, missed Ned by inches, colliding with the General Store building. The entire shop exploded with intense flames, sending fragments of wood and iron into the air, flinging Ned like a rag doll in Jacob's direction.

Ned landed with a sickening thud onto the ground three yards in front of Jacob.

Hui-ying raced to Jacob's side. "I took care of four more. The rest have fled," she said, panting.

Jacob walked slowly to Ned and found the outlaw still alive, lying on his back. Surprisingly, the man was still whole, having been largely flung by the percussion of the blast. He was singed all over, but his left side was seriously burned. The man could live with help and luck.

Ned opened his eyes. "You bastard. You son of a bitch. Make it quick."

Jacob drew his revolver with his left hand and aimed it at Ned's heart.

Hui-ying was conspicuously silent.

Jacob's finger tightened on the trigger. Anger coursed through his being, wanting to blot out the leader of the gang that had caused so much pain and embarrassment to him.

Ned stared at the gunslinger, resigned to his fate.

Jacob released the tension, and holstered his Peacemaker. "I can't kill a man in cold blood. No more. I've got nothin' to fear—I'm goin' to be leaving soon and won't be coming back to Clifford. Killing you, Ned, would just be an act of spite."

"Kill me!!!" Ned hoarsely screamed, his cracking, blackened face made him look like a Chinese demon.

"No."

Jacob walked away.

* * *

A few hours later they all met at the *Iron Queen*.

"I don't understand," Sir Thomas said. "Are you saying that the Emerald Stone isn't in Clifton?"

"Correct," Hui-ying replied. "There are only two Chinese families living here, and they are hardworking people, with no knowledge of the Sacred Stones. They are not of the Society of Heaven and Earth. I do not sense it being near; the Sacred Stone is not here."

Jacob was sitting, finishing re-attaching his arm. The rifle shot had only left a small dent on its superstructure.

The princess took the large sapphire from Sir Thomas' navigation chamber and displayed it on the palm of her hand for all to see. "Jacob was transported by this Sacred Stone to Arizona Territory, and we assumed it operated the same way as the other Stones—seeking the next in the eternal circle. We found the sapphire two times by using the diamond, the first getting us to Mongolia, and the second time to find Jacob encased in ice."

"And….?" Sir Thomas asked.

"We are assuming that the Sacred Stones only have a single property. All the legends talk about immense power in them, bestowed by Quan Yin, goddess of mercy."

"Mercy," Jacob echoed, eyes widening.

"Mercy," Sir Thomas repeated. "I am beginning to understand."

"And rightly so," Hui-ying said. "You are the preeminent scientist of this century. Yes, mercy. For reasons that I cannot fathom, Quan Yin is testing Jacob's caliber. He was transported to his homeland to face unfinished business, and to test that he has truly learned to value life, to be able to act with mercy. This is important to Quan Yin, a virtue that represents her very essence."

Jacob said, "I wanted to come back, after I joined your team, after my arm was … fixed—after I understood my feelings for *you*, Hui-yin. But the mission was more important than anything else."

Sir Thomas joined in the thread of conversation. "And Quan Yin, or perhaps her essence imbedded in the Sacred Stones, forced the detour. Splendid!"

Hui-ying nodded, acknowledging the solution to the puzzle, allowing a smile to radiate her face. "And I believe that if we use the Sapphire Elemental Stone now, it will take us to where the Emerald lies."

"Well," Sir Thomas said, "what are we waiting for? Let us embark on the next stage of our adventure!"

Nick had shared the satisfaction of understanding the meaning of Jacob's appearance on his parent's ranch, but quickly realized his own adventure was nearing its conclusion.

Hui-ying warmly caressed Nick's face. "Young boy, you have been so helpful to us, and have shown a true spirit of adventure, worthy of The Righteous and Harmonious Three."

"Can I join you, then?" Nick asked timidly. "My ma and pa trust me to rustle Long Horn on my own for up to a week at a time."

To his surprise, no one laughed. They took him seriously.

"No, not yet," the princess replied. "I believe the Sacred Stones do nothing by chance, and Jacob was transported to your property for a reason—and not just to acquire your local knowledge, Nick. I think you have a part to play, but you need time to grow. Besides, we need to return you to your parents' home, as they will soon become worried."

Nick was devastated by the news; he nodded, red-faced.

Jacob stood and placed his living hand on Nick's shoulder. "Boy, you've got what it takes, I've no doubt about that. Your ma and pa need you, and you've got to do the right thing by them. Believe me, we will meet again."

Nick knew that Jacob and the others were right, and poignantly sensed the honesty of the gunslinger's words.

The *Iron Queen* drew water from the river that was Clifton's water source, and left the ground when the hydrogen balloon was filled. The crowd seeing them off was twice as large as when they first came to town, and the folk were happier, having been rid of a long-term yoke around their necks.

The trip to the Triple C ranch was far too quick for Nick's liking, but he was happy to see his parents and younger brother and sisters … and the look on their faces when they saw how he got there. After a few hours of lunching and enjoying the ranch's hospitality, The Righteous and Harmonious Three bid everyone adieu and entered the *Iron Queen*.

Nick entered the carriage one more time to make his farewell more personal. "You will come back for me?" he asked.

"Of course, my boy," Sir Thomas replied. A red light suddenly flashed on a small console. "What the—?"

A blue haze surrounded them, and the engine built up steam.

Sir Thomas smiled wryly. "And it seems, my dear friends, Quan Yin has intervened again."

About the Author

Gerry Huntman is a writer based in Melbourne, Australia, living with his wife and young daughter. He write in all genres of speculative fiction, and many sub genres and cross-overs. The majority of his stories tend to be dark. Recent sales include: Stupefying Stories, Lovecraft eZine, BLEED charity anthology, Night Terrors III pro anthology, Black Beacon's Subtropical Suspense anthology, and a weird western in Railroad! Celebration Station interlude to Tonia Brown's serial series. He has been a judge in the Australian Shadows Awards for two years running.

COSMIC DOPPELGANGER

Mike Chinakos

ir Percival "Percy" Cox looked down the barrel of the .45 caliber Colt Peacemaker, not liking what he saw. The dark eyes of the stranger holding the pistol spat hatred and anger at him.

"I assure you that you have mistaken me for someone else," Percy said evenly.

The man holding the pistol looked ready to pull the trigger. Percy sat perfectly still at a saloon table, with his back to a badly plastered wall. He kept his hands resting on either side of a cooling cup of black tea, where the pistol wielding man and his three compatriots could see them. The other three men carried weapons as well—one a Sharps rifle, one a shotgun, and the third a scarred truncheon as long and thick as a logger's forearm.

All four men scowled at Percy, making their intentions to do him harm very clear.

"Get up," commanded the man with the Colt. "Slowly."

The man's thick black mustache twitched at the corners of his thin lips. Long locks of oily black hair fell in front of one of his brown eyes from beneath a battered brown bowler hat. Everything about the man indicated to Percy that his apparent adversary meant business and considered himself fully in charge of the situation.

Percy raised his hands slowly above his head before stretching to his full six foot height. He cautiously moved out from behind the table. The men stepped back, guns never leaving their target.

"Again, gentlemen," Percy said with a tight smile on his clean-shaven angular face, "I don't know who you think I am, or what you think I've done—"

"This is the guy, Chief Lappeus," the man holding the rifle interrupted. "This is the bastard that shot Charlie."

"Sir," the apparent chief said to Percy, "you are under arrest for the murder of Officer Charles F. Schoppe of the Portland Metropolitan Police Force."

"I think, had I shot and killed someone since arriving in this fair city, I would recall such a misadventure," Percy told the men. "Once again, I think this is a case of mistaken identity. My name is Sir Percival Cox. Percy to my good friends. I'm the captain of the H.M.S Steamship *Titan*. We are in port after charting portions of the Northwest Passage simply to pick up lumber for trade across the Pacific. You can check with the dock master to see that no one from my ship has run afoul of any trouble since we arrived here in Portland."

"Shut your pie hole, Brit!" the rifle wielder snarled.

"You can tell us all about it at the station," Chief Lappeus concurred. "Turn around and put your hands behind your back."

Percy frowned at the chief. He knew he didn't have much choice in the matter. He was unarmed and outmanned. Steeling himself against whatever indignities might follow, the captain of the *Titan* turned his back to his captors and crossed his arms behind his back. He heard heavy boots on the dirty wooden floor of the saloon, and then his arms were seized roughly. Looking over his shoulder, Percy saw the wielder of the truncheon standing behind him. With a metallic clank, cold iron manacles locked around his wrists. The man with the Sharps rifle had stepped up closer to keep an eye on Percy.

The few saloon patrons in the early hours of the morning sat watching in silence at the spectacle. The bartender pursed his lips and shook his head.

"And to think all I came ashore for this morning was to stretch my legs and get a spot of tea," Percy said to no one in particular. The bartender nodded sagely as if the comment had been made for him in passing conversation.

"Sir," Percy addressed the man behind the bar directly, "if you could get word to the first mate on my ship about my predicament, it would be greatly appre—"

The butt of the Sharps rifle cut the captain off in midsentence with a hallow thud of wood against flesh and bone. Pain lanced up the side of Percy's skull. The world went black, and he barely felt or heard the table breaking beneath him as he collapsed into unconsciousness.

* * *

The long Bowie knife felt right in his hand. Something about the curve of its handle and the balance of its weight seemed to fit more than just physically. The knife became a part of him. The bare steel matched the sharpened edges of his keen mind. The cold feel of the blade echoed the coldness in his heart.

He stepped out of the shadows of the Shanghai Tunnels into a room of slatted wood, moldy plaster, and dirt floors. An oil lamp sputtered on a small table next to a narrow cot, casting the claustrophobic room in pale yellow light. A young girl in tattered knickers and an open Oriental waist coat sat on the cot, smiling at him. She might have been considered very pretty at one time, but the life she led beneath the streets of Portland had prematurely robbed her of her youth and beauty.

Not that he had come here for her beauty. Or any other physical pleasure the harlot had to offer.

Closing the rough-hewn door behind him as he entered the room, he was careful to keep the Bowie knife out of sight.

"Hello, love," she said. "Looking for anything special?"

"Just you," he answered.

"What a charmer you are," she said with a smile that revealed yellowed teeth. "Nice accent. British?"

He nodded as he stepped up to her, stooping slightly due to the low ceiling. She looked up at him, parting the waist coat further to show him her small breasts.

"See anything you like?" she asked.

"Plenty," he answered, looking into her dull green eyes. Her pupils were dilated. From the cloying sent of opium floating around the Portland Underground, he could guess why.

Looking deep into those black orbs, he saw exactly what he came for. Down through those opaque windows, beyond the limits of the flesh, past the aether of the human mind, he saw the truth of existence: fear was power on all levels. Political, spiritual, personal and public. Fear rested at the center of all creation and all life. That terror equaled power if one knew how to harness that particular humor from the aether.

And he excelled at cultivating and harvesting fear.

His free hand shot out suddenly, clamping over her mouth, while he wielded the Bowie knife in front of her wide eyes.

"Scream and I'll gut you," he warned her.

The whore's hands gripped at his strong forearm in vain. She scratched him, leaving ribbons of blood in her fingernails' wakes on his skin. The pain drove waves of ecstatic pleasure throughout his body as he squeezed tighter, feeling her jaw crack under the pressure. She whimpered as he pushed her back on the cot, straddling her.

"Fight me and I'll make this last forever," he told her.

The fear in her eyes gave him all the power he needed to continue. The fear he would pull out of her would give him all of the power in the world.

* * *

Percy awoke from the disturbing dream about the poor prostitute with a throbbing head. He chalked the strange nightmare up to taking one hell of a hard blow from the butt end of a Sharps rifle.

Aware that he lay on cold, dank bricks, he slowly opened his eyes. A thick black rat stared back at him a few feet from his face. The rat's nose twitched a couple of times in Percy's direction before the vermin lost interest and scurried off through a hole in a wall of grey bricks. Water dripped somewhere in the distance, and the place smelled of mildew and straw. He had read in the *Oregonian* newspaper that Portland had been named "the most filthy city in the Northern States." At the moment, Percy wouldn't argue against that description.

Muffled voices spoke a few feet behind him. Percy lay quiet as if still sleeping and strained to hear what the voices were saying.

"We can't let him go," one voice said with contempt. Percy recognized him as the man who had belted him with the rifle.

"And I'm not sure if we can hold him," Chief Lappeus answered. "Not after last night."

"Are we sure the witnesses got it right, Chief?"

"Several witnesses saw the exact same thing in the tunnels. They all described the same man. Two of them even identified the assailant directly as Captain Cox. Now how is that possible when Cox was right here in our jail cell last night?"

"Maybe they got it wrong," the rifleman sighed. "Maybe it was a case of mistaken identity?"

Percy decided he had heard enough.

"Exactly as I asserted," Percy interrupted loudly. The sound of his own voice echoing in the cell caused his head to pound harder. He pulled himself up far enough to turn and face the men before slumping against the cell's back wall.

The two police officers looked at him through black iron bars.

"It sounds like you had more trouble with a man fitting my description," Percy told them with a smile.

The chief looked down at his muddy boots, his cheeks flushing red with what Percy thought was embarrassment.

"Perhaps," Lappeus said. "Or maybe you have a twin travelling with you."

"I'm the middle child between two sisters, Chief. Did anyone summon my first mate?"

Again, Lappeus flushed red.

"Yes. He said that at the time of Officer Schoppe's murder, you were overseeing the loading of supplies onto your ship. Several deckhands corroborated his statement, but we had some further investigating to do."

"In light of my confirmed whereabouts when your officer was murdered and the crime committed last night—whatever that may be—"

"A prostitute was savagely murdered," Lappeus said bluntly. "Her procurer caught the killer in the act and was murdered as well."

Percy's head suddenly stopped pounding. The vision of the girl in his nightmare floated in front of his eyes. He felt the Bowie knife in his hand and looked down, expecting to see it covered in blood. His hand was empty, but he could not shake the feeling of the knife's weight. The chief had been talking, but Percy had no idea what he had been saying. The sudden jangle of keys brought him back from the precipice of the nightmare and into the reality of the damp cell.

"I'm told that your ship will be in town for two more days," Lappeus said as he opened the cell door. "I've informed the dock master that the *Titan* has been quarantined and not to let her leave until I say otherwise. You're free to go for now, Captain Cox. I'll have a man escort you to the *Titan*. You are to stay on your ship until I say otherwise. Men will be watching to make sure you adhere to my terms."

Percy started to stand before realizing he was missing his pants. And his left leg. He hoped the chief and his men hadn't harmed it.

"I'll need my leg back," Percy told them through tight lips.

Lappeus stepped back with his fellow officer, waving someone to the cell.

A short, well-dressed man in clean leather shoes wearing wire bifocals entered the cell. He carried a long package wrapped in Percy's trousers under one arm, and a large leather satchel under the other. The police officers turned and left as the short man kneeled in front of Percy and greeted him with an easy smile.

"Good to meet you, Captain Cox. I'm Socrates Cayce, at your service."

Socrates unwrapped Percy's missing leg from his pants.

"Remarkable device," Socrates said. "The design is genius." The man stroked the steel frame and gears of the outside of Percy's leg lovingly. "I really wanted to crack it open and take a look inside, but I didn't want to violate your privacy. I felt bad enough when the chief had me take it from you."

"Thank you," Percy said reluctantly. "Will you be able to reattach it without difficulty?"

"Yes, yes. Nothing to worry about, Captain. I think I understand the basics of the interface quite well. The leg seems to operate on a combination of the mind and body's natural electrical pulses along with radium battery fuel cells and fluidized coal. I was very careful to study the attachments to your hip closely so that I could reattach the leg if needed."

"Much appreciated," Percy said with a touch of relief.

He placed a hand on Socrates's shoulder as the man opened up his satchel to reveal an array of tools. Socrates looked at him and smiled again before starting to work.

"I'd be interested to find out how you came to be here in the wilds of the Pacific Northwest with your obvious talents, Socrates."

As the man bent over the mechanical leg began to work, he waved a tool dismissively at Percy. "That's a story for another time. I'm more interested in talking about *your* predicament, Captain."

"I see no predicament, Socrates. I'm going to do as the chief ordered, and then I'm going to take my ship across the sea to Japan as planned."

"I don't think it will work out for you that way, sir."

"Why not?"

"I think I know who has been committing these crimes, and I'm afraid if they don't catch him, you will be the only one left to blame."

"If you know who did this, why not tell your chief?"

Socrates stopped working for a moment and looked up into Percy's eyes. The captain saw a vulnerability there that went along with the kind of mind that lived behind those eyes. A vulnerability that lesser men would take advantage of, or see as a weakness in the young engineer's character.

"The chief uses me when he sees fit, but he doesn't have the kind of mind to grasp the amazing times in which we live, Captain. He doesn't understand the power of steam, the complexities of engineering or the mysteries of the aether. I have theories about the crimes, but they're theories that only an open mind could comprehend."

"Try me," Percy answered.

"I will," Socrates assured him as he sat up from his work. "All done. Let me help you up to make sure the leg is working properly."

Percy came to his feet with the engineer's help. The leg seemed to be working perfectly as he walked around the cell testing it.

"Fantastic work," Percy praised him.

"Thank you."

"Now your theory, Socrates."

The young man's face lit up.

"I'll do better than explain it to you, Captain. I'll meet you at the *Titan* within the hour and show you!"

Picking up his tools and stuffing them into his satchel, the engineer hurried off, leaving Percy standing amazed in the cell. He felt a genuine admiration growing in his heart for the young man.

Percy began to leave. An uneasy burning churned in his stomach, and he felt a heavy weight in his right hand. Too heavy to be the weight of the Bowie knife. With a dream-like feeling washing over him again, Percy looked at his hand and saw he was holding a single shot, breach-loaded pistol. Though Percy knew it was impossible, he brought the pistol up and aimed it. Down the long barrel he saw the startled eyes and face of a man he knew must be Officer Charles F. Schoppe.

Then the pistol and the apparition of the officer disappeared.

"Come on," Socrates said as he stuck his head back into the cell. "I'll show you the way out!"

In a daze, Percy followed the young engineer.

* * *

Socrates Cayce boarded the *Titan* juggling his tool satchel and a large box. Percy watched with an amused smile on his face, afraid the young engineer might take a spill into the Willamette River and be swept down into the great Columbia River, and then all the way to the Pacific Ocean.

Somehow, Socrates made it onto the main deck of the steamship.

"Welcome aboard," Percy said, greeting him with a firm handshake.

"Thank you, Captain."

Percy's first mate, Alex Cross, steadied the engineer by taking him by the elbow. Alex started to take the box from the engineer, but Socrates shrugged him off with a curt nod. The first mate nodded in return, stepping back to his captain's side. Percy gestured toward his cabin.

"If you will join me in my quarters, we can discuss your theories."

"Actually," Socrates said, setting his satchel down on the freshly swabbed deck, "I think it might be better if I explained out here."

Percy looked over the rail of his ship to the man on the dock that Chief Lappeus had assigned to keep an eye on him. He recognized the man as the shotgun wielding police officer from the saloon. The officer had taken an interest in Socrates coming aboard the *Titan*, setting aside the newspaper he had been pretending to read as he stood to try and get a better look at what was happening on the steamship.

"Are you sure?" Percy asked.

"Don't worry about him," Socrates assured. "Even if he sees what we're doing, he won't comprehend it."

"Please, proceed then," Percy answered.

Socrates wasted no time. He held the box in front of him. Percy took a closer look at it. The box was encased in leather with binding that reminded him of a steamer trunk. Upon closer examination, he could see a brass locking mechanism and what looked like a few buttons and small levers. The engineer pushed one of the buttons, and four metal legs sprang forth from the bottom of the box with a metallic clang. Socrates sat the box down on the deck. It stood waist high to the engineer as he began to look around.

"Do you have a stool?" Socrates asked.

Percy titled his head at Alex Cross, and the first mate barked an order at a deckhand to fetch them a stool.

Satisfied, Socrates fished out an iron key from inside his vest and inserted it into the box's lock. He opened the case, detaching the lid completely, and set it on the deck next to his satchel. Percy stood back with his first mate, watching in wonder as the engineer went to work. Percy loved watching men like Socrates at their craft. There was a certain awe and mystique that accompanied the work of the truly scientifically gifted that men of intellect and adventure such as Percy could admire. Percy considered himself a man of the Age of Reason, but he knew there were certain aspects of mechanics and the sciences that he could appreciate, but never fully comprehend.

Percy knew his place in the modern world, but he still held onto the days of fisticuffs and adventure that had driven early explorers such as Sir Francis Drake and Lewis and Clark.

He watched as Socrates pulled out what looked like a small-sized vanity mirror attached to scissor springs from the box. Percy could see complex clockwork springs, gears, and wires in the box attached to the mirror. The engineer turned dials within the box at the base of the mirror-holding springs. Satisfied with whatever adjustments he had made, Socrates looked up at the captain with his easy-going smile. He then spun the mirror and box to face the city of Portland, toward China Town and the heart of the young city.

The deckhand appeared with a stool, and Socrates thanked him before taking a seat in front of the mirror.

"Captain Cox," Socrates said looking up at Percy and the first mate, "before I show you this, I think some explanation about my theory and the working ideas of this device should be explained."

"Go on," Percy told him.

"For months I've seen unusual things here in Portland. People walking the streets in apparent good health that I know have been long dead because I attended their funerals. Other people that seem to appear in two places at once. Fellow Oregonians I've known for years that seem not to know me at all—some of them appear to be almost lost in a city they've called home for decades. And when I speak to those same people later, they have no recollection of meeting me when I had previously encountered them. They all claim to have been elsewhere in the city during those times, and others can account for their claims when asked."

"Doppelgangers?" Alex asked.

Percy shrugged the question off. He knew the strapping young seaman came from folksier stock in the English countryside—the kind of folks that still believed in Faery Rings and pots of gold at the end of the rainbow.

But Socrates didn't ignore the first mate. He addressed him directly.

"No. Not doppelgangers. Not in the mythic sense. But much the same."

"Socrates," Percy said, "I'm not a superstitious man."

"I'm not either, Captain. This is science."

The engineer pulled a lever on the side of the box, and a small humming noise filled the air. Percy could smell the acrid stench of burnt ozone in the air. The hairs on his forearms stood on end. The thrum coming from the box throbbed throughout his body like the bass drum of an African witch doctor. He watched in amazement as the mirror showing the reflection of Socrates became a swirling fog.

Socrates turned a dial and the foggy vortex solidified into the image of the docks beside the *Titan*, complete with bustling porters and the watchful police officer.

"Amazing," Alex gasped.

"An outstanding trick," Percy said skeptically, all too aware of the parlor tricks used by spiritualists and magicians that fooled so many aristocrats back home in Britain. "A two-way mirror? Some sort of projection being fed from the backside of the mirror for us to see?"

"No," Socrates said, evidently not bothered by Percy's skepticism.

The dapper man adjusted a dial, and the image in the mirror changed like quicksilver. The docks and the city disappeared. Percy could see brown-skinned coastal natives fishing on the banks of the Willamette River. Cottonwood trees lined the shores, lazy puffs of white seeds drifting from their branches through the air and covering the grass and sand along the riverside.

Socrates adjusted the dial again. The scene shifted and then refocused. This time the docks and the city returned, but Percy saw the waterfront filled with British soldiers looking like they were preparing to go to war.

The engineer kept changing the picture. Portland's appearance shifted every time. Sometimes larger, sometimes smaller, other times not there at all.

"I don't understand what I'm seeing," Alex Cross admitted.

Percy had a few ideas but looked for guidance from the engineer.

"Please explain," the captain said.

Socrates drew himself up very straight, tugging at the lapels of his vest as he gathered his thoughts.

"Captain, I believe what we are seeing is a variety of realities. Some are similar to our own. Some distinctively different. I've been experimenting for years with many different methods of harnessing the energies of the aether for various scientific purposes. Much of my experimentation has been with the sciences of wave particles. I feel strongly that the aetheric energies exist as wave functions that contain every possible event and outcome of every possible situation existing in physical reality."

"This is far above my pay grade with the Explorer's Society," Alex joked with a confused smile.

"I think I see what you're getting at," Percy said. "Please go on."

"I think," Socrates continued, "that these waves of energy never collapse and never end. Picture them as a river with many branching tributaries. Since these energies exist without end, but contain many outcomes, certain events can alter the course of portions of the river, but never completely stop it. Thus these tributaries parallel one another without interacting. In essence this means that every possible outcome of every event is realized in a separate but non-communicating physical reality that exists alongside our own."

"You mean to say that many other realities exist unseen to us?" Percy asked.

"Yes, Captain. Many worlds. Some very much like our own, but some not at all."

"What does this have to do with all of the doppelgangers you've been seeing?"

"I think that although these worlds are parallel and not meant to interact with one another, somehow the aether between these worlds has been pierced in Portland. Somehow the worlds are crossing over— bleeding into each other—colliding, if you will."

Percy took it all in for a moment as he heard Alex take a deep breath of realization beside him. If these many worlds did exist and were now interacting with one another, then he could truly be in many places at once, and he *could* have committed the crimes he was accused of. If every event, outcome and situation were possible through these never ending aetheric waves, then it meant that he would have done, or will do, everything he could possibly conceive of—including cold-blooded murder. The differences among the many Percy's that existed might stagger the imagination. In this world he was a knight, a captain and an explorer. In another he might be a beggar. Or he may have died of some disease as a child. The possibilities were as endless as the stars in the night sky.

"We have to stop this other version of me from killing again," Percy told them.

"Captain," Socrates said with a dark look on his face, "we have to stop him and find the point where the realities are colliding. We have to seal the breach into our world. If we don't, I fear that it may spell disaster for all of creation. Whether by divine intention or the laws of nature, these many worlds were meant to be kept separate. If they continue to bleed into each other, it might mean the end of all existence."

"In that case," Percy clapped the engineer on his right shoulder, "I hope you have a plan, my friend."

Socrates smiled at him, a gleam of scientific giddiness sparkling in his eyes.

"Do you have any dynamite on board?" he asked.

* * *

Both murders happened in or around the infamous Shanghai tunnels stretching far beneath the streets of Portland, beginning in China Town and ending at the docks beside the Willamette River.

Socrates had proposed somewhere in the maze of tunnels that the Cross Rip—as he was calling the point where realities collided—had occurred. This meant they needed to gain access to the Portland Underground, which meant they needed access to the criminal organizations that ran the tunnels. Working closely with the Portland Metropolitan Police gave the engineer a greater insight into the darker side of the city than most. It only took a few well-placed bribes and some slight threats of possible police involvement for Socrates to arrange getting himself, Percy, and two men from Percy's crew into the back card room of a seedy saloon called Madam Woo's off of West Burnside Street.

Madam Woo herself guided them into the room, her silk robe trailing behind her on the dirty wooden floors. The room was empty, lit only by two oil lamps that hung above a stained card table. The stern proprietor spoke little English but knew the language of currency fluidly. She gestured to a spot directly behind one of the chairs surrounding the table. Percy could see the cracks of what looked like a trap door that a man intent on cards and deep into his cups would never have noticed. He felt sorry for the poor souls who probably passed out around the table, only to wake up somewhere at sea in the Pacific, unable to return to America and living out a life of forced labor aboard some criminally enterprising ship.

One of his crewmen managed to get the trap door open with some more gesturing from Madam Woo. Below the door about ten feet or so, a dirty mattress would soften the fall of someone being deposited down the hole. Percy and his party climbed down into the netherworld of the Portland Underground.

He looked up at the unsmiling face of Madam Woo as she shut the door above them. The clap of the wood slamming down made Percy feel suddenly imprisoned.

Quickly, he located a small lever above one of the tiny room's walls and pulled it. The wall slid to the side on unseen pulleys. Beyond the room, a tunnel trailed off into the maze of the underground warrens. Socrates had told them to expect to find many tunnels connected to illegal establishments, which included more than a few brothels that were run by the competing criminal elements of Portland. They had decided to start their search for the Cross Rip near the brothel where the last murder had occurred.

Percy sent one of his men ahead as a scout and told the other to take up the rear. He watched as Socrates wrestled with the straps that let him carry the box containing what the engineer called his Mirror Obscura in front of him. With everything in place, he looked like a typical street vendor hawking his goods on the corner of a big city street in a place like London or New York. Socrates pulled up the mirror and activated it.

"With the adjustments I've made, I should be able to detect the energies emanating from the rip," the engineer told them. "We need to move slowly enough for me to look around a bit. Again, remember that the people down here are not friendly to outsiders wandering amid the tunnels. Proceed with caution."

Percy followed his crewman at an even pace, keeping the man in sight at all times. Socrates and the man at the rear fell in step behind them.

The ceilings were low, causing Percy to lower his head. All around them the tunnels were reinforced with railroad ties, slatted wood and crumbling plaster and mud. The place stank of mildew, decay, and a pungent earthy aroma. The floors were mostly muddy with long planks of warped wood running down their centers. Oil lamps hung on the walls casting deep shadows everywhere. They passed tiny side rooms here and there as they moved from one tunnel to another. Some of the rooms had closed doors, locked with rusty padlocks. In others Percy saw men on bunks, lost in sweaty opium fueled dreams. The sweet smell of opium smoke did little to mask the dank odors threating to overwhelm his senses.

They explored the underground for a half an hour, following Socrates's instructions when he told them to turn here or pause there, while he swung the Mirror Obscura around hunting for the Cross Rip. Finally, the engineer told them to halt with a tense excitement in his voice.

"Look at this, Captain," Socrates said.

Looking at the mirror, Percy saw the tunnel they were in. A soft blue light sparkled along the wall the mirror was aimed at.

"These are residual aetheric energies caused by the rip. We're getting close. As we near the rip, I should see stronger traces of the energy. Sparks of white light in the blue."

"Let's keep going then," Percy told them. "Billy," he commanded the scout, "be careful. We don't know what to expect if we stumble upon the rip itself."

"Yes," Socrates agreed, "anything is possible where the realities meet. Don't forget that we walk in these worlds just as the citizens from the other side walk in ours. Don't trust what your eyes and ears tell you."

Billy nodded that he understood and moved around a corner. Percy hurried to keep Billy in sight.

He rounded the corner and came face-to-face with a wall of wet earth. Billy was nowhere in sight in the dead end of the corridor. Percy stood perplexed as the other two joined him.

"What happened?" he asked the engineer.

Socrates looked at his mirror and then at the dead end, his face frozen with shock.

"We're closer than I imagined! According to the mirror, this corridor goes on! I can see Billy moving ahead. There's no tunnel here in our reality, but somehow he's continued into another world!"

Percy moved to look at the mirror. He could see Billy cautiously moving down a corridor that didn't exist for them.

"Billy!" Percy shouted. The crewman kept moving down the tunnel, oblivious to the call of his captain.

The crewman stopped at the corner of his corridor, looking back over his shoulders. Billy's face registered a surprised look as he took a few hesitant steps back toward Percy and his partners. The seaman called out for them but couldn't be heard in their reality.

"He doesn't see a dead end on his side," Socrates explained. "To him it appears that we have disappeared."

"Perhaps if he keeps walking this way, he'll pass back into our world?" Percy wondered aloud.

They watched as Billy stopped about ten feet away from what was the earth wall on their side. He seemed to be shouting for them now. Percy saw a shadow appear behind Billy at the end of Billy's tunnel. The crewman spun around to face that way, completely blocking their view of the person coming toward Billy. He went to meet the newcomer halfway down the passage.

When they met, Billy turned to point back the way he had come. Percy got a look at the man being spoken to and felt his breath catch in his chest.

There stood Percy's cosmic doppelganger, smiling at Billy, clapping him on the shoulder.

Even though the captain believed in everything Socrates had theorized about the murders and the collision of alternate realities, the ideas had all been in Percy's head and imagination. Seeing the spitting image of himself talking to Billy brought the situation into a new light. The theories had become reality—a cold, dark reality that gripped his mind like an iron gauntlet.

Whatever explanation Percy's twin gave the crewman, Billy seemed to be buying it. The young man returned the other Percy's smile and went to take the lead again. The dark captain suddenly grabbed his shoulder, spinning him back around. The other Percy's right hand struck out suddenly. A glint of light flashed off the long Bowie knife in the instant before it was driven hard into Billy's belly.

"NO!" Percy cried out in vain.

Billy's eyed widened in pain and surprise as the doppelganger pushed the blade to the hilt, drawing the young man close to him. Percy and his companions watched helplessly as Billy died on his feet. The evil captain yanked the knife out, blood splattering the floor as he whipped it back. Billy's body fell hard to the muddy floor.

The doppelganger turned to face Percy's group. He smiled, cold and cruel, as he held the knife up in mock salute.

"He sees us!" Percy's other crewman—an old salty dog named Clive— shouted with a quiver of fear in his gruff voice.

Percy looked up from the mirror. The dirt wall remained in front of them, but the man from another reality could see through into their world. Percy felt anger surge in his blood, and he wanted to tear down the walls separating them—both physical and aetheric. They watched the mirror helplessly as the anti-Percy turned on his heels and disappeared into the dark underground city.

"But why would he kill Billy?" Cliff asked.

"He seems to know that we're looking for him," Socrates offered in explanation. "But how?"

A cold realization settled in the pit of Percy's stomach.

"I think I know how," Percy said darkly.

Mike Chinakos

* * *

The darkness embraced him.

He felt at home in the shadows. The shadows were like an extension of the dark corners of his mind. He had been living in the darkest parts of his own head and heart for so long that the bright world and brighter thoughts of humanity had become a distant dream. He had no wish to return to that world, especially now that he had found this underground paradise full of shadows, dark deeds and black souls like his own.

In some ways the Shanghai Tunnels of Portland reminded him of the twisted streets of White Chapel back in London. The tunnels were just as dirty, cramped and disreputable as those foggy city streets. He had been forced to leave White Chapel and had travelled to all parts of the globe before ending up in the wilds of the Pacific Northwest. But retired Captain Percival Cox of the Royal Navy knew he had found a new home in Portland.

At least for a while. Maybe longer if he could pin the murders he had committed on the man who shared his face.

Percival thought he understood what was going on. He wasn't about to turn a blind eye to this unexpected blessing. He didn't know how he could see through the eyes and hear through the ears of the stranger from another reality. But Percival took full advantage of that ability. In many ways, he was jealous of this other version of himself. He hated the man because he captained a steamship and commanded the respect and admiration of others. Just like Percival had once done, many years ago.

After losing his leg in the Crimean War, Percival had never been the same. He had developed a taste for exotic pleasures such as opium and murder, and he never looked back on his days serving Queen and country. If the other Percival wanted his old life he could damn well have it, but he would spend the remainder of his days behind bars. Or better yet, at the end of a hangman's noose, or impaled on the end of Percival's Bowie knife. Either the man would be tried for the crimes Percival had committed, or the retired naval officer would leave the man's body to be found in the tunnels next to his murdered companions. The local constables would have their ounce of flesh and revenge, leaving Percival to stalk the underground city at will.

Percival watched from his shadowy hiding place. He could see the door to the prostitute he had been carefully stalking for the last two days. She was a dwarf with fiery red hair and a deep laugh who called herself Toni Malone. Many of the dockworkers and seamen that came to the

48

underground city called on her frequently. Whether it was for an exotic encounter or because she loved to drink and smoke cigars just like the roughest of her customers, Percival didn't know. But he did know that he had never swum in the blood of someone like her, and the darkness living in his head compelled him to take her life next.

The compulsion to watch her writhe beneath his blade was overwhelming his body and common sense as he heard her moan through the thin door. Percival knew he should be hunting his twin, but the thought of her—the smell of her cheap perfume and sweaty sex—filled him with such yearning to make her bleed that he decided he could let his impostor wait for a while. He had seen her procurer passed out drunk in a card room in another tunnel. When Toni's customer was finished Percival would begin.

Percival sunk deeper into the shadows as he waited. The handle of the Bowie knife seemed to writhe with a life of its own in his right hand.

* * *

"This should put you in a state where you can see through his eyes like you did in the dreams and visions you described," Socrates told Percy. "Yet you should remain lucid enough to help us track him down."

Percy looked at the needle in the scientist's left hand.

"But what if he's still seeing through my eyes?" the captain questioned.

"I think that neither of you have complete control over this ability to see through each other's senses. This has something to do with the crossing of worlds and your proximity to each other. It's a chance we have to take, Percy. If not, we could wander around these tunnels for hours, risking getting separated from each other and suffering the same fate as Billy."

"Do it then," Percy told him, rolling up the white cotton sleeve of his uniform.

"This is my own concoction of opium and laudanum," Socrates explained as the needle pierced Percy's skin with a sharp prick. "Not as severe as a straight shot of opium. This will help you maintain some of your faculties while we hunt for your doppelganger."

"Why on earth would you have something like this in your tool bag?" Percy wanted to know as a warm sensation flowed up his arm.

"Sometimes I use it to help me when I'm stuck on a particularly difficult scientific equation or theory. It helps me expand my mind and vision."

"If you say so," Percy said with a giddy tone in his voice.

A feeling of elation, utter relaxation, and freedom from all physical and mental pain washed over Percy. The euphoria was intense, painting his vision of the dark tunnels in a different light. Things seemed brighter, like a wonderful watercolor painting. He suddenly felt very warm, his skin tingling as he became flushed. Although he could feel drowsiness creeping over him, he also found his senses sharply acute. Percy heard water dripping from the tunnel walls all around him. He could smell decay permeating the air like the perfume of the bowels of Hell.

"This is some sensation," he said. His mouth felt as if full of cotton, and he hoped that his companions could understand his words.

Socrates looked at him and smiled. The engineer seemed far away, as if he was standing at the end of the tunnel instead of right next to Percy.

"Captain, try to ignore these sensations. Try to focus on your other self. Let your own senses go. Channel his perception, Percy. See what he sees. Hear what he hears. Feel what he feels."

"I will."

Percy closed his eyes and the darkness spun around him.

"He's waiting," Percy said softly. "To kill again! He hungers for blood. That hunger burns through him so completely that it consumes his every thought. He knows he should be hunting us as we're hunting him, but he's obsessed with killing some prostitute. He knows he won't have to wait for long, and that excites him."

"Can you see this prostitute?" Socrates asked. "Do you know what she looks like?

Concentrating hard, Percy tried to see deeper into his evil twin's mind. The bleak, murderous thoughts he found in that head scared the hell out of Percy. Even though he had seen plenty of murder and death in his years serving his country as a soldier and an explorer, the cold thoughts of his other self were so dark that they unnerved him.

Finally through the mind's eye of his doppelganger, Percy saw the next intended victim. He quickly described the woman to Socrates and then willed himself back into his own body.

"I know her well!" the engineer exclaimed. "Toni Malone is infamous around these parts."

"Then we must hurry to save her!" Percy said as the tunnels seemed to tighten around them.

"This way!" Socrates commanded.

Percy and his crewman, Clive, hurried on the heels of the engineer. Percy hoped they would find the girl in time.

* * *

Toni Malone let out a blood-curdling scream.

Percy kicked down the flimsy wooden door to her room, knowing it might already be too late to stop his counterpart from claiming another victim. He ducked under the door's arch, entering the cramped room brandishing his Mark III .450 Adams Service Revolver.

In the dim light of an oil lamp, he saw a dark figure pinning the naked prostitute to a stained mattress. She struggled to pull herself out from beneath a massive man—clearly not Percy's twin.

"Help me get this bastard off of me!" she shouted at Percy, evidently not concerned that she didn't know him, or that he had a pistol aimed in her direction. "He puked on my bed and passed out on top of me!"

Holstering his sidearm, Percy stepped up to the bed and pushed the man off of Toni with his knee-high black leather boot. The man rolled onto the floor with a thump and then began snoring loudly. Toni quickly pulled a dirty blanket up to her bosom, as if she had suddenly become shy.

"Who are you?" she asked.

"Sorry to bother you, miss," Percy apologized as he bowed his head. "We heard you scream and came to give assistance."

"Thank you," she said and smiled. "You're an unusually kind gentleman for these parts. But you should probably go. My procurer will be along shortly, and he ain't the kind of man that will take kindly to this situation. Especially since you broke my door down."

Percy backed out of the room with a bow. He turned to find Socrates standing behind him smiling broadly.

"Hazards of her trade I guess," the engineer quipped.

Despite the dire situation, Percy couldn't help but smile back. Then he realized Socrates was standing in the tunnel alone.

"Where is Clive?" Percy asked.

They both looked up and down the tunnel but didn't see Percy's crewman. A sudden moan came from the mouth of a dark corridor adjacent to the prostitute's room. Clive stumbled from the darkness, clutching at his stomach. Blood trickled out from between his fingers as he fell to his knees, and then face first into the mud. Percy and Socrates rushed to his side.

Clive's eyes fluttered open, and he coughed mud and blood as Percy rolled him onto his back.

"Sorry, Captain," the crewman moaned. "Someone called my name from behind. The bugger was hiding in the tunnel. Didn't see him until he pulled me in and stabbed me."

"It's alright, Clive. Hush. Rest and conserve your strength."

As Clive closed his eyes, Percy looked up into the concerned face of Socrates. The engineer had set his Mirror Obscura aside and was digging through his tool bag for medical supplies.

"Stay with him," he told the engineer. "Keep him alive. He has a wife and five children back in England. I'm going after the murdering bastard that did this to him."

"But Captain—"

Percy silenced his new friend with a hard stare.

"Be careful, Percy."

Nodding, Percy leapt to his feet and grabbed an oil lamp hanging from a railroad tie above his head. He moved cautiously into the darkened corner. The shadows cast by the lamp danced around as it swung with his every step. They seemed to move with a life of their own, and he shook his head hard, trying to clear the cobwebs of opium and laudanum from his mind. Drops of blood ran down the middle of the dirt floor. Cautiously, he drew his pistol and pointed it in front of him. The lamp swung to his left. Then back to his right.

He caught a glimpse of his doppelganger dodging around a corner and into another passageway.

Percy hurried up the hallway, slowing down as he neared the corner. He listened intently but only heard the dripping of water and a creak of the timber supporting the walls and ceilings of the Portland Underground. Taking a deep breath, he spun low around the corner, lamp held to his side, pistol ready to fire.

A short, empty corridor stood in front of him. Lamplight reflected back at him from a tarnished and battered full-length mirror at the end of the hall.

"Damn," he muttered to himself. Apparently another obstacle had been thrown in his way by shifting realities. He approached the mirror for a closer look, pistol still held in front of him.

Percy wondered why anyone would put a mirror at the end of a passage like this, but he also realized the maze of the underground made no logical sense in many ways. The mirror was held in an ornate wooden frame, gold paint chipping away in large chunks. It had been a fantastically crafted piece at one time. He stopped in front of it, squinting his eyes to ward off the glare of the lamp being cast back at him.

Two hands suddenly reached out from within the mirror, roughly grabbing Percy's wrist and pistol. The hands pulled hard and the captain lost his balance, falling into the mirror. He passed through the looking glass as easily as a ship through still water.

On the other side of the mirror, Percy looked into the grinning face of his alternate self before being thrown hard onto the floor of another tunnel. The oil lamp clattered to the floor but kept burning. His pistol slipped from his grasp right into the hands of the doppelganger. Scrambling to his feet, Percy backed up, looking around for something to use as a weapon.

"That's far enough," his other self commanded.

Percy froze. He looked at his own reflection standing a few feet away. The doppelganger's khaki navel pants, white shirt and boots were covered in mud and blood. But he had the same intense blue-green eyes. The same sandy blonde hair pulled back into a pony tail. His high cheekbones spoke of his connections to the royal bloodline. His thin lips twitched into a sardonic smile, and that's where Percy saw the difference between himself and the man from another world.

The man's smile held no mirth. The cruel smile went straight up to his equally malevolent eyes. In those eyes Percy saw murder and madness.

"What happened to you?" he asked his twin.

"I could ask you much the same question, Captain," the other answered.

"I mean, *why*? What would drive you to such madness and mayhem?"

"You ask me that? After what we've seen in our days as soldiers? After everything we did to survive in Crimea? I lost more than my leg there, Captain. But I gained a better understanding of the world and my place in it. Life is pain and suffering. Death and decay. And it's better to be the one inflicting the damage than receiving it. Better to be death's messenger than to be reaped by the black angel himself. That's where true power lives."

"You're completely insane!" Percy cried.

"But not stupid, Captain. I'm going to kill you and drag you back to that whore's room. I'll take my time carving her up before I put your gun in her hand. When they find both of you dead, the authorities will think she killed you in self-defense before dying. They already harbor suspicions that you're a murderer. Once they find you, they'll close the case. I'll lay low for a while here, adopt a new identity, keeping my face hidden, and soon I'll be free to kill as I please down here. I like it here, and I could see living in these tunnels for the rest of my life. Moving between worlds, leaving death and chaos everywhere I go."

"You would damn yourself to all this decay and darkness?" Percy questioned, trying to keep the man occupied while his mind raced for a way out of the situation.

"You know what they say, Captain. Better to reign in Hell than to serve in Heaven."

His doppelganger pulled the trigger.

The hammer fell with a loud click but wasn't followed by the thunder of a bullet leaving the barrel.

Misfire!

Percy kicked the oil lamp on the ground in front of him. It flew into his evil twin's face. Following the lamp, Percy charged headlong into the doppelganger. The man swatted the lamp aside, losing his grip on the pistol. It clattered into the mud as both men grappled with one another. They spun against a wall, colliding into it with a thud. Percy struggled to hold onto one wrist of the madman while punching him in the gut. A vicious headbutt slammed into Percy's forehead with a crack. His already drug-addled head spun more as he struggled to keep his footing.

The other Percival broke free enough from the captain's grasp to quickly draw his bloody Bowie knife and thrust it at Percy's head. Percy caught the knife-wielding arm by the wrist and pushed back. His attacker kneed him hard in the gut and Percy slid down the wall, fighting off the knife all the way to the floor. The doppelganger straddled Percy's chest, now driving the knife down toward his head with both hands.

With his right arm pinned beneath the left knee of his assailant, Percy pushed back with all the strength he could muster in his weaker left arm. He dug deep into himself, searching for every ounce of willpower to survive. The dark Percival leaned all of his body weight behind his arms. Inch by agonizing inch, the long blade moved toward Percy's face. Percy tried harder to free his other hand, but he couldn't shake it loose. His vision began to swim, affected by the drugs coursing faster through his body with exertion and the air being pushed from his lungs by the man sitting on his chest.

"Shhhh," the grinning demon told him. "It'll all be over soon. You can rest soon."

Percy's left arm quaked with fatigue. The blade quivered a half an inch from his left eye.

A gunshot rang out, strangely muffled by the mud walls surrounding them and by the thundering thud of Percy's heart beating in his ears.

The doppelganger suddenly sat up straight, pulling the knife away from Percy's face. A red blossom flowered in the middle of the madman's chest. He looked at it in surprise, and then looked down at Percy. For a moment, Percy could see himself through the other man's eyes. Sweat beaded on his forehead and shock played across his face.

The Percival from Hell looked at him, not liking what he saw. Percy's eyes showed compassion, goodness and pity.

Then Percy was back in his own head as his counterpart fell dead with a wet thud onto the floor.

Percy pulled himself up to his knees, struggling for breath as he looked to the source of the gunshot. He saw two men coming down the tunnel. One was his first mate, Alex Cross. The other his newfound friend, Socrates.

"Alex, how did you—"

"I'm not your Alex, Sir Percival. My name is Captain Cross of the steamship *Titan*."

"Of course," Percy smiled. "Please call me Percy. And I guess you are not my Socrates then?"

The engineer shook his head, a dire look on his face that was the opposite of the smile and wonder of the Socrates Cayce he had come to know.

"We've been tracking down our murderous retired captain," Alex told him.

"And you know about the Cross Rip between realities?"

"Yes," stern Socrates answered. "The mirror behind you seems to be the nexus point between worlds. We have dynamite to seal the tunnel here in hopes that it will close the breach forever."

"As does my Socrates on the other side of the mirror."

"I bid you farewell then, Sir Percy," Alex told him. "And I hope we never have to meet again."

"As do I," Percy said with a grim set of his jaw. "I fear that if we do, it will spell the end of existence as both of our worlds have come to understand it."

"We'll be sealing this side of the breach when you leave," Cayce said as Percy gathered up the oil lamp and his pistol.

"We'll do the same on our side."

Percy stopped to give one last glance at his dead self. He thanked the Fates that his life had taken a better turn after losing his leg in the war than the life of his doppelganger. He left their world behind, passing through the mirror and back into his own reality.

* * *

"I've convinced the chief to suspend his investigation of you," Socrates Cayce told Percy. "You're no longer a suspect."

Standing on the dock below his steamship, Percy clapped the engineer on his shoulder.

"Well done. Did he believe your theories about the Cross Rip?"

Socrates smiled. "Of course not. But with conflicting eye witness reports and my report of the real murderer being buried under an *accidental* collapse in the Shanghai Tunnels, he had little choice but to close the case."

"You're a good man, Socrates. Chief Lappeus has no idea what kind of asset you are to his police bureau."

Gazing up at the stacks of the ship, Socrates had a longing look in his bright eyes.

"What are your plans, Captain?"

"Once the timber is loaded, I'll be sailing for Japan to trade. Commodore Perry of the American Navy opened that country up nicely, and I feel it's time that I pay the Land of the Rising Sun a visit."

"I've always wanted to see the Orient," Socrates admitted.

Percy looked at his friend and smiled. He had been hoping to question him about his employment with the city police, and now the young man hinted that said employment might not be as binding as one would think.

"How would you like to serve under a captain who appreciates and respects your opinions? One who realizes what an asset you are to his crew?"

"My bags are already packed, Captain. I'll write the chief a resignation letter and post it before we set sail."

Socrates turned to hurry back into the city and collect his belongings.

"Don't forget any of your tools, Engineer," Percy called after him. "I think we're going to have need of them when we get to Japan."

Percy watched his friend disappear into a crowd of dockworkers loading various ships. He turned and bounded up the gangplank and onto the deck of the *Titan*. From there he could see Socrates making his way into the city. He watched until the engineer faded from sight.

He really did hope the man remembered all of his tools.

Although Percy doubted that steam powered suits of samurai armor were more frightening than the knife-wielding nightmare of his dark side, he suspected he would need the brilliant scientist's help once again.

About the Author

Mike is a self-proclaimed Metal Maniac. He's a lover of all things Horror, Sci-fi, and Fantasy and has authored the novels *Hollywood Cowboys*, *Kiss of the Traitor*, *Dead Town*, and *Terminal Horizons*. His numerous short stories have appeared in a variety of anthologies and online magazines.

A proud father of two, he lives in the beautiful Pacific Northwest. He is hard at work on the final *Hollywood Cowboys* novel, *Season of the Dead*.

Mike is the past president and cofounder of the Northwest Independent Writers Association.

You can follow Mike on Facebook at:

https://www.facebook.com/pages/Mike-Chinakos-Author-Page/119409624782484?ref=hl

Or visit his website:

http://mikechinakos.weebly.com/

DEMONWOOD

Mark Everett Stone

Hickok, I'm calling you out!"

James Butler 'Wild Bill' Hickok sighed heavily through his thick mustache, staring glumly at the cards he held in one rough hand. Aces and eights. The game was an inch from him, the pot fat and ready to be scooped up, but now it would be divided among the three players who stared at him in alarm.

"Gentleman," he said quietly. "It appears I have business." A soft sigh. "Although it's come sooner than I would have liked."

"You could just leave," said Captain Massie, one of the other players. His eyes were wet with worry. "Grab yer horse and get the fuck out of town."

"And how would that look, Captain? Me, running like a fucking coward?" He shook his head sadly. "Naw, a man's gotta take care of business."

Hickok strode calmly, confidently out of the dim light of Nuttal & Mann's Saloon with shoulders thrown back and head held high, straight into the bright light of an August noon. The muddy town of Deadwood stretched to the left and right, the wooden faces of the buildings like moldy teeth burst from the dark gums of the earth.

People lined the wooden sidewalks. Clothed in rags, finery and all matter of dress in-between, they waited silently with pensive faces and fidgety motions. It wasn't a festive mood that hung thick in the air. Silence gripped them like a resolute fist, and Hickok fancied that he could hear their collective breath, the slow inhale and exhalation of a giant beast crouching, waiting to pounce.

But what drew his eyes was the figure standing still in the mud, head down, tan ten-gallon hat obscuring its features.

Black leather vest, dun colored trousers; blue bandana around the neck and heeled boots clothed the thing that wore a man's shape, finished off by brown leather gloves and gun belt. A long-barreled Colt rested along his right hip in a worn holster, the leather discolored and ratty.

"'Bout time, Hickok," said the figure in a voice that sounded like hacksaw blades caressing piano wire. "I almost came in looking for you."

Hickok stopped a few inches from the end of the walk. "I came, demon." He pointed to a body at the figure's booted feet. "What happened there?"

The demon toed the body of a youngish man covered in mud, but even with the thick coating it was easy to see the harsh angle of a broken neck. "This one was set to kill you, Hickok. Shoot you from behind like a coward. I couldn't have that."

Hickok sighed. "You killed him so you can kill me?"

The figure shrugged, not bothering to look up. "That is what I have been ordered to do. If he were to kill you, then I would have failed." The ten-gallon hat tilted up as the demon looked square at Hickok. The people nearest to the famous gunslinger gasped. "I never fail."

A lesser man would have shuddered and looked away. For Wild Bill Hickok, showing such weakness was throwing blood into the water and waiting patiently for sharks to arrive. Still, his eyes narrowed, whether in disgust or dismay no one could say.

Blankness, blackness, a featureless skull-shaped void that seemed to drink in any light that dared shine near. The demon was as expressive as a mannequin, yet somehow managed to radiate an almost palpable menace and evil that had the crowd of onlookers take an involuntary step back.

Then it smiled.

The void split, a parting where lips would have been, wide and long, stretching almost to the back of its 'head', revealing large, shining teeth like the ivory keys of a piano. It was a smile of near transcendent joy and malice, the grin of a serial killer as he slices into a victim, the smile of a sadist torturing a cat.

"You ready, gunman?" asked the demon in its jangly voice.

Bill nodded. "Reckon so." He took a squelching step into the mud. The foul stuff smelled of horseshit and fear. "Got a name, demon?"

That horrendous smile never wavered. "Why?"

"If'n I die, I want to know who's doing the killing."

"Zztagalothz."

"Well, ain't that a mouthful."

That ugly smile grew larger until the piano key teeth seemed to circle the void of the demon's skull. "There are shades of sound you flesh sacks fail to appreciate."

"That's enough goddamn jawin'!" hollered a voice from half a block away.

Hickok's eyes tracked to Al Swearengen standing on his third-floor balcony of the Gem Theater, coffee in one hand, the other buried deep in the front pocket of his trousers. Even from a hundred feet away, Bill could see the hate in the man's dark eyes.

Ellis 'Al' Swearengen was built like a wrestler with broad muscular shoulders and massive forearms. At thirty-one, the brutal owner and pimp was a legend in Deadwood for the cheap whisky and pussy to be found at the Gem and also for his total lack of self-restraint when it came to violence. Swearengen lured desperate young women to Deadwood and bullied and beat them into becoming part of his stable of prostitutes. It was rumored that his scarred fists put more than one man deep into the Dakota soil.

"You're master is jerking your chain," said Hickok to the demon.

A harsh, wobbly clamor filled the air, rising and rising until the residents lining the streets clapped hands over ears. The noise was a mixture of a demented calliope juxtaposed with a screaming rabbit. Quite a few women fainted. It took Bill a few seconds to realize that the demon was *laughing*.

"My master ... for now," it replied.

The fact that it could simultaneously talk and laugh unnerved Hickok more than its unnatural appearance. He went for his Smith & Wesson.

Wild Bill was quick, his hand a blur and the pistol spoke in a roar.

Peg-like teeth shattered, spraying the mud with ivory fragments. The demon's head whipped around 180 degrees before slowly rotating back, its smile still intact despite the fragments shining in the mud.

"Well ... shit," muttered Hickok. The S&W smoked in his hand, his finger no longer pressing on the trigger. What was the use?

"You are the first to shoot me in the teeth," said Zztagalothz in a tone that sounded eerily like ... respect. "That was smart, but not good enough. I am immune to ordinary weapons."

"So I see."

"Get on with it!" yelled Swearengen.

The demon slowly drew his pistol, revealing that it was not a Colt, but a Colt-shaped conglomeration of bone and sharp-edged obsidian. Jagged pieces of volcanic glass ridged the gray barrel from which a foul, black sludge dripped slowly onto the muddy street.

It hesitated.

Hickok sighed. "Might as well get it over with."

The ten-gallon hat tilted as the demon cocked his head. "You are not afraid?"

"I knew this was to be my last camp."

"Interesting."

The crowd held its breath, readying for the familiar sight to come.

Black flame shot from the bony barrel of the weapon, a liquid insult to the fabric of reality that snapped forward like a striking rattler to touch the famous gunfighter on the forehead just below his hat.

Wild Bill Hickok's head exploded in a welter of gore and bone fragments.

Act II

PanDEMONium

One last shovel full of rich Dakota dirt and the grave is finished. My hands burn like they have been dipped in fire, blisters already forming on the balls of my thumbs. It has been a while since I put to some physical labor.

The mourners are long gone. They came more to be at the gravesite of a legend than out of actually feeling some sort of sadness at his passing.

Fuckers.

Sol stands next to me, shovel in hand, jacket folded neatly by the grave marker. Sweat beads from his high forehead and plasters what is left of his hair to his round head. He is a good man, a better friend than I deserve.

"Pity," he says, wiping his mustache.

"More than that … it is a crime."

"All for stopping a man from beating a woman to death in the middle of the street."

I spit a thin ribbon away from the grave. "Seems that Mr. Swearengen thought Hickok might get a notion to becoming a lawman again."

Sol shakes his head and gives me a look of exasperation. It pinches his thin face something awful. "We been in town for a whole day now, coming across the country from the Montana Territories avoiding Sioux and Crow shamans and their magic, only to come to Deadwood where worse magic abounds." It is his turn to spit, and he does it well, going for distance instead of accuracy. "Demons, Seth. How are we going to build a hardware store in a town filled with demons? And why is it us burying Hickok, a man we met only just yesterday?"

"Because I volunteered. Because a former lawman should be put to rest by a former lawman." It is not a good explanation. In fact, it is terrible, but it is the only one I have. How could I tell my best friend that the man I met yesterday seemed more a brother to me than my own kin? Perhaps it is part of the magic that sweeps this wild country.

"Yeah, well Al Swearengen has demons, and if he finds out that you used to be a lawman, he might set one on you. He hates lawmen that much; they're a threat to his power. In Deadwood, Al Swearengen calls the shots."

"He won't know I used to wear a star on my vest unless someone tells him, so I am not worried about demons."

"Yet."

I nod. "Yes … yet."

"Excuse me, gentlemen." The voice comes from behind and it startles me, my hand flying to my hip, ready to draw. I just manage to stop myself before my fingertips hit the ivory handle. I swear at myself. Far too nervy—I need a drink of something fierce. As for Sol, he startles easy, but he doesn't carry a gun, so I don't worry about him plugging anyone.

"My pardon, Messieurs, I did not mean to startle. I was told I could find Monsieur Hickok at this location." It is an older man who speaks in a heavy French accent. He is perhaps in his forties, well dressed, with a full, graying beard and a glint of humor in his eyes. Something about him puts me at ease. There is a large trunk behind him, almost too big for one man to carry. He extends a blunt hand toward the grave. "I pray this is not he."

"I am afraid so," Sol says. "Mr. Hickok was killed today at noon."

The gentleman sighs heavily. "That is a shame. I have traveled a long way to meet the famous Wild Bill Hickok."

"From France, I suppose?"

"But of course, Monsieur, as I am French, so my point of origin was France. I traveled by airship to that stinking pesthole, New York. From there I took a steam carriage to Omaha, and from there I was forced to travel by stagecoach. Stagecoach! Can you believe it in this day and age? Such a barbaric means of conveyance." He shakes his head in disbelief. "Mankind has conquered the skies and the land, but we still must rely on brutes to convey us upon face of the New World!"

"That's because the Indians use their magic to blow up steam engines," says Sol. "Horses don't explode, no matter how much magic you throw at them."

"Pfaw!" tutts the tall stranger. "Magic! The tool of barbarians! It is science, my good men, that will elevate Mankind."

"Beggin' your pardon," I interject, head smarting with all the talk of science and airships and such. I never could cotton to such strange and wondrous things. Give me open air, a good horse, and the stars anytime. "But if you don't mind, there are introductions to be made. I am Seth Bullock, and this is my friend Sol Star. Who do I have the pleasure of addressing?"

"Ah, my apologies." The strange Frenchman stands taller, resplendent in his black suit, his graying beard bristling with bonhomie. "I am Jules Verne."

* * *

"Why are we in a tent in the middle of town?" asks Verne, tearing into a steak with great gusto.

"It's where we live," says Sol, waving a hand. "Until we build the hardware store."

The tent is grand by camp standards, a cloth enclosure over a wooden frame. We purchased the lot the second we reached town, the best spot for a store, clean straight across from the Gem. It cost most of our lucre, but I feel it is a worthwhile investment, and I told the Frenchman so.

We'd retired to the tent after purchasing meals at the hotel, which was full of eager prospectors looking to strike it rich down in Deadwood Gulch. The odds of becoming wealthy from gold mining are long, seeing how there are savage Indians about as well as the elements and wild animals, but gold brings a fever reason cannot counter.

Our new French friend listens to the story of Hickok's death in fascination and horror, at times forgetting to eat. Sol can sure spin a tale, it is a gift I envy, having no tongue for yarns. Hellfire, I watched the damn thing happen just a few hours ago, and I still sit here spellbound as Sol flaps his lips.

"Well, that is quite the story," Verne says, wiping his mouth. While not fat by any means, he is a big man with a big appetite. The buttons on his vest strain to hold the fabric together. "It was for this very reason Hickok contacted me, to help him rid this primitive town of the demon. Although I do not know how this Swearengen controls a demon."

Sol speaks up, his voice filled with authority. "He has the demon's true name." His brown eyes glitter. He is in his element, this learned partner of mine, filled with the knowledge from dozens of books. "Once you know a demon's true name, you control it."

I snort. "Hell, Sol, I heard the name the demon gave Hickok! Sounded like a man gargling with gravel with all those Zs and such."

He shook his head. "That was its second name, not the true name, the name of power. Question is, how in the name of all that is holy did he get a demon's true name."

I turn to Verne, "Why would Bill Hickok contact you, sir? Not that you don't seem a man of great reason and science who can perform great wonderments."

"I'm thinking that Hickok read Mr. Verne's story," Sol says suddenly. "Those newspaper articles about that man with a ship that sails underwater, killing all those slave traders." He snaps his fingers. "I read that other story. Did you really circle the globe in less than three months?"

"*Oui,*" says the Frenchman proudly. "However that is a tale for another time. I have grander things to show you."

"Fair enough."

Now my curiosity was piqued. "Grander?"

"*Oui, Monsieur!* Grand things indeed." He pats the great trunk at his side. We'd helped him move it to the tent, and it is a heavy piece of luggage. That man has a serious amount of muscle under his fancy French suit. "Wild Bill did indeed contact me after reading my account of Professor Lidenbrock and his journey beneath the crust of the world. He thought that I might have insight on how to rid the town of a demon due to my underground adventures." Verne throws up his hands, perhaps in disgust, perhaps in incomprehension. "I think he believed that demons came from Hell and that Hell resides in the deep places of the Earth. I, however, was intrigued at the notion of a demon plaguing this quaint frontier town and asked a wonderful young friend of mine, a man I met on my travels in a little town called Smiljan. I was quite struck by his intelligence and ingenuity, so I booked passage on an airship and paid the lad a visit. Upon hearing of a demon, he was skeptical, but at my urging, bent his great mind to crafting a device to defeat a being of unearthly origin." Once again he pats the trunk gently. "Nikola possesses a mind that few in this world have ever seen. A modern day Da Vinci, or Galileo."

Of course! I think. Hope blossoms in my chest. "He did it. He did it and you have it right there."

Verne smiles.

* * *

My stomach hurts, a queasy sharp pain that starts feels like a shit-ton of acid, and it burns way to my throat. It is hard not throwing up, to let fly with vomitus and decorate the drying street. I wipe my lips and find them desiccated.

I am no longer a lawman, yet I stride across the street filled with a myriad variety of humanity, dead set on performing a lawman's duty. Perhaps walking headlong to my death, but I can't stop myself. Wild Bill Hickok is dead because of Al Swearengen, because of the pimp's madness, and I have to do something.

Killing him would be easiest, putting a bullet from the Winchester in my hands straight between my eyes, but that would make me just like him, a murderer. Besides, he might sic his Hell servant upon me before that could happen, or maybe it lurks about in the shadows waiting for someone to foolishly try to kill its master.

There's the Gem, filling the night with raucous laughter and the smell of bad booze. The second floor lights are blazing as the girls inside earn top dollar for the pimp, and I wonder how many will be sporting bruises in the morning. It is that thought that spurs me on.

Through the door, and my blood begins to sing. I am excited despite the fear that pebbles my skin and raises the hair on the back of my neck. The wooden stock of the Winchester is a comfort, and validation for what I do this evening.

There are screams as people see a tall, slender stranger in a black suit bearing a Winchester. A man behind the bar ahead and to the right of me draws a pistol, but I shoot first, the rifle bucking in my hands. Bits of his left ear go flying, along with a goodly amount of blood. He drops the weapon and falls behind the bar, screaming. With a solid *clack*, I cock the Winchester, readying another round.

Another man comes at me, bearded face flushed with anger and an ax handle in both hands. I don't want to hill him, so I duck the swing and plant the butt of my rifle in his prodigious gut. He folds around the stock, mouth agape, spit flying from his teeth and then drops, wheezing. I step over his body toward the stairs.

"Swearingen!" I holler. "AL MOTHERFUCKING SWEARINGEN!"

Two more men rush me, but the sight of the rifle bearing their way stops them cold. They stare at the muzzle as if it's a rattler.

I smile, and I know it's not pretty. "Better get a move on." My voice is barely audible above the screams of whores and the stampede of patrons out of the Gem. I am giddy with reckless abandon. I could die this night, and that would be fine and dandy with me, as I have become a perverse thing, a demon of self-righteousness and wrath. The irony amuses me.

"SWEARENGEN!" My voice is thunder.

"What the fuck are you on about?" It's Al Swearengen himself striding down the stairs without a care. For me, it is proof that the demon guards him.

I look around, but I can't see the unclean beast, only Al strutting slowly and lighting a cigar. For a moment I am taken aback. He is younger than I expected. Younger and more brutal-looking. I had only seen him from afar, and up close I see his thin, black moustache tries to hide bloodless lips like worms squirming above his chin.

He is powerful. He radiates strength and is probably stronger than I. It hits me that without my gun and without his demon, he could probably rip my head clean off my shoulders without too much effort. The thought sobers me, and the feeling of might slowly bleeds from my body, leaving tremors that I savagely clamp down upon. I will not appear weak in front of this man.

"You and me, Swearengen….noon tomorrow."

He cocks his head. "Why the fuck would I do that?" His feet finish walking down the stairs, and he faces me square. Short and powerful, like a badger.

"I aim to be the law in this town, Al, and I want you to turn yourself in to me tomorrow noon in front of God and the good citizens of Deadwood."

"There ain't no fucking law in *my* town."

His town. The arrogance angers me. "Just because you know a demon's name doesn't make you a king here."

Swearengen's eyes fly open wide. "How the fuck do you know that?" He slaps his forehead. "That Jew partner of yours, Star. Has to be. Looks like I will have to kill a Jew as well."

I look around. The place is empty except for the man behind the bar shrieking about his ear and the idiot on the floor, gripping the ax handle and still trying to catch his breath. "Between you and me, Al, how the fuck did you get a demon's true name?"

He purses his lips for a second, sizing me up. "All right. Seeings how you're a dead man, I don't mind telling you. A lazy drunken fuck named Lentz, a fucking Jew, owed me big, several thousand lost in gambling and I needed to collect. Turns out he was kind of a Jew mystic and had possession of the creature's name, only he never used it because of the fear of losing his soul. One night while being a fucking drunk Jew he told me about it, and I said if he gave me the name we would be square." Swearengen laughs. He is amused by his tale, and I can tell he loves to hear himself jaw. "Hell, I said if he gave me the name, not only would we be square, but that I would give him ten-thousand fucking dollars to get out of my fucking town and never return."

Sol is right ... Al has a demon's true name and considers himself king of the hill. Seems like time for this reign to be over.

"Noon, Al. Noon. Come quietly and I will treat you fair."

"You are deluded, Mr....Mr ... " He snaps his fingers.

"Bullock," I say, shouldering the Winchester. "Seth Bullock."

Act III

CounterDEMONstration

"Seth Bullock, I'm calling you out."

It is the demon and not far outside the tent. My gut churns with bile as fear momentarily unmans me. *What am I thinking?*

"Don't worry, Seth," Sol says, adjusting a strap. "I have faith in Mr. Verne here. He sure is a smart man."

"*Oui*," comments Verne with a smile. "I am very smart, and my young friend Nikola who invented this apparatus is very smart as well."

It is easy for them to talk about a surplus of brains when they aren't readying to face off the demon who killed Wild Bill.

"Seth Bullock, I'm calling you out." The demon's voice tears through my ears.

"Just hold your water," I say, very happy my voice does not quaver. "I am coming out very soon." That would hold it for a couple of minutes, but no longer.

Checking my pocket watch, I see it is a minute until noon. Of course the demon is early.

"There you go, Seth," says Sol with a smile. He slaps my metal-clad shoulder. "You are ready, my friend."

I look at Sol Star, my best friend, and I see the worry in his eyes that does not make it to his voice. A glance at Verne shows me a big man who seems utterly confident, even serene.

"There is no doubt I look like an ass," I say, adjusting my holster. It is large and clumsy, and the weapon inside is uncomfortably heavy.

Sol smiles. "Yes. Yes you do. Now go kill a demon."

"No time like the present."

Verne's heavy hand finds my shoulder. "Remember, Seth, do not let it shoot you above the chest."

I nod. "Of course." There was no desire within my breast to become the second gunman in as many days to lose his head.

My boots hit the streets. They are dry today, the churned mud from the day before has dried into a treacherous landscape of foot-snagging holes and ridges. Again the citizenry lines both sides of the street in hushed expectation. They gasp and cry out as I emerge, standing tall. A few giggles and titters as well.

Can't say that I blame them. My torso is covered in a vest of silver and copper wire that spins round and round my chest and belly. Leather straps hold the strange garment together, and two long wires trail from the back to drag against the ground. Silver knobs the size of Double Eagles run across my chest beneath round glass dials whose purpose seems to measure something, but what I can't say. There is a foot-long copper box affixed to my back by more leather straps. The outward face of the box is made of thick glass and one can see strange gears and cogs inside made of several different kinds of metal, not the least of which is gold.

I sure looked a sight, a half-metal gunslinger from one of Verne's travelogues.

Hung at my side in a holster constructed of thin copper sheets and rivets is my weapon. Twice as long as a Colt, it also is made of a variety of metals, and from the butt trails a long, black cable that attaches to the bottom of the box.

"Mighty fancy getup," drawls the demon, who is just twenty short feet away. "Might I ask what for?"

I finger my new weapon. It is unnaturally cold. "No."

"Have to say I am mighty curious." The demon grins wide and once again I see those ivory peg teeth and shudder.

"Tell me your true name, then."

It sighs, sounding like the breeze through an abattoir. "Guess I will never know."

"You gonna stand there like a couple of nancy boys in love or are you gonna shoot already." It's Swearengen, standing on his balcony drinking coffee and looking like he wants to stare a hole clean through me.

"Your master urges," I say.

The demon nods. "He does."

"Want me to shoot first or are you going to?"

I barely see him draw, it is *that* fast. The barrel of the bone gun is a big black hole that leads straight to Hell, and I know the flame will hit me in the throat. I stand tippy-toe as fast as I can.

The gun spits darkness, and there is the feeling of being hit in the chest with a hammer accompanied by the sound of bacon frying. Underneath the sizzle are subtle screams, as if the gun is powered by the wails of the damned.

I jigger and judder and my heart races as strange energies flow through me, contracting my muscles and near setting my hair on fire. Sharp hot pain radiates from just below my collarbones throughout my whole body, but sets up at the base of my skull, threatening to tear bone apart.

My teeth feel like they are about to explode and strange *pops* and *whirrs* come from the box on my back. Against all odds, neck muscles feeling shredded and torn, I turn my head and seen the hellish black flames trickle down the two dangly wires into the hard soil of the street. The wire begins to melt from savage energies.

It is over and I take a long breath. The demon tilts its head.

"Interesting."

For once Al Swearengen says nothing.

I draw my weapon. It is a clumsy, slow move because my hands are twitching and fingers shaking, but I manage to hold the heavy weapon out in front of me, pointing more or less at the demon.

Thin copper tubing wraps around a long barrel, and instead of a hole at the end, there is welded a small round plate made of silver. Three one-inch prongs spaced evenly around the plate point at the demon, who is staring in what I assume to be fascination. There is no trigger guard, no trigger. Just a button beneath a small brass box from which the barrel emerges.

I push the button.

There is no sound from the weapon, no bark of gunpowder, no spitting of lead or flame. Instead the demon explodes with a harsh *clap* into a cloud of noxious black liquid that spatters everyone within thirty feet. It smells like brimstone and assholes. What's left of the demon's clothes is burning in the street. A rank, rancid smell arises from where flame touches black liquid.

I am shocked, momentarily stunned at the violence of the reaction. One minute ... demon—the next ... not. Black liquid drips from my heavy metal vest and my moustache. I know my hat will never be clean again.

Striding over to the spot where the demon stood, I step into more black fluid that squelches loudly beneath the heels of my boots. Nothing left. Except a head.

That head is still smiling, but it is stiff and lifeless, like a hell-crafted doll made of frozen tar. I don't bother to pick it up, because I have no desire to foul my hands.

"I reckon you're aiming to kill me," Swearengen yells belligerently. "Well come on up and try."

I am dirty, reeking and tired, my body suffering from lack of sleep and the effects of black fire and exploded demon. There is no more humor in me to tolerate Al's bellicosity. All I want is a bath.

"No Al," I finally say after a long pause. "I am no lawman, so I have no desire to arrest or kill you." He relaxes a bit at this, but tenses up at my next words. "However, the good people of Deadwood whom you have been bullying for the past few months might think differently about being forgiving."

I walk away, the sound of muttering and cursing following me into the tent, quickly drowned out by Verne and Sol's glad cries. I think Al might not be such a big shot in Deadwood anymore.

If he survives the next few minutes.

About the Author

Born in Helsinki, Finland (The Land of the Uncommonly Stubborn), Mark Everett Stone arrived in the U.S. at a young age and promptly dove into the world of the fantastic. Starting at age seven with the Iliad and the Odyssey, he went on to consume every scrap of Norse Mythology he could get his grubby little paws on. At age thirteen he graduated to Tolkien and Heinlein, building up a book collection that soon rivaled the local public library's. In college Mark majored in Journalism and minored in English. The newspaper business wasn't for him, so he did what every good writer does: find work in a wide variety of fields that included catering, bartending, and restaurant management. After getting married, he sold Hyundais (before they became popular) and, because he lives in Colorado, Subarus. Eventually he matured enough to be able to sit down and just write. Currently Mark is working on his latest novel "Omaha Stakes" and has two more in the works: "The Spirit In St. Louis" and "The Judas Codex". Both from Camel Press. Recently, he has been featured in the Arts and Entertainment section of the Denver Post.

OF FATE AND GEARS

A.L. Kessler

Felisa leaned against the wall and watched the man round the corner. After another item, she assumed, glancing up at the airships circling the area, preparing for landing. The docks made the perfect place for a thief; between the crowds and confusion, he could slip something out of a pocket or even a purse with ease if he was skilled enough. And this man was. He was also fated to die. She didn't know how yet, but as Fate it was her job to mark him for Death, once she figured it out.

Following him down the alley, she took in the way the leather trousers hugged his body and tucked into his black boots. His white shirt was stark against the black leather belt holding his gun. A strange contraption designed at the rise of technology, it was a weapon where a bullet was discharged through the pressure of steam. His deep auburn hair was long and pulled back at the nape of his neck, the fashion that most men wore in this time, and he pulled it off with great distinction.

He paused and studied his surroundings. She prayed he would think her a passerby. It wasn't often a human could see her, but in this strange time of technology and magic, anything was possible. When his blue eyes met hers, her heart pounded against her chest. He could see her! He could see through her magic, which meant he saw the white hair and swirling green eyes that made up her true appearance. She knew it by the way the color drained from his face. What was she supposed to do? Her sisters would tell her to run, but his gaze held her captive. They stared at each other for a moment before he turned and ran. A very human reaction to what she was.

She let out an annoyed huff of air and heard the mechanical flutter of wings before feeling a tiny weight on her shoulder. A creature made of magic and gears landed on her shoulder and whispered in her ear. "Your sisters wish you to return if you have not marked him yet. They have something important to speak to you about."

The mechanical fairy was nothing more than an annoying leash her sisters used to keep tabs on her. Felisa resisted the urge to swat at the thing. "Have they seen something?"

"It has to do with your sentence." The creature chirped, a bit too happy for Felisa's taste.

Her sentence, the thing that doomed her to this life. You defy your own fate and everyone gets their panties in a bunch. "Great. I'll be there in a little bit." Her eyes remained glued to the direction where the man disappeared.

"Don't you think about going after him," the fairy squeaked.

Felisa let out a sigh and held her hand out for the creature to walk on to. She met the red glowing gaze of it, lecturing would do nothing, but she entertained fantasies about smashing it. Shame it was a living creature, despite being made of gears and scrap metal. No bigger than the palm of her hand, Trix would be easy to crush with a simple clap. Her wired wings stretched out behind her, buzzing as if she could read Felisa's malicious thoughts. The gears ground and shifted with each tiny movement of the creature, and even though Felisa knew magic brought it life, she always marveled at the creation.

"I'm not. I'm wondering why he could see through my guise." She put the fairy back on her shoulder, rethinking her desire to scold the creature. "It's rare."

The thing snickered. "Maybe you are loosing your abilities. Perhaps your sentence could be nearing its end!"

Impossible. "Stop joking around." She spun to go the opposite way of the guy. Her heels clicked against the cobblestones as she walked. The sun started to sink behind the horizon, and the airships settled into their docks on the river as she walked by. Pulling her shawl tighter around her, she tried to think of any other reason he would be able to see her. Two came to mind, but she could accept neither one.

* * *

Luke turned the corner and headed further into the city from the airship docks. Holy cow that woman was strange, with her flowing long white hair. White as if the gods had drained it of all color, he'd never seen a human being with such color ... and her eyes. They caught his attention, but he found it strange that no one else seemed to notice her. He swore she was following him. She'd been behind him when he snatched the last purse. Was she another thief? Someone working for the police? She wore a key around her neck. Maybe she worked for some unheard of department? No, she was just a crazy woman, someone not from around here.

He glanced over his back and found himself alone. Heaving a sigh of relief, he doubled back. With the airships landing for the night, he could pick a few pockets while he made his way home. Sure enough, people filled through the square: women with their fancy bustles, bags, and clutches. Their parasols blocked their fair skin from the setting sun, and many of them locked arms with handsome men. Luke imagined that they would go home to their fancy houses and enjoy an evening in front of the fire.

Slipping his hand into the pocket of a gentleman, he unclipped the clasp of a pocket watch and slipped the thing out of its hiding spot. He dropped it in his own pocket and continued on.

They would enjoy tea and talk about the flight they just took, probably a vacation of some sort since air travel was normal for long distance. He, on the other hand, would return to his little house that he shared with his sister and mother, bringing home what he could to help provide for his family.

He finished winding through the crowd and made his way through the industrial area, finally ending at his house—one of the small two-bedroom ones in a row. Copies of the house lined both sides of the street within a few feet from each other. Luke entered and called out for his mother.

"In the kitchen," her chiming voice answered. That was his mother, always up-beat and sing-song even on the darkest day. He pulled his boots off at the entry and went to find her leaning over the coal stove. "Soup again?"

"Porridge."

He cringed, "Same thing. How is Anna feeling?"

"Still weak, the doctor said she will be until this illness goes away." His mother's voice hesitated, betraying her lie. The doctor knew that it wouldn't go away without some type of medicine, and if they weren't able to get it, his sister would die. He cursed fate and took his belt off.

"Watch your language, Luke. You maybe half past twenty years, but you will learn not to speak to me as such."

"It wasn't towards you." He kissed her cheek. "I was cursing fate."

She chuckled. "You be careful with that as well, those who curse fate or deny it tend to get in trouble."

Yeah, like he believed those old stories—mere children's tales to scare them into behaving. "Yes mum." He peaked into the room he'd abandoned to his young sister and found her sleeping in her bed. Her red hair stuck to her fever soaked forehead, and her chest struggled to rise with each breath. He leaned against the doorjamb, studying; he knew he'd do anything to keep his sister alive. Their father had been killed in an airship accident, leaving the family on their own. Not long after, his sister came down with this illness, and the doctors were stunned and wanted to try a new medicine, but they couldn't afford it. It was all Luke and his mother could do to get food on the table.

He locked his jaw, mentally cursing fate again as he turned away. His sister had her whole life ahead of her. How could this happen to her? At ten years old, she should be attending school, not be bedridden. He closed the door behind him, leaving it cracked so they would be able to hear if she called. "She looks worse."

"It's just the fever, it'll fade soon." His mother promised. "It fades and rises as it does with any illness. You know this." Her eyes flickered to the weapon at his waist. "You'd better put that away."

He nodded and started to take the belt and holster off. "Did you have much work today?"

"A few of the ladies came by with their dresses for the ball."

"Which ball?" He crinkled his nose; he never understood the need for big fancy events.

"This one is to celebrate the newest mayor. It's still a few months away, so I expect business to pick up, which means that you can … go out less."

He made a noise of agreement. "There was a woman today. She stood out from the crowd."

"Stood out how?" His mother snapped to attention. Turning to him, she locked her blue eyes on him. With her silvering hair tied up on her head in a bun and her eyes narrowed to slips, she set her hands on her hips and asked again. "How, Luke?"

"She had white hair and swirling eyes. Her dress was one without a bustle, but it had a corset. Her skirts were layered, and she wore a shirt with long sleeves that bellowed around her wrists. It's like she's not from this time. There was a key on a necklace that laid on her cleavage."

His mother ticked her tongue in disbelief. "There is no such woman in this town."

"She was by the docks, I suppose she could have come from somewhere else, but I swear I saw her, though no one else seemed bothered by her."

His mother turned back to the soup. "You would be wise not to go back there." The tone of her words told him they were done talking about it, but he couldn't get the woman off his mind.

* * *

Felisa stormed into her house and walked to the back. Ignoring her belongings and rooms, she headed to the big brass door at the back. Made of a series of gears and locks, she studied the ugly thing and took the key from around her neck. Running her hand over where the knob on the door should be, she summoned the keyhole and used her key to unlock it. When she turned it the gears on the door turned, whirled, and clicked. The door split in the middle and opened. She walked in and tried not to jump at the sound of the door slamming shut and locking behind her.

Two women stood in front of her, and she tried not to sneer at them. The one on the right had tightly wound silver gray hair piled on the back of her head. She wore a black robe with a sash around the waist. Her skin was wrinkled and flawed, and her glazed-over blue eyes still seemed to see everything around them even though Felisa knew the woman was blind. The one to the left had flowing black hair, ending at her waist. She couldn't have been more than six and barely came past Felisa's waist. The girl's eyes swirled with green, and she wore the dress appropriate for the times, with a big bustle on the back and her little, high-heeled boots. Felisa found the look ridiculous on the child.

"You called?"

"Have you seen how the man is going to die yet?" The old one asked.

Felisa shook her head. "No, but I know there is something that is supposed to happen to him. I only assumed death because of the dark aura he has around him."

"He is a thief, that is enough to taint anyone's aura. Of course you should know that."

She snorted. "I did what I had to in order to survive."

"You still stole." The young one chided. "But we don't think it is him that is destined to die."

Felisa tried to hide the ticking of her eye. She hated the games her so-called sisters played. Unlike her, their jobs as fates were permanent, and they carried no respect for the fact that Felisa was serving out her sentence. At this rate, she would never find someone else to deny their fate.

"Then what do you want me to do? The assignment was to track him, find out how he was supposed to die, and then mark him for death. If he's not supposed to die, what the hell am I supposed to do?"

"Follow him and find out what he is destined for. Neither of us can see it, and only you can see his aura and the silver string that leads him."

Great. "So you want me to what? Get close to him? Stalk him?"

"Follow him, use the gifts bestowed to you years ago." The young one stomped her foot. "Do what you do best."

She wrinkled her nose. "One problem with that, he can see through my guise."

"What did you do to get close to your marks before you took this job?"

"Job," as if she had applied for the position. "I seduced them, does that really matter here?"

"Do what comes natural." The old one said. "Follow his string with him and see what his destiny is. This one is special."

Felisa nodded, not keen on the idea, but these women ruled her fate. She bowed her head. "As you wish."

She turned away and knew they disappeared. Growling, she unlocked the geared door again and went into the main part of her house. This time she turned to the kitchen and started making tea. She took her time with filling the kettle and setting it on the stove to boil. Going through the motions calmed her nerves. Her mind focused on the sound of the water starting to boil, and she went to get a steeping ball.

With no guest there was no reason to get the fancy pot out, so she just needed one cup of tea to help her sleep. Filling the ball with chamomile leaves, she thought about the man. Seducing him was an option, but with him seeing her true self, it wouldn't be as simple as if he saw her as a normal woman. Grumbling, she poured the boiling water over the steeper and waited. "Shame that one of my gifts isn't to see into the future." No, despite what the mortals believed, she only got glimpses. It was normally the other two who could see the full future. The fact that they could not see Luke's was startling and unsettling.

* * *

Luke studied the people walking along the docks and spotted another constable lingering. It was the third one already, and Luke hadn't managed a steal yet because of them. He had some jewelry left to sell, but he would have to wait until the evening when the drunkards were out and willing to spend money. Giving up on the morning crowd, he turned down an alley and paused when he almost ran into the woman from the night before..

"You again," he muttered, but she glanced at him and he knew she'd heard him..

She gave him a grin, and he paused. He hadn't meant it to be a compliment, especially with the way his mother reacted, but the woman seemed pleased to see him. "Me again."

He hated to admit it, but she was beautiful in her own right, even if she was otherwordly. "Who are you?"

"I'm Felisa and you, little thief, are Luke." She walked towards him, a sway in her hips, and she reminded him of the rich women he often robbed on the docks.

Disgust filled him. "How do you know that?"

"I know a lot of things, and how is no concern of yours." She stopped, realizing he wasn't impressed. "I saw you in the square yesterday. Why do you steal?"

"You always this forward?" he asked with a snort. "It's not your problem."

She raised a brow and put her hands on her hips. Despite her strange clothing, he had to smile. She moved like an enchanting woman, but the switch in her attitude told him she held fire. "Not my problem? Maybe I'm just trying to get to know you or start a conversation. It's not like you can talk to anyone else."

"And what says that you aren't going to run to the authorities? What says you aren't the authorities?" Luke braced himself, ready to run at her answer.

"Because I don't like the authorities, in fact I downright hate them. They've done nothing but get me in trouble." She put her finger to her chin, pretending to think. "Yeah, hate would probably be the best word for that."

He chuckled at how she appeared cute with the simple gesture. Shaking his head, he tried to clear it, but it had been a while since he'd thought of anything but stealing. "I'm not into sharing details of my life, now excuse me, I have to get going." He pulled his jacket over his gun as he moved past her. She followed him, and he tried to think of how to get rid of her, but something told him that wouldn't happen. "Look, what do you really want? Clearly you have some invested interest in me, if you're following me. And how come no one else seems bothered by how you look?"

A few beats went by before she answered. "Because my magic keeps them from seeing me. They see what I want them to. You, however, actually see me, and that is why I'm interested in you."

"Magic? You're kidding me. You're what? Some type of witch?" The superstition was probably why his mother warned him to stay away. "People like that don't exist, and those who claim to be such get killed." Persecution of witches had come and gone as a fad, but there were those who still liked to take into their own hands the task of killing them.

"I'm not a witch, I'm ... " she hesitated. "I'm Fate."

He nearly tripped over his feet. Stopping, he spun around to face her. "Now I know you are mad. Fate is a mythical force that people blame when things go wrong."

"Yeah, and no one remembers when things go right." She grumbled. "You really think that? I mean, every myth has a personification of the gods. Why not Fate?"

Luke tried to recall the origins of fate as he continued walking with the woman following him. "The Greeks believed that there were three women who controlled fate. You are merely one."

"They had that part right. There are three of us, but two of them stay hidden. Think of me like the one in the field. I get to roam around amongst the humans."

He raised a brow; he didn't remember any of those in the Greek myths. "So you do what while you're masquerading?" He couldn't believe he was having this conversation.

"That's enough about me. I've shared plenty." Something sharp in her tone made him glance back at her. Her smile had faded, and she'd gathered her skirts up as they walked through the industrial area to keep them from dragging in the dirt. She stood out against the gray metal of the buildings and the steam rising from the factory. Her eyes cleared of their swirling color for a moment and remained a steady green. Spotting a faint flicker of grief, he felt guilty for bring up the questions.

Swallowing, he turned to continue but waited for her to catch up to him. "I steal because I need items to sell. My father was killed in an accident and left my mother, sister, and I in poverty. My mother barely makes enough money to put food on the table, and my sister is sick." He sighed. "I do what I can. Some days are better than others, but I'm hoping to make enough to pay for the new medicine that's supposed to help her."

Felisa switched her grip on her skirts and bit the inside of her cheek to hold her comment. She hated this part of her job. If he believed her story about her being fate, he would inevitably think she could change his sister's. Chances were the girl's thread was short and would come to an end soon. It often happened with the circumstances he'd told her. An annoying flutter came by her ear, and the slight pressure on her shoulder told her Trix had shown up to join the party. Everything would get back to her sisters, and Felisa knew it wasn't their ideal plan, but it was better than trying to seduce someone who did not want to be seduced. "That is tragic. Sadly, everything has a price."

"'Everything'? Even the things Fate can control?" he asked, his voice bitter. She knew what ran through his mind. Always better to blame fate for things you can't control.

"I don't control everything. In fact, I can't see most people's destinies." No, normally only those who would die or those she was granted access to their strings. She rubbed her eyes, and when she opened them the faint glimmer of a string caught her eye. A strange silver thread connected her and Luke together and continued through the slum neighborhood they had arrived at. She glanced over at Trix who seemed to shut down on her shoulder. The stupid mechanical fairy had fallen asleep. Maybe that would be for best, fewer things to report back to the sisters.

"Then what good are you as Fate?" He snorted and went to enter a house, pausing at the door. "My mother doesn't like visitors."

She tried not to lose her temper with him. "I guide people when I know what their destinies are, that way they don't fight against fate. Your mother won't mind me, it's not like I'm planning on eating or anything. Though I'd like to look at your sister."

"No." He clenched his fist. "My sister needs rest and doesn't need to be bothered by someone who can't help her."

Well, so much for finding out that destiny. Maybe she should have stuck to her plan of seducing him. She shrugged. "Fine, no seeing your sister."

He opened the door and called out to his mother, but no answer came. He went to the kitchen and she followed. There on the counter was a note. Felisa waited for him to say something. He glared up at her like he wasn't pleased with her being there. "She went to a client's house to hem a dress."

"Convenient." She forced a grin, her mind still occupied by the thread.

He cleared his throat and her eyes shot back to him. "What did you mean when you said fight against fate, is that possible?"

Felisa nodded, "There are even certain people who have been able to deny their fate."

"Something tells me that isn't a good thing." He chuckled. "What happens to those who deny it?"

She licked her lips as a nervous habit, "They get sentenced to work for the sisters." She grumbled. "And there's only two ways out of that."

"Which are?"

"Trick someone else into denying their fate, or serve it out." She glanced away from him, her eyes following the line of the silver thread. In order to figure out his destiny, she needed to follow it and put the pieces together. Why was part of his thread attached to her?

He made a hmm noise as she refused to meet his gaze. "Something interesting?"

"No, but I need to get going." She bowed her head and smiled at him. "I'll be around though, Luke." Waving, she walked out of the house. Out in the silent night she took a deep breath, a tugging sensation told her to go back into Luke's house. That's where she needed to be, but she refused to believe it. A woman came ambling towards the house, a bag clutched in her hand, and Felisa ducked into the shadows. The woman walked into the house, calling for Luke, and Felisa knew it was his mother. She turned from the house and headed back to her own, her mind stuck on the man.

* * *

Felisa got back to the house in the evening and growled when Trix's wings finally fluttered to life, brushing against her ear. She'd forgotten about the annoying fae while she was at Luke's. "Did you have a good nap?" Leave it to a mechanical being to sleep the whole day.

The whirling gears and buzzing metal settled after Trix moved from Felisa's shoulder to her head, sitting on her black hairpiece. "It was nice, but I'm sad that I missed what happened between you and Luke. Did you find out what his destiny is?"

"No, but I can see the string now. All I have to do is follow it and piece together what I know." She gazed at the strand wrapped around her wrist, and her voice hesitated. There was no feeling to accompany the thread, but a heavy weight landed in her heart. "I think he's someone who can deny fate."

"Oooo, and what makes you think that?" The wings came to life again, and the fairy hovered in front of Felisa's face.

She resisted the urge to swat at the creature like a bug. "Because I've seen not one but two strings, but it's too early to tell, those two strings may intertwine together." Though she couldn't imagine how. Maybe he'd be the one to free her from her sentence. "Is there something about this job that I need to know about?"

The fairy put a tiny finger to her lips and rolled her eyes to the left, pretending to think about it. "I know your sisters are very concerned about this case, and that is why they put you on it instead of one of the underlings."

Underlings, people who bargain with Fate with the price of working for them. Felisa ground her teeth, thinking about having one of her underlings do this job. It wouldn't work. "Interesting. I have work I need to do."

"I'll come with." Trix's voice rose a pitch.

"No," Felisa responded almost too quickly. "You stay here and watch the house." She didn't need a tail on this, especially Trix. "I'm just going to do some foot work, nothing too in-depth, since I need him in order to see the string."

Trix snorted, "Did you seduce him like you were told so that you can spend time with him without looking like a creeper?"

"No, and I hate to break it to you, but I always look like creeper. Now stay here," Felisa snapped and walked out of the house. She followed the shimmer of silver from her into the town. With the lack of airships, the only noise in the night was the steam engine and factories far off in the distance. She shuffled through the darkness, knowing the town by heart. It was the place she grew up, married, and with all intents and purposes, died. Bitterness filled her as she passed the tavern her unfaithful husband owned. Her string led her to the entrance, and she snorted at the disgusting urge to enter. She'd have to see him tending bar with a new woman on his arm, though there was always some satisfaction of seeing the scar on his face she'd given him.

Someone behind her cleared their throat and she spun around to see Luke there. "What are you doing here?" She asked.

"I came to try and sell some of the things to the drunkards here. What are you doing here?"

She shrugged. "Taking a walk down memory lane, I suppose. Shall I leave you to your work?"

"Why don't I buy you a drink? The barkeep here knows me well, so normally they're free." He winked at her. She didn't want to, just contemplating walking into the tavern made her stomach churn.

Luke raised a brow, "You paled, you alright?"

She couldn't let this get in the way of her job. "Yes, let's go in." She forced a grin before looping arms with him.

He chuckled when she led them inside. The bustle of the early evening crowd seemed quieter than normal, but there behind the bar stood the man she hated. The man who had been fated to kill her. He locked eyes with her; even though she appeared different, she swore he recognized her. His dark hair was cut neat and slicked to one side with an off center part. His grey eyes bore into her, and the only thing that marred his handsome face was the scar she had given him. Her fist clenched as she remembered holding the kitchen knife she'd use to deliver the blow. Fated or not, she had refused to die that night.

Luke tugged her forward and up to the bar. "Come on. We'll get you a drink, and then I'll show you how I do business."

"Why don't I grab us a table while you get drinks?" She gave him a smile, but her eyes darted towards Warren.

Luke followed her gaze. "Sure, back table, dark corner. It's the best place to do business."

Of course. She let go of his arm and made her way back to a square table, hidden in the shadows and away from the fire place. She settled down and tried not to make a disgusted noise when a woman came over and kissed Warren. When the light caught the gold band around the woman's ring finger, Felisa wondered if the woman knew about Warren's infidelity issues. Luke sat down next to her and handed her a glass of wine.

"You really don't like this place, do you?" he asked and pulled a bag out from under his jacket. He placed it on the table with a clink.

She wouldn't meet his gaze. "This place and I have a history." She shrugged and raised a brow when a man started towards them. Burley and stumbling, she wondered how much he'd drank, but she spotted a thread leading from him to Luke. "Here comes your first customer."

The man sat down and riffled through the bag on the table. He pulled out a gold pocket watch. Covered in a strange red haze, it caught Felisa's eye. She almost snatched it away, objects with a red haze normally brought death. She pressed her lips together as the man examined it.

"Ye donna have this ta oth'r night." The man's heavily accented voice carried as he held the watch towards the firelight.

"It's a new item, acquired two evenings ago," he said with a smirk "It's a nice piece, one of the better ones. The craftsmanship is flawless, and the chain gold."

The man nodded and pulled out a handful of notes, throwing them on the table. "If ye keep getting quality items like this, ye might sell more." He stood and took the watch with him. Felisa cringed when the red haze surrounded the man. Death would soon come knocking at his door, and she knew it was best that Luke got rid of it. She frowned at the strange sense of overprotectiveness.

"Something wrong?" Luke asked, drawing her out of her thoughts.

"No. Just thought I saw something," she murmured and tried to sink into the shadows when Warren marched over to the table.

He pulled up a chair and sat at the table with them. "Who's your friend Luke? Someone else in your line of … work? Or paid company?"

"She's a friend, not a whore," Luke snapped back without hesitation.

Something welled in Felisa, and she sat up straighter. She wanted to say something to Warren but knew she'd been warned about doing such by the sisters.

Warren raised a brow at her sudden shifting. "Right, I just wanted to tell you that authorities have been checking in on this place. They have recovered a number of items reported stolen from patrons of my bar. No one has dropped your name yet, but it's just a matter of time."

"Have any of the patrons ended up dead?" she asked before she could stop herself.

"Not that I know of, do you know something we don't?" he growled at her. "How do I know I can trust you? You're a stranger here."

Luke's eyes shifted towards her, and she knew she'd have to explain how she was connected to the bar. She met Warren's gaze and gave him a smile. "I'm a stranger to you, sir, not the city, and certainly not this bar. You can trust me though."

"I trust her," Luke chimed in. "She wouldn't put me in danger."

He was putting a lot of faith in her. She blinked, seeing the silver thread wrapped around Warren's wrist, between the three of them hovering above the table she could see the three threads intertwined.

Damn. She needed to figure this out and fast. A familiar buzzing filled the air, and Trix landed on the table.

"Isn't this interesting!"

All three of them glared down at her.

"I told you to stay home." Felisa snapped.

"Who is that?" Luke asked.

Warren snarled, "The better question is what."

Trix crossed her arms and glared up at Felisa with her tiny eyes. "You didn't tell them about me? What are you even doing here, you hate this place."

"Yeah, well you totally just ruined it all, you pesky little fairy." She growled at it. "Excuse me gentleman, I must go, I have a feeling my sisters need me." She stood and scooped the fairy up, placing the creature on her shoulder. As she walked out, Trix hummed in her ear some strange melancholy tune. "I know that song."

"It's the one played when they lowered your empty coffin in the ground." Her voice held too much joy for the subject.

Felisa shook her head. "That's morbid, I don't want to think about that."

"Why did you go there tonight?" The fairy asked.

Felisa shrugged. "I felt like something was calling me there, and now I think I know why."

* * *

Luke watched Felisa hurry out of the tavern. So many questions rushed through his head, but he needed to focus. Warren's admission about the authorities meant trouble

"That girl is going to get you caught. You can't trust women who want to meddle in your work." Warren's gaze was still on the door. "I don't know what it is, but there is something about her."

Luke snorted. "Funny, she didn't seem too fond of you." He knew better than to share Felisa's secret. Besides, if he went around talking about fate and magic, he'd likely be locked up in the asylum. "She said that she had history with this bar."

"I don't recall her, but so many women pass through here. I can't keep track of them all ... but back to business. I have seen several officers in here asking about stolen goods. I know you keep to the docks, but if I catch you stealing in here it will be your death."

Luke believed him, Warren didn't exactly have a reputation of being kind to those who broke the tavern rules. "I've never stolen from your patrons, at least not here. I've only sold goods. You said no one has ratted me out."

"Yet, Luke, yet. You don't understand the trouble you're bringing by stealing so often. I know that you're trying to get more money for your sister, but you need to lay low until the authorities back off."

He shook his head. "You know I can't do that. She needs the medicine soon, the longer we take in getting the money the greater chance of death. You've buried a loved one … you know that grief. My mother will not survive that again. I will not lose my family to illness," he snapped.

"And if it's deemed by fate?" Warren asked, and his eyes clouded with something dark. "You know no one can deny fate."

He knew otherwise, but he couldn't say such. "I don't believe in fate." Doubts about Felisa started to fill his mind.

"Just think on it. I'd hate to see you end up in the jail, or worse, in a grave." Warren stood and went back to the bar. Luke leaned back in his chair and wondered what he was supposed to do. He wished Felisa wouldn't have left, perhaps she could have told him what his next step was. He grabbed his bag of loot and left the bar. His mother would expect him home, and he didn't feel like scrounging up anything at the docks. Something told him all the answers lay with Felisa.

* * *

Felisa walked into the summoning room and glared at the two figures there. "I have news."

"Trix said you left her at home tonight. There was something you were following that you didn't want her to know." The young one said.

Felisa tensed. "I was originally going out to clear my mind. Something pulled me in the direction of the tavern off Main Street. I ran into Luke there. I've seen strings of fate between he and I." Both the sisters gasped, and Felisa crossed her arms. "Better yet, they are intertwined with my ex-husband who tried to kill me."

The younger one giggled. "Well isn't that interesting! Best find out why and how this all works out."

"I was working on it until Trix came into the bar and spoke in front of them. She almost spilled who I was to Warren. If he finds out that I'm not dead, even in this form, he will try to come after me again."

The older one shook her head. "He cannot kill you in this form. The only way he can kill you is if you become mortal again. You know the chances of that happening."

Yes, she did. "Can't you help me with this? I don't know what to do. For the first time in this job I am lost."

"You must discover your own fate in this one, Felisa. You have your choice to follow it or not. The choice you make decides Luke's. Just remember that." The two of them faded and Felisa cursed.

She hated thinking about her own fate. She remembered something she had been told when she first took up service, something the younger sister said.

"Fate is not always written in stone. It flows and changes based on choices we and others make. That is the only way one can change their fate without actually denying it. Only certain events are set."

Like her death. She managed to deny her death, but in the end the coffin was buried and she disappeared, becoming fate, but what if this wasn't the same? Luke's face flashed in her mind and an urge to check on him filled her, to make sure he hadn't done something stupid. She rushed out of the summoning room and to the front the door. Throwing it open, she balked, seeing Luke standing there.

His eyes were red and swollen from crying, and his fists clenched at his side. "My sister … she's worse. Please Felisa, there has to be something you can do to help." His voice cracked, and she knew she couldn't deny him this. His handsome face had crumpled into a grieving brother, and her heart broke.

"Let me grab my bag and Trix." She wanted to wipe his tears away. It was rare for a man to show such emotion, and she didn't want to add to the raw hurt he'd shown her by pointing out the tears. Grabbing her bag from beside the door and the sleeping Trix from the planter, she followed him out.

The evening rain had come in, as was typical with the season, but they ran in the mud. She gathered her skirts with her free hand and tried to keep up with Luke. "What is going on with her?"

"She's gasping for breath and the fever has spiked. Shivers have over taken her body and she can't keep anything down."

She hardly heard his words as they ran, but she repeated the symptoms over in her head, already trying to formulate a plan. If anything, the teas and herbs in her bag would postpone death and give Luke a chance to get the rest of the money. Lightning flashed, and a vision surrounded her.

Gone were the muddy streets and the rain, replaced by cold stone and bars. She glanced at her hands only to see the strong rough hands of a man. Luke's hands. She was having a vision through his eyes. A jail cell, with guards standing outside the bars. A wailing of a woman could heard in the background, followed by a drunken laughter she knew too well. Warren.

The vision faded and she came back to the muddy streets at midnight. Luke had stopped ahead of her and turned back, his brow drawn in concern and his face pale.

"You disappeared for a moment." He shouted. "What happened?"

She swallowed. "I was taken into a vision. Do not worry about it." She gathered her skirts again and ran to him. Eventually the mud gave way to the pathways to the homes. He led her to his house once more. When he opened the door his mother greeted them.

"Who is this?" She asked, pulling Luke into her arms. "You bring a stranger into our home while we should be grieving?"

Felisa took the chance to catch her breath as Luke explained. "She is special, Mum. Please, let her look at Anna."

The older woman flashed her a skeptical look. "You don't strike me as anything special. Luke, is this the woman you told me about before?" He nodded and she hit him over the head. "You fool, you have brought Death to the door."

"No. I haven't, she is not death. Please!"

Felisa cleared her voice. "Trust me, ma'am. Death is a whole different person than I. If anything, I would like to see if I can prolong your daughter's life."

"You may see her," the woman finally whispered. "If you are death, at least her suffering will be over."

Felisa closed her eyes, and she hoped she would not be seeing the reaper tonight. With a deep breath, she opened her eyes and entered the other room. She found the pale child on a cot, gasping for breath as Luke described. Sweat dripped from her forehead and her body shook. "Start some water," she ordered. She dug in her bag and pulled a pouch of tea leaves. "This will help bring down the fever and help with the chills." She searched wherever she could to see a thread, but it wouldn't reveal itself. She cursed under her breath when Luke took the leaves from her and headed towards the kitchen.

"Who are you truly?" His mother asked when Luke left the room.

Felisa shook her head. "I can't tell you that."

"I can see you, truly see you as Luke does. That must mean something."

Felisa put her wrist to the girl's head. It did mean something, their family was special. They could deny fate, but she wouldn't allow that to happen, not at such a high cost. She remembered when she first spotted the Fate before her and how confused she'd been, until she realized why. Closing her eyes, she took a deep breath. "It simply means that your family is special. That is it." She stood. "Give her the tea, followed by some broth. The fever should edge and the broth will help restore some of her strength."

Luke came in with a cup of tea and handed it to his mother as Felisa walked out of the room. Quick footsteps told her he followed, with a deep breath she turned to him. "Something is going on, and I don't quite have it figured out."

"You look like you thought of something." He put a hand against her cheek. "For a moment you looked angry, and now there's a sadness in your eyes."

She turned away from him. "I can see a string connecting you, Warren, and me all together, but I don't know why. Your sister has no string, and I know without the medicine she won't win. I know that if you continue to steal you are bound to get caught."

"Then what do you suggest I do?"

She licked her lips and gave a wicked smile. "I know the way in and out of Warren's house, I suggest you make that your next target. He won't report the crime, because the amount of money he has is from blackmailing constables and political figures."

"How do you know this?"

She crossed her arms, "Because I was his wife, and I discovered that he was running a brothel out of the bar. He blackmails his highest paying clients. When I figured it out he tried to kill me and failed."

Luke stared at her. She couldn't be serious. Warren's wife died of suicide. Everyone knew it. She'd gone crazy and went after him with a knife, then she gutted herself on his floor. It was a grizzly death and no one ever talked about it. Even Warren mourned in private and never brought it up. "You can't be her. They buried her."

"In a closed coffin ... that was empty. Get him drunk enough, he'll tell you that I attacked him with a knife when he tried to poison me. I was warned that night by someone who told me that I could change my fate. After I wounded him, he took after me with a knife. I disappeared before his eyes. Because I denied my fate of death, the other person was set free and I took her place. So here I am. Warren made up a crazy story about how I killed myself, and the sisters gave me a new identity and look in order to hide amongst the people. I'm not always in this place or time, but this is where I like to dwell still. You see me as this." She gestured to her skirts and corsets, "Others see me as just a plain middle class woman walking the streets. No one ever stops to talk to me, because they don't know me. It's part of the magic."

"But Warren talked to you—"

"Because I was with you. Now, do you want to save your sister or not?"

He pressed his lips together. Out of everything she'd said and told him, he found this hardest to believe. Warren had always been willing to help people out. Not a killer and not a blackmailer. Of course ... if breaking into his house would save his sister. ... "What is my fate, Felisa?"

"I won't tell you that," she whispered and looked down. "I won't let you end up like me."

That tugged on his heartstrings and he rubbed his chest. "Is it really so bad?"

"Having to figure out people's fate? Good and bad and watching it play through? Only a few years have passed here, true, but I have seen centuries of lives and deaths happen since I've died." Her eyes darkened with something he couldn't place.

"So what?" he asked. "I have to choose my own fate then and hope it's the right one?"

She nodded and started out of the house. He gave a nervous glance to the door of his sister's room, grabbed his pistol off the table and followed Felisa out. Her quick strides meant he had to run to catch up with her. "Are you sure about this?" He couldn't believe he was going to follow her in this, but the idea of being able to pay for his sister's care kept him going.

"Yes." Her fists clenched her skirts, turning her knuckles white and he wondered if she knew something he didn't.

* * *

When they approached the city square, shouting echoed through the streets. Felisa put a hand out to stop him behind her. They both leaned up against the wall of the alleyway and she peaked around. The man Luke sold the pocket watch to stood arguing with a man in a suit. Their screams couldn't be deciphered completely, but she caught enough words to know the man in the suit noticed the pocket watch. *His* pocket watch. She bit her lip and waited. The man would surely point Luke out, and she couldn't risk that. Glancing down at her wrist she saw the string leading across the square, but not stopping at the man, but they couldn't cross. Not right now.

"What's—" Luke started to speak, but she shushed him, still watching the scene. The man in the suit pulled out a pistol and shot the other one. Luke jumped behind her but remained silent. The man swept down and removed the pocket watch, continuing on like nothing had happened. Luke finally pushed past her, but stopped dead in his tracks when he spotted the body. "That's the man from earlier."

"Yes it is." She sighed. "That watch had a bad aura around it."

"Why didn't you say something about it?" He growled. "He's dead because I sold that watch to him."

She shook her head. "He's dead because he decided to buy a stolen watch from you. Not your fault, you're doing what you have to. He was an idiot waving it around the square."

"The authorities will be here soon, someone had to have heard that shot."

Yes, even with the steam-powered guns, someone would have heard the ruckus. She cursed and grabbed his wrist, dragging him across the square. "I don't like them being so close, but we'll make due."

He followed her without a word. Running across the square, she led him down another alley and stopped in the middle, standing in front of a large door. She traced the engraved wood squares and tried to push the memories away. The enchanting nights that she spent curled up by the fire, naive and blissfully unaware of everything going on. She clenched her jaw and pulled out a key from one of her pouches.

"You still have a key to the house?" He muttered in disbelief.

She chuckled. "I had it on me when I died." She unlocked the door and put her weight against it to open it. Luckily for her, Warren hadn't expected her to return.

Luke muttered something unintelligible as he followed her into the house. The only light came from the fireplace and a few lit candelabras. Tall bookcases lined the walls of the back foyer where they entered. The dying fire proved no one was working in the house. Good, they would be able to get in and out without a worry. Voices and shouting came from outside, and she knew the body had been found. They needed to move.

"Follow me," she whispered and led him through the foyer into a dark hallway. Everything remained where it was before, each decorative item, collectable and furnishing cast familiar shadows for her to follow. Her lonely nights wandering the house would pay off as well as her past thieving skills. She paused and started tapping her foot on the floor.

"What are you doing?"

"Looking for the boards I need to remove. I know he hides it here. I walked in on him when he was stashing it all," she muttered and paused when she finally hit a hallow part. Bending down, she pried the wood up. Piece by piece she revealed a hollowed out section where bags gathered.

Luke took a sharp breath and Felisa smiled, but her smile faded when the buzzing of tiny wings filled her ears.

"What do you think you are doing?" the mechanical fairy snapped, landing on Felisa's shoulder. "This is not what your sisters had in mind."

She knew that, but she wasn't breaking any rules. She wasn't forcing him to deny his fate, she gave him the choice and when the time came down to it, she believed he'd make the right choice. "Back off Trix." The fairy gave an angry buzz but settled on her shoulder.

Shuffling of the bags meant Luke was digging through them and taking what he could. Felisa kept an eye down the hall. With the authorities so close, if Warren walked in, they wouldn't have a chance to escape without getting caught. "You have enough?" She asked.

"Yeah, let's go." He climbed up out of the hole and started back the way they came. She grabbed his wrist. "The authorities will be all over the square. We need to go out the front."

His eyes widened, but she gave him a warm smile. "Trust me." She led him down another hall towards the front. Paintings and a few photographs dotted the walls, but she paid them no attention. She didn't need to see her old life again. No. She needed to get Luke out safely. She shoved Luke into a closet when the front door clicked open. Ignoring his protest, she leaned against the door and willed her magic to change her appearance to what she was when she had been human.

Warren walked in and froze when he laid eyes on her. Felisa smiled and gave him the barest of nods to let him know she was real. She ignored the buzzing protest of the fairy in her ear; the squeaking voice whispered that she was crazy. Maybe the rumors were true and she carried that into being a Fate.

"Five years and you've decided to return?" he snarled. "The authorities—"

"Are investigating a death in the square." She walked towards him, putting a seductive sway to her hips. "Someone was killed over a pocket watch that was sold at your establishment."

He swallowed and backed away from her, fear flashing in his eyes. "How long have you been back in town?"

"I've always been here, you've just never seen me, but it seems that the Fates aren't done with us yet." She glanced down at the silver string connecting her to his heart, and she knew what needed to be done. Luke would get out safely and live freely. Warren needed to die and she would kill him. It would add to her sentence without a doubt, but she couldn't care less. She trapped him against the wall, her body pressed up against his. A tremble went through him as he met her eyes. She wrapped her hand around the pistol at his waist, knowing he always kept one there. She pulled it out of his holster while her other hand traced the scar on his cheek.

"Not so strong now when your wife comes back from the dead, are you?"

Confusion creased his brow and he shoved her away. Felisa stumbled back but aimed the weapon at him. The steam compressor hummed and hissed when she pulled the hammer back to start the reaction, but before she could pull the trigger a shot rang out behind her and Warren jerked.

Blood exploded and blossomed over his white shirt. His hand shot up and touched the wound, coming away covered in red, with wide eyes he gazed past her and at Luke. "You."

Felisa spun around to face at the thief, who pocketed his pistol with a blank face. The silver thread between Luke and Warren faded, as did hers, but the one between Luke and her remained. Trix fluttered up and tugged on Felisa's hair. "Now would be a good time to leave, before you get caught."

Felisa nodded and stuck the pistol in her waist band. Luke stuck his back in the holster and grabbed her hand, running into the streets and into an alley. He had the bag slung over his shoulders and started back in the direction of his home, but Felisa stopped him. "My place is closer. It'd be best to not let them find us wandering the streets."

He gave her a small nod, and she knew he was close to shock. Tonight was the first time he'd killed.

* * *

Felisa brought Luke a cup of tea, and he settled on the couch. "Why did you shoot him? I shoved you in the closet for a reason."

"I don't know, it seemed like a good idea at the time. When we were going through the halls I saw the paintings of you and him, and you looked truly in love with him, but I could see that he wasn't with you. He married you, was unfaithful, and hiding things from you. It was a moment of anger when I came out of the closet. And then I saw you aiming at him and I knew that I couldn't let you do that. You'd never forgive yourself if you killed him."

She knew he was right, but she worried he'd denied the fate laid out for him. Of course, the thread between them remained. "He stole my heart when he caught me trying to steal his watch. Warren insisted on trying to save me from a life on the streets ... and he did. For that I owe him a lot." She shrugged. Trix came and landed on the table in front of them.

"The sisters have requested your presence."

Luke glared down at the thing. "Will you tell me what that is now?"

"In layman's terms, it's a magical mechanical fairy that was created to be my baby sitter." She sighed and stood. "You sit here and drink your tea. I'll return in a little bit. Tomorrow we'll work on getting that money to the doctor for that medication."

Assuming there would be a tomorrow for him and he wasn't turned into a Fate like her. She gave him a weak attempt at a smile and walked to the back of the house. Taking the key off her neck, she opened the door and stepped in.

The younger one giggled. "Very brash."

"I followed the strands, isn't that what you wanted me to do?" She clenched her fists in her skirts, trying to keep her temper. "It lead me to Warren, a string to the heart meant he had to die."

The older one nodded. "Yes, he had to die and everything worked out as it should."

Her heart leapt. "So Luke is free to live the rest of his life?"

"Yes, but listen to me closely Felisa. You denied fate when you were a mortal, and you followed it as you are now. You let Luke choose his own way instead of nudging him to denying it. He made the choice to kill Warren when you were determined to do it, but both of you made a selfless choice. You could have tricked him into taking your place, but you didn't, and he chose to murder someone even though you tried to secure him a safe getaway."

"Everything was predestined, but each choice changed that destiny. Today you and Luke followed the path that would lead to your happiness instead of his downfall." The younger one gave a single clap true to her childlike nature.

Felisa bowed her head. "I merely did what I'm sentenced to." Though she resisted the urge to trick Luke, she knew she couldn't condemn anyone to this life.

"And for that your sentence is over," the old one whispered.

Felisa balked. "What?"

"Your sentence as Fate is over. You are free to live your life where you left off, that is unless you chose to go elsewhere or choose to continue as what you are."

Glancing behind her, Felisa tried to weigh her choices. To continue a new life, possibly with Luke or on her own. Even with the strange events surrounding her, the town might learn to accept her after being gone for five years, presumed dead, or they may label her a witch. Or she could continue as Fate, watching centuries of events go bye. Every event tore her soul or made it soar. She closed her eyes and tried to see Luke's fate if she left. His sister would heal, his mother and his sister would start their own dress shop, and the family would thrive. Luke would quit thieving and take over the tavern.

But no matter how hard she tried, she could not see her own future with him. She would have to trust her life to the fates, again. With a deep breath she laid her key down on the table between the two sisters. She would have to take her chances and not screw up her second chance at life. Giving the two a slight bow, she knew her choice had been made the moment she spotted the silver string for the last time. Her final test of following her fate, her destiny. She left the room and the door closed behind her.

In an eerie sweep of wind, the door disappeared, leaving a blank wall behind.

With a deep breath she went back to her greeting room to find Luke sitting on the couch, sipping his tea. She smiled at him. "I've been released of my duties."

"Who is taking your place?" He asked, his eyes tinted with fear.

She shrugged. "It doesn't matter, what matters is I'm here and I can live my life again."

"Should be interesting to explain it to the authorities ... where you came from and why your husband is dead and not you." He snorted and stood.

With a gentle push, she put him back on the couch. "I'll handle the authorities, and tonight I'll be making a payment to the doctor for your sister's medicine. I know that she'll heal and your family will be fine." She didn't know how things would work out between them, but she didn't care. Now she was free, Luke was safe, and her husband had paid for what he'd done.

About the Author

A.L. Kessler is a paranormal romance author residing in Colorado Springs. Since she was a teenager she's loved weaving stories and spinning tales. When she's not at the beck-and-call of the Lord and Lady of the House, two black cats by the names of Jynx and Sophie, training a playful puppy named Zelda, playing with her daughter, or killing creepers and mining all the things with her husband of 4 years, she's either reading, participating in NaNoWriMo, or writing in her Blog Writing Rambles.

www.amylkessler.com

SINKING TO THE
LEVEL OF DEMONS

David Boop

Deputy Matthew Ragsdale considered the sheriff's badge mocking him from the desk of his dead boss. He swore it even laughed at him, but then realized the sound came from his daughter Trina playing back by the jail cells. His wife Sarah, hovering anxiously near his side, took a tentative step closer and laid a hand on his arm.

"What are you going to do?"

"I don't have a choice."

Water pooled at the corners of Sarah's eyes but refused to become actual tears.

"You can wait for a new sheriff from Tucson, or marshals from Denver."

Matt thought about that, but the longer they waited, the more likely Jimmy Kettle's Claw Rock Gang would come back to town. They were satiated on blood, alcohol, and women for the moment. But how long would that last?

His mentor, Sheriff Levi Fossett, had laid out what it'd take to bring the outlaws down. A plan that would put Kettle in his grave with little risk to either of them.

Too bad the Claw Rock Gang gunned down the unarmed man outside of church. Fossett's body cooled in the freshly covered grave. Sarah, Trina, and he still wore their Sunday best, all three having just attended the funeral. As the reverend spoke his words about death and resurrection, the town folk looked to Matt, and their eyes asked unspoken questions, "Are any of us safe?" or "Are you man enough to stop the madness?"

He stood in the sheriff's office pondering that very same question. He'd been like them, when his family first moved West on the first expansion. His father, a trader, was one of the original settlers of Drowned Horse. Matthew's strict upbringing carried over into a love for law and order, a love Sheriff Fossett picked up on and nurtured.

Trina emerged from the back and sidled up to her daddy. She hugged his leg, her ever-present rag doll he'd made for her hanging from her tight little palm.

"Someone has to." He picked up the badge with conviction. "No. I have to. I have to finish Fossett's work. I know the plan."

The plan wouldn't work just by himself. Deputy—No. *Sheriff* Matthew Ragsdale would need help. However, he wouldn't get it from most of the men in town. The outlaws had terrorized the locals going on two months, and more than a few died standing up to Kettle and his gang of fiends. Leaving the town unprotected while he rode to Flagstaff didn't bring him any comfort either.

He didn't need many men. One more should do it.

* * *

Adoniram G. Craddick nearly swallowed his mouthful of square nails when the newly christened sheriff poked his head around to the back of his business.

"Ram."

"Shaywiff."

Matt stepped into the room. "Now don't start that shit up. Don't matter what title they hang on me. We've been on a first name basis since we married sisters. That's what? Going on ten years now."

Lanky, but not skeletal, Ram righted himself to his full six foot three frame. He examined the project he was abandoning, and then gave his guest his full attention. After setting down his hammer, Ram spit the nails into one hand. The other he offered to Matt.

"Yeah, I s'pose I'd never get used to calling you that, anyhow. Offer you some lemonade in the parlor? Sadie just made it this morning."

Matt looked down at the item Ram had been working on. "There isn't a rush on that, is there?"

"That?" Ram indicated the coffin. "Nah, just planning ahead. With the Claw Rock Gang around, it pays to have stock."

The statement stung Matt visibly, and Ram quickly backtracked. "I mean, not that it'll always stay that way. I'm sure they'll get their comeuppance before long."

Matt removed his Stetson and stared at the rim. "Yeah. Sorta why I needed to talk to you."

Drowned Horse's undertaker raised a wary eyebrow at his best friend. "Sounds like I might need to make that drink a bit harder." He opened a clay urn and pulled out a small flask. Ram blew off what Matt hoped was only dust. "Whisky?"

* * *

Claw Rock hadn't been named because it looked like a claw, or a hand, or anything remotely claw-like. It got its title from the gouges outside the red sandstone cave. Word had it the Apache drug prisoners into the cave and slaughtered them; a brutal tradition dating back before a single settler set foot in the area.

Kettle and his men chose to hole up near the *Wiipukepaya*, the tribe that moved in when the Apache left. The gang traded food and money to the Indians for the right to claim the cave as their own. Starved and desperate as the *Yavapai* Nation had become, they didn't care if one group of white men killed another. While the natives still considered the area sacred, Matt had a sneaky suspicion that the Wiipukepaya knew what everyone else suspected; the U.S. Military hovered just on the other side of the horizon, planning to drive them from their homes just as they had the Apache.

James "Jimmy" Kettle was a former military man. Despite the informal nature of the outlaw life, Kettle ran patrols that walked a perimeter around the Claw Rock at night. They patrolled in pairs, each watching the other's back. So, Matt and Ram moved as a team, with the notion of taking out both guards less one get off a shout. There was enough of a moon out that a posse would've been seen moving through the brush, but two men crawling stealthily could be missed. The odds were still in their favor.

"I'm not so sure 'bout this, Matt," Ram said in a whisper, "I'm more used to buryin' dead men, not makin' them."

"We need to take out four, maybe six men to get to the place we need to be," Matt returned the hushed tones. "If this works, then the town's safe."

"If? You didn't say nothing 'bout no 'if'!"

Matt pushed his brother-in-law's face into the sand because Ram's voice crept up more than the sheriff thought advisable. Directly into Ram's ear he whispered, "Shush! They'll hear." He let the man's head back up and Ram spit sand from his lips. "There is always ... how do those generals say it? Oh, yeah ... a margin of error."

The undertaker shot daggers at Matt.

The sound of approaching footsteps signaled the men to roll in separate directions, positioning themselves on either side of a small mound. While Jimmy Kettle might be smart, his men were not so much. They followed a well-worn path around the rocks which made it easy for Matt and Ram to lay a trap.

As soon as the outlaws stepped into the snares, the lawmen pulled them tight, tripping the guards. Matt and Ram were on them before they could call out. Bringing the butt of their six-guns down decisively on the patrol's heads, the lawmen knocked them out quietly.

"See?" Matt badgered, "That's two we didn't have to kill, Deputy Craddick."

Ram huffed. "Don't call me that."

The next set of guards' pattern would take them too close to the cave's entrance to risk any sort of protracted attack. Fortune had it that they'd stopped by a large rock to roll a smoke. Matt and Ram slipped rags over their mouths and slit their throats. They fell without a sound.

Ram stared unblinking as their blood stained sand and rock.

Matt whispered, "These men raped two of the Sagebrush's whores, beat them bloody and left them for dead. That's no way to treat a lady, even one who sells her body. Every man in Kettle's gang has blood on his hand. If we end their reign tonight, the blood on ours might just be justified. Ain't this worth it to not have to fear Sadie's gonna end up raped or worse?"

Ram shot back, "Yeah, yeah. That's how you got me out here in the first place, damn snake oil salesman that you are. I just never had to take another man's life before. Give me a moment."

Matt gave him all the time they had to spare. Ram must have come to terms with his problem, because he helped drag the bodies behind the rock.

The late Sheriff Fossett covered everything in his plan, including spots to get an unobstructed view of the entrance of the Claw Rock cave. The height of the opening was easily thirty feet tall and curved out like a shell in the sand. The rock itself had a plateau above it where two more guards watched the grounds. In front of the cave, an area had been cleared of rock and debris, becoming a communal meeting spot. Nearly a dozen men milled around a cook fire, acting bored.

That bothered Matt, as they'd most likely be riding back into Drowned Horse soon.

Kettle's gang held a gallery of wanted men, each more mean than the next. One in particular stood out; a black man the likes of which Matt hadn't seen around those parts. Stocky and wearing a stove pipe hat, his ears were pierced with bone. The man stared into the fire like it contained a whore dancing on a stage. Seeing something he apparently didn't like, he spat into the fire pit, got up and entered the cave. He didn't reemerge, which gave Matt the willies.

Ram exhaled long and hard. "I think that's a black magic man. Like the witch doctors you read about in adventure magazines."

Matt asked, "How do you know?"

"I'm an undertaker. We know the people in our trade. Voodoo men from Louisiana, like him, specialize in death; creating it, worshiping it, fighting it."

"Fighting it?"

Ram shivered. "It's said they know death's face, and when he comes for you, a voodoo priest can scare him away."

"Why would Kettle have one in his gang?"

"Scare people. Keep his men in line. Who knows? It gives me the creeps, though."

"Me, too. Let's get this over with."

They made their way around the back of Claw Rock and scaled up the side thanks to a series of stacked rocks. The guards stood there, looking out at nothing, paying no attention to the lawmen approaching their backs, their complacency a result of Kettle's dark shadow. Who'd have the cojones to attack such an evil son of a bitch?

Keeping their hats tilted low, Matt and Ram spoke in turn.

"We're here to relieve you."

"Yeah. Boss wants a word."

The guards turned without a concern in the world.

"You're earl—" one started to say, but the sheriff shoved a knife through the bottom of the outlaw's jaw, pinching his mouth shut and driving the tip into his brain.

The second guard, however, was quicker and caught the undertaker's hand before it could plunge in. They grappled and it became quickly evident Ram was outmatched.

Matt moved up fast to wrap an arm around the man's throat, silencing him.

The guard was strong and, despite being outnumbered two-to-one, he held his own. He pushed backwards, dangling Matt over the rim. The sheriff looked down briefly at the campfire below him, but God's mercy kept anyone from looking up. Ram pulled them back from the edge. Matt tightened his chokehold, but the burly bad guy showed no signs of surrender.

The outlaw let go of Ram, twisting the undertaker's knife out his hand in the process. He swung it wildly at Ram, driving him back toward the opposite edge. Suddenly, he turned the knife around and stabbed Matt's arm. The lawman let go with a holler and dropped to the rock. Changing targets, the outlaw looked to send the blade right through Matt's heart when a gun went off and a red geyser spurted from the guard's forehead. The sheriff rolled out of the way as the dead man fell forward.

Moving fast as lightning, Matt grabbed a bundle of dynamite from the satchel they'd brought along. Ram did the same with a second bundle. They placed them where Fossett had predicted an explosion would bring the whole cave down.

After lighting the fuses, they hopped down the backside like mountain goats. Kettle's men made it around the bend in time to see the duo reach the trail. Bullets bounced against stone. Matt and Ram retreated, doing their best to keep cover between them and their pursuers. They returned fire as often as they could.

The explosion, when it came, took the top off of Claw Rock like a volcano. The lawmen didn't get as far enough away from the blast as they wanted, and they hit the ground hard. Dirt and gravel sprayed over them. Matt came up first, spitting sand from his mouth. Ram rolled on the ground, laughing.

The round-up didn't take long. Most of the Claw Rock Gang had gone inside seeking cover, not expecting the whole entrance would come down around them. According to the surviving crew, Jimmy Kettle, including his voodoo man, had been inside when the explosion sealed the cave. No one was coming out of that alive.

Matt's satisfaction in seeing Fossett's plan through to the end kept a smug grin on his face as they escorted the remaining criminals off to jail.

* * *

Drowned Horse gave Matt and Ram a hero's welcome. Music wafted from the Sagebrush Inn for the first time in weeks. The owner, known only as Owner, made the first round of drinks on him, and both men felt duty bound to imbibe.

Sarah and her sister Sadie, upon hearing of their men's return, came rushing over and lavished both lawmen with a public display of affection. Embarrassed, Matt blushed, but Ram jokingly asked Owner if he and his wife could use one of the rooms upstairs.

"You takin' to this deputy stuff, after all?" Matt ribbed.

Ram gave his new boss a mischievous grin. "If it's all free beer and taking down men like Kettle, then hell yeah, I'll be your partner." He held up his hand as a warning. "Part time, at least. Still got a business to run and all."

Matt handed over a tin star he'd grabbed while at the jail. "Let's make it official, then." He settled the crowd and spoke loudly. "Today we saw the last day of the Claw Rock Gang and the first day of Deputy Adoniram G. Craddick, my brother-in-law."

The Sheriff pinned the badge on Ram's pocket, and the crowd whooped and hollered. Sadie gave her man a big kiss. Sarah lifted a sleepy Trina onto her daddy's shoulder.

"Now, take good care of our town while I'm escorting these ne'er-do-wells off to trial, 'k, Deputy?"

"Sure thing, Sheriff."

They slapped each other on the back, and all was right with the world.

* * *

Sherriff Matthew Ragsdale returned from Flagstaff two days later to find what was left of Ram dead in the middle of the street.

Blood splattered the area surrounding the body like the pattern on a Navajo blanket. Matt scanned the street to find pieces of Ram scattered to and fro; a rib over by the water trough, a foot near the porch to Mrs.

Harris's clothing store. As close as Matt could guess, a pack of coyotes had ripped his deputy apart. He couldn't understand why the body rotted in the center of town.

There were signs of chaos, overturned chairs, broken windows. The town appeared as it did after the Claw Rock Gang went through it. The town's padre approached Matt with a message that turned the Sheriff's blood to ice.

No one was to touch Ram's body on orders from a very much alive Jimmy Kettle.

Before the Father could explain further, Matt rushed home to find his home ripped asunder. He raced through the three rooms and to the back yard. There were no signs of his wife or child.

At Ram's funeral parlor, an inconsolable Sadie tore at him as soon as he stepped through the door, alternating between beating Matt and trying to gouge his eyes out. Visiting nuns from the church managed to get her restrained.

"What happened? Where are Sarah and Trina?"

The holy women crossed themselves, and Sadie composed herself enough to speak.

"This is all your fault. If you'd done left Kettle alone, he would have bothered us for awhile, and then moved on when he saw there was nothing else for him here. But no! You had to play the hero and you just had to drag Ram along. Wanted to make a big name for yourself, didn't ya? Bigger than Fossett. Bigger than God! Look where it got us!"

He grabbed her shoulders and shook his sister-in-law. "Where. Is. My. Wife?"

"They took her," one of the nuns began. "Unholy creatures."

The other one picked up with "'And it is said in the last days, the dead shall rise and walk the earth.'" She pointed at Matt. "You've brought on the apocalypse, Sheriff. Kettle has unleashed demons. He is in league with Satan! And it's all because of you!"

Matt looked at Sadie. "What is she talking about?"

Sadie wept. "Kettle came back into town. He had men with him. His gang. Some were alive. Others ... "

Not understanding, Matt asked, "He brought dead bodies with him?"

"Walking corpses they were. Their souls are in hell, but their bodies still moved, possessed by demons!"

"Sister, there is no—"

"Tell that to the dozens who saw them, Sheriff! Tell that to the priest who soiled his cloth. Tell that to your brother-in-law!"

"They came at Ram and he fired," Sadie interjected, "He kept firing, but they wouldn't go down. T-they weren't alive. They swarmed him, about six of them. He k-kept fighting as they tore his body apart." She sobbed. "Kettle told us to not touch the body. That it would be a lesson to us all. Not even death would stop him."

Matt thought back to what Ram had said about the voodoo man. There had to be a connection. Could he really bring back the dead? Even just their bodies?

"Sarah and Trina. What happened?"

She could barely get the words out. "H-he took them. Left a message for you to come to Claw Rock, alone. Or he'd kill them."

Matt turned and double-timed it from the funeral parlor.

Sadie followed him to the porch. "You bring her back! Even if you have to die, yourself. Don't come back without them! You hear me, Ragsdale? Don't show your face in this town again if you don't bring them back!"

The words echoed in Matt's ears as he loaded his saddlebags with more guns than he thought wise to carry. He had no plan for his return to Claw Rock, only a target.

He stopped by the Sagebrush. No music wafted through the rafters. Men huddled over drinks. Women consoled each other, dabbing eyes. Most of the town was in attendance.

"Who's with me?"

No one would meet his eyes.

"They've taken my family. *Your* families will be next." He spoke slowly, but forcefully, "Who is with me?"

Frank Chalker, the town's blacksmith, spoke up, "We've seen what happens when someone rides with you, Sheriff. Best you be off, now. Go."

"Cowards!" Matt spat on the floor. "You let them walk into our town. Beat our women. Kill good men. Take whatever they want, including a child. And you won't lift a finger to help? You hide, afraid for your lives. What kinda life is that?"

Another man called out. "Kettle's got demons or something riding with him now. We can't fight that!"

Matt moved around the back of the bar where Owner kept a bible. He grabbed it and flung it hard down on the counter.

"You tell me, in this book you all profess to believe in, where it says evil is stronger than good. Anybody?"

No one spoke, nor moved, nor barely breathed.

Disgusted, the sheriff went to the front door. With his back to the crowd, he removed his badge and tossed it away.

"Y'all are dead to me. Dead as those things Kettle calls men."

* * *

Matt moved forward through the brush much the same way he and Ram had the other night, painfully putting into perspective why he was back there so soon. The patrols were no longer two men marching side by side, but one undead creature that used to be a member of the Claw Rock Gang.

Their milky white, sunken eyes never blinked.

Matt tracked them from Fossett's lookout as they moved slowly in formation. He spotted the two he and Ram had killed by the flapping neck flesh and then counted six more in various states of damage and dismemberment; from missing arms to crushed skulls. Not all the gang had been killed, several still living outlaws could be seen. Those among the still living were Kettle's voodoo priest and Kettle himself.

Matt discovered the walking corpses didn't hunt by sight or smell. When he'd taken a step towards one, it turned slightly. Stepping back, it returned to its original position. Step forward, turn. Step back, return. He deduced they must have a sense for the living, as if his beating heart drew them. That changed his tactics.

Sadie said that guns had little effect, but Ram had a Remington while Matt brought his father's Sharps Big 50. He considered what the walking corpses would do without their heads?

Somebody behind Matt kicked a rock, so he rolled and drew. A Wiipukepaya scout held his hands up to show he wasn't armed. Matt uncocked his sidearm with a sigh of relief. The scout motioned for Matt to follow, and the former lawman figured he had nothing to lose.

* * *

The late afternoon sun always made the red rock of the area glow, as if the heat absorbed by the stone monuments was released back into the world.

Matthew Ragsdale walked right up to the villain's camp unarmed. He hadn't set two feet into the area before he was set upon by living corpses.

He wasn't attacked in any way, just subdued and led forward. He tested their grip on him and it was if his arms were in irons.

Matt took in the scattered rocks that circled the front of the cave. Blood and scratches coated the many of the large boulders.

A devil's laugh bounced off the red sandstone walls of the cave.

"You're late."

Kettle's granite form stepped out from the darkness of the cave. Built like a lumberjack, Kettle's muscles appeared ready to burst from the seams of his shirt. He cinched his belt closed as he approached Matt. "I've already finished. I expected you to hear her screams when you arrived and do something stupid." He grabbed Matt's chin and tilted it up. "I really wanted you to do something stupid."

Understanding the implications of Kettle's words, Matt lurched at the outlaw, pulling with everything he had to break free. His futility brought amusement to Kettle's face. The former lawman cursed and foamed at the mouth.

"You cocksucker! You're a dead man! You hear me? If you hurt her in any way, I'll rip your balls off with my bare hands!"

Kettle moved to a chair that sat waiting for him on his imaginary stage. "Oh, she struggled at first, mind you. But I think by the second time, she quite enjoyed it. Turns out she'd only been with boys, not a real man like myself."

"Sarah! Sarah! I'm here! Where is she you fucking monster?"

The outlaw made a motion, and two of his living gang went into the cave. Moments later they dragged Sarah Ragsdale's partially conscious body out. Her clothes were torn, and when they dropped her in front of Kettle, Matt could see blood on the inside of her leg. She made little choked sobs, and her husband couldn't tell if she knew what was happening anymore.

"Oh, my god! Sarah. Sarah!" Tears of futility ran down Matthew's cheek. He shook them free and glared at Kettle. "You goddam bastard. If you touched my daughter in any way … "

The voodoo man followed shortly after Kettle's men, pushing Trina forward. He had hands on her shoulder and steered her until they stood beside Kettle. Cheeks stained from crying, Trina held her rag doll tight against her chest, like a cross to ward off evil.

"I haven't done anything to the girl, yet. She's too young. After you're dead, I plan to sell her to a whore house. Once she bleeds, I plan to be the first one to taste her flesh." Kettle gave a pensive look. "I wonder which one will be better? Mother or daughter?" He glowered over Matt. "I'm sure it'll be your daughter. She'll be fresh, unspoiled. And after she watches what I do to her daddy; obedient!"

The two locked eyes, testing the seriousness of the other's will; hatred radiating off their bodies like the desert in summer.

As to accent the tension, thunder rolled in the distance. To the north of their position ran Oak Creek and from there the trail up to Flagstaff. A storm rolled down the mountain.

Everyone alive could taste death in the air. Gang members, licking their dry lips, backed away from their boss, the voodoo man held tighter to his charge, and even the walking dead seemed nervous.

Matt gave first. His head dropped to his chest and in a voice, barely over a whisper, he pleaded, "What do you want? I'll do anything. Just let them go."

Kettle leaned forward. "I'm sorry. What was that?"

"I said, 'You Win!' Take the damn town. Take whatever you want. Take me, my life. Just let them go!"

The madman stood. "I don't need your permission for that, Lawman! I never did. What I need now is payback. You tried to kill me. Nearly succeeded. All I want now is revenge."

"Then take it. Do whatever you want. Beat me senseless. Kill me in the most spiteful way you can imagine. Just let them go."

Kettle scanned his two hostages. "No, I don't think I will. Your wife will recover and I think I can get some more use out of her before she's unable to walk. And I already told you what I have planned for your little girl. No, I think I will kill you, just as you suggest. Slowly. Painfully. And all the time, you'll know that I have your family."

He walked up close to Matt again and said, "I nearly lost all hope in that cave, you know. Luckily, I had my witch doctor with me. He didn't like being trapped anymore than I did."

To accentuate the point, the voodoo man slid his hands closer to Trina's neck.

"He brought my dead men back to life. Controls them now, he does. They don't feel pain like we do. Dug us a nice tunnel out. Of course, Claw Rock has a few more claw marks in it now."

Matt's face took on a strange mix of confidence and satisfaction. Kettle took a step back, his brow furrowed.

"So, the voodoo man controls the corpses, huh?" Matt asked.

"What?"

110

"Your lease's been revoked, Kettle."

Matt gave a whistle that was answered by two whooshes as a pair of arrows flew in. One struck the voodoo man in his upper torso. He fell back against the rock, releasing Trina. The stocky man staggered, but kept standing. Matt cursed it wasn't a killing blow.

The second arrow hit the walking corpse to Matt's right. The charge that burned on it was small and the fuse short. The explosion that followed had just enough to blow the once living killer apart. The creature on Matt's left didn't react at all, still holding the former lawman tight. With one arm free, Matt tried to escape, but the death grip remained.

Kettle ran to where Sarah slowly got to her knees. The gang leader yanked her up and held her like a shield in front of him, one meaty arm wrapped around her waist, his pistol draw and poking her in the side.

More explosions could be heard, as the Wiipukepaya took out the walking abominations.

"Call them off, Sheriff! I'll kill her! You know I will!"

Awareness returned to Sarah face. Her eyes darted wildly, finding her husband. Shame, anger, and pain marred the face that once only showed him love and laughter.

Matt reached a hand out toward her.

Sarah mouthed, "Save Trina" and then reached back to where Kettle's Apache knife pressed against back. She fumbled it free from its sheath and, cocking an arm behind her head, cut Jimmy Kettle from ear to jaw. The outlaw threw Sarah down, holding his free hand to his gushing face. Snarling, he fired three shots into Matthew Ragsdale's wife.

Noise stopped. Matt could no longer hear the cries as Indians appeared everywhere to shoot the living and dead members of the Claw Rock Gang. He couldn't hear the moans as the walking corpses attacked, shrugging off damage and ripping warriors apart.

All Matt could hear was the blood pumping through his ears as his wife's arm dropped limp and lay there motionless. He barely noticed when the Wiipukepaya chief chopped his jailer corpse's arm free from its body. Suddenly released, Matt ran to his wife, clinging to the hope that he'd find a spark of life there, but finding none. He pulled her to his chest and cradled her.

Sound returned as Trina called to him.

"DADDY!"

Wildly he searched. Kettle was gone. The monsters fought the Yavapai warriors, one corpse to five warriors, and the corpses were getting the upper hand. Their number seemed to increase and Matt swore he caught a fallen Indian rising out of the corner of his eye.

Just in time, Matt saw the Voodoo man dart into the cave with Trina.

Not wanting to be distracted any further, Matt searched for a gun, knowing his grief would have to wait and, upon finding a fully loaded Colt, set off after his daughter.

* * *

The tunnel extended farther down than Matt would have expected. An escaping flicker of light below meant Matt would also need a torch to follow them. He found a lantern with busted glass, but still contained oil. He lit it, hating the fact that it'd make him a target.

A dozen feet. Two dozen feet. He lost track how far down he went. The path opened up on a cavern easily as big as the Sagebrush. Stalagmites and stalactites made a cobweb of stone throughout. In the center, a locomotive-sized pit yawned.

"Dad—" The word was cut off, but a decidedly male, "OW!" followed it.

The voodoo priest stepped out from behind a pillar, shaking his hand. Trina looked scared but smiled when she saw her father. The black man took a knife and pressed it against Trina's collarbone. The wound in his chest still seeped, but he didn't show any signs of slowing or passing out.

"Let her go, and you get to go. Simple as that." Matt had the borrowed gun drawn, but both he and the voodoo man knew he wouldn't pull the trigger. Matt changed tactics. "What do you want?"

With a decidedly Creole accent, he said, "Your head. You done left me in a hole to die. Now I'm gonna leave you in one to die. I dunna care about da girl. Kettle can have her, or da reds. I jess wanna see you jump in dat hole over dere. Den I let da girl go."

"My life for hers? You swear?"

"I swear."

Matt walked over the edge and peered over. It was blacker than a starless night. He kicked a rock and never heard it hit bottom. He turned to say goodbye to his daughter when a large explosion rocked the ceiling above.

The voodoo man smirked. "I lay a curse on the whole area. Any who die around here come back as zhombie. Da reds be killin' da living, dey come back. The zhombies be killin' da reds, <u>dey</u> come back. Hope everyone got enough boom powder."

Another explosion and one of the stalagmites near the black man fell to the ground, forcing him to move Trina and himself closer to the pit.

Matt seized an opportunity. He dropped his lantern, extinguishing it, then drew and fired, knocking the torch from voodoo man's hand and down into the abyss.

"And I hope you can see in the dark."

The room went black. Matt fired a second shot at the spot where he visualized the black magic wizard to be. The man cried out in pain, but Matt didn't hear a follow-up "thump" indicating he'd been killed.

"Trina! Crawl to me, baby!"

The former lawman fired twice more. Once to find the voodoo man in the flash, the second to shoot that direction. He missed, but he caught Trina moving toward him. Matt crouched down and crab-walked her way. A clink of metal hitting stone reverberated through the cavern, and Matt realized his enemy stabbed the ground in hopes of piercing the girl.

Two bullets left, Matt thought.

He fired once more, finding the villain poised to bring the knife down on Trina's back.

Matt leapt forward, covering his daughter. The weapon entered near his left shoulder blade. In agony, he twisted, pulling the voodoo man over him. They wrestled, rolling one way and then the other. The blade tore its way out causing Matt more pain as his flesh ripped.

Matt lost track of where the pit was until his leg crossed the rim and hovered over the chasm. A moan reverberated through the cave, and it wasn't one of theirs. The shuffle step of one of the undead told Matt the voodoo man had called for reinforcements.

"You hea dat? Dat's death coming for you and your little girl."

Matt got his legs under the larger man and donkey-kicked him up and over his head. The voodoo priest sailed into the pit and Matt said, "Not if you die first."

Matt had no less than a breath to enjoy his victory before he heard his daughter.

"Daddy! Help!"

"Trina!"

He had no idea where they were. He scrambled around until he found the lantern and relit it. The zombie held Trina and stood poised in mid-action near the edge, like its last orders were cut off. Terrified, Matt cautiously moved closer to his daughter. The zombie was one of the guards he and Ram bled.

"Easy now, big boy. Don't do anything you'll regret." Not that talking to it would help the situation. To Trina, he comforted. "It's okay, sweetie. Just hold your hands out for daddy. I'm coming to get you."

Bravely, she extended her arms, rag doll fisted in one.

"I need both hands, honey. Can you let Miss Molly go for a moment?"

She hesitated, unsure what to do. Slowly, she nodded and released the doll.

The zombie stepped off the edge.

Matt dove for Trina, but he wasn't close enough. Their fingers grazed and he watched her vanish into the black, a scream taking his heart along with it.

Matthew Ragsdale wailed, his anguish magnified by the cave's echo. He rocked back and forth, rag doll clutched tightly to his chest.

* * *

The zombies stopped moving upon the death of their master. The remaining Yavapai dismembering them with no problems after that. They followed it up with a purification ritual. The smell of burnt carcasses filled the air.

Matt's original Indian scout pushed the former sheriff's shoulder flesh together and field stitched it closed. He wrapped a bandage about Matt's neck and torso and told him that he needed a doctor to sew it properly back together.

But Matt didn't acknowledge him. He walked to where he'd left his horse and mounted. By the time he'd gotten to Oak Creek, rain fell in sheets. Oblivious to the cold, Matt let it numb his body as a partner to his soul.

The trail rose steeply the farther up the trail he rode, becoming increasingly treacherous. Much to many a traveler's surprise, Arizona wasn't all dessert, and the path Kettle took had killed many who were unprepared. Matt found spots where Kettle's mount slid in the mud. Within a half hour, two sets of tracks, man and horse, were barely visible.

Not much else was in the torrential downpour. Matt dismounted and grabbed his rifle and two pistols. He wacked the horse's butt, and it went back down the way they came. It wasn't five minutes later the former lawman moved out of the way to let a second horse come down the trail.

Kettle was close. Even through the rain, the increasing dark, Matt had a sense of him, as if their fates were tied.

A shape moved ahead. Too small for Kettle. A river otter heading down to the swelling creek below.

A blow sent Matt to his knees. It'd come from the rocks above. Two fisted. Hard. It landed on the lawman's shoulder—his bad one, and Matt roared. The next strike came from a boot to his back, and Matt went all the way to the ground. He felt the stitches in his back pop free. Blood would flow. Matt didn't have a lot of time.

He rolled to his right in time to miss being shot. Matt kicked upwards and knocked the wet gun from the outlaw's hand. He kicked again, boots landing on Kettle's gut and forcing him back a couple feet; just enough for Matt to get up.

Kettle drew the long Apache blade and squared off with Matt. Sarah's wound to his face no longer bled, but it burned red across a wet, angry face.

"Don't 'spose there's much to say at this point, is there?" Kettle asked.

Matt drew his Bowie, much shorter than the one the outlaw wielded.

"No. I recon there ain't."

They circled each other, gauging their mettle, neither at their best.

Matt went low, hoping to gut the larger man. Kettle tucked in, barely avoiding the knife, his own swing taking off Matt's hat. Matt jumped back as Kettle kicked forward, but took the boot to his shin. It stung, but not bad.

Kettle bull-rushed Matt, slamming into him before the former sheriff could get his knife positioned. They hit the side wall together and air escaped Matt's lungs. In retaliation, Matt brought up his knee as hard as he could, hitting close enough to a sensitive spot that Kettle rolled away. The larger man swung the blade around and Matt ducked in the nick of time. Matt's blade connected with Kettle's leg, sticking in and coming out bloody. The outlaw grunted, but managed to slice across Matt's right arm.

They stepped back from each other. Bleeding and woozy, they staggered, trying to stay upright.

Lighting struck a tree a ways from them. Matt, facing that direction, was momentarily blinded by the flash. A dark shape moved towards him. Matt dropped his knife, using both hands to grab at Kettle's blade arm. The force was too much and he could feel Kettle's blade pierce his left side down to the bone. The sharp pain brought inhuman strength. Matt rammed his good shoulder into Kettle, forcing them both to the ground.

The weight of their drop caused a chunk of the trail to drop off into the ravine below. Matt had Kettle's arm pinned to the ground, but the other was free to land punches to Matt's kidney.

The gorge hung next to them, and Matthew Ragsdale had a momentary flash of Trina as she fell into the darkness. Rage strengthened him as he twisted the outlaw's arm, forcing him to drop the knife. Matt rained blows on Kettle's face; one after another, after another. Kettle's nose and jaw broke. His teeth cut Ragsdale's hand as he pummeled the defeated man's mouth. Kettle held up his hands to defend himself, but nothing stopped the onslaught.

Ragsdale pictured his wife's eyes the moment before her death. He recalled the way his heart sank when he found his best friend laying in the street. The fear in Trina's eyes. His own failure to save all of them.

He didn't notice as his and Kettle's bodies slipped closer to the muddy edge.

Kettle got out a garbled, "Stop!" just before they both went over.

They landed on a lower level of the winding trail. The former sheriff propped himself up along the wall, forcing himself to his feet. Kettle clawed his way to standing.

Jimmy Kettle, drawing from reserves no man should have had, spun with a hold-out gun in his hand.

Ragsdale, gun still on his hip, drew at the same moment.

Thunder muffled the gunshot, but the blossoming bullet wound in Kettle's chest proved Ragsdale the quicker draw. Kettle wobbled for the moment, and then toppled over the edge. The former sheriff watched him plummet three hundred feet into the raging waters of Oak Creek, swallowed whole and gone.

Ragsdale sat, the deluge doing nothing to fill the well inside him. Nor did Kettle's death seal the hole that was as big as a locomotive and as dark as a demon's soul.

* * *

Frank Chalker pounded the glowing-red horseshoe three more times before dropping it into the water to cool. It'd been three months since the end of Jimmy Kettle and the Claw Rock Gang, and business had finally picked up.

Oh, sure, there were still rumors about Drowned Horse being the place where the dead roamed free, but the town had always been the stuff of scuttlebutt and gossip. A new sheriff had been expected for days, but that was bureaucracy for you.

It was fine, though. Peace reigned over the town—a pleasant change.

"Pa? Mom wants you in for dinner."

"Be right in Nate," Frank called to his son.

Chalker thought about his boy. The kid hadn't taken to smithing, yet, but he had one hell of a dead-eye when it came to hunting. Maybe he could get the boy interested in making rifles instead of railroad spikes and they could expand the business.

Chalker and Son Weaponry. It had a nice ring to it.

The sound of a boot scuffing the dirt came from the entrance to the workshop.

"Almost done—"

When Frank turned, his blood ran cold. He dropped the towel he had been cleaning his hands off with.

"Sheriff Ragsdale."

No expression showed on the man's face.

"Not Sheriff anymore. Y'all seen to that."

Frank held up his hands. "Matt, listen … "

But the man didn't seem to be in a listening mood. He drew a pistol and aimed it at the blacksmith's chest. Frank caught a glimpse of something tied to the belt opposite the holster.

A rag doll.

"It wasn't my fault. T'was none of our faults, what happened to your family. Kettle, he had monsters. How do you expect … "

The man cocked the gun.

"Be reasonable, Matt. This isn't what your family would have wanted."

"They're dead. So is Matthew Ragsdale. So are you and every man who stood by and let Kettle leave this town alive."

The gunshot drew Nate from the house in a sprint. The man, gun still drawn, reflexively brought it around until he saw it was Chalker's kid.

Nate spotted his father's body and ran to it yelling, "Pa! Pa! Pa!"

The man tracked the boy, deciding whether to cover his tracks. He'd hoped not to be seen so quickly. He chose to holster the gun and walk away. Nate called after him, tears in his voice.

"Why? Why?"

The man stopped. "Revenge. Isn't it always?"

The boy cradled his father's head and between sobs asked, "Who are you?"

The man tilted his head so he could peer back over his shoulder.

"Tell everyone a vengeful spirit has returned from his grave. Tell them …

"The Rag Doll Kid is coming."

About the Author

David Boop is a Denver-based speculative fiction author. In addition to his novels, short stories, and children's books, he's also an award-winning essayist and screenwriter. His novel, the sci-fi/noir *She Murdered Me with Science*, debuted in 2008. Since then, David has had over thirty short stories published and two short films produced. He specializes in weird westerns but has been published in many genres including media tie-ins for *Green Hornet* and *Honey West*.

2013 saw the digital release of his first Steampunk children's book, *The Three Inventors Sneebury*, with a print release due in 2014. David tours the country speaking on writing and publishing at schools, libraries, and conventions.

He's a single dad, returning college student, part-time temp worker and believer. His hobbies include film noir, anime, the Blues and Mayan History.

You can find out more on his fanpage:

www.facebook.com/dboop.updates

or

Twitter @david.boop.

THE SPIRIT
OF THE CRIFT

Sam Knight

Spiritualist and Medium," Georges deciphered aloud. The hand-painted sign was decorated with so many flourishes that the storefront name had been rendered nearly illegible. He turned his attention away from the row of businesses lining the street and grinned at his brother Yves. "I believe we have found our next benefactor."

Yves smiled back. "Mother would be proud!" The two looked nothing alike. Georges was dark haired, dark complexioned, and kept himself immaculately groomed, while Yves had a mop of dirty blond hair, grimy fair skin, and teeth that would make a wart-hog jealous.

"You really think so?" Georges looked quizzically at his brother. "I mean, we are kind of cheating...."

"Honestly! Worried about cheating the cheaters? How could you forget the look on Mum's face when she realized she had run out of money, giving it away to swindlers like this?" Yves pointed angrily at the little shop.

"Out the way!" A voice cried out behind them.

Yves and Georges hurried out of the cobblestone street just as an ice wagon raced past. Both brothers gestured rudely at the driver who had not only failed to slow, but had flicked the reins to speed the horses up. The improper gesture befit Yves ragged appearance, but it was comical when matched with Georges' pinstriped suit and gentlemanly façade.

"Bastard!" Georges called after the horse and wagon, knowing the insult fell on deaf ears. "I hope your ass freezes to the buckboard!"

"Let it go," Yves patted his brother on the shoulder. Georges could easily work the minor incident up into a major occurrence that would overshadow the next few days. "It's not worth it."

"Still. He's a bastard. Acting like he owns the streets."

"Well, we were just standing in the road gawking like village idiots." Yves's pale countenance went slack-jawed as he made a blank expression at Georges.

Georges reluctantly smiled. "All right, then. Let's go make some money."

"Now yer talkin'," Yves replied in a slurred voice to match his idiot persona. "Oh, wait." He dropped out of character and patted his pockets. "Do you have a kaleidoscope? I don't think I have one on me."

"I've got one. Do you have the ghost-scope?"

Yves rolled his eyes. "I've *always* got that."

"All right then. Again. Let's go make some money."

Georges glanced up and down the street to make sure no more carriages would try to run him over before stepping back out onto the cobblestones. He straightened his jacket cuffs, adjusted his waistcoat, and corrected his posture to be as stiff as possible. He strode across the street with an air of dignity.

Yves followed, slouching and swinging his arms like the hunch back of Norte Dame.

The kingly fashion in which Georges entered the shop was wasted on the unoccupied room. The show Yves put on, attempting to open the door Georges had allowed to shut in his face—by using only the backs of his hands—was also wasted. Neither brother was discouraged in the slightest.

Looking around at the shelves and glass display cabinets full of expensive oils, potpourris, and incense, Georges smiled to himself. This place obviously made plenty of money.

"Ahem!" Georges cleared his throat in the rudest polite way possible.

On the other side of the room, Yves began picking at the seat of his pants with one hand while stretching up on tip-toe to try to reach glass baubles off the top shelf of a display with the other. When no one emerged from the back, Yves went ahead and knocked a few of the curios off.

The resulting sound of shattering glass quickly summoned two people; an overweight middle aged man wearing standard homemade burlap pants and shirt, and an attractive young woman in a velvety red dress befitting a spiritualist. The man wore a sour look and had a small club clenched tightly in in one fist. The woman, wild-eyed, held the top of her bodice together with one hand while frantically trying to button it up with the other.

Georges had a hard time deciding which of the two he most wanted to keep his eyes upon. Fortunately, Yves chose that moment to curl up on the floor and begin wailing like an infant.

Rolling his eyes up toward the heavens, Georges assumed the look of someone so disaffected he might die just to relieve his boredom. "Oh, puh-lease! Not again. Three times in one day is quite enough!"

Georges spun on his heel and marched over to Yves. "Here." He pulled a telescoping brass tube from his coat pocket and held it out.

Yves peeked through his fingers to see what was being offered before he stopped crying. When he saw the kaleidoscope, he snatched at it instantly. Tears a thing of the past, Yves put the tube to his eye and grinned as he looked around the room.

With a heavy sigh, Georges tiredly turned back to the other two people in the room. "I am terribly sorry. I will pay for whatever it is he has broken."

The heavy man's knuckles returned to a normal color as he relaxed his grip on the club. The woman turned her back to Georges and Yves and quickly finished buttoning up the front of her dress.

"I've got it, Papa," she whispered.

The man eyed Georges, then Yves. Yves eyed him back through the kaleidoscope with a silly grin. Grunting, the man returned to the back room.

"Please, sir," the woman called Georges attention back to her, "allow me just a moment to clean up the glass." She bent down behind the sales counter.

As soon as she was out of sight, Yves put the kaleidoscope in his pocket and pulled out an identical looking brass tube, his ghost-scope.

The woman came out from behind the counter with a broom and dustpan and began sweeping up the colored shards from the wooden floor.

Yves followed her every movement with his scope. Georges was hard pressed to keep a straight face as Yves waggled his eyebrows at the young woman's lithe form.

A nearly overwhelming scent of perfumed flowers and fruits filled the air, mixing with a horrid burnt smell.

"Dear God!" Georges covered his nose with the back of his hand. "What is *that*?"

Yves retreated to the farthest corner of the shop and began feigning retching noises. At least Georges thought Yves was pretending.

"I'm terribly sorry, sir!" The woman continued cleaning. "Some of those oils were quite rare and valuable because of their strong scents."

"Hmph!" Georges almost sniffed in disgust, but thought better of it. "*Of course* they were."

With an apologetic smile, the young woman finished sweeping up the shards and took them into the back room. When she returned, she opened windows and used a small wooden stool to prop open the front door.

Yves went back to looking at everything in the shop through his mock-kaleidoscope, although he continued to make quiet gagging noises.

Georges, still holding the back of his hand to his nose, was on the verge of gagging himself. "Perhaps I should return later, after this has aired a bit."

"Oh yes, sir," the woman bowed slightly. "That might be a wise choice."

Georges narrowed his eyes at her. "Are you trying to get rid of me?"

"Oh, no—!"

"Do you find you have difficulty hiding your disdain for my poor brother? Do you think it improper that a wealthy family would keep one if its own around instead of putting him in an asylum or turning him out to the gutter?"

"Sir! I—No!" The woman's face turned red as she became flustered.

"You'll not be rid of me that easily! I came here to speak with the dead, and I'll not leave until I have!"

"Please, sir. This way." She pointed to a wooden door in the back. "We hold our séances back here where the bright of day doesn't interfere as much."

When Georges didn't follow her gesture, she led the way.

"Come, Tomás," Georges said to Yves. "Let us go see if Mummy will talk to you here."

"Mummy!" Yves spoke for the first time since entering the shop. "Mummy, Richie! Mummy!" He jumped up like a child and danced over to hug Georges.

"Yes, Tomás, Mummy." Georges stiffly hugged Yves back for a moment before pushing his brother away again and straightening his jacket.

"Where? Where Mummy?"

"In there, Tomás. In that room. Let's go."

Yves stopped and looked around with a confused look on his face. "No Mummy?" he said to the air. He frowned deeply. "No Mummy!" he told Georges and stomped his foot.

Georges sighed. "Let's go see anyway, Tomás."

"No, Richie! No Mummy!"

"Please, Tomás. Let's go see."

Yves pouted. "Richie. No Mummy."

Georges put his arm around Yves. "Please. For Richie? Come on." He began gently pulling Yves toward the back room.

Georges gave the woman a weak apologetic smile as they crossed the threshold to enter the darkened room. He looked over his shoulder and quietly whispered "Tomás thinks he can talk to an invisible lady named Angelica, and she tells him things. Right now she seems to be telling him we will not be seeing our mother here."

"The spirits do as the spirits wish, sir." The woman seemed to plead with her eyes. "We will see what we can see."

She followed them in, and the room went dark as she closed the door. A clicking sound repeated three times as she twisted the key on the wall to light the gas fueled sconce. A warm glow filled the room as the flame came to life and revealed the dark red velvet drapes that hid the walls. Mostly filled by a large round table with a glass ball for a centerpiece, the room also held eight chairs, gathered around the table, and a large portrait of a scowling older woman.

"Please, sit." She gestured to the chairs.

Georges led Yves to a chair and put him in it before sitting himself. The woman took a moment to straighten her dress and her hair, and then, with a flourish, she walked around to the large leather covered chair that established the head of the table.

"I am Madame Limatana, and here, in this room, the spirits do *my* bidding." She waved her arms wide and looked upwards with a distant gaze. Yves followed the pretty young woman's every movement through his kaleidoscope so intently Georges began to worry Yves might break character again.

Madame Limatana seated herself in the leather chair and placed her hands upon the table. She began murmuring a rhythmic chant and swaying in her seat while sliding her hands around on the table.

The light abruptly dimmed. The two men could barely make out the woman's silhouette. Yves made appropriate frightened sounds and leaned into Georges for comfort.

The slight glow from the eye piece of Yves's ghost-scope caught Georges' eye, and he quickly put his hand over it. Yves pulled away sharply, as though he thought Georges was going to take Tomás' precious kaleidoscope away from him, but he had gotten the hint and the scope disappeared into his pocket, hiding the faint luminescence.

"Spirits! I sense your presence!" Madame Limatana opened her eyes and looked around the room. "Reveal yourselves to us!"

The glass globe in the center of the table began to glow a faint blue. Madame Limatana reached out and caressed the ball with her hands.

"I see your mother ... " Her whispered breathily. "She is not happy. She has been trying to contact you, but something has been stopping her. I can hear her ... She is saying ... Richie. Richie. Richie." As she whispered the name, it echoed faintly from elsewhere in the room, imitating her tone and cadence. "Richie, why won't ..." Madame Limatana's voice faded out as the other voice grew to a whisper.

"... you listen to me? Richie? Your brother needs you to be strong!" The voice seemed to come from above them. It was just loud enough to be heard, but not loud enough to recognize the identity of the speaker.

Madame Limatana's eyes were focused upward.

Georges pretended to look up as well, but kept his eyes upon the young woman.

"Not Mummy," Yves whispered to himself and cradled his kaleidoscope. "Not Mummy."

"Tomás? Can you hear me, dear? Tomás?" The voice faded slightly, making it even more difficult to recognize. "Are you being good for Mummy?"

Georges saw Madame Limatana do something with her hand next to her ear, and he knew she was ready for the next trick. Under the table, he nudged Yves' foot with his own to give his brother warning.

"Are you...." The overhead voice faded.

"… being good for Mummy?" Madam Limatana finished the sentence with her eyes closed. "I need you to be a good boy." The chair Madam Limatana sat in began to slowly rise, taking her up into the air with it. It stopped when her knees reached the height of the tabletop. She shook her head from side to side, as though trying to wake up. "Be good for Mummy! Mummy has to go now. Be good!" She opened her mouth and a ghostly white form began to emerge from within her.

Slowly coming out like smoke, the pale form seemed to expand and rise as it materialized from Madame Limatana's body. Madame Limatana's form undulated eerily slow and fluidly, as though underwater, seemingly trying to wake herself up.

"Not Mummy." Yves voice was quiet, yet carried the shrill edge of panic. "Angie says not Mummy."

"Shhh! Tomás. Everything is all right." Georges whispered.

The last of the ectoplasmic form came out from Madame Limatana's mouth, and her eyes flew wide open as she jerked awake and her chair crashed back down to the floor.

"Angie says not Mummy!" Yves stood up angrily. "Angie says man and woman trick Richie! Angie says fake!" He threw his kaleidoscope through the ghostly apparition floating across the room. The brass tube hit the middle of the suspended cloth, tore a hole through it, and continued on into the curtains covering the walls where it hit with a loud *thud*.

"Yi!" A figure cried out and stumbled out from behind the curtain.

Georges stifled a grin. Yves' marksmanship was good.

"What the hell is going on here?" Georges stood up angrily.

"Papa!" Madame Limatana rushed to check on the man who had held the club earlier.

"You have deceived us!" Georges pointed with a shaking finger.

"Fake!" Yves yelled again and pointed at the glass ball on the table. "Fake!" He pointed at the chair Madame Limatana had been sitting in. "Fake!" He went around the room pointing at things, both seen, such as the scowling portrait, and unseen, such as the curtain he pulled open to reveal a woman who looked just like the portrait.

The woman shrieked and covered her mouth with her hands, unable to decide whether to go help the injured man or try to hide.

"Mama! Papa's hurt!" Madame Limatana called to her.

Georges strode over to the gas light on the wall and turned the key, brightening the room.

"Fake!" Yves tugged on strings that pulled some sort of balloon out from behind another curtain.

Madame Limatana's father finally managed to stand upright. A rivulet of blood ran down his cheek from where the kaleidoscope had struck his eyebrow. "Stop," he called out.

"Fake!" Yves pulled a hidden lever and a wind started up, blowing the curtains and the fake ghost with a rippling effect.

"Stop!" The man roared and stomped toward Yves. "Stop!"

Yves fell into a ball where he was and began sobbing loudly.

"How dare you!" Georges approached the man threateningly. "You charlatan! How dare you try to take advantage of us and then yell at my brother as though *he* has done something wrong!" Georges raised his hand as if to backhand the man.

"Stop. Please stop." Madame Limatana put herself between the two men. "Please."

The older woman ran over and protectively placed herself between Georges and Madame Limatana.

Georges lowered his hand and pulled himself up erect, straightening his coat. "You have not heard the last of me. You will be hearing from my solicitor." He stiffly walked over to where Yves was still crying on the floor.

"Sir, please," Madame Limatana followed him, "allow me the chance to explain."

Georges ignored her. "Come, Tomás. Let us get away from this place. I'm sorry I didn't listen to what you said about Angelica. She was right. I will listen in the future. Come on." He held out his hand.

Yves began reaching up, but stopped, his eyes upon the kaleidoscope he had intentionally stomped upon while yelling 'Fake!' and exposing the rigged props. His mouth dropped open and his eyes went wide as he pointed at the broken toy. His jaw began working, but no sound came out.

Georges followed Yves pointing finger until he was looking at the glass shards and smashed brass tube. He allowed his own countenance to darken into a hopeless despair. "Oh dear God, no."

Yves let loose with a mighty ear shattering wail and began crawling toward the broken toy.

Georges blocked his way. He bent down and scooped the man up like a child, holding his crying countenance into his shoulder. He turned, glaring with burning eyes, and hissed. "That was the only thing he had from our mother. It was the only thing that calmed him."

"Sir, I am so sorry...."

He turned his back to them and carried the sobbing Yves out the front door and into the street.

"God Almighty! How much farther? You weigh as much as a mule," he grunted into Yves ear.

"Go 'round the corner," Yves sobbed into his shoulder as he kept an eye on the store's front door.

Georges made his way between buildings, dropping his brother the instant tapped him to let him know they were out of sight.

"Oh, thank God. My poor back."

"How'd it go?" Yves asked. "Did they look worried?"

"Not as worried as I would have liked, but enough I think. You might have ruined it by scoring the man in the eye!"

"Not like he didn't have it coming. He's back there bilking money from poor old ladies who believe in his malarkey. They're not any better than the people who took all of Mum's money pretending they were talking to Father."

"Let's circle to the back of the building and see if we can figure out what they are up to." Georges suggested.

Yves nodded and pulled his ghost-scope out of his pocket. It looked just like the broken kaleidoscope. As they neared the back of the building, he extended the scope to its full length and began looking through it.

"Anything?" Georges asked.

Yves shook his head and passed the ghost-scope over.

Georges held it to his eye and examined the view of the world it provided.

The back of the building became as if nothing more than a yellowish shadow, revealing other, darker yellow shadows within. Georges could make out three figures moving around, and he could even tell which was Madame Limatana and which were her parents, but was hard to tell what they were doing. The man waved his arms quickly and angrily as the women followed him around the shop, appearing to talk and lay hands upon him to calm him, but beyond the movements of their shadowy outlines, details were lost.

"The walls are too thick." He handed the scope back to Yves. "Did you have any trouble using it inside?"

Yves put the scope in his pocket.

"A little. Not too bad. I could see well enough to find all of their tricks. How long do you think we should wait before we go back?"

"What do you want to try to get? Hush money or part of the business?" Georges' eyes gleamed with excitement.

"I still feel trying to get part of the business will come back to haunt us one of these days. I still think we are better off just taking money and never having anything lead back to us. If someone gets really upset about paying us off every month, they could track us down through a bank deposit."

Georges frowned. "In that case, I say we go back tonight."

"Sir! There you are! Please! You didn't give me a chance to explain!" Madame Limatana had turned the corner and spotted them.

Georges cursed under his breath as Yves quickly pretended to be quietly sobbing.

"Please, come back." The woman hiked the edge of her dress up as she hurried over to them. "Please. I can put this right if you will just give me the chance."

Georges glanced at Yves who was having a hard time hiding a satisfied smirk as the woman closed in on them. Yves nodded slightly.

"And just how do you intend to 'put this right'?" Georges asked.

She stopped and curtsied as she reached them. "I am so sorry about your kaleidoscope," she told Yves, who refused to meet her eyes. "We can see about getting you a new one. Maybe a better one, even."

Turning back to Georges, she bowed slightly again. "Please, sir. Please come back."

Georges sighed exasperatedly. "I will give you five minutes. Come, Tomás."

Yves resisted, shrugging off Georges' hand. "Not Mummy."

"I know. But let's go see what they have to say. Please. For Richie."

Yves reluctantly followed Georges and Madame Limatana back to the shop. He made retching sounds as they walked through the lingering odor of the spilled oils.

Madame Limatana's parents were waiting for them. The man's eyebrow had stopped bleeding, and the blood had been mostly cleaned off his face.

"Sir," began the man, "We are terribly sorry for any distress we may have caused you and your brother. It's just … " he broke off looking for the right words.

"It's just that you are frauds, bilking good honest people out of their money with your petty lies designed to give them false hope." More bitterness from his own history crept into Georges' voice than he had intended.

"Oh, no sir." Madame Limatana stepped forward again.

"We have found," interjected her mother, "that most people who claim they want to speak with the dead truly do not. They want to feel released of burdens and obligations to the departed, but they rarely want to actually speak with the deceased."

"Which is why we installed our diversions and gimmicks," Papa finished. "To allow us to grant them that peace of mind. But if you truly wish to speak to the spirits of the departed, we can accommodate you." He pointed back to the room Yves had nearly torn apart and eyed Georges challengingly.

Georges hesitated for a moment, but Yves made the decision for him by marching into the room muttering "Fake."

Georges followed. Madame Limatana was the last to enter the room, closing the door behind her parents as they followed Georges.

Mama seated herself at the head of the table where Madame Limatana had been before. Papa and Madame Limatana followed suit, sitting to either side of Mama, who gestured for Georges and Yves to sit as well.

Yves noisily wiped his nose on his sleeve and climbed into a chair, sitting while holding his knees close to his chest. Georges managed an affect of impatience as he seated himself.

"No need to turn off the lights?" he asked snidely.

"No." The old woman's answer was neither terse nor acquiescing. "The spirits care not." She held out her hands to her daughter and husband, and they took hold of them. Papa offered his hand to Georges while Madame Limatana reached for Yves'.

Yves grabbed the young woman's hand with a silly childish grin that Georges thought was likely less than half faked. With a sigh, Georges took Papa's hand and then took hold of Yves other hand, completing the circle.

Mama closed her eyes and bowed her head, muttering a chant. The room grew cold, and the gas light fluttered although there was no breeze. Her voice took on an ethereal quality, a lilting timbre beyond the capability of a human voice.

"Georges? Georges, is that you?" The voice came from the woman, but seemed to be all around at once. Georges went pale at the sound of his real name.

Yves' eyes went wide and flashed from Georges to the woman leading the séance.

"Oh, my poor, poor little Georges."

As something touched him, Georges jerked upright and pulled his hands back, turning to see behind himself, and feeling the back of his head.

"Yves! For shame!" the voice continued.

Yves nearly fell out of the chair trying to turn around.

"Why do you lead your brother around the country like this? It's not good for either of you. And don't get me started on how you are wasting your father's invention!" The room grew frigid as the ghost scope lifted up out of Yves' pocket and hovered in the air before them.

Yves grabbed at it, but then dropped it on the table, as though he had been burned. Frost rapidly grew like ivy across the brass and filmed the lenses.

"So many good things you could have done with it. You could be helping doctors heal people. You could be letting others see it to learn how to make another. But no. My children use their father's greatest gift to them for petty extortion and cheap thrills with poor unsuspecting women."

Yves face jerked as an audible slapping sound filled the room. His hands flew up to cover his reddening cheek.

"God Almighty!" Georges eyes were wide in fear.

Madame Limatana's hair swirled behind her head as though someone were lovingly stroking it. She was unfazed by the ghostly touch and even gave an appreciative smile to the air above her.

"Lavinia. Boamos." Madame Limatana's parents both looked up. "You do a good thing here. I am sorry my sons have caused you so much trouble. They didn't understand what you do. They will fix everything they broke and pay for everything they can't."

"*Sastimos, Didikai,*" Mama said with a gentle smile.

The wind ruffled Mama's hair and then a cold chill surrounded Yves and Georges. Both of their chairs began to rise into the air and they grabbed the edges for balance.

"Mind your mother, boys," their mother's disembodied voice warned. "Put this right, and get your lives straight before it is too late."

The chairs slammed back to the ground, nearly sending Georges and Yves falling out of them. And then the presence was gone.

Georges' breath came in rapid pants in the silence that followed. Yves scrambled to grab the ghost-scope off the table and held it to his eye, searching desperately for any hidden mechanism that could have lifted his chair.

Madame Limatana and her parents stood up with gentle, yet self-satisfied smiles upon their faces.

"You can start by re-hanging the curtains," Papa told them and left the room, followed by Mama.

"And I'll thank you to never look at me with that scope again." Madame Limatana's cold gaze and tone of voice froze Yves where he was.

Georges shakily got out of his chair and imitated Yves by examining it, but his examination was cursory. "I think that really was Mother," he whispered. "We shouldn't have been doing this. I told you! We were the crooks all along. How many people have we … ?"

Yves grabbed Georges' shoulder and spun him. A huge red welt in the shape of a handprint covered his cheek. "If that was really Mother, then why did she slap me for being a Peeping Tom, but not you for blasphemy?"

"I didn't blaspheme!"

"Yes you did." Yves waved his arms angrily. "When I got slapped you yelled out 'God Almighty!'"

A slapping sound filled the room and Yves' head jerked sharply to the side. When he looked back at Georges, he had welts on both sides of his face. He glared at Georges. "Mother always did like you best."

About the Author

A Colorado native, Sam Knight spent ten years in California's wine country before returning to the Rockies. When asked if he misses California he gets a wistful look in his eyes and replies he misses the green mountains in the winter, but he is glad to be back home.

He claims to still be able to remember the look, feel, and smell of some books, and has been spotted sniffing books as he ruffles the pages. Once upon a time, he was known to quote books the way some people quote movies, but now he claims having a family has made him forgetful, as a survival adaptation.

As a writer, Sam refuses to be pinned down into a genre and writes whatever grabs his attention, be it horror, children's books, or a Cthulhu chess story. He has spoken at Denver and Salt Lake City Comic Cons, as well as numerous smaller conventions, and is part of the production team at WordFire Press.

Sam can be found at SamKnight.com and contacted at:

Sam@samknight.com.

❦ THE TOY MEN ❦

David B. Riley

He reflexively tugged on his graying beard as he surveyed the situation unfolding in front of his ship. Commodore Atticus Minturn lowered his field glasses. This was not looking good.

"That damned Quimby will get us all killed." So much for the reconnaissance mission. The sailors were leaving Quimby far behind as they raced across the ice. Minturn doubted anyone cared if Quimby took a bullet up the ass, but the paperwork would be a bear to complete. Better some bureaucrat from Washington than one of the commodore's sailors, though. How could that man move so slowly? People were shooting at him.

The first sailor, Midshipman Reynolds, hauled himself up the ladder. He was so out of breath he could not form any words. The cold air did not help with the breathing. The rest of the team was racing for the USS *Wanderer*. And their pursuers were right behind them.

Finally, the sailor gasped out, "Sir, they hid under the ice. Popped up behind us. It's a miracle no one got hit. They're using carbines—limited range and accuracy."

Veritable popguns. "Lay down some cover fire with the Gatling," Minturn ordered. "Let's show them what the big kids play with."

The gunner's mate cranked the handle, and the weapon erupted with its fearsome volley. Mounds of ice and snow simply exploded. "Sir, I can't

see a target. There's too much snow in the air. Can't see a damned thing."
They'd never been in an arctic environment before.

"Well, that may do just as well," Minturn said. "If we can't see them,
they can't see us."

The five remaining sailors from the reconnaissance team scurried up
the ladder. A bullet ricocheted off one of the metal rungs. At least no
hands were missing.

"Then again, we're a damned big target just sitting here," Minturn said.

Mr. Quimby finally made it up the ladder. He, too, was gasping for air
and struggled for words. "They had guns," he finally sputtered out.

"I can see that," Minturn replied.

"They seemed to know we were coming," Quimby added. He brushed
the snow off his parka. He noticed a bullet hole and stuck his finger
through the material. "Damn. I just bought this one."

"I gathered as much," Minturn said. The commodore pondered the
irony. If only that bullet hole had been two inches to the right, then the
silly-looking twerp with his handlebar moustache and bald head would be
back out on the ice bleeding to death instead of inside, telling him how to
run his airship. No such luck. "Commander Hastings, get us underway.
We are in range of those carbines. I'd hate for Mister Quimby to take a
stray bullet up the ass," Minturn ordered his executive officer. The airship
jolted a bit as its kerosene powered engines kicked in and it began to
ascend up from the arctic ice it had been parked upon. "We're above
them now. Open fire."

"They're gone, sir," the gunner's mate replied. "I have no target."

"Heading, sir?" Petty Officer Watson, the helmsman, asked.

"We're going to … " Something caught his attention. "What have we
here? It's him!" Minturn pointed at the strange flying vehicle that was
powered by animals. "Intercept course! Full speed ahead!"

"Answering full speed ahead," the helmsman replied.

"If we don't get him fast, once they get to altitude we'll never be able
to catch them," Quimby said.

"We know that, Mister Quimby," Minturn replied. "We got the
intelligence briefing too."

"Sir, they're picking up speed," Commander Hastings said. "He's
getting away."

"It's amazing how fast those flying beasts can move. Gunners, open
fire. I know we're out of range. Fire anyway," Minturn ordered.

The ship's two Gatling guns roared to life and belched out their banquet of smoke, fire and lead. There was a spark as one of the bullets struck one of the runners on the strange big red sleigh. The man in the red suit piloting the fleeing vessel gave them a discourteous gesture with his left hand, snapped the reins, and they were gone.

"Damn," Minturn said. "Crafty bugger."

"Orders, sir?" Commander Hastings asked.

"Turn us around, Mister Hastings. Prepare to attack the village," Minturn commanded.

The *Wanderer* tilted slightly as it turned sharply, then they began to descend. The buildings were arranged in an H-shaped pattern. One large structure sat in the middle. The village seemed to have been designed for a flying vessel to easily come in and land on the unusually wide street.. They would use that feature to their own advantage.

"Damn!" Quimby yelled. "Look at all the tracks in the snow. It'll take hours to round them up."

"Quimby, we do not have the manpower to hunt them all down. It could take days. They may even have a snow cave to hide in. We may never find them. And we're trespassing in a foreign country. Once you give away the advantage of surprise, this is the mess you end up with." Minturn gave the area a quick scan with his field glasses. "Put us down right in the middle of the village, in that open area. They didn't have much time to pack. Maybe we'll get lucky."

A bullet cracked one of the windows. His men opened the firing portals on the side of the airship and returned fire with their rifles. Within a few minutes there no longer was any resistance coming from within the village.

"Secure the village," Minturn ordered. "Come on Quimby. Let's see what we've got here. Mister Hastings, the ship is yours."

"Aye Captain," the XO acknowledged. "And should the Mounties show up?"

"Defend your ship, Commander," Minturn said. He pulled out one of his beloved cigars from the breast pocket inside his immaculate blue uniform and lit it. He grabbed a hooded parka off the rack near the hatch.

"Aye Captain, the XO replied."

"Is that wise?" Quimby asked. "Shooting it out with the Canadians could be problematic."

"Problematic!" Minturn nearly swallowed his cigar. "Problematic! It was your insistence we bring you up here, practically to the North Pole.

You had to go and give away our position so you could look them over. Now it's problematic!"

"Well, I'm just saying," Quimby muttered.

"Fan out men. And remember, these little runts have guns," Minturn said.

It only took a few minutes to secure the village. The sailors only found four residents that were still inside the settlement. The prisoners were taken into a large room that was decorated with gingerbread houses and Christmas trees. A fire still crackled in the brick fireplace.

Quimby looked at the prisoners. "So, you're an elf."

"So you're an asshole," came the quick reply.

That response brought the butt end of a rifle to the side of the elf's head from one of the sailors, though the elf did not seem to care. He tried to spit in contempt, but nothing came out of his mouth.

"Looks like your boss ran off and left you," Quimby said. "He was heading toward Russia."

"The Tsar loves Christmas," the elf replied, "unlike you people."

"We're the ones who love Christmas—the real Christmas," Quimby said. "Before your Santa Claus tried to replace it with himself and change a sacred holiday into a commercial orgy."

"What are you going to do with us?" another elf asked.

"Hang you," Quimby decided.

"On what charge?" the elf asked.

"Charges are for the courts. This is a military matter" Quimby turned toward Minturn. "Commodore, hang these hell-spawned midgets and burn this place to the ground."

"Do Bertha and Sam know what you're doing?" a third elf asked.

"You know my children's names?" Quimby asked, then regretted it.

"And where they go to school," the elf added. "And you're away from home a lot, Nathan Quimby, special advisor to the president. It would be such a shame if something happened to those children. How would your wife feel if they disappeared one night? Or never came home from school?"

"That changes nothing. I will not be intimidated. Hang them," Quimby ordered. "Right now."

"Of course, Mr. S does Mrs. Quimby every year right in your home while you sleep upstairs," the third elf said. "While you sleep he's banging her on the floor right by the Christmas tree."

Minturn seemed to be turning a shade of purple. "Hang them!"

The sailors all looked at Minturn for guidance. The commodore gave a simple nod. Ropes were tossed over the biggest branches of the largest Christmas tree.

"You'll never find him. Are you going to invade Russia?" the loudest of the elves asked. "The Germans gave up. You will too."

"Ah, the Germans make quality toys," Quimby said. "They didn't want your crap any more than we do."

"You're Americans. You don't have quality anything," the elf said.

"Maybe so, but we're not the ones getting strung up now. You are. Get this over with," Quimby said.

All four elves were quickly strung up. Their feet danced around in the air for about a minute, then it was over.

Midshipman Reynolds came in from outside and snapped to attention. "Sir."

"Yes, Mister Reynolds?" Minturn asked.

"We've scouted the complex. There's nothing of real value here. They have a simple living quarters and several storage buildings filled with wood and paint. Oh, and a room full of toys just behind this building," he reported. "Do you want us to try and salvage anything?"

"We could only take on a few hundred pounds. We're already near our weight limit," Minturn replied. "It doesn't sound like it's really worth it."

"Burn this wretched place," Quimby demanded.

The men again looked to Minturn for guidance. Minturn again gave a simple nod of acquiescence.

As the flames engulfed the workshop, storage buildings, and living quarters, the crew of the *Wanderer* marched back to the waiting airship. The powerful engines fired up, and the greatest airship the world had ever seen began to climb into the arctic sky. The dancing fingers of the aurora borealis looked like they were going to reach down and touch them as they powered their way up from the frigid world below.

A convoy of perhaps ten dog sleds was approaching the burning village from the south. The men driving the sleds all wore the distinctive crimson uniforms of the Canadian Mounties.

"Canadian scum!" Quimby said. "Harboring vermin like those elves. Send them a few rounds, Minturn. Maybe break out that 20 millimeter cannon we got from the Germans."

"Helmsman, set a course for Washington, standard speed," Minturn ordered.

"Washington! We have to go to Russia and hunt down that criminal," Quimby demanded. "That damned Tsar will give him asylum."

"That damned Tsar has more airships than we do," Mister Quimby. "Leave it to the State Department."

"I am the State Department," Quimby protested.

Minturn let out a sigh. "Oh, yeah, I keep forgetting what it is that you do. Commander Hastings, I'll be in my quarters. If Mr. Quimby wants to go to Russia, show him the door. He's free to jump out. Perhaps the Mounties will take him," Minturn said.

"Damn you Navy people!" Quimby snarled. "If only the president would've placed this vessel under Army control."

"I doubt the Army could've even found this place, *sir*," Commander Hastings said.

"Well put Mister Hastings," Minturn said with a sudden smile on his face.

"Aye, sir," the XO replied. "South by southeast, Mister Watson."

"Answering standard speed," the helmsman replied, "south by southeast."

About the Author

David B. Riley is a Colorado author and editor who writes horror, science fiction and steampunk. He has edited six horror anthologies and is the author of three novels and over 100 short stories.

ᲢHE HOUNDS
OF VAUDEVILLE

Jezebel Harleth

Gunshots were normal in the Black Hills, and single percussion sounded far away. Charlotte didn't think much of the noise. She was too busy trying to fix the lock on her handcuffs for her escape act for The Wild Wolves of the Wild West show that night to really pay it much mind.

Charlotte's mother, Esther, glanced up from the red silk brocade she was repairing on her stage costume and cocked her head to one side. "Which way did Petey go?"

"I don't know, mama," Charlotte responded, fastening her handcuffs on her wrists. "You can smell just as well as I can." Still, Charlotte scrunched up her nose and followed her little brother's scent. She sensed, just as her mother did, that he had gone east. The gunshot, though it echoed through the town's wooden buildings, leaving false impressions of its origin, had almost certainly come from that direction.

She met her mother's terrified eyes. Deftly, she freed herself from the stage cuffs. "I'll go check on him."

Esther set aside the brocade. "I'll go too."

Charlotte fetched a shawl off the top of their traveling trunk and held up a hand. "You have to finish the costume for tonight."

"I'll finish it," her mother said firmly, exiting the tent ahead of Charlotte.

They were in town, so they remained human as they raced through the streets. Their skirts and petticoats fought against them, and the boning of their corsets made it difficult to breathe. Sometimes Charlotte didn't know what was worse, being human or being a woman.

Petey's scent led them to a small wooded area next to a cattle pasture where the smell of dung and sweet grass pervaded the air. The Black Hills that surrounded them were more purple than black as the sun inched further west, and the thick underbrush impeded their progress. The smell of copper and salt entered Charlotte's nostrils, subtle at first, but unmistakable by the time she reached the banks of a small creek in the pasture.

"Petey!" she cried out as her mother howled in anguish.

Petey, little Petey, lay in the mud, pale and unconscious with blood pooling around his right shoulder.

"We have to call the others!" Charlotte cried, lifting her head up to the sky.

"No," hissed her mother, gently picking up her younger child and clutching him to her bosom. "The hunters could still be here. Get rid of the dress as soon as you hit the trees so you can shift, and tell the others I'm right behind you. Be stealthy, my love. Be the wind."

Charlotte swallowed and nodded. Then, she ran faster than she had ever run in her entire life.

* * *

"Shot? Shot by what?" demanded the troupe leader, Wyatt Sherman, his big red handlebar moustache quivering on his top lip as he sputtered. "We have a show tonight!"

"Wyatt, don't be so human and help clear a bed," admonished Gailene, their sharpshooter. She was a silver wolf, and despite her young face, her hair was as grey as limestone. "The show will go on with or without Petey."

Charlotte bit her lip, eying the tent flap nervously, waiting for Wild Eyed Jane to come with the medical supplies. Charlotte had only just put on a frock after shifting back into a human, and she hadn't bothered to tie the lacing in the back. "I don't think it's a normal bullet wound," she said. "He wasn't awake when we found him."

"Nonsense. He's a pup," Wyatt brushed her aside. "He'll heal, or I'll dock his pay for shirking."

Charlotte growled and glared at Wyatt until he met her eyes.

"And I'll have none of your guff, youngin'. Respect yer elders," he rumbled.

Wyatt was powerful. He stood six feet, with fiery red hair and a large potbelly. His arms were as thick as tree trunks and just as strong. Everything about him was big … and unmovable. As a wolf, he was nearly the size of a bull. On stage, he was simply called The Redwood.

Charlotte sensed all of this as they stared at one another, and she could feel the years between them weigh on her, pressing against her until, finally, she looked away.

The flap to their tent tore inward. The canvas from the door trailed over Esther, red-faced and out of breath, as she entered holding Petey in her arms. Charlotte could see her mother's muscles shake. Petey was twelve years old and heavy enough to be a burden.

Wyatt's eyes trailed over to Petey, and they widened.

"I smell … " Gailene started but didn't finish as she pressed herself against the canvas of the tent, narrowly avoiding Wyatt as he stepped forward and took Petey from Esther.

"Where is Jane?" he bellowed, laying Petey down on the bed.

"I'm right here." Jane appeared in the doorway. She was a petite blonde and already wearing her costume for the evening, which was a pair of ridiculously wide chaps, an oversized belt buckle, and a hat that was two sizes too big for her head. In her hand she held their medical kit, such as it was. The worn leather pouch contained a pair of tongs, tweezers, some cloth, and wolfsbane tincture.

Her nose scrunched up. "Is that … " She rushed to Petey's side.

Charlotte sniffed again, trying to determine what they were smelling. She sorted out the salt of her tears and the musty fragrance of leather. She worked past all the familiar scents of the others in the troupe, from Wyatt's meaty breath to her mother's perfume. Finally, she detected the scent. It had a tinny, metallic aroma. She assumed it was from the bullet, but she knew the strange odor wasn't iron or lead.

Jane pulled the tweezers out of her pouch and called for some whiskey. Without hesitating, Wyatt strode over to his stash of alcohol, which he usually stole from the local saloon the moment they stepped into town, and handed her a half-drunk bottle of mountain howitzer.

Petey didn't move as Jane poured the drink over his shoulder. Now, the room stank of dirt, blood, booze, and that strange metallic smell. Charlotte worried that maybe Petey was already dead. Focusing on his chest, she saw it move weakly up and down. Petey's eyes shot opened, and he howled when Jane dug around in his shoulder with the tweezers.

"Shut him up," growled Wyatt.

Jane ignored him and fished around in the wound. "Got it." She pulled out something small and bloodied. Wiping the object on Petey's shirt, she held it up in the dim light of the kerosene lamp. Esther gasped.

"It's silver." Wyatt's eyes glowed in anger.

* * *

"The show must go on," Wyatt said to the troupe. Nearly thirty people crowded around him, a few as wolves, all wearing their costumes for the night. Some were Indians of an indeterminate origin, and others were dressed as geishas from the Far East. Most donned bowlers or leather chaps.

"Without Petey? He's the stagehand!" exclaimed Tom, one of the actors.

"We'll manage, Tom," Jane said, replacing the bandages on Petey's wounds.

"Look, he's all right," persisted Tom. "Silver's got him low, but he'll recover eventually."

Charlotte watched the exchange furiously. She kept one ear trained on Petey's small, stuttering breaths and the other outside, listening for any sort of footsteps. From the look on her mother's face, she could tell she was doing the same.

It was clear to Charlotte that Tom was exaggerating. Petey wasn't going to recover eventually like it was no problem. He was a pup. Even with the silver removed, the poisoning could have been too much for his body to bear. She could almost feel the heat radiating off of him as a fever raged through his bones.

Tom caught her look, and ignored it. "The show must go on."

"I think you're missing something," interjected Jane, pushing back her oversized hat. "There are hunters in this town, and they found one of us. What's to stop them from gettin' the rest of us now?"

"They shot a little boy. I'd like to see them take on a pack," interjected Gailene, baring her teeth.

"Calm down, Gailene. We aren't all sharpshooters like you. We may be werewolves, but that doesn't make us exactly equipped to handle hunters. We're vaudevillians for God's sake."

"We've got a few hours before the show, Wyatt. I say we find the scent of the bastards that shot Petey and take them out."

The werewolves all nodded their agreement and looked to Wyatt, who had been silently observing their discussion. It all depended on him. "The show must go on," he decided. "But let's go get those sons of bitches. Charlotte, Gailene, go find the scent. Gailene's act can go anywhere in the show, and Charlotte, I don't think you got it in you to perform until you see some blood."

* * *

It was hard for Charlotte to return to the scene. There, on the rocky banks of the creek, was Petey's blood, cooled, purple, and gooey in the crevices of the pebbles.

Only this morning, Petey had begged her to go out to play with him. "There's a crick, sis!" he had said excitedly.

"I've seen cricks before, Petey. Why dontcha just go on now by yourself."

Petey's eyes had shown as he grinned. "By myself? Really?"

"Sure, we're close enough to the humans that I ain't worried about some other wolves. I have to fix the lock on these handcuffs. They come off before I want them to, and we're going to have a whole lotta people wanting blood, and not just the troupe."

Charlotte bit her lip at the memory. She had told Petey to go off on his own, and this was her reward. But how had they known he was a werewolf? Did he let his youth get the best of him and transform in the meadow? Or had they been tracking the troupe before they even entered town?

She and Gailene circled out from where Charlotte had found Petey's body, using their noses and sweeping larger and larger concentric areas. By the treeline, Gailene shouted out, "I got gunsmoke!"

Charlotte raced over. The terrain was thickly wooded. She scratched her arms on the brambles and tore a hole in the lace at the bottom of her skirt as she struggled over to Gailene.

As Gailene said, the burnt smell of powder tainted the air. Charlotte got down on all fours and sniffed for anything else.

She immediately disregarded the pine needles and the moist earth, honing in on the foreign scent of the hunter. Wrinkling her nose, Charlotte pulled back. "Disgusting."

Gailene covered her nostrils with one hand. The smell of rotting onion and cheap cologne pricked at their noses. "Good news that son'a'bitch don't shower," she said.

Charlotte nodded and turned to follow the scent that oozed lazily through the air. The two tracked it to the main road into town. Every step they took, it was harder and harder to detect one form of stale body order from the next. By the time they reached town, it was a faint whisper of scent that led them past the peeling paint walls of the sheriff's and on to the doors of the local hotel by the train station.

"A hotel? He been tracking us?" Gailene growled. If she were in any of her wolf forms, her hackles would have been raised.

Charlotte shook her head. "How could he have been? I've never smelled his scent before. We'd have recognized it."

Scrunching her nose, Gailene nodded in an agreement. "We better go tell Wyatt."

"Why? The hunter's in there. We can take 'im now."

"Don't get so excited, pup."

Charlotte winced. At eighteen, she was definitely no pup.

"We can take him in his sleep tonight after the show," Gailene said, turning around.

"Our third act goes well into midnight," objected Charlotte.

"Exactly. He'll be asleep."

Charlotte crossed her arms and frowned. "I don't see why we can't do it now."

"This is a pack decision, Charlotte. You know that, even if you are human most the time. We'll ask Wyatt. "

Charlotte rolled her eyes. Gailene was human just as much Charlotte was.

* * *

"Esther, he's going to be sick or well whether or not you're here." Charlotte's hand stopped just before she touched the flap to enter her tent, and she listened. Though muffled by the canvas, Charlotte recognized Wyatt's voice and scent. "The show ain't no good if we don't have the Whore with the Heart of Gold singing."

"I swear to God, Wyatt," Esther responded quietly, "if you say the show must go on, I'm going to … "

"You're going to what? Look, Esther, you were my packmate before you ran off to the city. I took you in even after you tried to live like you were a human. I even took in your cubs when they didn't know a tail wag from an ear prick, but the show is the show. It's the only way we keep living even if some of us don't make it. You get that, Esther. You don't forget it."

"We are werewolves, Wyatt. The show is always on for us, whether it's with the wolves or with the humans. We always gotta be pretending we are what we ain't."

"Finish your dress then. Keep your mind off things."

Before Esther could respond, Gailene pushed passed Charlotte and into the tent.

"We found 'im, Wyatt." She sat down on a trunk, pulled out a gun from her holster, and checked its chamber. "He's at the hotel by the station."

"When do we get him?" Charlotte asked, moving over to her brother. She thought maybe his breathing was a little louder, but he was still pale.

"You looked at the main tent, girl?" Wyatt responded. "It's starting to fill up. We get 'im tomorrow."

"Our troupe is called the Wild Wolves of the Wild West, Wyatt," interjected Gailene. "I hate to say it, but even a dumb hunter might put that together. He shot Petey with a silver bullet. He's gotta know that the pack is here. Hiding in broad daylight only works if no one suspects you in the first place."

Wyatt glanced over toward Gailene. "We'll deal with it after the show. Esther, you're on first tonight."

Esther nodded, squeezed Petey's hand, and went through the tent flap that Wyatt held open.

* * *

"How did you mess that up?" yelled Tom, pulling off his shirt that had been reddened with clay to make him look more rugged. "You're our escape artist, Charlotte. You is supposed to escape."

"Look, no one knew. Everyone thought it was a joke," Charlotte spat back. "You're the one that forgot half his lines in a two minute sketch."

"Your brother wasn't there to give me the right props. It's hard to croon about whiskey when the bottle on stage is clearly for perfume."

The wolves next to her whined at each other about the third hoop missing from their agility acts.

"Enough!" Wyatt bellowed. The room fell silent. Clothes were half off, and the performers still in wolf-form paused and sat down. "It was not a great show, but we managed fine. We are professionals, and we make mistakes part of the act. We did that tonight, and you know for damn sure we'll be doing it other nights. Don't mess up tomorrow's show, though, or I'll be looking for new performers."

The room was still. When it was evident Wyatt was finished, they went back to changing out of their stage clothes, emotions now more subdued.

Charlotte changed into a pair of breaches and a dirty blouse, and made her way out to the performance area once the backstage tent had cleared out. The last stragglers of the audience had finally left, and the other wolves returned to their own tents, the lamps still burning, all on high alert.

Wyatt stood in the middle of the ring, a second person on his right. Charlotte expected it to be Gailene. Instead, she saw a tall, pale man with yellow hair. She hardly recognized him, but she knew his scent.

"Frankie?" she asked.

"Hello, Charlotte," responded the pale man.

Usually, Frankie, stayed in his lupine form of a light colored wolf. He was in the Cowboy Versus Wolves sketch and did a few other tricks in between acts.

"You do the talking, Frankie." Wyatt commanded. "In case you run into trouble, no one will recognize him enough to point fingers at us. As for you, especially after you brought down the house with your failed escape artist trick, you're gonna need to get your mama's costume and put makeup on your face. You'll just be another prostitute. That should distract them enough."

Charlotte almost objected, but the look on Wyatt's face told her she shouldn't. The expression also told her he noticed her that she was close to pushing back, and that he was going to remember her disobedience, whether it was voiced or not. She averted her eyes.

"Fine," she said.

She strode purposefully back to her family's tent where her mother had escaped to during the intermission.

"How is he?" Charlotte asked, though she could tell from the smell that he wasn't much better.

"Jane flushed the wound out with more wolfsbane, but we don't have a lot left," Esther said, smoothing Petey's hair. "I've spent my whole life trying to keep you out of danger, you know."

Charlotte didn't know what to say.

"I tried to make everyone think you were a human. Raised you to be one as best I could." Esther closed her watery eyes.

"Mama, why are you telling me this?"

"Because I did everything I could to make sure you and Petey would never have to live in fear of hunters like I did. Like your pa did. But it don't matter. Petey's been shot. We aren't safe."

146

"We're going to be. We're going to take care of the hunter tonight. I'm going to need your whore costume, though."

Esther looked up at Charlotte and cocked her head.

"It's a disguise," Charlotte explained. "Wyatt thinks we'll attract less attention."

Esther nodded, stood up, and began undoing the laces on her corset.

"And then, the show must go on," Esther sighed wistfully. "So you are going tonight."

Charlotte nodded. "I'm the only one who can pick a lock."

"Help me unlace, dear."

Esther held her hair and turned around, her eyes on her young son.

"And before you say it, you ain't coming with," Charlotte said, loosening the ties until her mother could get out. "I need someone to come home to if I live. Petey needs you if he lives."

Charlotte pulled the dress down off her mother and stepped into it. In silence, Esther helped her tighten the corset. Then, wordlessly, she turned her around. Still in her petticoat, Esther fetched her makeup and painted Charlotte's face.

Esther placed her hands on Charlotte's shoulders and looked gravely into her eyes. Pulling her daughter into an embrace, the steel bones of her mother's corset digging into Charlotte's ribs, she said, "Be safe, little one. I love you."

When she let go, Charlotte looked into her mother's hazel eyes one last time before leaving to get Frankie. It was only when she left the tent that she realized her mother was never going to offer to go in the first place. Simple wolf instinct was to protect the youngest cub. Charlotte shook her head. There she went, thinking like a human again.

* * *

"Would you stop itching?" Charlotte growled under her breath as they stalked down the hallway toward the foulest concentration of the odor of Petey's would-be killer.

"I ain't wore clothes for three months. It chafes," Frankie moaned. He was supposed to be standing watch, but Charlotte thought his mind was more dedicated to scratching then watching her back.

"Shh." She edged her way past the last three doors and took out her pins.

Bending down to put her at eyelevel with the lock, she got to work. The stink of her prey wafted through the keyhole.

"I think this looks pretty suspicious," uttered Frankie. Charlotte gave him a warning look, her eyes wide and her brow furrowed. "Oh can it, will ya? I'm talkin' quiet 'nough no one but you and me can hear."

Charlotte rolled her eyes. "Undo your pants, and face towards me. Use your ears to listen for someone coming. It'll look like we're ... we're doing something else."

Frankie raised his eyebrows. "How you know about fellatin'?"

"How do you, Frankie?" she countered.

Frankie shrugged, and Charlotte went back to trying to pick the lock. The mechanisms weren't anything like the ones she used on her handcuffs. On those, she just had to press on a certain area and she was free. Grimacing, she realized that maybe real locks were actually meant to keep things ... well ... locked.

"Why ain't it open yet?" Frankie asked, throwing a look over his shoulder while a drunkard stumbled down the end the hall. He caught Frankie, seemingly in the act, and threw him a thumbs up before struggling to open his own door.

"Hush," replied Charlotte.

Charlotte's pin slipped, and it made clicking noise as she did it. The two werewolves froze and listened. To them, the sound was deafening. Hardly breathing, she listened to the other side of the door. A rustle of sheets and a scraping noise of wood against wood alerted them that they'd been heard.

Exchanging glances with Frankie, Charlotte stood up, leaving her pins in the door, and Frankie hitched his pants up and turned on his heel. She heard the door open just as they cornered the stairwell. They raced outside, and she smelled the hunter leave his room and enter the bar on the first floor.

Charlotte gritted her teeth. They had failed.

* * *

"What do you mean he ain't dead?" Wyatt didn't roar, like Charlotte expected. He was quiet, and it was far more menacing than when he yelled.

"I messed up picking the locks," she said, keeping her eyes low.

"You losing your touch, pup? You pick locks all the time."

"Stage locks," hissed Charlotte. "They ain't really locks." The mechanisms on most of the chains they used on her popped open easily to pressure.

"What are we going to do?" whined Frankie. He tore off his shirt, and pulled down his pants.

Charlotte jerked her eyes away as he transformed into a wolf.

"It's our final show today," said Wyatt. "We'll kill him tonight and go on to Deadwood."

"And if he shows up before then?" Charlotte asked.

Wyatt grinned, baring two sharp canine teeth. "Well, the show must go on, now don't it?"

* * *

Charlotte slept very little through the remainder of the night. She dozed off sometime around dawn and startled awake when someone shook her shoulder.

"Time to wake up, love," said Esther, a smile gracing her tired face. Confused, Charlotte stared at her mother quizzically before she realized the putrid smell of fever was no longer in the room. Her eyes widening, she barely dared ask. "Petey?"

"Hey, sis," came a weak voice.

Overcome with joy, Charlotte tore her blanket off and rushed to Petey's bed. "Hey, pup. You feeling okay?"

"Not really," he grumped. "Not dead, though."

"Yeah, you definitely ain't that." She smiled. Esther put a comforting hand on her shoulder. "How long you been up?"

"Longer than you," he joked, his voice still quiet and fatigued.

"Let's let him rest a little," Esther cut in. "He's going to sit in the audience tonight so I can keep an eye on him, and I'd like him to be awake for most of it. Don't look good to have a sleeping audience member."

Charlotte placed her hand on her mother's and squeezed it. "I gotta ask him a question first."

Esther frowned.

"It's important, mama." Turning her face back to Petey, she smiled gently. "Petey, what were doing when you got shot?"

Petey's eyes drifted off to the side, and he stared at the ground.

Swallowing, Charlotte pushed. "Petey, this is important. What were doing when you got shot?"

"Playin'," he said softly.

"Playin' what?"

"Deer hunter."

"As what? A wolf or a human?"

Petey frowned, and refused to look at her.

"Petey, as a wolf, or a human?" she pressed.

"I didn't think anyone was around," he said inaudibly, his voice quaking.

Placing her hand on Petey's forehead, Charlotte stroked his hair. "It's all right. We'll fix it. Now get some sleep."

Charlotte stood up, feeling relieved. The hunter hadn't been tracking them. He had just lucked on Petey playing in the field.

"I'm going to get ready for the show," Charlotte told her mother.

* * *

Despite the mistakes of the night before, the crowd was even bigger for this show. They packed into their seats and chattered excitedly. At least Charlotte thought they were excited. They seemed to be smiling well enough some pointing at the curtain as it went up, elbowing their neighbors to pay attention. But Charlotte was concentrating on the smells that filtered through the tent, hoping that in the mess of dirt, perfume, liquor, and humanity, she might be able to discern the hunter's scent if he was fool enough to interrupt their performance.

Jane, in her oversized hat, did the first sketch, trying to mimic the werewolves dressed as cowboys' back flips across the stage. Every time she attempted one, her hat would fall off, and she'd run and retrieve it, tripping the other acrobats. The audience roared with laughter at every failed flip.

If Charlotte's mind weren't on other things, she would have enjoyed watching it too, even from the wings. Jane changed what she did every show. Sometimes she would bumble into the acrobats, and other times she'd land herself into the audience trying to imitate their tricks. Somehow, the joke of her losing her hat never grew old.

But Charlotte was thinking about Petey, who sat in the front row to the right, looking bored by all the acts he's seen far too many times. At the end of Jane's sketch, he half-heartedly clapped, and Esther took the stage.

Petey shrank into his chair and covered his face with his hands as she, in her low-cut dress that made her breasts look twice as big, sang to the crowd,

"Make it beat, little lover, with your coins,
And it'll beat for you and your loins,

Cuz I'm your lover, and my heart's made of gold,
Give it what it needs, or it's gonna withhold."

Charlotte covered her mouth to stifle a laugh at Petey's red face. She supposed it was one thing to know your mother sang a song about being a prostitute, but it was quite another to see her do it instead of being backstage.

During the intermission, she caught a familiar scent, like rotting onions, and she scanned the crowd uneasily. She never saw the hunter, so she didn't know his face. There were too many people in the audience for her to discern which one was him.

Gailene walked up to her, her rifle at her side. Though Charlotte's heart was racing and her breathing fast, Gailene was hard as a stone.

"Do you smell that?" Charlotte asked urgently under her breath.

"I do." Gailene nodded.

"What do we do?"

"The show must go on." Gailene cocked her gun, and took a bowler from the wardrobe.

"Wait, you ain't in Cowboys Versus Wolves," protested Charlotte.

"Neither is you, but we're going to improvise."

The curtain went up, and Tom's voice echoed across the tent, silencing the chatter of the audience. Quickly, Charlotte shed her dress and transformed into a wolf.

"Man has come up against many great enemies," pronounced Tom, "but none so great as his archrival from the past: the wolves."

Frankie, Charlotte, and two other wolves stalked up on stage. The audience gasped. On the other side, primitively dressed actors strolled out, their faces painted in dirt and their clothes ragged and made of furs.

"What are you doing here?" Frankie demanded, using the non-verbal communication of wolves.

"Can't you smell him?" Charlotte returned.

Frankie paused and lifted his head. Then, he growled, "Yeah."

"Just play along for now."

"At first, man was no match for the beast's vicious fangs," rang Tom's voice. Frankie lunged at an actor, and the man dramatically died, a pool of fake blood spilling out from his strategically placed flask.

Again, the audience gasped.

"You have every right to be scared!" shouted a man from the audience. He stood up and strode down the aisle, an insufferable smirk on his face. As he neared the stage, his disgusting odor washed over

Charlotte, and she knew this squat, balding man was their hunter. She was surprised at his forthrightness, to stand up and accuse them of being werewolves with so many ready to tear him to pieces.

Then it occurred to her ... the bastard thought the werewolves wouldn't dare do anything to him in front of all these people. It also helped to take down a pack of werewolves if you had a whole crowd of townspeople to help mob them.

"Th-then," Tom's voice stuttered, "came weapons."

The hunter got up on stage, his putrid scent wafting into Charlotte's nostrils, making her feel sick. Out of the corner of her eye, she saw Petey's face blanch. He recognized the smell, too.

Gailene strode out on to the stage with her gun aimed.

"We do have every right to be scared," she said in her stage voice. It boomed across the audience. "These wolves threaten everything we are."

"Oh, madam," smirked the hunter. "Do not lie. You are a wolf as well."

"Indeed you are right, sir," she replied carefully. "With guns, we can finally be equal to the wolf. It is because I have this rifle that you feel safe amongst the pack. We are all wolves now."

The hunter quirked a quizzical brow at her.

Gailene glanced over at Charlotte, and aimed the rifle at the hunter and Charlotte.

Charlotte's eyes widened and tried to convey to Gailene that she didn't understand.

Gailene's trigger finger twitched, and she nodded at Charlotte again. Heart beating fast, Charlotte did what the show taught her to do, she improvised. She lunged at the hunter, and a shot rang through the air.

Some members of the audience screamed, and others gasped. Charlotte fell to the ground, pushing the hunter's body down with her own. Blood, flowed out from below her. Gailene grinned, and set the butt of her rifle down on the ground. Charlotte lolled her tongue out, and played dead as best she could.

"I was wrong. With guns, we became not equal to the wolf," she proclaimed. "We got better."

Then the curtain fell. The room filled with applause, and Charlotte hastily got up as the actors scurried off stage, confusion clear in their eyes. The sketch was wrong from the beginning, and there was supposed to be at least three battles before the wolves were overcome.

Beneath Charlotte, the hunter lay still with a clean bullet wound in his head. Charlotte transformed back into a human as they pulled his body off the stage. "Damn, Gailene. You are a good shot."

"It's my job." She shrugged, grabbing a towel and sopping up the blood while one of their singers sat in front of the curtain on stage crooning about the full moon being an Indian's only friend. His voice, Charlotte noted, sounded a little shaky.

Charlotte stared at the hunter's body, unsure of how to feel. For the past two days, all she could think about was sinking her teeth into his throat for what he did to Petey. But there he was, with a bullet hole between his eyes. It felt satisfying, but not as satisfying as tearing him limb from limb.

"What do we do with the body?" she asked as they dragged his body off stage. Moments later the curtain went up, and three wolf performers went out with their "trainer," and proceeded to jump through fiery hoops and balance on the backs of chairs. "Where's Wyatt?"

"I'm here," Wyatt whispered. He was halfway through a costume change, and his bare chest was covered in bright red hair.

"The hunter tried to—" Charlotte started.

"I know what happened. Quick thinking. Both of you. Put some clothes on. We'll stick him in a trunk for now, and on our way to Deadwood, we'll dump in a river." Wyatt walked away and put on the last half of his costume, which was a large top hat and a jacket made of beaver tails.

Charlotte nodded. It took a while for her and Gailene to manhandle the hunter's body into one of their trunks, and by the time they had finished, so had the show. Charlotte and Gailene raced out to join the ranks of the troupe for the final bow. In the corner, Petey stood, clapping. Behind him, the rows followed suit. It was not The Wild Wolves of the Wild West's first standing ovation, and it certainly wasn't Charlotte's, but this one felt better than all calls for encores she had ever been a part of.

Wyatt put his arm around her and gave her a squeeze before they bowed a third time. Petey smiled at her as he applauded, and she grinned back.

The show must go on.

About the Author

Boom Baumgartner, writing as Jezebel Harleth, is a science fiction analyst and writer for ScienceFiction.com. Her favorite things outside of Science Fiction include British panel shows, writing young adult stories, reciting the Fresh Prince of Bel-Air opening theme in attempt to be ironically cool, and sketch comedies. You can find her musings at LovingTheAlien.net.

THE BANKER, THE ZULU & THE EMPIRE MAKER

Jason Henry Evans

rthur looked at the pall of cigar and cigarette smoke blanketing the room, disgusted. The bitter, sour taste of the African tobacco reflected his thoughts. *I should be grateful. I have had more opportunity than most.*

"Another cup, sir?" the African man asked formally in his stiff uniform.

"Yes, thank you." Arthur was courteous to a fault. He was also observant. Arthur scanned the office As the African poured another cup of *Darjeeling* tea. The three desks on this floor were tidy, as he demanded; a messy desk was a sign of sloppy bookkeeping, and sloppy bookkeeping could ruin a banker. . No, *his* office would be neat; neat and scandal free.

"… and then the man actually started talking about the Zulu war again, as if it had ended yesterday!" Arthur wasn't listening.

"Mr. Tolkien, did you hear me? I told Mr. De Groot that there was nothing I could do; I could not authorize an amount that large, regardless of his service to the crown."

"Yes, of course. I do hope you were polite about it, Gerald. He is an old man, you know." Arthur replied.

"Of course I was polite," replied the young fair-skinned banker, "but I just don't see the point. I mean he's mortgaged up to his neck with that farm."

"Oh, Robert, be kind." Said the third man. "It's all the man has. You speak as if he's plumping it down on race horses—he's just desperate." Arthur was surprised to hear sympathy in a bank.

"Oh *bother* his desperation, Richard. He should have managed his accounts better."

Arthur poured some milk in his tea and began to stir.

"You know, we might be better served if we remember that this was *his* country before it was ours. And the Boer's have done good service, fighting the Zulu's and all that." Arthur then took a sip of his tea. That set off a war of words between the three Englishmen. A re-occurring drama would occur during the afternoon tea they took once the bank closed at 3 P.M. By 4 P.M. the curtains would be drawn on their little Greek drama; they would then process the paperwork and go home. The same thing happened every day. The heat of South Africa seemed to stir their passions, or maybe it was the absurdity of drinking hot tea in a country where the temperature was over 100 Fahrenheit thirty0 days a year.

On his way home, the heat began to wane as the sun set over the mountain range. His house was about three miles from the bank and Arthur always walked. Even as a child, Arthur had walked. It invigorated him.

As Arthur entered his home, the heat from the kitchen hit him flush in the face. The baby was crying while the African housemaid tried to soothe him. Arthur quickly adjusted to the heat and only then began to smell the roast beef that was boiling on the stove.

"Arthur, is that you?" a woman's voice shouted out from the kitchen.

"Yes, dear, it's me." His heart flipped in his chest as it always did when he heard her voice. Arthur made his way down the narrow hallway and into the kitchen.

"Dinner will be ready in about half an hour. M'Dalla," his wife said. "Please go get Mr. Tolkien Scotch. Serve him in his study. Dear, your mail is on your desk." Arthur was relieved that his she ruled the household with such an iron hand. He was very proud of her and the household she kept.

As was his habit, Arthur went to his office, laid his briefcase down and glanced reluctantly at his mail, which was lying next to a well-worn copy of *King Solomon's Mines*. A letter with the seal of the British Crown in Africa sat neatly on top. He began to untie his preposterously tight necktie as he sat. Arthur opened the letter anxiously.

Dear Mr. Tolkien,

Your presence is required at the Office of the British Ambassador to the Orange Free State on September 3rd, at 9 in the morning. This meeting is of a sensitive nature and requires the utmost delicacy. Your discretion in this matter is required. Please bring this correspondence with you. *Speak of this to no one.*

Speak of this to no one. The words lingered in Arthur's mind as his heart slowly but steadily crawled out of his chest and into his throat.

Do they think I've embezzled money? Do they think I've been lax in my oversight? What? Arthur's mind raced with the implications and he picked over every possible oversight that would command this kind of attention. *Good Lord, the meeting is in two days!*

The knock at the door barely entered his mental inspections.

"Mr. Tolkien, your Scotch,"

"Oh, yes." Arthur responded distractedly. One of his servants entered the room carrying a small silver tray with a glass of Scotch on it. How did his wife always seem to know exactly what he needed before he did? For a brief moment he felt the relief of having such an amazing wife, and then the fear of a scandal and what it would do to her his heart in a vice. He would endure anything to avoid that.

* * *

Arthur had never sat in a chair so comfortable before. Waiting in the British Embassy, with its cut velvet couches, leather chairs, and porcelain vases distracted him from the comfort of that chair. *I do not belong here,* he thought to himself. Arthur was a small man, from a small family who grew up in a small town. Being a banker was a dream come true for him. Sitting in that embassy made Arthur's dreams feel small, too.

Please God, let there be no scandal, He thought to himself. *What do they want from me?*

Suddenly a door opened up and a man in a black suit walked towards him. "Mr. Tolkien? Mr. Cavendish will see you now. Please, walk this way."

Arthur stood with all the grace he could muster and followed the man while carrying his briefcase. The trepidation was mixed with dread. *Am I going to be deported? Arrested?* He thought again of his wife and all the things, great and small, she did for him. A scandal would hurt her. The man he followed opened the door and motioned to Arthur. Inside was a large room, with generic paintings in gilt frames along the wall depicting nature scenes from South Africa. In the middle of the room was a large walnut conference table inlaid with Brazilian wood. About a dozen chairs fit neatly around the table. On the far end of the room were four seated men. Two were dressed in morning suits; the attire of the ambassadorial class. One man wore a simple brown tweed suit, while the last man wore a military uniform. He looked familiar for some reason. One of the men in a morning suit stood up.

"Mr. Tolkien, Mr. Arthur Tolkien?"

Arthur crossed the room to shake his hand. "Yes, that's me."

"I am Mr. Cavendish, you'll excuse me for not making other introductions; we have to be quick." Arthur nodded.

"Please sit. It says here that you've been in South Africa for three years now?"

"Yes, that's correct."

"It also says that you come from Staffordshire?"

"Yes, the village of Handsworth." Arthur replied.

"And that you come from a family of *piano tuners?*" the man in the uniform groaned. He was given a sharp look by the other man in black, while the fourth gentleman simply smiled to himself. All of this made Arthur very uncomfortable. Why, he could not say.

"May I inquire why you gave up the family business?"

"I like numbers."

"Ah." Cavendish replied. "Your bank superiors have the highest praise for your dedication, your loyalty, *and your discretion.*" Arthur sat up a little straighter at the compliment.

"Thank you, Sir. Mr. Cavendish, has there been some misunderstanding at the bank?" Arthur's throat was dry. At that all four men looked at each other and began to laugh. This confused Arthur.

"No. No. Nothing is wrong at the Bank of Africa, Mr. Tolkien. But something is very wrong in *Rhodesia.*"

"I'm sorry, Mr. Cavendish, I don't follow."

"Cecil Rhodes is one of the most powerful men in the world. Ever since diamonds were found in Africa he has been instrumental in securing the continent for the United Kingdom. He is celebrated, admired, and since he owns *de Beers*, rich."

"I've heard of Governor Rhodes, Mr. Cavendish, but what does this have to do with *me?*"

"It doesn't, directly. You are the misdirection," said the man in the uniform.

Mr. Cavendish continued. "Arthur Tolkien, this is –"

"General Kitchener! I thought I recognized you!"

"The general is here because of Governor Rhodes. There have been unsubstantiated rumors coming from Rhodesia. Unfortunately, his capital is so remote it's very hard to get any solid information. That is where you come in, Mr. Tolkien."

"Me?"

"We would like to send you to Rhodesia on a standard accounting trip. You are to audit his records. You will do this as a representative of Her Majesty's Government. We will, of course, supply you with all the credentials you will need to gain access. Watch his response to your arrival carefully. Note any oddities or discrepancies you find in his books. This man here is Reginald Dalton. He will pose as your assistant. As you look for things wrong in the governors books, he will look for things wrong, *everywhere else.*"

Arthur was confused for a moment. Then things began to make sense. "You're asking me to participate in espionage against a British governor?"

"No, Mr. Tolkien, we're asking you to audit his books."

"Why me?"

Mr. Cavendish lit a cigarette as he spoke.

"Spies are suspicious of everyone, Mr. Tolkien. Bankers, on the other hand, must be good judges of character, or else their banks fail. Your betters say you are a good judge of character. Above all else, this is what we need. You are also a small man from a small family. No one would suspect you." At that, Cavendish looked at Reginald, who smirked.

"You will be handsomely reimbursed for your trouble, Mr. Tolkien. Will you help?"

Cavendish took another puff off his cigarette. Meanwhile, Arthur's head began to spin.

"I don't know; this is all so sudden. When would I leave?"

"Tonight by dirigible. You would be in Rhodesia by sunrise."

"Tonight? I have to have to tell my wife! Pack clothes! Write instructions for my employees at the bank!"

"There is no time for that, Mr. Tolkien." Cavendish took another puff from his cigarette. "I know this is sudden. I also know you are a man of duty and responsibility. That is why we ask you. But today, a higher duty calls; to queen & country. Will you help us?"

Arthur's heart, (which had been in his throat all morning,) now dropped unexpectedly into his stomach. Immediately he counted the costs and advantages in his head. This was not his job. He had worked hard to secure his position at the bank, and they had no right to whisk him off to Rhodesia. Alan Quarterman stories were one thing, but this was different.

Then he thought of England. He would still be the son of a piano tuner had this opportunity abroad not existed; had there been no *Empire*. His marriage, his career, his successes were because of the Empire. *You owe to the crown, which has given you so much.* He thought to himself. As it dawned upon Arthur that he would go, he smiled and thought *Well look at me. I guess I am a patriot.*

"Alright"

That afternoon was hectic as Arthur tried to prepare. Men went to his house to pick up clothes. Waiting for him on the gang plank of the Zeppelin was Mr. Dalton.

"Mr. Dalton, I see you have my travel bag."

"Yes sir. And please, call me Reggie." The man was slender and nondescript. Someone you would never suspect of being a spy. *I guess that would be the point, wouldn't it?*

"There's plenty of room on board, but we'll be bunking together tonight so we can talk, *privately;* nothing serious, just going over the trip, sir." Reginald lead the way as the two men walked to their cabin. It was very small, smaller than a train birth.

"Where are you from, Reggie?"

"West end of London, sir,"

"Please, call me Arthur."

"Alright, sir—I mean, Arthur."

With that they went over the plan. The only thing that changed was the warm friendship that grew between the two men in a matter of minutes. The sun set while a ship mate came with cold sandwiches and beer. Both men were hungrier than they had imagined. Before they ate, Reggie removed his coat and Arthur gasped.

"You're wearing a pistol?" Exclaimed Arthur.

"You can't be too careful in this business; best be prepared." Reggie took the shoulder holster off, unloaded the revolver and handed it to Arthur. "I brought an extra one for you!"

Reluctantly, Arthur held the pistol. It was heavy and unbalanced.

"That there is the Enfield Mark I revolver, she's a life saver, she is."

"I don't think I'd like to carry this; I think I would lean to one side." Both men laughed.

"Well then, if it's too big, try this one." Reggie opened his pack and took out a small pistol along with a mechanical contraption.

"What is that?" Arthur asked.

"That is the Remington Derringer 95 concealable pistol."

Reggie then placed the contraption on Arthur's arm, loaded the small pistol in its place and stepped back. "Now Arthur, straighten your hand out quickly."

The spring loaded little pistol jutted forward into his left hand. "Oh my!" he exclaimed.

"This way you can have a little protection and it won't be noticeable."

"It doesn't really feel comfortable. Must I?"

"I must insist." Arthur understood and began testing the spring action, while Reggie helped himself to a sandwich. The two talked amicably for an hour or so before the weariness of the day overcame them. They finished the beers & sandwiches, pulled out their murphy beds from the walls and quickly found sleep.

The next morning Reggie tried to prepare Arthur. "Now, Arthur, Ft. Salisbury is no Cape town, or Pretoria. It's doesn't even look like a small, English village; this is a boom town. The roads won't be paved, the sidewalks will be made of rough wood, and the people there will be desperate men and women; miners mostly. Have you ever read those American Western Novels? It will look a lot like that."

"Why go by dirigible, then? I mean, we are spies, aren't we? Isn't this a bit conspicuous?" Reggie smiled at the question.

"That's *exactly* the reason why. We *want* to be noticed; a big show, with you as the main attraction. While everyone is looking at the accountant from Whitehall, that being you, very few will notice the accountant's assistant, me, which frees me up to see what they're trying to hide." Reggie grinned as he chomped down on what remained of his biscuit.

"And all I have to do is show these letters to Mr. Cecil and look at his books?"

"No. I doubt he will be in Fort Salisbury; your job is to present the letters to whoever is in charge, and look at the books. We do really need to see if there is any evidence of malfeasance. Your presence should to unnerve them."

Before Arthur could ask another question, the porter returned to tell them they would be landing soon. The two left their cramped cabin and walked down the small hallway to bridge of the air ship. They were so close to the ground that they could see the tiny people leave their buildings and point at them in the sky. Men on horseback were beginning to ride out to where they would land. Others followed them.

By the time they were within 40 feet of the ground, an armed escort from the fort was standing at attention in their faded red British tunics. Simply dressed men and women waited behind them, by the dozens and dozens.

"Landing in thirty seconds, Captain," called one of the crewmen.

"Brace yourselves," The captain barked.

BOOM! The ship shuddered as it hit the ground. Arthur lost his balance and landed on his side. He could hear a crack as he did. *Oh no! I've broken the derringer!* Quickly he patted down his left arm to see if anything was bent or broken. *Fortunately, it doesn't seem to be too bad.* Reggie helped him up, along with one of the ships crewmen.

"Ready?" Arthur took a deep breath at the question.

"Yes."

"Porter, see to their bags," barked the captain. The door from the air ships bridge swung open and a gangplank was lowered to the ground, four feet below. Outside were the British troops, dressed in faded red tunics and black slacks. Besides them were rough looking men with carbine rifles on horseback. Behind them, a motley bunch of civilians.

As they walked down the gangplank, a rather large bull of a man with a heavily waxed handlebar mustache and ruddy cheek's stepped out of the British soldier's line and presented himself. "Color Sargent Braun, at your service," he saluted sharply.

Here goes everything, Arthur thought. "Good Morning, Color Sargent. Would you happen to be the commanding officer?"

"No Sir! That would be Lieutenant Angel. He's off hunting right now, Sir. May I enquire as to whom you are, sir?"

"My name is Arthur Tolkien, this is my assistant, Reginald Dalton. I am a civilian banker, here to audit your financial records."

"On whose authority?" piped up a man dismounting his horse.

"Mr. Tolkien," Sargent Braun barked, "This is Mr. Frank Johnson. He has no official title, other than confident to Governor Rhodes."

Johnson walked over to Arthur. He wore black wool trousers and a tan cotton shirt with four pockets on it. Over that was a brown leather vest and on his head was a broad brimmed brown hat, like a cowboy would wear, with the left side folded up and pinned to the hat. He wore one revolver on each hip and had a rifle strapped to his horse. He wore a grizzled beard of stubble. The man marched right up to Arthur, which scared him.

"B-By the authority of Her Majesty's government, Mr. Johnson"

"I AM her Majesty's Government! Out here, at least; do you have any documents to prove you are who you say you are, Mister, what was it? – Tolkien?"

"Y-Yes sir. I have a letter from Whitehall, and my royal warrant here." Arthur fumbled for a few moments with his bag. *Dear God, get me through this!* Arthur prayed. He pulled out a billfold with everything in it. Frank Johnson snatched it from his hands and opened it. After scanning the documents he clenched his jaw.

"Braun, take these two *gentlemen* into town and find them lodgings. Porter, when will your ship be leaving us and where will you be going?"

"In an hour or so, sir. We're headed back to Cape Town, Sir."

"Good, do not leave without a letter from me, understand, boy?" the scorn in his voice was evident to all. "Governor Rhodes will hear of this." With that, Frank Johnson walked back to his horse and road off in a huff.

Soon the crowd departed and the platoon of soldiers marched back to the fort. Up close, it was clear that this town was full of shanties and hastily erected large buildings. They passed several ale houses which were still open from the night before. *It's not even 9 A.M.!* Arthur thought to himself. Soon, they were at what looked like the most reputable building in the town—which wasn't saying much. It was two stories high, decorated with wooden columns out front, and was freshly white-washed. In front of the building was a billboard with a painting of a Zulu warrior in full war regalia.

"The Assegai's Point?" Arthur asked.

"It has the best rooms in town, sir," was Sargent Braun's reply.

The three men, followed by British soldiers carrying their bags, entered the saloon on the first floor. The smell of cooking bacon filled the air. Arthur showed his credentials a second time, and the manager told them it would take some time to ready the rooms.

Sargent Braun informed both men that Mr. Johnson would send for them that afternoon, after they got settled. He and his platoon then left. Arthur and Reggie found a table far away from the bar to sit and wait.

"I'm sorry I fowled that up, Reggie."

"What are you talking about? That was PERFECT!" Reggie's eyes beamed with excitement.

"But I stammered and fumbled my papers." Arthur looked confusedly at Reggie.

"Yes. But it worked out. Don't you see? This Frank Johnson fellow was clearly unsettled by our arrival. However, you played scared so well, that he doesn't think you're a threat."

"But I *was scared*." Reggie laughed quietly at that.

"Don't worry Arthur. This Johnson person right now is afraid of the authority you represent, not of you. We have him at a disadvantage. He's more concerned with what you're going to find then he is of you. He thinks you are some low level paper pusher, someone he doesn't have to fear."

"Which means he won't be sizing me up?"

"Yes! And, as *your assistant,* it also means he won't be sizing *me* up; that gives me a freer hand than I normally would. Arthur, you did well."

Soon the room was ready and a native boy carried their bags upstairs. The rest of the day went by quickly. At 11 A.M. they were invited to dinner with Lt. Angel, who had returned from hunting that afternoon. The meal was homely but filling. Angel was a young man, no older than 25 or 26, freshly graduated from Sandhurst. Mr. Johnson made his apologies for not attending, but was busy across the Zambezi River, dealing with the Ndebele.

"I thought the Ndebele were peaceful?" Arthur asked.

"They can be. We've had several incidents of late. Nothing unusual for Zulu's I suppose."

"Are the Ndebele part of the Zulu nation?"

"No. They broke away before the consolidation under the great king Shaka. They have settled the area and turned to farming. They apparently don't like the heavy machinery being assembled for mining—it spooks them." an African boy, no older than 16 stepped forward to open the wine. An African woman in her mid-twenties came forward to remove the dishes. Her complexion was dark brown and her eyes were hazel. The curve of her hip and bosom were unmistakably distracting.

"Well, this has been pleasant. Thank you, Lieutenant Angel, for your hospitality." Arthur was courteous and bowed low while trying to catch a glimpse of the girl again, to which the Lieutenant bowed in return. *This part of the game, I can play,* Arthur thought approvingly.

The next morning, bright and early, Arthur woke up and got ready to do his job. After breakfast both men walked right to the Fort to see Mr. Johnson.

"I'm sorry sirs, but he's not here. But he asked me to take care of whatever needs you have." The boy was not a soldier, but a secretary. He had blond hair and a clear complexion.

As the secretary opened the door, Arthur was surprised to see it decorated like a hunting lodge. A large stone hearth stood at the back of the room; when lit it would warm the whole building. Zebra pelts & lion skins adorned the walls, along with the heads of gazelles, antelope, and even some elephant tusks. On the far side of the room were two crossed assegai, the Zulu short spear, and several well-crafted daggers with carved animal antler handles. Finally, there were two ornate desks in this great room, plus a large, old leather sofa, worn in spots. Next to the hearth was a shut door, spaced at the mid-point of the wall. Next to it was another door, which led to a kitchen. On the far right wall was a third door.

"The books are kept in that third room, over there, sir." Arthur nodded at the secretary.

"Well, let's begin." All three men headed for the third door.

The secretary opened the door to a dark room with several locked trunks, a filing cabinet and a small dust covered desk. On the desk was a bust of Queen Victoria, in bronze. Coldly, the boy remarked that the records were all here, but they weren't well organized.

"We can see that." Reggie said.

"When can we expect to see Mr. Johnson?" Arthur asked.

"He will either return tonight or tomorrow morning. I will be out here if you have any questions for me. The office closes at noon for lunch and at four for the day. Tea will be served immediately in the officer's mess hall at the end of business." With that, the boy left the small, dusty room and sat at one of the desks.

Arthur sighed and began to take his coat off. Reggie put a hand on his left breast pocket and shook his head *no.* He then tapped Arthur's left forearm. *The Derringer,* Arthur realized. He nodded at Reggie and put his jacket back on. They opened the chests and found bundles of tied paper mixed in with hundreds of half crumpled loose sheets. The lone filing cabinet was the same way.

The mess of random sheets began to take a bizarre form of order as Arthur & Reggie made stacks upon stacks of papers. Without knowing it, they had worked the morning through.

"Mistar ToolKEEN," A feminine voice called from the main room.

Arthur and Reggie both left their work to see who it was.

It was her. The beautiful native serving girl from the night before; she was even lovelier in full day light.

"LOOTINANT An-GAL would like to know if you would prefer lunch here, or with the officers?"

"We'll have lunch here, thank you. I'm sorry, I didn't catch your name."

"It is not important." She cast her eyes to the floor when she spoke.

"Everyone has a name." Arthur said smiling. *Am I flirting with her?*

She smiled, coyly. "I am called Amehlo, Sir."

Reggie looked confused at Arthur. "Yes. As Mr. Tolkien said, if you'd fetch our lunch, we would be grateful." Amehlo bowed her head and left.

"What do you think you're bloody well doing?"

Arthur turned red with embarrassment. "I know, you're right, that was childish."

"What have you found in their records?"

"Well, I saw records indicating the purchase of copper wire and copper tubing—lots of it; by the ton." Arthur was thinking now. "What about you, Reggie?"

"Correspondents with a man named Albert Vickers."

"Isn't he an industrialist? Why would he be corresponding with Rhodes, and why would the letters be here?"

Reggie continued. "That's not enough evidence."

"I also found some letters in French, and in German. I don't speak either."

"I have returned with your lunch, gentlemen." That got both men to stop talking and re-enter the office space.

Amehlo served both men cold fish, pickles and hard boiled eggs with a pitcher of beer. They ate quietly in her presence. Arthur could not bring himself to make eye contact with her. *What am I doing?* He thought. *I am a happily married man. I made a vow, and I intend to keep it.* Although some Europeans would argue that native girls did not count.

When lunch was over, Amehlo gathered up the dishes and left the room. Soon, the secretary returned and all three men went back to work.

It wasn't long until four O'clock came and the two men prepared themselves to leave.

"Shall we go to tea?" Arthur asked quietly in the room they were working in.

"Why don't you go; I'll excuse myself as having to do more paperwork."

As they walked outside, Reggie walked towards the exit while Arthur walked towards the officer's mess for tea. Inside were Lieutenant Angel, the small secretary they had met before, and the newly returned Frank Johnson. All of them stood to greet Arthur.

Mr. Johnson was considerably calmer now. "Mr. Tolkien, please join us. We have the rare pleasure of Chinese Orange blossom tea today."

Why does his smile look like rows of sharp hyena teeth?

"How goes the battle of paperwork hill?" asked the lieutenant. All laughed at his joke.

"Slowly. You would think a major business concern would be more organized."

"That is my fault," Johnson replied. "I've been more an adventurer than a governor and I simply do not care for that part of the job." Those teeth were showing again.

"May I ask about the tons of copper wire and tubing?" Arthur tried to play innocent.

"We plan to string electric lights here in the near future, Mr. Tolkien. The tubing is for running water. Fort Salisbury will be big one day!"

"And you and Governor Rhodes keep correspondence all sorts of people. I found letters in English, French and German."

"You'll have to speak with Governor Rhodes about that, those are his letters."

"Who is Albert Vickers?"

"He produced the Maxim Gun," blurted the lieutenant.

"You mean the machine gun? The one Kitchener used in the Sudan?" Johnson replied as he sipped his tea. "The very same."

"How many do we have here?" Arthur asked.

"Just one," Johnson replied.

"We only need one." Lt. Angel chimed in.

The four men talked amicably for half an hour before Arthur excused himself. As he walked back to the Assegai's Point to confer with Reggie, things began to race in his mind. *Why would he need more than one of those machine guns here? The Ndebele were peaceful, weren't they? So what was going on?*

Arthur arrived at the hotel, went upstairs and ordered hot water brought for a bath. As the sun started to go down, the native servants came into the room and lit all the lamps. Reggie entered the room as they left.

"Well, *your Grace*, enjoying your evening bath?" Reggie grinned.

Arthur returned the look by rolling his eyes. "I was unbearably hot, so I decided to behave like a gentleman and clean up. What have you learned?"

"There are no diamonds here. At least that's what the miners complain about while they drink. These miners have been working at a full scale operation for over a year and have nothing to show for it."

"That is odd." Arthur got up out of the tub and began to dry off. "The old timers at home say that before Rhodes consolidated operations, the smaller diamond miners would take out a loan for 3-6 months. If they didn't find anything, they would close up shop. Yet they've been here a year"

Both men paused to think.

"Rhodes must be certain he has a claim, or else he wouldn't keep digging."

"The miners are also frustrated that they can't go over the great river, the Zambezi." That sounded odd to Arthur.

"Why not?"

"The army says it's too dangerous, according to the miners. Some have even stopped mining and are now farming."

Then Arthur had a flash. "What did Lt. Angel say at dinner? That the natives were spooked by the machinery? Why is there machinery being crossed over the Zambezi River, when no mining is done for safety reasons?"

"What was that?" Reggie asked. Arthur continued to get dressed as Reggie pulled his Enfield pistol from his chest holster. He slowly opened the door and saw a man running downstairs. Quickly, he ran after him, leaving the door ajar.

Arthur finished dressing and followed down the stairs. The saloon was full of miners and off duty soldiers. Reggie made eye contact with Arthur and shook his head no. Arthur met him downstairs and agreed to eat dinner there, in the saloon.

The next morning they two men made their way to the fort again to continue their accounting. Frank Johnson's young secretary greeted them at the gate.

"I'm sorry gentlemen, but Mr. Johnson had to leave early this morning to go hunting with the lieutenant. He won't be back until noon." Somehow Arthur was not surprised. The three men walked in silence until they got to the office again. Arthur and Reggie went right to work.

"Here's something interesting; Vickers donated £4000 for Christian missionary work. That's an awful lot of money for bibles." Both men's interest piqued at that. They continued to work on the records.

"I'm going to the loo." Reggie announced. Arthur continued to read.

Bags of cement, moved out here? Why? Vickers Bibles?

Reggie returned from the bathroom and stood in the door.

"Reginald, come, look at this." But Reggie just stood there.

"Reggie, come here." Reggie took one step forward and fell, face forward, onto the floor. In his back was an Assegai.

Arthur stopped what he was doing and dashed towards Reggie's. Gently, he turned the spy over enough to look him in the face and talk to him. Reggie's eye's opened, but did not meet Arthurs.

"Reggie! Reggie! Look at me, Reggie! Look at me!" But Reggie's eyes did not look at Arthurs. Then he saw it, reflected in Reggie's eyes; another man in the room. Remembering his derringer, Arthur gently laid Reggie on his side, turned quickly and thrust his arm up to trigger the pistol: nothing.

"Don't you know it's not polite to point?" It was the secretary! He had one of the wall mounted daggers in his hand. His grin had a predatory feel to it. Quickly he launched himself at Arthur, who was on one knee.

The two men wrestled around and over Reggie. Arthur had no time to mourn his new friend. The boy was on top of him, struggling to get his right arm free from Arthur's grasp and plunge the dagger into his chest. Suddenly, the secretary's left arm came free and found its way to Arthur's throat. He tried pulling it off with his right hand, but the youth had leverage.

The lack of oxygen made Arthur's heart and head pound wildly. It was hard to concentrate. His mind and muscles started to weaken and he began to see stars. He thought of his home, his friends at work, but most of all he thought of his wife. The tender smiles and the pompous way she ordered her servants around. He was going to miss her.

Mabel! Fight Arthur. Fight for Mabel.

Arthur snapped back to reality and realized his right hand was free. He punched the secretary right in the nose. He punched him again: And Again. And Again. Soon, the grip on Arthur's throat weakened as blood from the young man's face dripped on Arthur's chin and neck. Arthur took his free right hand, placed it firmly on the boys left side and pushed.

They were now on their sides; Arthur on his left, the secretary on his right. There was blood everywhere. *I broke his nose.* Arthur thought to himself.

WHAM! Arthur hit the boy in the mouth—and stunned him. That gave Arthur time to get up. He was just to his feet when the boy started to get up too. Arthur looked around for something to hit him with.

As the secretary gathered himself he saw an opportunity. Arthur's back was turned to him. A little dazed, he realized he had dropped the knife. He bent over to pick it up. The last thing he ever saw was Arthur Tolkien holding that bronze bust of Queen Victoria over his head, ready to smash him with it.

Arthur leaned against the desk in the dreary office and tried to catch his breath. *Someone must be told!* He thought to himself. All around him the neatly piled papers were strewn over the floor, covered in blood. He ran out of the room and towards the front door when he had a thought.

They're all involved, everyone; the Lieutenant, the soldiers, but especially Frank Johnson. If I go out there now, I'll be detained and convicted of two murders.

Looking around wildly, the first thing Arthur did was lock the door.

Think Arthur. When a man comes into the bank, sweaty, fear in his eyes, do you give him a loan? No. Desperate men do stupid things. Don't leave this building looking desperate.

Arthur took a deep breath, went back into that hated room and began to collect documents. He then went into the kitchen, found a pitcher of water and rubbed his face and head with it. He then combed his hair and straightened his tie.

Arthur had calmed down enough to walk out the front door, although his hands were trembling terribly. He took a deep breath and walked back, one last time, into the room where the dead men were. He sat Reggie's corpse up against the filing cabinet, and looked at his friend one last time.

"Sorry, old man." With that, Arthur took the Assegai out of Reggie's back. He took Reggie's suit jacket off, unbuckled the shoulder holster with its Enfield pistol still in it. He then removed his jacket and put the shoulder holster on. Arthur then left the room, shut the door, and put his jacket back on.

If I have to shoot my way out of here, I'm a dead man. Be calm, stiff upper lip.

Calmly, Arthur unlocked the front door. Slowly he walked out of the office and towards the front gate. *You can do this, Arthur.* Closer and closer he inched towards the gate. Arthur was aware of everything: his breathing, the warm breeze chilling the sweat running down his face, even the pace of his walk. He wanted so badly to run, but that would look very bad.

Arthur's heart leaped as he made it to the guard house.

"Mr. Tolkien." It was color Sargent Braun. Arthur sighed heavily.

"Yes, Sargent."

"Lovely whether today, isn't it?" Arthur looked up.

"Yes, it is, isn't it? Although we could use the rain," the Sargent added at that.

"Leaving, so soon?"

"No. I was just going to retrieve my reading glasses. Silly me, I forgot them." Arthur tried to smile blandly.

"Oh, very good, sir. We'll see you soon." Braun nodded to the guardsmen and Arthur was allowed to pass.

I'm not out of this yet. His mind kept repeating that over and over again as Arthur calmly walked to the hotel. It wasn't even 10 AM yet.

When he got there, he walked right to the saloon and ordered a bottle of scotch. He was shaking violently now. Trying to calm himself again, he walked upstairs and waited for the drink. Pouring over his notes he tried to make sense of it all. When the alcohol came, he poured himself a stiff drink to calm the shakes he was suffering from.

He started to cry. *I am not a spy! I am just a banker!* He poured himself another drink, then a third. Arthur then began rummaging through his things.

There it is. The revolver Reggie gave him. It too had a shoulder holster. He then rummaged through Reggie's bag for ammunition. Two boxes full of cartridges. That would help. He took that, the information he had brought from the fort, and tried to figure out his next move. Something inside Arthur shifted. With a savage clarity, he planned his next steps.

The only way out is to get back to civilization. I'll go to the river, follow it until I can get to another settlement.

Just then he heard a commotion coming from the hallway. Was that Color Sargent Braun's voice? A loud knock came at the door.

"Mr. Tolkien, are you in there? MR. TOLKIEN! You need to come with us sir." He could hear the door being unlocked. Frantic, Arthur grabbed the bag and headed for the window. It faced the alley. His heart once again made its way into his throat as he climbed onto the small ledge. The door opened and shots were fired at Arthur. He saw no escape.

"Mr. Tolkien, you are under arrest, in the name of the Queen!" Braun bellowed. Across the alley was a sturdy one story building. Arthur threw his bag onto the roof and jumped, propelling himself onto the other roof.

Gunfire thundered as the soldiers aimed from the window. Arthur gathered his bag and leaped on to another rooftop. He could see a soldier climbing out of the window and onto the first roof he had landed on.

Oh bother.

Arthur jumped onto another roof, surprised it held his weight. The young soldier took a shot at Arthurs head. Frantic, he was just about to jump a third roof when he heard someone whistle. In the alley was a mysterious, small man on horseback, holding the reigns of another horse. Without thinking, Arthur leaped from the roof and into the saddle of the second horse. The two galloped away as the sounds of gunfire intensified behind them.

They road for almost two hours without stopping; at first the horses sprinted, but that ended quickly and they began a brisk trot for the next hour or so. Neither person spoke to each other that first hour, nervous that the British Army was galloping upon them. They both sat on their horses in the silence. It was Arthur who broke it first, by pulling a gun. There was a look this side of madness on his face;

"I don't want to seem ungrateful, but you'll have to forgive me for the revolver. I have been chased, nearly strangled to death, and I watched a friend die today. So please, let's dispense with the pleasantries and answer my questions; who are you and why did you help me?"

The hooded figure next to Arthur answered in a woman's voice. "I helped you, Arthur TolKEEN because in helping you, I help my PEEpole." Then she pulled back her hood and revealed her face.

"Amehlo!?" Arthur asked in shock. "But why? How are you connected to this all?"

"Come with me Arthur TolKEEN, and I will explain. My people need you." Her eyes were full and round. The desperation in her voice was too great.

"Alright, Amehlo, I will come." With that, the two rode on. She never said how far her village was, but she seemed to know the way. Arthur was glad for it though; the riding gave him something to do with his hands. His mind, however, was a tumultuous sea of thoughts.

Like any banker, he logically went over a ledger of facts in his mind. He thought about the evidence he collected. But what was so dangerous that it cost Reggie his life? How did he get here? Then Arthur thought of Amehlo.

What was so alluring about this African woman? She was beautiful, yes, but there was something more. There was a sultriness he had never experienced before. There was also a strength there, not unlike his wife's. As he watched her ride, he realized hers was an exotic beauty, foreign and alluring to him. And when she practically *begged* for help, a mixture of English chivalry, lust, and *the white man's burden* overcame him.

They stopped once at the Zambezi River. There, they watered the horses, and themselves. It was about 8 PM and the moon was high. They forded the river at a spot that was safe for the horses and continued to ride into the bush. It was almost 10 PM, according to Arthur's watch when the Kraal came into view. Night fires had been lit so the whole kraal glistened with light.

The two were stopped about 1,000 yards away from the entrance by guards.

Soon, other men with the fierce assegai came to greet the two and walk their horses into the kraal. The whole place smelled like cow dung. The Ndebele, like their Zulu cousins, were cattle herders and cows meant wealth. It wasn't a bad smell to Arthur. In fact, it reminded him of England and small country farms.

Once inside, Arthur could see the huts, great and small, that made up the Kraal. There were about 100 huts, grouped together in certain ways oblivious to Arthur. Their placement around the wooded fence seemed to suggest some sort of street design, with broad avenues for cattle every four or five groupings of huts. He could see the glow of fires coming out of most of them. *This is just like King Solomon's Mines,* mused Arthur.

The men who were leading the horses were taking the two of them to the largest hut, more like a wicker pavilion, in the middle of the Kraal. In front of it were dozens of men and women looking on. It was only then that Arthur realized that the women—all of the women—were topless. *Don't stare, Arthur, this is their home.*

An older man, covered in animal skins and black feathers was waiting for them, sitting upon a great throne. He stood as they drew closer. Amehlo jumped from her saddle, walked up to the man and then prostrated herself on the ground in front of him. There was much talk among the crowd; some of the women cried. The man rose from his seat, grabbed her shoulders and made her stand upright so he could hug her. They clutched each other. Amehlo began to speak her native language again and point at Arthur.

"You may dismount, Arthur." *Finally,* Arthur thought. As he swung his right leg over and dropped to the ground, five men surrounded him and pointed their spears at his throat.

"Amehlo, what is the meaning of this?"

"No weapons except his own must be near my father, the king. Give these men your pistols and you will be given hospitality. No harm will come to you, Arthur TolKEEN, as long as you turn over your guns."

He slowly took his jacket off and unstrapped both holsters from his shoulders & handed them to anyone who would take them. He smiled blandly as someone took the revolvers and the assembled crowd cheered.

"Thank you, Arthur TolKEEN." Amehlo said.

Both were ushered inside the king's large hut. It looked more like a Vikings long hall to Arthur. They were seated on mats, given water to drink and wash their faces. Amehlo excused herself to speak with her father. Food was prepared and given to Arthur. He had forgotten how hungry he was. There was fresh milk to drink, roasted strips of steak and corn porridge with bits of vegetable and meat in it. Arthur had eaten his fill when he realized that Amehlo had returned. He did not want to be rude, so he said nothing.

"Arthur, would you come with me?" Amehlo voice was behind him. He got up and turned around to see Amehlo dressed in her traditional tribal attire. Her feet now had sandals with anklets of gold on them. Her waist was covered with a cowhide skirt embroidered at the edges with beads of different colors. She wore a belt of gold links. Her hair was combed out and wild, while on her chest laid dozens and dozens of necklaces of white beading.

Amehlo took him to see a hut filled with half a dozen sick boys, ages 13-19. They all looked like they had some kind of burn on their bodies. They were coughing and sweating. Great Fires had been set up for them inside a large hut while their mothers cried over them. The great king stood before Arthur with several guards. He began to speak and Amehlo translated.

"These men were captured by the men in white at the Great stone building, south of here. They were gone for many months. Now they return- sick—with the fever of the White demon and his yellow rock. Others are still there, but they have the rifle and other mechanical monstrosities. We signed a treaty of peace with the British and they steal our young men, make them work until death, than they steal more. My daughter says you are good man. If this is so, help us."

All Arthur could do was touch the young men and look into the eyes of their weeping mothers. As the King spoke and Amehlo translated, Arthur felt many emotions rolling over him; pity, rage, fear and sadness; most of all, Arthur felt shame. He thought of all of the stories he read about the British Empire, how it was benign and helpful. How the Empire taught civilization to these *savages. Yes, but at what cost? I have benefited greatly from the Empire. But if this is the price, then they can have their thirty pieces of silver back!*

The next morning, at dawn, Arthur awoke and got ready. Amehlo came to him as he was dressing and spoke.

"Our scouts will take us to this place and you will see for yourself, Arthur TolKeen. We will have to walk, as the horses will be seen from a distance."

"I understand, Amehlo. I will need my pistols back."

"Once we leave the Kraal." Amehlo replied.

Both mounted their horses and trotted with a vanguard of 4 Ndebele warriors. The warriors walked while Arthur rode for over four hours as he tried to put the pieces of the puzzle together in his head.

What is Cecil Rhodes doing out here? Why did they try to kill us? Why all the foreign correspondences? Who are those people? Why were the Ndebele getting sick? Why all the secrecy?

All these thoughts swirled in his mind before the biggest thought of all; *What were Vickers Bibles? Why would Vickers donate so much to the Methodist Church in South Africa? Could I kill a white man or a British soldier?*

And then he thought of Reggie, and the casual callowness his class allowed him in South Africa, in the Empire. He thought of those Ndebele boys who had been used. He thought of his own desire for Amehlo, and how if he had wanted her, it would have been a simple thing to do, to take her honor for his pleasure. Not even his wife would question it. It all sickened him. For Arthur, Cecil Rhodes and that camp began to symbolize everything wrong with Empire.

I have had enough. I will do what needs to be done, for Queen & Country, and if they hang me for it, I don't give a damn.

"Arthur TolKEEN, time to leave the horses."

And with that, they dismounted. Once on foot, Arthur checked both revolvers and his derringer. The spring-loaded mechanism *still didn't work.* They walked another half hour or so before they saw it on the other side of a berm: a gleaming white building. It was three stories tall with wings on either side of a great atrium. Mounted patrols of men all dressed in white crisscrossed the front of the building. To the North of the building was a small mountain, no more than a foothill really, but there was a mining entrance. To the South of the building was a wagon train, forty wagons long. Some white men dressed in all white, along with African porters were off loading the merchandise and putting it into the white building. Tied to the top of the building was a small dirigible. As they party crept closer to the enormous building, they saw a water wheel to the North, almost behind the structure, feeding off of some tributary of the Zambezi.

"Well, well, well."

"What is it Arthur TolKEEN?"

"I do believe they are using that water wheel for electric power." Arthur rummaged through his knapsack and found Reggie's field glasses. He took a look.

"Well, I was right. They are generating electricity with that water wheel. Amehlo, this is serious." Arthur took out his notebook and scribbled something in it. "If I don't make it out alive, make sure you get this to the British Embassy at the Orange Free State. Understand?" He handed her the notebook while she nodded her head.

The party crawled the last eight-hundred yards on their bellies in the tall grass. Arthur motioned the others to stay in place. He crept to within eighty yards of the farthest wagon. There, he slowly stood up, dusted himself off, and proceeded to walk normally to the other wagons. The African workers paid no attention to him, as he thought they would. The doors were the size of barn doors and they were open, too. Once inside he could see great electrical lights illuminating a great warehouse. There was grain, metal girders, copper wire and tubing, along with bags of cement and pix axes. There were gallons of paint and long crates named "Vickers Bibles" stacked ten feet in the air.

The warehouse ended and he went through a door into a hallway. There were large doors on either side of the hallway. Arthur peered into one and saw two old men in white lab coats reading and taking notes on a chalk board. The symbols and numbers meant nothing to him. On the other side of the room was a man dressed in a white uniform and white pith helmet carrying a holstered sidearm. Arthur took a deep breath and turned the door knob, walking in.

"I'm ever so sorry, but this is my first time hear and I had a question?" Arthur tried to look as menial as he could. The guard, however, was having none of it and rushed over to the door wear Arthur stood.

"What do YOU want?"

"I'm sorry, but there was no one to sign these invoices. I went looking around, but saw no one of station, sir. Would you mind?" Arthur pulled his notebook from his pocket and gave it to the guard. The guard snatched the notebook to read it. Arthur walked to the guard's side, who was originally facing him, and pointed something out to him. While doing this, Arthur slowly pulled his Enfield Revolver out with his right hand and hit the guard on the back of the neck with the heavy pistol. The guard collapsed immediately. Arthur shut the door and turned to the two amazed men in white.

"LISTEN. I only hit him, but I will SHOOT you! Answer my questions quickly. Who are you and what is this place?"

One of the men started speaking in German. The other man tried to calm the first one down. They argued in German for about ten seconds, then were quiet. The second man spoke in broken English.

"I am Dr. Ludwig Boltzmann, this is Dr. Bernstein. You are not wif de English?"

"I am English, but no, I am not with these men."

"You MOOOst help us! Some of us have been here for years, others a few months. This Rhodes is MAD!"

"You mean you've been kept here against your will?" Arthur was shocked.

"Ja-Vol! I have been here 2 years, Dr. Bernstein, 6 years. Dere are oters!"

"What is this place? Why are you kept here?"

"Dis es un laboratory for *military research*. Dis Frank Johnson makes us design veapons here!" The Dr. was getting visibly upset. Tears began to stream down his face. "He works us like slaves. He vants *super veapons!* There are oters! Please, take us vit you!"

Arthur didn't know what to do. Then an idea came to him, a grim idea.

"No. I can't take you back. But, spread the word: I will return—soon. Tell the others to be ready. It is the best I can do. I'm sorry." Arthur didn't even stay to hear their objections. Quickly, he put his revolver away and walked back to the warehouse. In it, several black porters were moving some sort of statue, 12 feet high, into place. It had articulated joints and a monstrous face. *Mad, they said Rhodes was.*

Just as he had made his way out of the building, he noticed a wagon with one crate in it. It said VICKERS BIBLES in bold letters. Arthur nonchalantly stepped up on the wagon, grabbed the reigns and began to turn the wagon around, a guard on horseback road up to him.

"Just where do you think you're going, MISTER!" With his left hand, Arthur pulled a revolver from his jacket and shot the guard in the face. The man fell to the ground and his horse shot off across the vacant field in front of the building. *Good. They'll think it was an accident. I'll be long gone before they ask a porter what happened.* "Yah! Getty up!" He called. And the wagon went forward.

The trot back to the Kraal was much faster, since they did not need to sneak back. It was afternoon when Arthur, Amehlo and the warriors returned with the wagon. It caused a great commotion as it entered the Kraal. The warriors at the gate tried to prevent it from coming in, but Arthur spurred his draft horse to go past them as they jumped out of the way.

Arthur then drove the wagon to the King's hall and spun it around. He was immediately met with threats in a language he didn't understand. He did not care. He climbed into the back of the wagon and looked around for something. A hundred assegai's surrounded him as the king came forth and Amehlo dismounted. There was a cacophony of noise.

Arthur looked around the crowd and saw a warrior brandishing his assegai by the wagon. Arthur swiped the weapon away and began to work feverishly to open the crate. When it popped open, all conversation stopped. There was silence.

"Great King, my people have wronged you. We are not all like Frank Johnson. Let me prove it to you. Go to war with me! If you do, I give you, in the name of my queen, this."

Amehlo spoke for her father. "Your gift is great, as are your words, Arthur TolKEEN. We will fight with you!" All began to cheer and say the Zulu war cry.

"Pie –A-Tey, UZOOTOO! PIE-A-TEY, UZOOTOO!"

The king dismounted his throne and walked towards the crate. His eyes sparkled as he approached, then touched the brand new Maxim machine gun.

* * *

Arthur didn't sleep all that night. The march to the building was quiet, too. *A mad man, they called Rhodes.* He thought to himself. *Good lord in Heaven, surely all the bad things I do here today will be wiped away when I rescue those other men?* Arthur thought of his home, and his wife.

Arthur and the Ndebele were arranged about two-hundred yards in front of the building.

"Amehlo, tell your father to start the attack when they hear the gunshot. Remember, *Horns of the Buffalo.*"

"I will, Arthur TolKEEN. But my father has something for you. A gift." Amehlo unfolded a soft calfskin to reveal a beautifully crafted assegai, the great weapon of the Zulu, with an ebony handle. It took Arthur's breath away.

Arthur took the weapon, felt its balance and tested it. Amehlo smiled at him. Arthur took her hand, and with tears in his eyes spoke.

"I'm no good with moments like this. I'm a banker, not a warrior or a spy. But in these last days my feelings for you & your people have grown greatly. In another world, perhaps, I will meet you again."

Amehlo smiled at him and kissed him softly, on the lips. Arthur, ashamed of his desire, turned and walked away. "Wait for the gunshot." It was not yet dawn.

* * *

Arthur crept up to the wagon train. This time it was being guarded by those Englishmen in white uniforms and pith helmets. He saw two, about ten yards away from him, so he drew both pistols. *Blessed be the LORD my strength, which teacheth my hands to war, and my fingers to fight.* Arthur stood up, surprised both men and shot them dead. The sun was rising over the valley, and Arthur could see the Ndebele aligning for battle. Another gunshot—the alarm! Arthur ran to another wagon. He figured they wouldn't be that closely guarded, this was, after all, a secret facility.

Two more soldiers ran towards the direction of the first shooting. They did not see Arthur hiding under the wagon and ran past him. Arthur rolled out, stood up and shot one of the guards dead. The other turned to face him.

"There's only one way you're getting out of this alive, boy. Drop your rifle." The soldier complied. "Now, take off your clothes." The soldier looked bewildered. Arthur told him again. This time he obeyed.

* * *

Amehlo and her people had arrayed themselves for battle. They sang the traditional war challenges, and the British complied. Within ten minutes approximately two-hundred riflemen in white lined up in front of them, about eight-hundred yards away. In front of the infantry roughly eighty men on horseback appeared. Amehlo and her people could see the Maxim guns being set up on the flanks of the British line on either side.

Her father had deployed his troops in the traditional Zulu fashion; one long continuous line of battle organized into three wings: One to the left, center & right. The one in the center had an additional flying wing of troops in reserve.

* * *

Arthur let the Englishman in his underwear run away from the battle. Now in a white uniform, he jogged passed the wagon train and into the warehouse. Men, black and white, ran everywhere. Arthur calmly walked over to the hallway from the other day and began looking into the rooms.

"Gather your things, we're leaving," he ordered. Everyone did as they were told. He then got to the other wing and saw the Ndebele boys who were being forced to mine. They were guarded by two soldiers.

"I have orders to release these men."

"Your daft! On whose authority?"

"This." Arthur butted one guard in the mouth and shot the other.

"Open the lock before you lose your life!" Stunned, the living guard opened the door then tried to stop the bleeding coming from his mouth. Arthur took his rifle and gave it to one of the boys. He needed no words. The boys ran down the hall.

* * *

Outside, the cavalry in white formed one line, eighty men and horses across, and began trotting towards the natives who were singing loudly, preparing themselves for battle. The trot turned into a gallop, which turned into a charge. The men took out their swords as they got closer to the Ndebele. The center ranks of Africans began to fall back, then completely run away. The cavalry soldiers thought they had won the day. That was when they saw the machine gun and heard it fire like thunder.

Within thirty seconds the cavalry was decimated. Where there had been eighty men and horses now stood fourteen still mounted. The rest were writhing on the ground, man and horse, screaming in pain. All fourteen broke in terror as the wings of Ndebele charged forward chanting their war chants.

The two-hundred or so infantry broke too; they never thought they would have to fight. *Natives always break in front of cavalry,* they were taught. Now things were different. The only white men who held were the machine gun crews. They began throwing back fire of their own. Dozens of Ndebele went down as the rest charged. Some of the infantrymen regained their courage and turned around to fight. The tide was changing.

That was when the freed slave miners showed up and rushed the machine gun nest on the left of the line. They strangled the crew of three with their chains and turned the gun on the infantry. Soon, they had turned the gun on the other crew. The battle was officially a rout.

* * *

Inside, Arthur had told anyone who spoke English and was a prisoner to head for the wagons. He told them to check the other rooms on the other floors. He then headed back to the wagons. What he saw outside was a bloodbath. English troops running in every direction, begging for their lives and being surrounded. They were murdered one by one.

I did this.

He couldn't think about it now, he had to grab his bag. It was still under the wagon. Arthur didn't put his holsters on, that would take two long, but he did put both revolvers into his belt and picked up his assegai, along with the bag.

Something was wrong though. There were no scientists outside. He ran inside the warehouse to find out what was going on. Inside was a squad of six men pointing guns at the scientists. Before he could figure out what to do, twenty or so Ndebele ran in screaming. The soldiers turned and began shooting. Arthur made his way across the floor to the scientists.

"Ve can't make it through der!" one of them said.

"I know! The Ndebele are slaughtering the soldier's, they won't be able to distinguish you from them! I know! Go to the roof! We'll use the Zeppelin!" Arthur began running up the stairs when out of the corner of his eye he saw one of the soldiers climb on top of a box, and then *into the ugly statue!*

What is he doing? He heard a *woosh* coming from the statue. Arthur did not understand.

"LOOK OUT! DAT AUTOMOTON IS COMING TO LIFE!" A scientist screamed this, but Arthur did not hear. All he could do was watch as the statue began to move.

The hisses and whistles of the machine clanking to life were terrifying. *WOOSH!* And the soldier swatted a half dozen Ndebele with his left hand. *SWAT!* And the metal giant crushed another two with his right hand.

Arthur pulled the trigger on both revolvers and watched as the bullets bounced off. It got the monsters attention and he smashed the staircase with his hands. Arthur crashed to the ground with the other scientists.

Dazed, Arthur saw a box of dynamite on the other side of the room. He dashed to his feet and ran for it. Meanwhile the scientists huddled and the Ndebele ran. Arthur reached the crate, pried it open with his Assegai and grabbed a stick. Frantically, he took the bag off his back, and searched for matches. One lit and so was the dynamite. The Ndebele continued to run into the warehouse.

Arthur then threw the lit dynamite at the feet of the metal monster.

"Everyone DOWN!"

BOOM!

The flame washed over the metal monster, but the thing was only dazed, although it's right foot was completely blown off. The soldier inside got it kneeled on one knee. Arthur could hear gears turning on the monster and saw something he couldn't believe; a Maxim gun popped out of its shoulder and swung forward. Then it started spitting forth its lead fury in every direction; Ndebele, scientist, soldier alike.

Blind fury took over Arthur as he charged the damaged machine. On one knee, it was only 9 feet tall, instead of 12. Arthur leaped on its chest and began to pound on the chasse. He was too close to be hit by the machine gun, and the pilot inside needed one hand to steady himself. The other hand was starting to wrap itself around Arthur as he began to punch the heavy metal head with his fists. Then it happened. The derringer on his left arm popped out of his sleeve.

Arthur angled the pistol into the pilots eye hole and fired its only round. The pilot shuddered and went still. The monster fell backward with a *CLANG!* and didn't move. Silence fell on the warehouse for a moment. It was broken by the cries of joy by the Ndebele. Some went to finish off the scientists, but Arthur got between them. He showed his assegai, which stopped the warriors.

"Who are you?" Once of the scientists asked.

"Just a banker."

* * *

The wood paneled room felt different this time. General Kitchener was there, as was Mr. Cavendish, and the other gentlemen, who did not speak. *Poor Reggie,* Arthur thought. He was giving his report on what had happened. Kitchener was frowning and shaking his head while Mr. Cavendish listened intently. The other man simply took notes.

"Why do all of this? Certainly the mechanical monster will be a great military break through, yes, but what were they mining? Why all the secrecy and the abducted scientists," Mr. Cavendish asked. Arthur was just about to give an answer when a commotion was heard outside and the door swung open.

"I'm sorry Gentlemen, he insisted."

"Quite right I insisted! I want some answers NOW!" It was Cecil Rhodes.

Every man in the room stood up, except for the silent man.

"Ah, Governor, how pleasant it is to meet you! Your presence is most unexpected, but welcome, nonetheless. Won't you sit down? Tea, perhaps? James, fetch the Governor some tea, and some biscuits, would you? Thank you." Cavendish was all smiles.

"I will not sit down. English blood has been spilled! My facility destroyed! And that new machine gun is in the hands of the Ndebele! Three of them!" Cecil Rhodes looked like his head was going to explode.

"Sit down, Governor," the first words from the silent man, who was playing with his top hat. The governor blustered a bit and then took his seat.

"That man there is responsible for the deaths of British soldiers, the destruction of my personal property and the murder of my man's secretary! He has committed treason and should be hanged! Why is he not in irons?"

Cavendish smirked, than spoke. "Mr. Tolkien was just about to discuss those things, weren't you?"

"Yes, I believe I was." Arthur's left arm was in a sling, he had been shot during the battle, but hadn't known it until his adrenalin had stopped pumping. It was pumping now, as he began to speak.

"My report will explain the death of Reginald Dalton, ordered murdered by Frank Johnson. The rescue of some famous continental scientists, some thought dead, others simply missing. It will also explain the irregularities in Governor Rhodes books and finances.

"Cecil Rhodes started up a secret mining facility in the middle of disputed African territory, in violation of several treaties, kidnapped European scientists and started slave mining all for this."

Cecil gingerly pulled a chalky yellow rock from his bag.

"What is that?" Mr. Cavendish asked.

"It's not what the rock is, it's what you can do with it. On our trip back in Mr. Rhodes Zeppelin, I spoke with several scientists. This all started some six years ago when Madam Curie was visiting London to give a talk to the Natural Society. At a cocktail party afterwards, Mr. Rhodes overheard her talking about a substance called *radium*. It was a natural material that glowed in the dark. She discussed the material with some of her colleagues. Mr. Rhodes became fascinated by it. He had her letters to other scientists intercepted."

"THIS IS OUTRAGEOS!" Rhodes bellowed.

"Be quiet governor," the silent man spoke again.

"Do continue," Cavendish asked.

"Some of the scientists seemed to think that you could refine this ore, and concentrate *radiation.*"

"What's radiation?" Cavendish asked.

"All energy gives off radiation, Mr. Cavendish. The burning logs give off heat and light, two forms of radiation. But there are other forms, too. Now, gentlemen, you must know these correspondences were of a highly theoretical nature. They were making hypothesis and extrapolations."

"What does this have to do with what happened, man, spit it out." A blustered Kitchener asked.

"Under the right conditions these scientists believe you could split an atom and gain unlimited power."

"What kind of power?" asked the silent man.

"Electrical power, I suppose. Whole cities lit, factories working round the clock, trains that didn't need coal, a new age of machines, gentlemen; all with this little rock."

"But some of the letters hinted at a darker potential. They talked about a bomb."

Kitchener stood up, and began to walk around the room. "A bomb, you say. What kind of bomb?"

Arthur took a breath and replied. "A bomb big enough to destroy whole armies, or fleets, or even cities. A bomb big enough to change the balance of power for a hundred years." All the men listening looked stunned, except for Rhodes.

"The Governor hear spent millions of pounds, redirected resources, used the British Army, and treated the natives like chattel, all to make a bomb so he could rule." Throughout, Arthur tried to be calm, but he failed.

"That little man is a traitor! He is responsible for the deaths of dozens of British troops. Look at him, he went native!"

"Better native than mad!"

"Oh, you love your little darkies, don't you!"

"They beat your army, didn't they?"

"Enough, gentlemen," the silent man said. "Governor, your actions were reprehensible! You stole from your investors, diverted resources away from the crown; put the lives of soldiers and subjects alike at peril. If it were not for your distinguished record, you would be in front of a firing squad, right now! But your love of Empire is well known and that should be taken into account for your many crimes. It is the kidnaping of citizens from Germany and France that grieves the crown the most. We almost went to war over those men! Let me assure you, Cecil, that a war with Germany *and* France is not one we could win! So, this is what you will do. Your political career is over. You will finish this term of office, but no more. You will pay reparations to the families of those scientists, and to the British soldiers who died. And the last thing you'll do is get those machine guns back from the natives! You may leave now."

"I am Cecil Rhodes! I will not be dictated too!"

"And I am Lord Randolph Churchill, Member of Parliament! I speak with the voice of the Prime minister when I say you will do as you are told or I will go public, and you will be ruined! What shall it be, governor?"

With that, Cecil Rhodes, gathered his hat, bowed, and left.

Arthur finished his report, shook hands with the gentlemen and began to leave. Before he did, Lord Churchill spoke one last time.

"Mr. Tolkien, in the Prime Minister's desk is an envelope which holds the names of every man who has won the Victoria Cross for gallant service. This list is secret. Please know, your name will be on that list. Your country thanks you for your service."

Arthur bowed solemnly then left the room. He took a taxi back to his home. On the way there, he thought of everything that had happened in that week. He thought of Reggie, and Amehlo, the Ndebele and the scientists. He thought of all the times he could have died. All these things made him grateful.

"Mabel, I'm home."

Jason Henry Evans

About the Author

J.H. Evans has been an educator for most of his adult life. He graduated from the University of California, Santa Barbara in 1996 with degrees in History & Renaissance Studies and began working in schools three years later. Moving to Colorado in 2004 at the request of his new bride, J.H. Evans continued to work in the classroom. He has always had a passion for history and for good fiction. Those two things came together in this short story. In 2013, J.H. Evans graduated from the University of Colorado, Denver with an MA in US History. He is currently working on his YA book, as well as a book on classroom management for new teachers.

THE VON HELSING CHRONICLES: BLOOD MAGIC

Peter J. Wacks
&
J.R. Boyett

From the personal journal (recorded 1840-1863), of Friedrich Von Helsing, PHD; Professor Emeritus of Supernatural Mythos, Kings College Cambridge; Inmate, Bethlem Royal Hospital, secure ward for the criminally insane.

~ ~ ~

Hell is not only reserved for those departed from the mortal coil. Having fought to reconcile my memories and choices with the perceived morality and understanding of the masses, I can say that Hell is not being able to trust one's own memories. I have delayed somewhat in recording this account as I have felt that the events contained herein required some degree of reflection, that I might not subject myself to a mistelling or altered account. Perhaps

I shall one day be fortified such as to find occasions of this nature less taxing upon my sensibilities. Although I do not consider myself delicate, I hesitate to think that I may come to find such things to be common, and I fear the state of a man that I should be if I should find such a day upon me.

I endeavor, therefore, to chronicle my observations such that I may reflect more fully upon them, should the need present itself as proper. From what I have seen thus far, I have come to know with certainty that the realities of this world are far more diverse then our sensible western minds care to warrant. Furthermore, the apparent frequency with which I have observed such matters causes me to conclude with a great deal of confidence, and no small amount of trepidation, that I should expect to encounter many more subjects of study before I depart from my current companion's company.

My colleagues and I started our adventures recently departed from university. Schooled as we were in matters of science, we had begun to dabble in the occult. We left our universities and, taking advantage of our station, we became adventurers. Our noble ambitions coupled with our foolish pride, we set forth with confidence in our knowledge of science. Science abandoned us, however, leaving a rift between the moralistic, logical thought which we had learned as proper young gentleman and the darker truths of the world. This rift proved deadly. While I have now come to terms with the demise of my troupe, it has been some short months since Markus and I set the last of my surviving cohorts upon transport to London.

His broken body, lain feebly upon the stretcher, had been granted refuge in the dusty and musty hold of a regional transport—affectionately termed by the masses as a 'city-hopper.' It had cost me considerably more than was just to persuade the Captain to set aside one half-dozen pallets of turnips to make space enough for Niles to lay in transit. Still, I would have paid far more had it been required.

It was, at that time, my intent to endeavor upon a voyage of my own, a return to the civilized lands at the heart of the empire. I had hoped that I might visit with my dear friend during his convalescence. I am, however, hesitant to depart from Markus for as much as a day. I have no shame in acknowledging that I fear that any segregation at this point may become permanent. I say this in part because I question my own resolve to remain upon my present course; should I find myself in the comfort of quality, I doubt that I could muster the resolve to return to this world of darkness and despair. Should that cast my will as weak, then I shall endeavor to show that it is not so; rather, that an adjustment to a world as morally nidorous as the truth thus shown to me is not a simple task.

My second reason for hesitance is that I am uncertain if Markus would allow my return, and I have full confidence in my own inability to locate him should he desire that I not. Although I have succeeded in convincing him to accept my services, I am still uncertain of the lengths to which I may press my companion's hospitality. It is clear to me that he is accustomed to a solitary life. I am uncertain if he has ever before had a companion such as I, but I have no doubt that my presence is yet another example of his peculiar generosity. I do truly aspire to deserve his affections, should I come to earn them, and I hope to one day serve him as the assistant for which I have named myself, but I know that I presently lack that which is required of this role.

My feelings are mixed with regards to failure. How easy it would be to simply fall short of his expectations. He would surely cast me aside, and I could then return to a world of pure science. But could I truly? Might I ever forget the horrors, if only for a moment, of which I am now aware? Might the images of my own actions pass from my dreams, or am I destined from this day forward to relive the nightmares which I have witnessed?

Regardless, I am certain that my association with Niles Byron is complete. Should he recover, God willing, and should I put aside my own phantoms, it is a certainty that further association between our families shall invariably lead to considerable distress. Aside from the stirring of memories which we would surely seek to transcend, the Lord and Lady Byron would certainly take offence to our continued fraternization.

It was myself, after all, who convinced Niles to join in our ill-fated expedition. The influence which I once asserted over their heir was poor enough when it was nothing more than a sophomoric distraction from the responsibilities of his estate. That he is now likely crippled beyond capacity is a blow for which his house will certainly suffer, and from which they may never recover. It would be foolhardy to think that I may again rely upon house Byron as a means of introduction to the imperial court. Both my father and my brother may disagree with my motivations, but I take pride in stating that a lost friendship is the greater of the two losses, regardless of the political gain which may have been secured.

* * *

How my mind wanders as I record these thoughts. As through a maze of memories towards twists and turns as yet uncharted, I have yet to evidence the discipline of a proper memoire. The purpose of this entry is not to chronicle my own lamentations, but to provide a proper account of my queer observations; observations of such curiosities as bring me to the precipice of doubting my eyes, my mind, my very soul.

I shall therefore endeavor to remain on task from this point forward, and I ask my future self to please forgive the immature and inconcise composition of my previously expressed thoughts. I had, at the time of recent events, come to accept the truth of our Hunt, though I still find myself in some degree of shock regarding the speed with which I had become involved in another ordeal. It is one thing to know that myths and monsters are more than mere fancy; it is another to witness such things in as short a period as recent circumstances have provided. Shining a light upon the darkness of the world does not simply dispel the shadow, it reveals what is hiding within; a sight for which one needs much preparation.

The subject of this particular study is more recognizable than that which brought me into the company of my companion, but is no less monstrous for this fact. If anything, the human characteristic of this subject makes the events recorded herein that much more monstrous in nature; for a beast at least is such by nature, but a man of this kind represents a much greater evil. True evil is the monster created, not the monster born.

It was November of 1839, not seven weeks following our departure from Prague, when my companion received correspondence from his Order. The Brotherhood, so far as my inquires have revealed, is a global network of those whom guard against the incursion of dark forces. As a Knight of the Order he is frequently the recipient of such dispatches; although, as I have so few travels with my companion I cannot speak as to the frequency with which he receives such correspondence. Nor can I speak with regards to the frequency with which such correspondence results in extended travel. What I can say is that this was the first such dispatch of which I was aware, and that what follows was the first ordeal with which we had engaged since Markus rescued me from certain doom.

I can only allude to the contents of this particular missive as I was not privy to the details, kept as I am from the sanctum of his deepest trust. I was thrust from the room, politely but firmly, as Markus spoke with one of his Brothers. Disguised as a Franciscan monk, an order which observes vows of poverty, chastity, and obedience, the man simply arrived at the door of our lodgings begging a moment of Markus' time. I can only assume that there is some form of secret communication which allowed these men to know of their mutual allegiance, for I am certain that neither had met the other before that day.

Such was my distress that I cannot speak to the duration to which I paced the hall as the two men talked. Alas, after a period far beyond my comfort, the Franciscan exited the room, closing the door softly behind. He paused in the hallway, staring solemnly at me before continuing on his way. I was called back into the room by a thoughtful looking Markus, who was then gathering his gear.

"We go to Germany," said he.

I nodded and began to pack my belongings, trusting that he would illuminate the mystery as he deemed necessary. I later learned that Markus had been informed of dark portents which required an investigation into the activities pertaining to a small Bavarian *stadt*. There were indications of a dark and foul magic, the source of which we were to identify.

These are the events which proceeded. Before beginning our journey, we acquired several items and materials. Some of which would be recognizable to any layman, while others were of a more specialized variety. These included such things as the staples of the road—dried meats, cheeses, and spare clothes—and such mundane sundries as any would need to embark upon a long journey.

To me this seemed in and of itself odd. Even while considering the infrequent intervals at which the small city hoppers ran, airship travel would make this a quick journey. But I did not question my companion and instead held my reservations in solitary confidence. Upon completing these mundane purchases, we finished our acquisitions by granting our custom to shops of both the holy and the occult. Conscious of the cost of air travel, we had endeavored to limit the weight of our equipment and had purchased only that which was not guaranteed to be found at our destination. And thus it was that we began the journey to Bavaria.

We approached the locale of our quarry from the southwest, disembarking the city hopper at the Nuremburg centrum. It was there that we secured the remainder of our supplies, the mundane from common vendors, and from the guildhall we acquired the more unique items of the trade. It seemed to me that Markus was oversupplying for this hunt, a most questionable tactic by my mind, but again I did not question his actions.

One particular vendor caught my interest, however, and I shall tangent slightly to remark upon this curiosity. I have recorded a portion of what I heard because of how the words stirred within me a sense of wonder. Knowing both the German with which the salesman spoke and the English which was his native language, I was perhaps more aware of the minor errors of translation which caused the passers-by to smirk at his vocal inconsistencies. I have for the most part recorded what he intended to say in his own language, rather than that which he actually said in my native tongue.

'Come one, come all. Come and be the first to witness the most amazing advancement of human ingenuity to grace these ancient hills. The power of the telescope has long been known to scientists, military commanders, explorers, and avian aficionados alike. But now you can possess this wondrous power in the palm of your hand thanks to the craftsmen of Wilson and Dixon. It is my pleasure to introduce to you for the first time the Binoculine Image Enhansor. With this portable wonder, you are the meister of your own fate. Be amazed as distances are made void by the wonder of this little gadget. The Wilson and Dixon Binoculine Image Enhansor : Strong enough for Wellington but small enough for Napoleon.'

It was a device of which I wished to learn more, but that desire required a more opportune time, as we were then in quite a hurry. Our hours within the walls of this great city were few and we shortly departed for Oberpfalz by means of the Amberg highway.

Amberg had been the regional seat of power until governance was transferred to Regensberg in 1810. Travel upon the highway was thus lighter than it had once been, though we did see a fair amount of both mercantile traffic as well as the transport of crops. Amberg, itself a quant city, offered us both respite as well as a chance to collaborate. Our pace thus far had been considerable, and we had found little occasion for privacy. At my companion's behest, I spent a portion of that evening on the town. There, in the cold snow draped streets, I discovered the warmth and hospitality of the Bavarian people. The lights and ambiance of the *Chrsikingle Markt* bestowed a jovial quality upon the evening, and the warm *Lebkuchen* reminded me of more pleasant times. It was from there that we turned north and ventured into the northern portion of Oberpfalz.

As a point of interest, it is my estimation that Bavaria has retained a certain degree of nationalist pride. Its Napoleonic release from the Holy Roman Empire and its subsequent independence as a Kingdom is a thing which I believe to remain a significant cultural factor. By and large its people are hospitable and warm, in that way which one finds only in rural districts. I find myself continually intrigued by the degree to which this is at odds with the urban centers of the northern districts. Bavaria is quite simply more pleasant, and its people more hospitable. Despite this, however, I could sense from the common man a hesitance which I attribute not to my high born inflection of the language, but rather to the bearing which I had acquired while studying among the imperials.

Questions of Napoleon versus George matter little to the masses as few people care to see any difference between one emperor or another; and whether it be by military dominance or by diplomacy, a conquest is still a conquest. I have in truth found little love for the imperials outside of Britain proper. Although, truth be told, popular support for the Imperial Court is not universal within Britain herself. I have no doubt that this is entirely due to that historic and audacious maneuver by Emperor George in 1783. But then, given both the lack of parliamentary confidence following the treaty of Paris, and the Constitutional Crisis two years later, perhaps it is not entirely surprising that the Crown moved so decisively against the Parliamentary body. Far be it from me to comment on topics for which I am no expert, but I have sometimes wondered if affairs might be different today had Parliament not sought to define as a high crime the Crown's influence regarding the Indian Controversy. Even with public disdain for parliamentary inefficacy, not to mention the loss of the colonies, I doubt that the restoration would have been successful, nor so swift, had Parliament not given the Crown cause to act. Of course, retaining the House of Lords as an advisory council proved invaluable during the reconciliation, and the loss of the colonies did rouse a certain nationalist pride which paired well with earlier imperialist policies, most notable of which was the colonial reconstitution of 1812.

But again to the task at hand; it should be no surprise that Markus remains a stranger to me. I have known this man for but a short time; and yet despite his age and apparent breeding, I am attracted to him by some strange charisma. There are moments in which I see in him something which defies the obvious. It is not merely the odd moment of wisdom—

such times as when his eyes assume the far sighted gaze of Methuselah—but also the volume and breadth of his knowledge. He is by all accounts a peasant, and yet there are occasions in which I sense within him a deep understanding of etiquette. I have on occasion had cause to suspect a wry grin or glance, as though he is privy to some secret jest aimed upon my attempts to maintain a semblance of civilized living, a jest for which I am ignorant by capacity alone.

As I have indicated, it should be no surprise that he remains a stranger to me, but it is the manner of this strangeness which is so ... perplexing. It is a deeper thing which continues to elude me.

But what troubles me is that I am as of yet incapable of defining the very nature of this abnormality which I sense within him. It is not simply that he is wise beyond his years. This, given his profession, I can understand. Rather, it seems at times as though he *is* beyond his years. It is not a thing easily put into words.

One such occasion took place in the heart of Vilseck, in the shadow of Burg Dagestein. We began the evening in question by securing lodging at the smallest of the stadt's inns, after which we visited the local canteen. Etiquette and custom vary widely from one region to another, and although I always strive to comport myself as a gentleman of the Imperium, Markus blended with the locals as though he had been reared in one of the local hamlets. Markus, without even a hint as to our true purpose, soon had the locals lifting their steins and sharing stories of supernatural lore, of which there were many. He sorted through these tales like a university scholar in a new library, tapping the knowledge of each person as though they were a tome before discarding the irrelevant and pursuing the next. Even knowing what Markus was about, it was difficult to see anything other than a man quickly making associations with the whole room. As for myself, I quickly recognized the potential harm of my own contribution, and so found myself nursing one of several bratwursts as a way of avoiding interaction with the peasants.

Markus had in short order found what he desired. It was barely one hour past the mid of night when he signaled to me that it was time to leave. We retired to our lodgings, at which time Markus saw fit to tell me some of what was to come. On the morrow we were to ride out, departing the now friendly townsfolk, and begin the hunt. There was in the stadt a blood magician, a thing which was most commonly known as a necromancer. He explained to me that a necromancer is one who uses magic to draw upon the energies of life, typically to harmful effect. He gave me then an example of an ancient account wherein a necromancer had enslaved an entire populous by binding their blood to his will. He stated then that this is among the most perverse of corruptions, and that it could very well prove to be a dangerous hunt. I must admit to some excitement upon hearing what our quarry was to be, as there was a part of me which was then naïve enough to think that such things are *adventurous*.

By weaving together the tales of the townsfolk Markus had determined that the magician was likely practicing to the north of the castle near the hamlet of Friehung, and that this was the area which we were to investigate. Some subterfuge was required as the quarry we sought was most likely one of the townsfolk, and were we to reveal our purpose, or to visit for too long, we may well have been found out. This could then have brought most dire repercussions upon us. I was warned then to rest well, for it might be some time before we were to enjoy such 'comforts' again.

* * *

Dawn soon came, and as it departed so did we. In the morning we rode west along Amberg Starsse, and through residential Vilseck where we then crossed the river. In a matter of minutes we had found ourselves isolated on the empty road. I was caught unaware when Markus then lead his horse off the track and into the nearby stand of trees. It was not long after this that Markus had located a small clearing, whereupon he dismounted. It was there that we began a most methodical pattern of examination. Knowing what it was which he sought, Markus began a process of magical soundings which he then used to triangulate a location of esoteric convergence.

Digging into his saddlebags he withdrew a curious brass device.

"What is that, Markus?"

He held up the device for me to see. It reminded me of nothing so much as a brass sextant with four silver wires attached to it. At the end of each wire was a golden nail upon which were etched archaic runes. "Traces energy. Watch. Learn."

I did so eagerly. Placing the device squarely in the sun, he carefully stretched the four wires until they were taut; he then gently pushed the golden nails into the ground, each one in precise alignment with the device. Though there surely must be a principal of natural philosophy or modern science which explains what happened next, I must admit that I am ignorant as to what it may be. The sextant began to spin in place, ratcheting back and forth, until the dial finally settled, pointing to the east.

I gaped. "What principal powers this device?"

Markus looked to me like I was a fool. "Magic."

When I responded it was somewhat derisive, but respectfully so. "Surely there must be some scientific principal which powers this device? Would not the demonstrations of Galvanni have been called magic one century past?"

He stared at me for a long moment. "No."

"But how does it work?" I pressed eagerly.

"There are in the world things ... how you say, conduits. It is like series of strings. These strings they ... converge at special places, yes? We search for this, this place where strings connect."

I ceased then in pressing for an answer as he stowed the device. A good portion of our day became a repetition of this ritual of placing the sextant, taking a reading, and departing. We were mindful of the farmers in their fields, and took efforts to avoid their interest as we cautiously circled north and east. We continued this process of drawing an ever clearer azimuth until near to sundown. The result of which pointed us to a location not far east and slightly north of *Burg Dagestein*. It was thus that we found ourselves on a small wooded hill above Friehung. There we found an ancient track which led from the hamlet to a nearly inconspicuous grove. The reason for the increased provisions became clear to me at dusk when Markus motioned us to stop and began to unpack a camp. It was there that we were to rest for the night.

I began to dig a small hole to make a fire, but Markus stopped me. "No light."

Refilling the crevice I inquired, "Is there danger?"

"No, Friedrich, I do think no. But fire may bring eyes to us."

I nodded in reply and continued then to help him assemble camp.

* * *

On the morrow we conducted a more thorough examination of the hill. Perhaps it was the dawn light, diffused slightly by both the trees and a light grey mist, which caused within me a strange stirring, but I must report that the place simply felt odd. It was sparsely littered with small stones, each the size of a man's fist. These, as it turns out, were placed in a vaguely circular pattern around the odd and partial clearing. So widely were the stones placed that were we not looking for such signs, we could have easily looked over the summoner's circle. In the center of this circle stood a rather large and nearly flat topped stone. So ancient were the marks upon its surface that they appeared to be the result of natural processes. But Markus' keen eye saw our surroundings differently. "This," he indicated to me in detail as he cautiously pointed to the effects of the ancient stonework. Most notable was the shallow depression upon the northern face, which lead to a slightly darkened seam along the right side of the boulder.

"This is where blood flows." Markus spoke in a deep whispered tone. "I would think that carving was made many centuries ago. Come. We must hide, or we spook fox."

We proceeded then to conceal ourselves much as a *Jägermeister* would while in pursuit of a stag. It was at this time that the purpose of the remainder of our supplies became apparent. Markus cut a swatch in some of the more dense foliage, replacing the missing fauna with the cloth which he had purchased. Stringing the cloth from tree to tree and throwing dirt and leaves upon the hanging fabrics, Markus constructed a cleverly disguised concealment.

To me, the educated city dweller, the concealment seemed obvious. When I brought this point to the attention of Markus, he calmly shook his head and spoke sagely. "Eye is deceived by imperfection. If we construct perfect duplicate of forest, we increase chance of notice."

"Are you sure, Markus? This all seems so … " I shrugged then, not sure of the appropriate words to use without delivering insult.

He pointed then to the hill. "Walk to top of hill. You will see."

I followed his instructions, climbing until I reached a point just below the grove. My surprise was considerable. Even with the aide of the sun, albeit low in the sky, as I could not easily find the camp. Knowing where it resided I was able to discern its location, but only with great difficulty. It was effectively invisible. Properly chagrined, I returned to our camp. Settling in upon the cold earth, we waited, exchanging but few words. Neither of us wished to risk our speech carrying too far or being overheard, especially at night when sound carries best. Over the course of the next two nights, Markus bided his time carving additional runes into the shafts of his bolts, oiling his weapons, and repeatedly checking each piece of his gear. For my part I buried myself in a copy of *Der Hexenhammer*. I had hoped to glean some material of tangible use, but I found that Kramer's work was incapable of such application. Much of the work is, in my opinion, dedicated to a patriarchal approach to a biased agenda; wherein the majority of the work is geared toward proving the existence of witches rather than addressing the means with which one may handle such persons.

This continued for two more nights, until finally, on the evening of the full moon, we first witnessed a form upon the path.

On the evening of the full moon, as the sun bled its last light over the horizon and the moon slid in to take its place, a lone man walked up from the hamlet below. He dragged behind himself a large trundle, nearly the size of a small cart. He was dressed in strange finery, the source of which I could not identify. Markus grabbed my arm as I started to move, cautioning me to wait.

"Let him begin ritual," he whispered, "then we ambush and disrupt magic."

I nodded and waited for Markus to decide our action. He had, without my notice, set to ground the sextant and was at that moment watching it with devoted intent. It was not long before my companion gleaned from his device some knowledge which I failed to comprehend, for he instantly rose and whisked me to my feet. I did my best at that time to merely emulate his actions. I stepped where he stepped, and when he froze I froze. It was not long then before we had crept our way to the crest of the hill, and were then watching the strange happenings within the grove. What followed next was a surprise to us both, although my companion covered his with remarkable ease.

As the full moon ascended its apex, the circle which we observed began to alight with a most unholy and red aura. Even the small stones which formed the circle assumed this unholy aspect. I have no shame in acknowledging my own fear, for I would not have been surprised if Lucifer himself were to then split the ground and descend upon us mortals. Fortunate as we were that such did not occur, I was not set to ease by what happened in its stead.

The air within which I crouched was filled suddenly with quite inhuman shrieks. It was the bleating if an ewe which had been pulled from the trundle. The Necromancer deftly held the creature within the crevice that I have already described, and with all the hesitation of a butcher, began the ghastly work of separating the still living creature from its flesh. This deed he performed as he chanted in some unknown and guttural language, not unlike that which one might expect to emanate from the lips of the damned and disowned souls of the abyss. I could dimly sense that I was enraged by this action, but such was the state of affairs that I was overwhelmed with disgust, and it was all that I could do to keep my meager rations within the confines of my stomach. As troubled as I was by the letting of blood, I should have found comfort in its completion; alas, the only thing more disturbing then the constant cry of the tortured ewe was the sudden silence which followed its death.

The Necromancer then turned to the trundle and, maintaining his chant, wrestled a larger form upon the stone altar. With clear effort, the fiend thrust upon that stone the form a slight and slender girl. She could have been little more than thirteen of age! I was frantic with anxiety and my heart quickened as I heard Markus calmly gather a breath beside me.

"We go." Quiet determination filled his voice. Markus calmly walked up the hill toward the Necromancer, who had now subdued his would be victim. Leveling his shotbow, he walked with determination. He pulled the trigger and a bolt flew from its perch. The mechanism beneath the weapon's firing rail clicked softly as the cylindrical magazines turned in time. A new bolt was secured upon the rail and the trigger clicked in preparation as the first bolt found its mark, burrowing deep within the Necromancers right forearm. The fiend spun then to face us, revealing his visage for the first time. As he held up his uninjured hand a red light shimmered before him, surrounding him with a barely perceptible mist.

Markus sighted down the rail of the shotbow. "Friedrich, right flank!" I moved to the right as I listened to Markus continue. "How many in your coven?"

The necromancer tilted his head, curious. "Why would you think I have a coven? Covens are for the weak, Hunter." Markus may have been surprised to hear from this man the inflections of education, but I was not. Upon first sight of his visage, I had recognized the features of the Bavarian aristocracy. "I have no wish to harm you, Brothers of the Blade. Leave me to my work and I will grant you shelter for the night. We can discuss this matter on the morrow."

Markus pulled the trigger again. A bolt flew forth but was deflected and sparked with a small wash of flame as the red mist momentarily solidified. "You steal blood of others. You take what is not yours, and defile purity of soul." Markus' response was cold and pointed. Were I to wager, I would hazard a guess that he was then speaking with a mind to some dark mystery of personal import.

"I take what I want, because I can."

It was then that I could no longer contain my disdain for this *man*. "These are people!" I screamed.

"They are cattle!" said he as he turned to face me. "People yes, but animals all the same. Do you think that Man is special because he can speak? Because he can reason?"

"You prey upon those who are weaker than you. You are a tyrant!" I felt my rage rise.

"Why should I be ashamed of my station? Why should the improbability of the heritage of my birth cause me to seek some indelible defense upon the behalf of others? Yes, I was born into heritage. Yes, this was by mere chance alone. This means nothing! Does the wolf lament the death of the lamb? Does the peasant lament the death of the pig ... or the King the death of the peasant? Do we mourn the death of that which we eat in order to survive? Why then should I be concerned with the death of those beneath me? Is the social order not a force of nature, sovereign unto its own principles? Tell me this, *Imperial*, if all men are equal and deserving of fair and *just* treatment, then why has every society developed a hierarchy of iniquity? Even dogs have an order to their pack, whereupon the lowliest mutt supplicates himself to the alpha. Does this not evidence the natural order of all things?"

"You rationalize your sins." said I.

"My sin.... Does the Bible not speak of sacrifice? Does not the Bible itself state the life of thing is contained within its blood? If you read Leviticus you will see that my art was once considered to be pleasing to your God. You are correct about one thing, though; Man *is* different, but it is a difference of degree, not a difference of kind. When the blood of lesser beings could not wash away the sin of the people, a man was hung upon a tree to be drained of his life. Why? Because Man is the pinnacle of creation ... and as such his blood holds the greatest value to the gods."

I did not know how to respond to this. I found myself acknowledging some value of the justification, but the level of my disgust was increased in seeing one who used the scripture to validate this manner of transgression.

"I know your mind, *Imperial*. I know what your *humanist* response will be, but answer me this: does being human absolve one of the First Law of Nature? No! Humans are humans. The fact that we speak does not make us special. I think therefore I am? Hah! I *BLEED* therefore I am! The only difference between you and a rat is the potency of your blood. Take it from someone who knows; I have delved the depths of the human *spirit*; I know what makes us different from dogs ... I have *tasted* it.

"Your rationalization is an abomination. You are simply evil."

"Evil? And pray tell my good sir, what is evil? Do you define evil by the arbitrary standards of an absentee god? Or do you impose a derivative morality as a categorical imperative? Tell me, what innate aspects do you assign to morality that allows you to call me evil? You have no answer ... well then allow me to enlighten you. Evil is nothing more than a fabrication of the weak. The very concept of good and evil is flawed because one cannot exist without the other. Take away evil and you have no good. Morality is little more than a social delusion. The Laws of Nature have no account for morality because it is a purely human construct. What does it matter then if I choose the path of *evil*, except to allow you to call yourself good?

"You call me evil but you know only my methods. You know nothing of my motives. Detestable as you find me to be, I am the defender of this land, a patron of its people ... my people. For thousands of years my family has been steward to this land; before Napoleon, before Charlemagne, before Rome itself! We are beholden to the bones of these hills, and indeed the bones within them! We bring the rains and repel the droughts. We embolden the soil and draw forth the harvest. We expel pestilence and strengthen the livestock. We are called one at a time, from father to son. We serve the land and by extent its people.

It was then that Markus interjected. "What do you mean ... steward?"

"Are you daft easterner?" He was not. I had deviated from our plan and this was his attempt to recover. His weapon was still leveled upon the Necromancer but he held it in check as I resumed my flanking. "Do you think the prosperity here is natural? Why is it do you think that the plague spared us of its deathly grip? One day the people of this land will remember the oath that binds us to them. They will remember our patronage and call upon us once more to lead them ... to protect them. They will know our loyalty and bow before us once more, as the master we are."

"I do not understand." Feigned my companion as I unsheathed the runic dagger with which I had been provisioned.

"Watch then as I do what I must, and you will understand the true order of the world." With these words he turned to the girl who was bound then by his magic. Her frail form was lithe underneath the thin gown as she struggled sheepishly against the unseen bonds. With his free hand he fondly, yet forcefully grasped her head as though he intended to mount her. With the bolt still firmly imbedded within his forearm, he brought the blade within his right hand to caress the girl's inner thigh.

It was then that I cut deep, as I had been instructed. I had been uncertain of my ability to do so, but I was compelled by altruism and thus gave freely of myself. I suspect now that Markus had deduced this of me and orchestrated his plan with an understanding of my persona which I myself lack. The blood began to flow immediately; deep crimson it fell from the wound which then pierced my forearm, much as the bolt had pierced the Necromancer's. Had I waited any longer I suspect that fear would have arrested me, but as it was I acted in faith upon the instructions of my companion. It was thus that I flung my blood at the fiend before me.

Even as I did so, his blade had pierced the soft flesh the young girl. One of the few things which I can recall with clarity was the fear in her eyes at that very moment. I could see no pain upon her face, but the fear was clearer than Austrian crystal.

There are moments when the human mind is overwhelmed by events and it races to understand them. It is at these moments that time seems to stop, or to slow. For me, this was one such moment. I did not know what more I could do. I had performed my task as instructed but feared that I had done so incorrectly, and that this innocent child would subsequently pay the price for my hesitation. I saw then her blood as it was pulled by some unnatural force from the small cut in her leg. It was forming a beaded mist around the Necromancer even as he moved to make a second incision.

What happened next is almost beyond human conception. My own blood, freely given, entered into the growing maelstrom and mixed with that of the virgin child. With all of its impurities and doubts, it seemed to dissolve within the magical energies which then surrounded the Necromancer. It was thus that I was pulled inextricably into the chaos. I was a leaf in a whirlwind. What I knew then, and what I know of it now is quite simply beyond words. The spell and I were one. I could *feel* the surges of the Necromancer's work as it was brought to conflict against the pulsating rhythm that was the cosmic heartbeat intrinsic to the conduits of which Markus had spoken. My understanding of maters preternatural was beyond comprehension. It seemed so clear to me then, and I can but grasp at the thinnest tendrils of this knowledge, like the tiniest wisps of smoke through my clumsy fingers. Even these descriptions lack substance when compared against my ever vanishing memory.

All that I can say is that a balance was corrupted. The fiend's spell surged where it should not, and it fluttered where before there had been stability. I can recall his increasingly feeble attempts to wrangle the massive energies, as well as an awareness of my own imminent destruction. That part of me which had become vastly wiser than any man, that part which was then no longer constrained to a single mortal identity, knew that I had been sacrificed by my companion much as the virgin had been sacrificed by the necromancer. My intended actions could have never resulted in that which I had been told to expect.

One could imagine then the perplexity which I felt when I found myself, bereft of my senses, staring upon the naked sky. Markus stood above me with that stoic non-expression. I was internally cold. I was confused. I was painfully aware of the utter stupidity of Man. My mind was dulled once more by the limitations of this shell, and I trembled with fear at the immensity of that with which I had nearly become a part. How he had removed me from that maelstrom I do not know, for in a state of perfect understanding such a thing seemed impossible; and yet, it was not.

When I awoke, the blade had already been removed from my arm, and though tender, I could find no physical evidence that it had ever penetrated my flesh. The child, I know not here name, had been draped in a thick blanket and stood near Markus, barefoot in the light snow. She was at that time more composed than myself, and I know not how much time had passed to grant her the opportunity to come to terms with what she had experienced.

What was left of the fiend was scarcely identifiable. His remains consisted of tattered remnants of cloth and small, assorted piles of meat. No attempt was made to collect the densely scattered remains. He had been, in his own words, little more than an animal. We left him there for the wild dogs, and I can think of no punishment more biblical or more fitting for one such as him.

We walked together then, the child, my companion and I; he a fierce predator and she a gentle creature at one with the ground under her feet. It was not long before we had gathered together our camp and set upon the track toward Freihung. Some short time later we had arrived at the home of her father. A small and quant dwelling, it was, in the manor of the region, located in close proximity to neighboring families. We encountered no one on our journey, and within the dwelling we could detect only the faintest signs of peaceful activity.

It was there that we departed from the child, trusting in her insistence that she was safe and that we need not worry further for her wellbeing. She touched my face lightly with her oddly warm fingers as we spoke our farewells, and I felt awkward because of the intimacy and affection which filled her eyes. Those eyes stirred within me affection of my own, and I feel even now as though she holds a part of me. It seemed to me then that she possessed a maturity which I would not have expected of one her age, and that she was not quite as helpless as I would have thought. She spoke to me fondly and said that our debt to each other was paid. She spoke hopefully of a time when we would be reunited, and reminded Markus of the honor of his oath. I can still feel that phantom of her touch upon my cheek.

* * *

The necromancer's words haunt me still, though. Where is that invisible line between good and evil? Morality and damnation? Science and magic? How do I explain what I saw that night?

As I grow to gain Markus's trust, I also chronicle these events in the hope that someday I will understand the science, the philosophy, behind these events. Surely there must be a rational explanation for ... all of this. Musn't there?

Then why does this memory fill me with such loss and emptiness?

Peter J. Wacks & J.R. Boyett

About the Authors

Peter J. Wacks was born in California sometime during 1976. He has always been amazed and fascinated by both writing and the world in general. Throughout the course of his life, he has hitchhiked across the States and backpacked across Europe on the Eurail. Peter writes a lot, and will continue to do so till the day he dies. Possibly beyond. Peter has acted, designed games, written novels and other spec fiction, and was nominated for a Bram Stoker Award for his first graphic novel Behind These Eyes (co-written with Guy Anthony De Marco). Currently, he is the managing editor of Kevin J. Anderson & Rebecca Moesta's WordFire Press.

J.R. Boyett was born on a rural island in the Puget Sound and spent much of his youth in the heart of Dixie. He enlisted in the U.S. Army at the age of 17, where he served for 5 years before suffering a career ending injury. In 2010 he received his Bachelor of Arts from Pacific Lutheran University and is currently pursuing a Master of Divinity at Fuller Theological Seminary.

A Philosopher and Theologian, J.R. Boyett follows in the long tradition of using fictional narrative to not only entertain the reader, but to examine essential questions about ourselves and the world in which we live.

Special thanks to Will Brown for his fantastic artwork!

Brown Takes to the Skies

J.A. Campbell

I hated leashes.

Elliott, my human, tried to argue that since we'd been invited to fly on the airship, I shouldn't have to be on a leash.

Captain Peyton, the owner, had countered that allowing me on board was exception enough.

Elliott had almost walked away. In the end it was my desire to fly on the airship that made him agree.

Besides, they had a ghost problem, and I was the dog for the job.

My human held my leash while I stood with my paws on the rail, nose to the wind, drinking in the glorious scents of the sky.

A few ladies tittered nervously as they strolled across the deck, distracting me from my nose. One glanced up at the air bag that kept us aloft. The other said something in soft tones, like Elliott might have used on nervous lambs, and they moved on.

"Sure is beautiful up here, isn't it, girl?" Elliott said.

I dropped my jaw in a doggy grin and wagged my tail before putting my nose back into the wind.

Though only a short time since we'd lifted off, already I felt at home in the sky. Perhaps it was strange for a dog to like to fly, but I'd done far stranger things recently, and I liked the scents the air brought me.

"We should begin our preparations," Elliott said.

Huffing, I dropped back to all fours and padded next to my human as we headed for the door that led below.

The ladies stopped us.

I sniffed, one smelled very nervous, the other merely annoyed. Both wore fancy dresses I associated with the clothing from back in the east where we'd come from, and they smelled faintly of flowers.

"They really let you bring a dog onboard?" The annoyed one asked.

"She does tricks." Elliott knew we weren't supposed to talk about the ghost, so he couldn't tell them why I was here.

Obediently, I sat up on my back legs when Elliott gave me the signal.

The nervous one laughed. "What's her name?" She held out her hand for me to sniff.

"Brown."

She glanced up at Elliott. "That's not a very original name for a brown and white dog."

He shrugged. "She's a Border Collie from the old country. They all have simple names."

The woman still held out her hand so I put my paw in it and she giggled. "How wonderful."

"She'd better not have fleas," the annoyed one said.

I flattened my ears.

"Easy, Brown. She takes exception to that, ma'am. Now if you will excuse us, ladies, we were off to find some lunch." He touched the brim of his round hat and I followed him away.

Lunch sounded like a fine idea to me. I hoped they had steak.

Elliott and I walked across the deck and down into the ship. It wasn't very large. I'd been on a steamship on the Mississippi river that was larger.

Captain Peyton, the owner of the airship, had approached us almost as soon as we'd gotten off the train in Denver. Apparently we'd made enough of a name for ourselves that he'd been looking for us and discovered we were headed for Denver. He hadn't wanted me to come along, not believing that I was part of the ghost-hunting team, but finally he'd consented, as long as I wore a leash.

Food smells, including meat, distracted me from my memory of the stinky Captain and how demanding he'd been when he asked us to banish his ghost. He'd smelled of sweat and fear and guilt when he'd told us of his problem. At the time I'd wondered why, but now I only cared about eating and handling the ghost problem.

Elliott left me outside the door to the room where they prepared the food. Sitting, I waited patiently until he returned with two wonderful smelling plates. Drool splattered the floor as I followed Elliott back to our room.

"Well, Brown. This should be straight forward." He stared at his great grand pappy's hunting journal while I made short work of my lunch.

"We should simply be able to summon, trap, and banish the ghost without much trouble." He put his plate down on a small table and rummaged in his hunting bag.

I rested my chin on the arm of one of the two chairs and stared at his half-eaten food. Surely he was going to finish that?

Kneeling next to the bed in the small room, Elliott shoved a small rug out of the way and cleared some space to draw. I knew I should be more concerned about what Elliott was doing, but the uneaten food had my nose's full attention.

"Brown, are you still hungry?" Elliott finally noticed where my nose was pointed.

Strictly speaking, I wasn't hungry, but there was always room for steak. He laughed. "Go ahead and eat that while I finish up this drawing."

Gleefully, I jumped into the chair and devoured his lunch. Once I'd licked the plate clean, I joined Elliott and looked over his drawing. I knew the circle with the strange designs was supposed to be complete, no breaks in the lines at all. Elliott had explained it all to me once. I looked closely and woofed quietly to let him know I thought it looked okay.

"Good girl, Brown." He scratched my ears and I thumped my tail on the ground before scooting back so I could watch for the ghost. It was my job to catch it with my Border Collie Eye and push it into the trap, the same way I herded sheep into a pen.

Elliott read from his book, trying to keep his voice down so passengers wouldn't hear, but also keep his voice forceful enough to command the ghost that haunted this airship to appear.

The air chilled and the gas lamps flickered. White smoke drifted in under the door of our small cabin and crawled across the floor. Jumping up, I got out of its path and growled, trying not to sneeze as the ghost's musty-ozone smell filled the room. Pausing in front of the trap Elliott had drawn, the smoke began to swirl as more continued to pour under the door. Finally, the smoke stopped flowing under the door and the white swirl spun faster like a dust devil. Many of the other ghosts I'd fought did the same.

Two eyes opened and stared at me. Growling when I felt the ghost's wind pull at my fur, I met its eyes and pushed. Most ghosts fought me when I caught them with my Eye, but this one simply floated backward until the trap sprung around it with an audible pop.

Sitting, I tilted my head while I stared at the ghost. I was very good at hunting ghosts, but it was never that easy.

Elliott frowned, as if he were also confused at how easy that was. "Good girl, Brown."

We both stared at the ghost, but it simply swirled contentedly in the trap, not howling in rage or otherwise trying to escape. Elliott glanced at me and I looked back and thumped my tail on the ground once because I wasn't sure what else to do.

According to the owner of the airship, this ghost was supposed to be extremely violent and had almost thrown him off the ship several times when they were high in the sky. It didn't bother passengers often, but it did chase the crew around.

This hardly seemed like a violent ghost.

"Well, I guess I'll get on with it." Elliott looked back at the book in his hands and said the first few words that, when complete, would banish the ghost.

"Ah, excuse me."

Elliott snapped his mouth shut and I yelped in surprise, looking around for the source of the voice. It almost sounded like one of the men who had taught Elliott about books and things when we lived back east, with words carefully formed and pronounced. Not like a lot of the people we came across in the west.

We both glanced wildly around before looking back at the ghost. It was no longer spinning and seemed to be more like the cloud of smoke from earlier. The eyes were gone.

"Who's there?" Elliott finally asked.

"Ahh! You can hear me. Excellent. Most humans can only see me."

Sniffing the air, I whined uncertainly. The only thing I could smell besides myself, Elliott, faint traces of lunch, and the background scents of the airship was the musty-ozone of the ghost.

The smoke drifted around the trap before becoming taller and almost human shaped. Wavering slightly, slits opened where its head would be if it were human, and formed eyes and a mouth.

"Hello."

I flattened my ears and stared at the ghost. I'd never seen one do this before. Sure, I'd had ghosts talk to me on occasion, but usually they hurled insults like squirrels. Though, once I'd met a friendly ghost. He'd looked completely human though.

Elliott lifted his book.

"Please, don't. Hear me out." Raising what looked like a hand, the ghost interrupted Elliott before he could begin the banishment words again.

"Okay." Elliott sounded uncertain.

The ghost made a sound like it was clearing its throat.

That seemed really strange to me.

"My name is … was Charlie Victors. I'm the owner of this fine ship."

"I see." Elliott took a couple of steps toward me, carefully stepping around the ghost-trap.

"That murdering bastard, Peyton, stole it from me after he killed me." The ghost shut its eyes for a moment, and the smoke swirled as if it were agitated.

Elliott shifted uncomfortably and smelled nervous. Pushing my nose up under his hand, I tried to reassure him by leaning against his leg. He scratched my ears, and that seemed to calm him a little.

"Yes, well, I've heard of you two and I hope you can help me."

"Heard of us?"

I tilted my head, wondering if I'd understood the ghost properly.

"Well, yes, even spirits talk amongst themselves."

"How?" Elliott sank down onto one of the chairs.

"That's not relevant at this time. Just that I've heard of you, and all that. No hard feelings of course, all of those you've sent away were giving ghosts bad names. As, I suppose, I was. Unfortunately, I was unable to take care of Peyton myself and now I need your help."

Elliott shook his head. "I'm sorry, this is a lot to take in. Exactly how do you think I can help you?"

"Why, prove that Jerrod Peyton murdered me of course. And then perhaps I can go to my rest instead of haunting this ship for eternity."

I whined.

Elliott was silent for a while before he glanced at me. "Mr. Victors, I'm sorry. I don't know how to prove that Captain Peyton murdered you. All we do is fight ghosts."

And demons, and Martians, and vampires, I thought to myself. For a while there, I'd wished for a simple ghost to fight after all of the strange creatures we'd encountered. If we could handle Martians especially, I thought maybe we could handle a murderer. Martians were worse than squirrels.

"Of course I'd be willing to help. I know where some of the evidence is. If it will see Peyton hang, I'll even pretend you've already banished me. I've only made myself a nuisance because I wanted to get rid of him."

Frowning, Elliott leaned back and rubbed his forehead with his hand. "What proof can you offer me that you're telling the truth?"

The ghost shifted around until its eyes met mine. I refrained from capturing its mind because it wasn't trying to escape. It studied me for a minute, and then did a curious thing. It spoke to me.

"Dog, can you understand me?"

I thumped my tail on the ground once, shocked. "Of course."

For some reason, though, I couldn't communicate directly with humans. Ghosts always seemed to understand me. "My name is Brown."

"Her name is Brown," Elliott said at the same time.

The ghost laughed, but it was a friendly laugh instead of the evil hate-filled ones most ghosts used.

"So she says." The ghost seemed to smile. "And you are?"

"My apologies, I'm Elliott Gyles."

"Nice to make your acquaintance."

Thumping my tail on the ground again, I woofed quietly, though I wasn't sure what to think about this very strange ghost.

"Brown, when you met Peyton the first time, did he seem strange to you?" The ghost asked.

"He smelled afraid, but most people are afraid of ghosts. He also smelled guilty." I glanced at Elliott, who was staring at both of us intently.

"Mr. Gyles, your rather fabulous dog says that he smelled guilty. Would he have smelled so if he weren't feeling guilt about creating a ghost?"

"Is that correct, Brown?"

I woofed once in agreement.

The ghost's eyes widened. "You already have a system of communication worked out?"

"Yes, of course," I replied. "Just because humans can't listen properly and understand animals, doesn't mean we can't communicate with each other."

"You are remarkable."

"That's all well and good," Elliott said. "But that doesn't prove your story."

"No," the ghost agreed. "But perhaps it helps. By all means, keep me contained in this trap, but go investigate my desk drawers in the office. You'll find documents that support my claim. He was an investor, to be sure, but he decided he wanted all the money for himself. Go on, you'll see. He should be enjoying his lunch at this time."

Elliott glanced at me before shrugging. "Very well. Come on, Brown."

"Ah, Mr. Gyles, if the door should be locked, there is a spare key hidden along the top of the door frame on a hook so it won't fall. I had a singularly bad habit of losing my keys."

Elliott nodded to the ghost and let us out of the small room.

"So, you can talk to ghosts?" Elliott glanced at me as we walked down the hallway toward the office Charlie the ghost wanted us to investigate.

I woofed quietly, once.

"Do they talk often?"

I woofed twice to say no.

Elliott was quiet after that, seeming to think. It didn't take us long to navigate the small airship. We knew which room to go to because we'd had a tour when we first came aboard.

Pausing outside, Elliott put his ear up to the door and listened.

"It's quiet. Do you hear anything, Brown?"

Listening and sniffing told me the room was empty, so I woofed twice.

"Good, watch and make sure no one comes this way."

I sat next to the door.

Elliott unclipped my leash and looped it on his belt. Then he knocked lightly on the door. "Just in case," he said, smiling at me.

I doggy grinned back, though he smelled nervous.

Elliott tried the handle but it didn't turn so he felt along the doorframe. Turning my attention back to the hallway, I listened with half of my attention to what Elliott was doing. He let himself into the office and opened drawers, muttering to himself. Finally I heard an 'ah-ha!'

I also heard footsteps coming down the hallway.

Alarmed, I woofed quietly.

Elliott shut drawers and rustled papers.

The footsteps grew closer.

Urgently, I woofed again.

Elliott left the office, shut the door and returned the key.

"Come on," he whispered.

We walked away from the office quickly but before long Elliott slowed and looked around as if he were looking for a ghost. I recognized what he

213

was doing and sniffed the floor, playing along.

"Mr. Gyles?" Captain Peyton said.

We both turned and I wrinkled my lips when I caught a hint of his sour scent.

To my canine nose, most humans smelled best after they hadn't bathed for a few days, but I wished the Captain would jump in a lake or do something to wash away the sour scent that clung to him.

"Yes, Captain?"

"I trust you are having luck searching for the nuisance?"

He called the ghost 'the nuisance' when guests could potentially overhear.

"Yes, we have had some luck. I suspect we will have success tonight."

"Tonight? Why not now?"

For a moment the Captain smelled suspicious, and his eyes flicked to the office door he stood near.

"It's the best time to capture a ghost," Elliott said.

"Of course." His scent eased. "Carry on then."

"Thank you, Captain." We turned away.

"Mr. Gyles."

Elliott stopped and looked back, his nervousness rising.

"Dog on a leash, please."

Sighing and smelling angry for a moment, Elliott clipped the leash to my collar. "Sorry, not used to using one." We quickly left the narrow hallway.

Elliott was silent until we were back at our room. He hesitated, hand hovering over the handle, before he took a deep breath and opened the door.

Pushing past him, I sneezed as the musty-ozone ghost smell tickled my nose. The trap still contained a swirling cloud of smoke that solidified into a sort of human figure when we entered. Two eyes opened and the ghost regarded us until Elliott closed the door.

"Well?" It asked.

"I've found enough evidence to suit me, but I'm not sure it's enough to see Peyton hang." Elliott took some papers from the inside pocket of his vest and waved them at the ghost before putting them into his hunting bag.

"Well, it's a start. What do you plan to do next?"

"If I let you out, will you give your word that you will pretend that I've banished you?"

"Yes, I promise. However I plan to monitor your progress and tell you if I see anything important."

Smudging the drawing with his foot, Elliott disabled the trap and it opened with an audible pop.

The ghost melted into a cloud and poured out before swirling around my paws.

Picking up my paws, I tried not to let the ghost touch me, but I could only lift so many paws off the ground. I whined.

"I quite like you, Brown," the ghost laughed, briefly flowing into a semi-human form.

Wagging my tail uncertainly, I tried to like the ghost too, but it was still a ghost.

"In the morning, I will tell Peyton I succeeded. We will be on board until we return to Colorado. I will try to question the crew and see if I can find any more evidence."

"Be careful. I'm sure I don't need to tell you that Peyton is ruthless."

Elliott nodded.

"Very well. I will leave you for now. Thank you." The ghost made a gesture similar to one Elliott made when he tipped his hat to ladies and melted back into a cloud of smoke. It crept along the floor and vanished into the wall.

"Well, Brown. That's a new one." Elliott took off his round hat and scratched his forehead.

Huffing, I sat and stared at the wall, head tilted, trying to figure out how we were suddenly working for a ghost instead of a human.

* * *

The next morning we found Captain Peyton on the deck of his airship. He stood toward the front, Elliott told me that was called the bow, and looked out ahead of us.

Sniffing the air, I could imagine what he saw, though I couldn't see it yet. What Elliott called cotton puff clouds would fill the sky. The sun shone brightly, and I scented water from far below. All the extra spring scents of the world coming alive after sleeping through the winter colored the air too. I loved the smell of spring.

Peyton glanced at us, checking to make sure I wore the leash. I glared at him, much like I stared at a recalcitrant sheep, except this time I really was angry. Quickly glancing away, he cleared his throat and addressed Elliott. "You did say she was friendly, correct?"

J.A. Campbell

Elliott glanced at me and shrugged. "You're making her wear a leash. She's not terribly happy about it."

"Well, it's not like I put it on her. She can't know it was my doing."

"She knows," Elliott said. "Regardless, we've handled your ghost problem."

"Oh, most excellent!" His scent shifted from nervous to relieved.

Elliott smiled, though I could smell his anger and uneasiness. He didn't show it though. Once, we'd convinced people we hunted ghosts that weren't actually there and he'd had to act all the time. Peyton would never know how Elliott really felt, especially since humans couldn't smell emotions.

"We will be in St. Louis shortly. The winds favored us in the night. We will head directly back to Denver once we've loaded cargo and passengers."

"Excellent. Thank you, Captain."

"Thank you, Mr. Gyles. I'm quite glad to be rid of the nuisance."

Continuing to glare at Peyton, I jumped when a quiet voice in my ear whispered … "I wonder if he called me that when I was alive, too."

Huffing in annoyance, I sat, looking around for the ghost. I couldn't see it anywhere, but the faintest hint of musty-ozone colored the beautiful spring scents. I sneezed.

Elliott glanced at me. "Come on, Brown. Let's get something to eat."

Turning, I walked next to him, sensing that the ghost trailed along with us.

* * *

Bright colors filled the sky and the sun had set by the time the ship landed. It was a noisy affair with men shouting commands, lines snapping in the wind and a sudden jolt when the ship finally settled and was secured. We picked an out of the way spot on the deck, watching while passengers got off. The two women from the first afternoon spotted me. The nervous one approached with the other lady trailing behind.

"My uncle, the Captain, told us how you helped," she said to Elliott. "We are so grateful. Brown, I have a treat for you." She held out a piece of cooked meat.

Normally I would have taken it without thought, but something smelled strange though I wasn't sure if it was her or the treat. Laying down on the deck, I covered my nose with my paws and whined.

"Oh," she tittered. "Maybe she's airsick."

216

"Maybe," Elliott said sounding suspicious.

"Here, you can give it to her later."

He accepted the scrap and watched as the ladies left the airship.

"You're not hungry?"

I whined.

After glancing over the side of the airship, Elliott tossed the scrap of meat away. "Never seen you refuse food before."

I huffed.

After the passengers all left, the crew unloaded the cargo.

"Brown, let's go inside. I don't feel well."

I followed Elliott to our room and watched as he collapsed into the bed. Jumping up next to him, I lay my chin on his chest. He smelled odd and I could feel his heart racing.

I'd been sleeping for a while when the ghost woke me up.

"What's wrong, Brown?"

"I don't know," I said. "Elliott's not well."

"I wasn't around for a short time," the ghost said. "What happened?"

I told him how we'd been standing on the deck of the airship and the nervous lady had tried to give me a scrap of meat and that I hadn't wanted it. Something had smelled strange. She'd given it to Elliott instead and shortly after he'd become sick.

"You didn't touch it?" The ghost asked.

"No I didn't. Elliott only held it and then threw it over the side of the airship."

The ghost swirled around in a cloud of smoke for a moment before solidifying into its human-like shape again. "Perhaps it was poisoned."

I flattened my ears. "Poisoned?"

"Yes, he could have gotten a little bit of it through touching the piece of meat. It's a good thing you didn't eat it, Brown."

I whined. "Is he going to be okay?"

"I don't know. We should try and find the antidote if there is one."

I tilted my head. "An antidote?"

The ghost nodded. "Yes some poisons come with a cure. Something that counteracts the poison. It's called an antidote. I don't know if this poison will have some, but it's a good chance that if Peyton is behind this he will have wanted something he could counteract it with just in case. Was the woman wearing gloves?" The ghost asked.

"Yes, she was."

The ghost nodded, or what seemed to be a nod with his smoky form.

J.A. Campbell

"Why do you ask?"

"I bet she's not now," the ghost replied. "Probably to protect herself from the poison, though why he'd want to harm you I don't know. Perhaps he simply didn't want to pay. Maybe he's suspicious that you know more than you should."

I huffed in annoyance. "Well, let's go find this antidote."

"Do you know how to open doors?" The ghost asked me.

I nodded like the humans did and hopped off of the bed. Waiting by the door for the ghost, I studied the doorknob. It returned to its smoky form and crept across the floor behind me. After a moment it disappeared, but I could still smell a faint hint of musty-ozone.

"The antidote, if there is one, should be in the office," the ghost said. "If it's not there it may be in his cabin."

Relieved to discover that the doorknob was one of the lever type handles, I stood on my hind legs and put my front paw on the lever and pushed down while pushing forward. It didn't work. The lever clicked but the door remained shut.

Remembering that the door swung inward, I knew I needed to pull instead. I hooked my paw on the handle pushed it down and hopped backward. This time the door opened enough for me to get my nose in it and to sneak out into the hallway. I stopped, looking and sniffing, but no one was around.

"I will keep my senses open, and if I see or hear anyone coming I will let you know. Things are different as a ghost, though, and sometimes I don't notice as much as I should. Stay alert, Brown."

I woofed quietly in agreement and headed back toward the captain's office. Of course, I had no idea how I was going to get in since I couldn't reach the key.

The ghost alerted me to several presences in the hallways, and we were able to take side routes. If it weren't so late, more people would have been out and would've spotted me. Perhaps they would have tried to capture me.

I wasn't sure what I would do if someone captured me or tried to. I'd have to fight back, and I didn't want to hurt people, but to save Elliott I'd do what I had to. It didn't take long for us to navigate the hallways of the small airship. Shortly I sat on my haunches staring at the door to the captain's office. After a moment's hesitation, I sniffed the knob and listened at the door. No one was there, and the knob smelled normal. I stood on my haunches again, my paw on the top of the knob, and pushed down. This type of knob was much harder to turn, and it was locked.

The ghost swirled into its humanlike shape, two eyes opening and staring at the door. I got the impression that it was significantly annoyed.

"I had forgotten about that. If I get the key down do you think you can open the door?"

I stared at the ghost, my head tilted, ears perked forward, trying to figure out what to say. I had to get the door open, but did I think I could do it? Not with the key.

Even though I didn't answer, the ghost seemed to understand what my hesitation meant. "Well, you are a remarkable dog, but I suspect using a key would be beyond your physical capabilities ... though I'm certain you understand how to use one."

"Yes, of course I understand how to use a key. I don't think I can actually do it."

The ghost considered the door for a moment longer and a mouth appeared, smiling. "Well of course," it said. "If I can get the key down for you, certainly I can manipulate a simple lock. I wasn't too terribly concerned about someone breaking into my office and therefore did not buy an expensive lock for the door. I merely wanted to deter curious travelers from disturbing me while I worked."

The ghost vanished before I could ask what it meant, and because I was listening very carefully, after a moment I heard the distinct click of the lock opening on the inside of the door. Surprised, I tilted my head and wagged my tail before jumping up on the door again and trying the knob. This time it turned easily and I was able to push the door open.

"Well done, Brown," the ghost exclaimed when I entered the study. "Shut the door behind you and let's look."

I used my nose and the ghost used whatever senses ghosts have. I caught hints of the strange smell I'd scented on the nervous woman, but every time I caught hints of it there was nothing in the drawer—or on the table, or on the shelf—that looked even remotely like it contained poison. I was careful not to touch anything just in case, at the ghosts cautioning. It, being already dead, took care of that part of the search for me.

After a while we had to admit defeat. Even the hidden compartments the ghost knew about were empty or only contained papers which were not at all interesting to me since it would not save my human's life.

"Well, Brown," the ghost said. "I do believe were going to have to try his cabin. Ah, that rankles me to say his cabin. It's my cabin, this is my ship!" The ghost's cloud swirled rapidly, the light smoky color darkened for a moment before it seemed to get itself under control and returned to its humanlike form. "Sorry, Brown. I had moment there. Very well, onward we go. I will lock the door behind you if you would shut it."

I stopped by the door, listening. I heard footsteps but they were far enough away that I should be able to get the door shut before they got here. I managed and dashed around the corner just as I heard the captain's footfalls and smelled his distinct sour scent come around the corner. He paused in front of the office door, and I hoped the ghost had gotten it locked before Peyton tried to open it. I heard the clink of keys, and then a soft wind ruffled across my fur.

"Brown, Peyton should be occupied for a while."

I followed the musty scent down the corridor toward the captain's cabin. We made it without any problems. This door was one of the lever ones and wasn't locked, so it was easy for me to go in. I wrinkled my nose in disgust at the scents from his room. It smelled even more sour than the captain himself. I sneezed I couldn't help it.

The ghost looked at me. "What do you smell?"

I wrinkled my lips and sneezed again. "His scent is very sour. Enough that he's the first human I've ever met that I actually wanted to take a bath."

The ghost laughed. "I seem to recall that he did stink, but your nose is much more sensitive than mine."

Once I was able to ignore the smell, we searched the room. My nose was impeded by not being able to use it completely, but finally I caught the scent of what I had smelled on the nervous lady and smelled hints of in the office. I woofed quietly to get the ghost's attention and it came over to me.

Gesturing with my nose, I pointed toward the cabinet.

He momentarily disappeared inside. "That's it Brown." He returned. "There are two bottles. They aren't specifically labeled poison and antidote of course but they're probably what we're looking for. You shouldn't touch them but now we know where they're at. Let's see if we can wake Elliott long enough to get him here, and then maybe he can give himself the antidote if that's what it is. If not it may not matter."

I flattened my ears at the ghost's words and whined. We had to help Elliott. The trip back to the room I shared with Elliott was short. It was late out and it seemed like everyone was sticking to their cabins or were up on the deck watching the night sky. I pawed the door open, ran across the room, and shoved my nose under Elliott's chin, whining and trying to get his attention.

He groaned and tried to push me away, but I was insistent and shoved harder at his chin with my nose.

"Brown, what are you doing? I'm trying to sleep."

I whined and tugged on his sleeve.

He pushed me away and rolled over.

I jumped up on the bed and put my paws on his shoulder, pushing him onto his back, and then I put my paws on his chest and licked his face.

"Brown, leave me alone. I'm tired and I don't feel good." His voice sounded weak.

I growled, knowing that would get his attention. I never growled at him. He was my human.

Elliott forced his eyes open and looked at me, clearly unhappy, but I tugged on his sleeve again. "Oh okay," he said. "I'll try. I know it's important. You're a good girl, Brown. I'm sorry."

Elliott sat up in bed and clutched his head. I tugged on him urgently, and he managed to get to his feet. He looked like he might fall at any moment.

The ghost swirled around my feet. This time I ignored it and it swirled toward the door. I understood that it wanted me to follow, although I knew where we were going.

I opened the door and Elliott stumbled after me. It was pretty obvious he wasn't paying attention to where we were going. Although he managed not to step on me when I stopped in front of him to let a lone passenger get down the hall before we entered it. The one stairway was a little bit of problem, and he almost fell halfway down but he caught himself on the railing and stumbled to the bottom. It didn't take long for us to get to the captain's cabin, and I opened the door.

Elliott seemed to be aware that we are doing something strange because he stopped and looked around. "What are we doing, Brown?"

I nudged him in the back of the knees, and then led him over to the cabinet where we'd found the poison. At my urging he opened the door and stared blankly at the two bottles that sat on the edge of the shelf. I whined in frustration but the ghost came to the rescue, solidifying next Elliott into his human form.

"Elliott you must look at bottles. We believe you've been poisoned. One is probably the antidote but you need to look and see. I don't read so well as a ghost. Brown smelled the poison so we know these are what we need."

Elliott perked up at the word poison but not by much. He carefully took the two bottles off the shelf, though his hands shook and he nearly dropped one. He held them both up where I could see. I pointed my nose at the one that did smell like the poison and growled. He put that one back on the shelf before looking closely at the other one.

"I'm not sure I can get my eyes focused enough to read the small label," Elliott said.

The ghost whirled around us and disappeared for a moment before returning. "Hurry, he's coming this way."

Elliott took the stopper off the bottle, sniffed, and then shrugged. "Well, I suppose it can't hurt me anymore than I'm already hurt if I have been poisoned."

Whining, I watched while he drank the contents of the bottle.

Elliott sputtered, wrinkled his nose and gagged. "That tastes awful. It must be good for you as bad as it tastes."

The ghost chuckled. "I don't suspect the effects will be immediate but we should get out of here. The captain is coming."

Elliott staggered to his feet and followed us out of the room. I was certain he was going to fall over, but he managed to keep his feet and we led him further way from the cabin. It would be obvious that someone had been there as we hadn't taken the time to shut the door, but there was little we could do about that now.

By the time we made it back to our room, Elliott seemed to be feeling better, and to my nose he smelled a little bit healthier. He sank down onto the bed and stared at me for a moment before getting back up. He washed his hands and face in the basin before coming over and wrapping me in a hug. "I don't know what I'd do without you, Brown. I can't believe they tried to kill you. It must have been the piece of meat you refused."

I woofed once in agreement and he buried his hands in my ruff and held me close.

"Thank you, Charlie, for helping," he said to the ghost.

"Of course, Mr. Giles. After all you're helping me as well."

"Please call me Elliott and I will continue to help you as best I can, but he's already tried to kill us once. We're going to have to lay low until we get back to Denver. I'm not sure if we'll be able to do anything right away, but I will certainly help you see him hang for trying to kill my dog and having obviously killed you. I have a friend in the area, a sheriff, and I'm certain he'd be willing to look into it."

"Excellent, Elliott," the ghost said. "Perhaps you should get some more rest. In the morning I would act as if nothing happened, otherwise the captain may become suspicious."

"What is this?"

Snarling, I spun but didn't launch myself at the smelly man. Two other men stood with him in the doorway. The ghost vanished immediately but the damage was done. Obviously Captain Peyton had seen him.

"So you banished the ghost, did you?" Peyton glared at Elliott.

Elliott climbed his feet and though he was steadier than before he still moved more slowly than normal. "You tried to kill my dog."

"Nonsense. Whatever are you talking about? I've done nothing of the sort, yet you are apparently conspiring with the ghost who you claimed you already banished. For a considerable fee I might add, that I was planning on paying you when we returned to Denver. Yet I hear you talking about seeing me hang for something I did not do."

Elliott glared at him but before he could say more the captain gestured. "Seize him and that dog."

"Brown, run!"

As the men came forward I darted underneath them. I knew Elliott was right, we couldn't overpower them right now, and as long as they didn't kill him they couldn't take him far while we were in the air. We'd be back in Denver soon. I had to stay hidden long enough to escape in Denver and find help. Although who would help a dog I didn't know.

I remembered someone from the last time we were in Colorado, a little blue cattle dog named Scoot and his person, Sheriff Tolbert, but they weren't in Denver and I had no idea how to find them.

I could tell the ghost followed me as I darted down the hallway, because I smelled the musty-ozone and felt a slight breeze through my ruff as it fled with me.

Men shouted and chased after me, and I had no idea what they did with Elliott. I darted around a corner, ran up a flight of stairs, and dashed down into the hold while the ghost whispered suggestions to me. Finally, finding a dark corner, I hid under a tarp. The ghost assured me that at least for the moment we had lost our pursuers.

"Ghost," I said.

"My name is Charlie."

"Charlie," I said, though it felt strange. "Can you check on my human and see what they're doing to him?"

"Of course, Brown." The ghost vanished.

Miserable, I curled up into a tight ball and waited. I didn't like not being able to help my human. The ghost returned a while later and actually seemed excited, for it swirled around quickly and its colors darkened in agitation.

"Brown, we can rescue him once we're on the ground. The captain doesn't know I can unlock the door. We can get him out once we land, and then he will be able to tell the authorities what has happened. I don't believe Peyton will let him go otherwise, so we need to act quickly. Do you remember where he put those papers?"

"Yes. His hunting bag."

"We need to get them before the captain searches his room. He hasn't yet, but I'm sure he will soon. I will make sure the way is clear."

I knew the ghost was right even though I didn't want to leave my safe hiding place, so I crept out from underneath the tarp and followed him back through the ship. Sticking to the shadows as much as I could to stay hidden from view, I ran, though the hissing gas lamps that lit the hallways made that difficult. Once we were back at the room, Charlie checked to make sure no one was inside before I went in. I found Elliott's hunting bag where he left it and clutched it in my mouth.

"Hurry, Brown. They're coming."

I darted out of the room, not bothering to close the door behind me, and followed the ghost as we ran back toward the hold. Picking another spot to put the hunting bag once we were at the hold, I scraped back some canvas as if I were burying a bone. Fortunately there were no squirrels to dig it up and steal it. I was starting to think I liked the captain less than I like squirrels, which was saying something.

"Should we rescue Elliott now?" I didn't want him to be captured any longer than necessary.

"He'll have to hide on the airship until we land if we rescue him now," the ghost said.

Huffing in annoyance, I glared at Charlie the ghost. "Isn't there any other way off of the airship?"

"Well, it is possible to make it land early, but who knows where we will come down. Brown, let me go investigate and see how far away we are. I overheard the crew saying that the winds were favorable. Perhaps we'll be down soon."

"Okay." Curling back into a ball, I tucked my nose under my tail and sighed.

Charlie vanished and I was again alone. I hoped once we had our sheep ranch in Colorado that Elliott wouldn't be in any danger anymore.

I didn't have to wait long before Charlie returned.

"Excellent news, Brown. We should arrive soon. Well, there is some bad news. We'll be landing during the day. That will make it harder for us to hide our escape."

"Just as long as it is soon. Please keep an eye on Elliott for me while we wait."

"Of course, Brown. Get some rest."

Shutting my eyes, I tried to sleep so I'd be ready to go when it was time to rescue Elliott and escape.

* * *

It seemed like I slept forever, but finally Charlie woke me.

"Brown, we're landing. Be ready."

Crawling out from under the tarp I hid under, I shook and listened carefully. Distantly I heard the crew shouting and a few excited noises from female passengers. The sounds of the airship changed, and my ears felt funny like they had the last time we landed.

Finally, the ship jerked and it felt like we came to a halt. I retrieved Elliott's hunting bag from its hiding place.

"Okay, Brown, let's go before the crew comes down."

We had to go up onto the deck to get from the hold into the main part of the ship, but in the chaos no one noticed me slinking along behind boxes and baggage. Creeping was awkward with the hunting bag clutched in my mouth, but no one was currently looking for a brown and white dog. They were all staring over the sides and marveling at the city of Denver or waiting for their turn to get off the airship. Sneaking down into the passenger area of the ship was harder, but I managed with Charlie's help.

"He's in here." Charlie led me to one of the passenger cabins at the very back of the ship.

"Keep your senses open," I said to the ghost. "They're probably expecting me to try and find Elliott."

The ghost swirled around me and then vanished into the wall. After a moment I heard the lock click, and I scratched at the door. Before long I heard the handle jiggle and saw it turn.

"Brown!" Elliott left the room and hugged me tightly. "Good girl," he took the hunting bag from me and slung it over his shoulder. "Let's get out of here."

J.A. Campbell

I woofed in agreement.

This time we were prepared when the Captain's men tried to capture us. I grabbed a couple of ankles with my teeth, tripping them, and if I bit a little harder than I would have on sheep, well, who could blame me. Elliott hit a few others and then we burst out onto the deck.

Not having much of a plan other than to run, I barked ferociously, scaring women and men alike as they scattered out of my path. Elliott sprinted behind me, and I could smell the faint hint of musty-ozone as the ghost fled with us.

People screamed, or yelled in anger and a few tried to grab me, but I was quicker and soon we had managed to lose ourselves in the bustling streets of Denver.

Elliott leaned against a wall and panted. "I think we need to find the police, and then I need something to eat. I'm sure you're starving too, Brown."

My stomach growled when Elliott mentioned food.

He laughed, but it was a bitter laugh. "Let's go."

I pressed against Elliott's leg while we walked, and though it made it harder for him, he didn't object. Finally, we found the police station and though I'm sure they didn't normally allow dogs, I wasn't about to stay outside. Besides, no one objected when we entered together.

"Can I help you?" The man behind the counter asked.

"Yes, I have a murder to report."

He smelled surprised. "One moment." He went further into the building and came back after a short time with another man. They both wore uniforms with shiny buttons.

"I'm Officer Toms. Please, come with me." He barely glanced at me, so I stayed pressed up against Elliott's leg while we went further into the building. We were shown into an office and Officer Toms gave me a dish of water.

Not having had any in a while, I was very grateful and wagged my tail at him while I drank.

Elliott told the story of how he'd overheard some of the crew talking about the previous captain's murder and how he'd stumbled on some evidence and then how we'd almost been poisoned. He left Charlie the ghost out of it. Finally, he presented the papers he'd come across in the office.

Officer Toms studied them for a while before nodding. "This will take some investigation of course, but I believe we have enough to arrest

Captain Peyton and keep his airship on the ground until we can determine more. Please, wait here."

"Officer, it's been several days since I've had a decent meal. May I go across the way to the café?"

"Yes, Mr. Gyles, but please, come back once you've eaten."

The thought of food drove everything else out of my mind, and I happily followed Elliott back out into the crowded streets. He left me by the door and apparently procured permission for me to enter, because he returned to get me after a moment.

Food occupied my attention completely, though I remained pressed up against Elliott's leg while we ate.

Charlie reappeared once we finished.

"They captured him. At first he protested, but then a couple of the crew who I'd hired spoke up and he confessed." The ghost cloud spun and seemed to laugh.

Someone gasped, and a woman screamed.

"Oops." Charlie vanished.

Several of the people in the restaurant stared at us. Elliott sipped his coffee as if nothing had happened, though I could tell he was amused by the slight tilt of his lips and his scent.

"Perhaps we should return to the station," Elliott said, his scent souring to nervousness.

I remembered that Elliott didn't really like the police. It had something to do with when we used to hunt fake ghosts for money.

After draining his coffee we went back across the street.

Officer Toms was waiting for us. "Thank you, Mr. Gyles. We've captured Peyton and he confessed. We won't need anything else from you."

"I'm glad to have been of assistance."

"Good day, Mr. Gyles."

"Good day to you, Officer Toms."

Elliott sighed in relief once we were outside. "Come on, Brown. Let's get our wagon and horses and head for Miller."

Musty-ozone filled the air for a moment, and Charlie swirled into view.

"Elliott," it said. "Might I trouble you for one more favor?"

"Of course."

"I was wondering if you had a spell other than the banishment that might allow me to cross over. My task is done, but still I remain."

"I … " Elliott frowned. "Actually, I believe I do. I was going to ask if you wanted to join me and Brown. We make a good team. I imagine you'd like to go to your rest, however."

"Yes, though I'm honored by the offer."

"I still need some supplies from my wagon, and I would like to put some miles between us and Denver. Will tonight be soon enough?"

"Of course."

"Elliott, Brown, I can't thank you enough. And there is little I can do to repay you."

"No need," Elliott said.

I woofed in agreement. I wasn't sure how I felt about Elliott sending Charlie away. I was getting used to having him around. I did know I would be glad to be out of the city though. Elliott scratched my ears and we headed for the livery.

* * *

"… and go to your final rest."

Charlie the ghost swirled one last time and vanished.

"Brown, I think we need a vacation." He sat next to the small fire we'd started and put his great grand pappy's journal into his hunting bag.

Woofing in agreement, I rested my chin on Elliott's knee. I liked hunting ghosts, but I didn't want my human hurt anymore.

"I'm going to miss Charlie though." He ruffled my ears. "But who needs a ghost when you've got the best dog in the world as your best friend."

Jumping into his lap, I covered his face in kisses, trying to tell him that he was the best human ever.

Elliott laughed and hugged me close. "We will go to Miller, get our ranch, and maybe you can teach that little dog of the Sheriff's how to herd sheep."

And maybe they'd have another ghost in the saloon. If they had a ghost problem, I was the dog for the job.

About the Author

Julie has been many things over the last few years, from college student, to bookstore clerk and an over the road trucker. She's worked as a 911 dispatcher and in computer tech support, but through it all she's been a writer, and when she's not out riding horses, she can usually be found sitting in front of her computer. She lives in Colorado with her three cats, her vampire-hunting dog, Kira, her Traveler in Training, Triska, and her Irish Sailor. She is the author of many Vampire and Ghost-Hunting Dog stories and the young adult urban fantasy series *The Clanless*. She's a member of the Horror Writers Association and the Dog Writers of America Association and the editor for *Steampunk Trails* fiction magazine. You can find out more about her at her website:

www.writerjacampbell.com.

THE HEART OF APRICOTTA

Mike Cervantes

A Letter from R.J. Bricabrac to George H.M. Entrils, Dean of Anthropological Studies, Interdimensional University:

Dear Sirs,

Thank you for providing me with another opportunity to present my findings. Unfortunately, I'm unable to do so in person, as I've come back from my latest expedition with a bad case of Portal Pox. I'm certain I'll recover in enough time to see you in person soon, but meanwhile I've been a bit too busy, quarantined in my dormitory while the faculty throw numerous parties around me, so that I may give the disease to the other little scientists.

It's just another one of the many small sacrifices that I, Rufus Jerome Bricabrac, Junior Explorer, Second Class, Undergraduate, Emeritus, of Interdimensional University, enjoys doing for his old alma mater. While I am always the first to admit that my tenure as a full member of the faculty was quite … unavailing, I still work hard daily to uphold the principles of our storied institution, or "Ol' Timesides" as the students like to refer to it.

From the very moment our founder, Professor J. Orenthal Ungrate, invented the Trandimensional and Interdimensional Machine Of Travel For History and Industry, or T.I.M.O.T.F.H.Y. for short, I, and every little wheel involved with the tenure of I.U. has worked tirelessly to keep a record of geography and history for every little sideways alternate reality that crosses into our stratosphere as a result of interacting with his wonderful invention. I remember being there personally the day the Professor sacked the entire geography department, scoffing at their ridiculous claims that we'd put the frontier out of business, since he had created a machine that could offer us countless, possibly infinite, frontiers to explore.

Ah, Professor Ungurate, may he live forever.... And one day perhaps escape the belly of the mysterious eldritch abomination who appeared in the portal and swallowed him whole in a vain attempt to absorb his inner power.

But I digress. One could certainly spend a lifetime explaining our glorious history, but one can also spend a lifetime attempting to add to it, which is precisely what I attempted to do with my latest expedition.

I chose to attempt something that my contemporaries had yet to conquer successfully: a thorough geographical survey of the dark, untamed, center of the continent of Apricotta. Located in universe quadrant 9-611, Apricotta, like our own Africa, is a wild, untamed, wilderness, filled with tall, ungroomed foliage, and any manner of monstrous untamed fauna, the likes of which we'll never see in our own dimension. A contemporary of mine, Hammond Wholewheat, was the last to attempt to explore these treacherous jungles and came back with only these three words to say about the whole of Apricotta: "It's the pits!"

Undeterred by my colleague's negative assessment, I immediately began to set my sights on finding the center of Apricotta. I collected my supplies: food, camping gear, and navigational equipment, as well as my trusty instantaneous daguerreotype maker, able to record images of the continent with a mere shutter.

Since I am currently not in any way tenured by the University, I had no resources to secure a proper crew, and instead I had to once again impose on the good nature of my trusted manservant Quee-Zay. A native of a savage version of Finland located in universe quadrant 11-11, Quee-Zay is a man who knows no fear. Literally, the concept of fear does not exist at all in his universe. He became indebted to me after I saved him from a rampaging Hunkabeast, and let me tell you, it was a hunk of a Hunkabeast, and he has been my loyal confidant in many an expedition. His skills compliment mine ideally, for as much I am intelligent, sophisticated, and worldly of mind, Quee-Zay is strong, wily, and interested in little besides his own self-preservation.

With supplies at the ready, we immediately passed through the T.I.M.O.T.F.H.Y. and found ourselves at a camp just north of darkest Apricotta. There, we met with the native Gelby tribesmen, who we've become allies with in the numerous times we've failed to find the center of the continent. We spent our first night in their care, partaking of wine in giant juice filled gourds and participating in a tribal dance performed by the chief in order to wish us a safe journey. At dawn the next morning, we set on our way while the Gelby stood at the border chanting "Ooba-Toohwa-Nawa," which I understand means "Good luck. You'll need it."

Aren't they sweet?

We began by venturing into the dense jungle, Quee-Zay hacking away at the overgrown foliage with his machete. I had my Instananeous Daguerreotype machine at the ready, certain we'd reach the vast, uncharted, center of the continent a lot sooner than we expected. But, no sooner had I thought that did Quee-Zay stop dead in his tracks, his spindle-thin body bent over two pairs of dense bushes I couldn't see over.

"What's the matter," I asked of my astute guide.

"Big water." He replied.

I stuck my head into the foliage at Quee-Zay's height and saw that indeed, we had walked a straight line into a steep cliff overlooking a gigantic waterfall. I quickly tossed a rock in order to determine the depth of the drop. To this day I wonder what happened to that rock. Anyway, I reasoned that since there is a waterfall, we must be standing on the very ground upon where the river decides life is no longer worth living. Therefore, we can merely walk along the edge of the cliff towards the waterfall to find a spot to proceed.

The detour took several hours, trudging in an ellipse around the cliff with Quee-Zay still hacking away feverishly at the native plant life. Finally, we could see a clearing. I practically jumped over Quee-Zay's back and ran towards the first thing we'd found in that godforsaken place to resemble a meadow. Eagerly I threw my hands into the river, splashed the water on my face and loudly exclaimed "We're free!"

That's when a hundred spears thrust out from the bushes in every direction, stopping just short of my neck. I instinctively began to follow standard "captured by natives" procedure by putting my hands on my head and slowly getting back onto my feet. Standing at my side was Quee-Zay, who was coaxed from hiding by yet more spears.

"We been bought," he quipped.

As we took the long walk back to the home of these ruffians, I got my first good look at them. They looked pretty standard for tribesman, hair bounded into braids tied with bones, bones in their noses, war paint across their faces, and nothing to hide their personal shame but a loincloth. That was all pretty standard. Their dark blue fur, white shiny fangs, and claw-tipped fingers, however, were enough to give me considerable alarm.

Once we were led to the center of the village, my eye caught sight of a giant black cauldron right in the center of the square. In any known universe, that spells "cannibalism." Oddly, I didn't feel afraid. Instead, I felt an enormous amount of indignant rage well up within me. I vocalized many times over how much I resented being eaten, and said many things to the effect of "I will not be a feast to these cannibals!" and "Don't these cannibals know they're about to devour a man of true genius?" but unfortunately, as our captors embodied the very definition of "primitive," my words were lost on them.

It wasn't until we began to be lowered into the water filled cauldron that inspiration struck me. I asked Quee-Zay if he could speak to them a few words in Gelby. Quee-Zay did so, and after many words exchanged in the interdimensional tongue. He turned to me and awaited my inquiry.

"So what did they say?" I asked.

"They not like you keep calling them cannibals," Quee-Zay replied "They don't have any interest in eating their own kind."

"If that's the case, why won't they set us free!?" I said, feeling my temper rising again.

"We not their kind."

I endeavored to protest again, but stopped as soon as I felt what could only be the sensation of a heavy pot lid slamming over the top of my head. Fortunately, I was still wearing my pith helmet, or I certainly would have spent the remainder of my soup-like experience as a helpless vegetable. As I sat in the center of total blackness, I allowed serenity to wash over me, and I recalled an important lesson relayed to me by my former professor, Chauncey Putz-Gamey: The best way to avoid cannibalism is to taste terrible.

I instructed Quee-Zay to join me in emptying our pockets for anything foul that might bring negation to our own flavor. I added paprika, fish bullion, removed my socks and underwear and wrung them into the cauldron water. Quee-Zay threw in the milkweed he frequently chews on for indigestion and an enormous cube of saltpeter he wears under his headdress for religious purposes. I came to a conclusion in the moment that perhaps an enormous amount of oxidant into a rapidly boiling cauldron was perhaps not a good idea, roughly around the time the pot began to boil over, blowing the cauldron lid clear off our heads and sending it sailing into one of the nearby thatched huts.

The natives looked oddly at us.

We looked oddly at the natives.

The natives looked meanly at us.

We looked affrightedly at the natives.

Thinking quickly, I informed Quee-Zay to commence "Operation Snail Shell," an improvisational tactic wherein we both tipped over the cauldron until it was standing upside down, then lifting the mouth of the immense appliance over both our heads and carrying it over us as we ran for our lives. It would have been successful, if not for the fact that this particular cannibal's pot was indeed very heavy, and we were only able to lift it waist-high. We nonetheless attempted to make a run, but just as I'd calculated we'd only made it a few steps before we crashed pot-first into a nearby tree.

I attempted to bargain with Quee-Zay to be the first to peek out of the pot to see how far we've gone, but he insisted that he chose paper over my rock, even though it was too dark inside to actually see our hands.

I lifted the mouth of the pot and was met with the sight of the cruelest pair of feet I'd ever seen in my days. These feet belonged to the tribe's chieftain, who I believe was a being composed entirely out of fat, fur, and anger. Quee-Zay's translations relayed to me that our self-interested attempt to avoid becoming appetizing had upset a tribal ritual, desecrated sacred ground, and angered a god whose only concept of mercy is the sending of plagues containing only tiny frogs.

"Does this mean we won't be eaten?" I asked sheepishly.

"They not want to waste the dishes. Now we will be sacrificed to big water." Quee-Zay said with a bit of native exasperation in his voice.

We were tied in a prostrated position against a bamboo raft and carried to a river. We lay completely helpless as the tribal chieftain made a heart-felt plea to his angry god to allow us to be perfectly acceptable in our role as an indecipherable smear on the jagged rocks at the bottom of the waterfall. With a salute, punctuated by a word that sounded like a punch to the stomach in Yiddish, the assembled tossed the raft in the river.

The roaring water at my ears was deafening. I tried to do what I could to signal Quee-Zay but was unable to do anything to outcry the river. I knew that I was on my own at the moment, locked in a battle of wits with a body of rapidly moving water, and currently losing. Things were grim. I had thought for a moment about making peace with my chosen deity, only to conclude that I was in another universe and had no real way of confirming that my chosen deity even existed here.

I reached down to attempt the sign of the cross with my right hand. It was then that I realized that the natives had tied the line binding my right hand somewhat loosely, and whenever I pulled down, the ropes around my left ankle would tighten. I attempted to free myself by doing the inverse: I pushed my right hand into the river water and attempted to wiggle my left ankle free from the slightly slackened vine. Presumably, it worked, and I victoriously lifted my freed left ankle in a 90 degree position from the raft.

That's when I hit the branch.

Indeed, a low hanging tree branch decided to rise in our way the very moment I shook my leg free. When it struck me, the pain was excruciating, but putting that aside in favor of not dying, I crooked my ankle and attempted to bring a stop to the crusading death trap. We were safe, but unfortunately still trapped, as I found myself at a loss to untie myself any further without losing my tenuous grasp on the overhanging tree branch.

I felt the raft rock. I turned my head to see Quee-Zay on his feet with both hands gripping the overhanging branch. At first, I was at a loss as to how he managed to get loose from his bonds, but, remembering what had happened a year ago while nearly burned at the stake in a Boston infested with mad Puritans, (I believe that was Universe 471-88) it's likely that he chewed the ropes off.

Now that I'd stabilized the raft, it was Quee-Zay's job to shimmy across the branch and carry me to safety. It was a slow and sensitive endeavor. He first raised his legs to meet his arms. Then he shimmied across the length of the branch, forcing it to bob up and down and nearly forcing me to lose my foothold on the branch. Once he got to the other side, I felt as good as saved.

Then he made a break for it.

I wasn't offended. I was certain that Quee-Zay was merely interested in securing a more suitable means of rescue.

And that would have been perfectly lovely, if the branch hadn't chosen that very moment to snap.

I sailed through the rough, deadly rapids of the river, foregoing my previous hesitation towards prayer while I was tossed right and left down a path of certain destruction. Not seeing another opportunity to catch myself, or really anything in the face of such a torrential whisking, I attempted to resign myself to my fate. In my panic I struggled to remember precisely what the five stages of grief were supposed to be, so I experienced denial, anger, gassiness, and that strange confusion you get when you feel you've left a door unlocked before finally achieving acceptance.

When the raft slid out of the river, I felt the sensation of flying several miles rapidly downward with the wind whipping across my soggy personage, so quickly I felt my clothing start to dry. Every muscle in my body tied itself in a knot as I braced for impact.

I felt a thud.

I felt a bounce.

I felt a thud.

I felt a bounce again.

I opened my eyes to see that I had landed in the center of a net made entirely out of jungle vines and bamboo posts. As far as I could see over the side of the raft, I could tell that this structure was built to protect anyone from falling into the bottom of the waterfall too harshly. My first instinct was to believe that Quee-Zay had saved my life, but he would not have had the time to run away, descend a cliff, and build this highly supportive structure in the time it took me to make peace with the universe.

My contemplation of this was cut short when the air above me was overshadowed by the tribal chieftan, who, while standing over me, emitted a belly laugh that was so immense it rocked the entire safety net and raft along with it. I was untied and taken back to Quee-Zay's side, and it was relayed to me that this whole business about sending foreign men over the falls was all simply an elaborate practical joke played on, as the chieftan put it "Any scrawny outsider without the stomach to become a proper meal."

We were escorted back to the village where our comedy act was revered by all the natives assembled. Our clothes were dried, we were fed frozen fruit paste and coconut stalks fried in oil. We were also given a daguerreotype taken of me mid-fall.

We were asked to possibly stay among the tribesmen as honorary spiritual leaders who were tasked with bringing their youthful female charges into womanhood, but, having had enough excitement for one day, we instead opted to return home. After bidding farewell to the tribe, we hiked through the now clean path out of the jungle and returned to the space where the T.I.M.O.T.H.F.Y would lock onto our coordinates and return us to our universe.

I'm reasonably certain that it was the combination of the native food with exposure to the torrential waters that has me in the condition I'm in at the moment. It has hurt me only in that I sincerely hoped to deliver these findings in person, but the need to bathe daily in kelp and be rubbed in goldfish oil has been preventing me to do so. While there's still much more of the continent of Apricotta to explore, I believe that the work I've done on this expedition has moved us progressively forward in our ongoing quest to better understand the wild dimensional continent. I also hope that this excursion has proven that I am worthy enough to once again be tenured by the university and be awarded a crew for purposes of further exploration.

Pretty please with sugar on it?

-R.J. Bricabrac

About the Author

Mike Cervantes is a graduate of The University of Texas at El Paso with a degree in Creative Writing. He is a participant in many of Denver's local Steampunk and creative writing conventions and conferences. He is currently writing an ongoing series featuring the adventures of The Scarlet Derby and Midnight Jay which you can find online at:

http://thescarletderby.tumblr.com

THE MURDER WHEEL

Kara Seal and L.H. Parker

Thunder drowned out the shrill screams of the horses as I sipped chamomile tea, mindful of the china's chipped rim. The whites of those dead eyes haunted my sleep and now the daylight hours too, so I averted my gaze from the steaming liquid's reflection. The spoon was tucked beneath my napkin, and I didn't dare glance at the kettle's polished exterior.

"I know the others will be upset." I paused as a low groan rattled the vardo's back door. "But I do appreciate you allowing me to visit, Tsura."

I felt Tsura's sharp gaze like the nick of a dagger. Reluctant to see what thoughts lay behind her all-seeing eyes, I fixed my sight on her wild mane. Two black braids threaded with grey snaked down her chest, uncovered against the elements. Even now she still wore her hair in the way of unmarried Romani women, a testament to her unfailing faith in traditions. I patted my silk top hat, ensuring the brass clockwork fascinator faced forward, my own hair pinned securely underneath. That uncivilized traveler's hairdo was the first thing to go when I moved to London.

"I remember our last conversation," Tsura murmured, fingering the worn leather putsi resting against her breast, a protection amulet she'd made herself when we were children. A lot of good that pouch would do her against the creature that now hunted me.

"That was two years ago." I sniffed.

"You called me 'filthy gypsy.'"

The flickering candles threw shadows across the red drapes drawn shut against the dark. I blinked. As in my nightmares, blood streamed down the vardo's walls, spattering my high-necked gown and streaking my elder sister's face. Her eyes bled red before reducing into black holes, just like....

Oh dear.

I closed my eyes and counted my breaths until the dizziness passed and the whalebone corset no longer dug into my ribs. Lack of sleep was catching up with me.

"You're unwell," Tsura said with that knowing voice I'd loathed as a child.

"Just faint." I opened my eyes. "The doctors are helping with my insomnia. I've not adjusted to the electroshock yet."

Lightning flashed outside the vardo's dusty windows, illuminating two rearing horses, neither of them the two automatons I purchased for this journey. Peering through the curtains, I spied a hunched figure leering at me through his long, dripping hair. The heavens boomed, jostling the wagon and setting Tsura's steeds into fits of fearful whinnies. Then the man was gone. I gripped my ultra-wave equalizer pistol from within the folds of my skirt.

"—push me away," Tsura said.

"I was grieving," I said, placing the tea cup on the table with a trembling hand. "You know I wasn't in my right mind when Niko—"

"Don't!" Tsura snapped. "Never speak the name of the dead!"

"Pardon me." I searched for words, but a squeal of twisting metal silenced me.

I glanced at my wristwatch; 7:02. The ticking cogs glinted, and I expected to see the dead man's eyes in their silver surfaces. The sun had already set; nowhere was safe.

With a final hiss of air, the beeswax candles extinguished, sucking the warmth from the wagon and blanketing us in darkness. I drew my gun, grateful that this time leather gloves steadied my sweaty grip.

Fabric rustled above me. A breeze caressed my face.

"Stay back!" I hissed, raising the equalizer. "I'm armed."

Cruel laughter cackled in my ear, the stench of rotting corpse filling my nostrils. The mullo grasped my wrist with an icy touch. Long fingers wrapped around my neck and squeezed until my heart sputtered. My undead husband eased me onto the wooden floor with gentler movements than he'd ever shown me when he was alive. I struggled to aim the pistol, but it slipped from my grip. *This time he will finish me*, I thought as my eyelashes fluttered shut.

A whispered incantation broke the silence.

Light burned the back of my eyelids followed by several strikes to my cheeks. I heard the rip of fabric. The decaying limb thumped my breastbone once, twice. I gasped for air. Oxygen burned down my throat, sating my aching lungs as the cold hands released me.

I watched my sister, the shuvani, through the blur of tears. A blue flame danced in the palms of her hands, emitting warmth far more familiar than the towering castles and steel inventions London promised me.

Tsura's scrutiny drilled into my soul and sniffed out my secrets faster than a pack of English Foxhounds on the hunt.

"Miri," she whispered. "What have you done, foolish child?"

* * *

My steam powered carriage bounced over the countryside's muddy roads, not as fancy without the mechanical horses, but the varnished oak wood accented with brass was much more respectable than a night in that weather beaten artifact my sister called home. And yet, for the first time in weeks, I'd slept securely in Tsura's vardo, safe behind blood warding spells. My undead husband, the mullo, paced a mere 50 yards away. Even in my dreams I couldn't escape those claw-like hands, stiff from death, or his gaping mouth, teeth rotting off the jawbone.

I braced myself against the morning downpour as rain collected on the rim of my hat and dribbled down the back of my neck. Once again I adjusted my cloak, balancing the instruction manual under the wool while gripping the steering wheel with my right hand.

Tsura grumbled beside me. Not from the rain—she was accustomed to the harsh elements—but from the rotating cogs and gears whirring at her feet.

"You could have taken your vardo and followed me," I said, suppressing my condescending tone as best I could.

Tsura shot me a dirty look.

"The horses are safer where I left them." She sniffed and readjusted her red scarf as rain dripped down her long nose. "The mullo hunts you and those that help you. Now, turn right at the fork up ahead."

"Where are we going?" I asked, following her instructions then pumping a foot pedal to increase speed. The carriage jostled, and I once again bemoaned the loss of my two automaton horses plodding along in perfect symphony. "How do we dispose of it?"

"Not with your useless gadjo gadgets," Tsura snapped, grasping her amulet. "A mullo only comes after the living for revenge. What did you do to wrong him?"

I swallowed, formulating my response as it came out in stuttered syllables. The million lies I've spun since settling near River Thames always came easy to my tongue, but this time the truth willed its way out.

"I killed the bastard."

A small laugh escaped my lips, and a smile pulled at my cheeks. I touched my jeweled cross necklace. Confession really was good for the soul.

"The way he drank, he didn't want to live." Tsura said. "It doesn't explain why he rose from the grave."

"I laced his beer with hemlock one night." I said. "Then watched his body convulse and gasp for air until he slumped to the ground and moved no more."

I could see my sister's brow furrow from the corner of my eye.

When I'd killed Niko, I never imagined he could hurt me worse from the grave. I simply wanted to put an end to the bruises and black eyes suffered from his raging fists.

"I'd do it again," I said, keeping my eyes fixed on the bumpy road. "I regret putting it off for so long. Being a young widow in high society makes life difficult."

"Yet still you suffer your husband's wrath," Tsura mused. "Did you burn all of his earthly possessions at the funeral?"

I stiffened.

After sewing the coins and baubles that hadn't been spent on drink into my ratty hem, I'd played the part of distraught wife, lamenting the sudden loss of my husband. Thanks to the superstitious nature of the Romani, no one dared investigate his cause of death. Instead, the kumpania elders gave him proper death rites, burying his body and burning our vardo, with all his belongings inside, to ashes. I never believed in the archaic folklore of my ancestors, but perhaps I should have listened closer to the stories shared around the campfire about the dangers of foregoing traditions.

"Everything but a few coins," I muttered. "They're gone now."

Tsura didn't respond at first. "I never liked him. I was sorry when Da forced you to marry."

Her unexpected approval pleased me.

"I didn't think you'd understand."

Tsura laughed under her breath. "You should have come to me before killing the bastard. We would have staked an iron needle through his heart so his soul remained pinned in the afterlife instead of hunting you."

"I thought mullos were an old traveler's tale," I said.

"Proper Roma know better than to taunt spirits." Tsura squinted at a point over my shoulder then grabbed my sleeve. "Stop here."

I pulled the brake lever and spun a second, smaller wheel. Steam billowed from the pipes above the wagon, hissing and spraying us with hot water. Tsura screeched and cursed at the chugging engine. I pumped another petal, flipped a switch, then another. Parting my cloak long enough to consult the crisp manual pages, I punched another button, and the vehicle shuddered then stopped in the middle of the wet path.

"Damn gadjo and their useless junk!" Tsura jumped onto the road, kicking the tire with a muddy boot.

"I'm not welcome here," I said, my eyes locked on the gaily painted wagons atop the grassy hill. "If they see me—"

"—Then let's make this quick." Tsura mopped wet strands off her forehead and held out her hand. "Give me your necklace."

"Why?" I clasped my cross with icy fingers. I didn't have a putsi full of rocks and animal bones to protect me, but I did have this cross I'd gotten from a gadjo church shortly upon arriving in London.

"I need to trade," she said. "Magic isn't cheap."

I tried to read her wrinkled face, admiring the steely resolve that reminded me so much of our long dead mother. Of course she knew how to barter for spells. Born with the dark Romani complexion and that wildness in her brown eyes that could never be snuffed out, she was a shuvani, a gypsy witch. Trained in the arts passed down by my great-grandmother, I only dreamed of having a pinch of the power emanating off of Tsura's being. Instead, I hid the dark skin my mother gave me under powdered makeup and dressed my unruly curls with the high fashions of an esteemed Victorian lady.

"What's a bit of jewelry's worth against ridding myself of that creature?" I unclasped the gold chain and handed the pendant to my sister.

Tsura twirled the gold chain, frowning at the glittering gems.

"Give me your watch, too."

"No!" I cradled my wrist to my chest. "This is a Milston Priceworth. People pay thousands for a custom piece. A dear gentleman gifted me this one earlier this year. I'll never see another like it in my lifetime."

"It's no good if you're dead," Tsura said, holding out her waiting palm.

Grumbling at the smug look on her face, I slipped the fine piece of workmanship off my wrist. Tsura snatched it from my hand, and I winced when she crammed it and the necklace in her soaking pocket.

"I'm sure a broken one will still fetch a pretty price," I said.

"Stay here," Tsura instructed. "Do not speak to anyone. Do not approach the others."

With a final nod, she stepped off the path and trudged up the grassy hill to the circle of colorful wagons. Campfire smoke billowed from the caravan and with it the mouthwatering smell of cooking meat—smoked rabbit and hedgehog. Half-clothed children giggled as they ran through the rain like wild beasts, escorting my sister to their kumpania. A couple of the elders eyed my fancy vehicle but were too wary to approach.

I drew my cloak tight around my shoulders, teeth chattering against the cold, and ignored the rumble in my belly. Thunder rolled in the distance, and a fat drop hit me in the eye before rolling down my cheek. I wiped it away, then frowned when the glove returned streaked with red. I rubbed my face with my other hand and more blood smeared the brown leather. Pinching my nose, I fumbled for the lace handkerchief I'd taken to carrying on my person.

Someone retched, a dry croaking sound that sent fear surging through my veins. The damned mullo crouched in the middle of the road like a rabid animal. Hollowed eyes burned through me. A wide, rotting smile pulled and puckered, yellowish skin taught on his cheekbones. I blinked. I never saw him move, but suddenly he stood three feet closer.

"You're not real," I whispered. "It's daylight."

He closed the gap between us, grinning. A scream bubbled up but stuck to the back of my throat. I fumbled in my skirt pockets for my pistol, but he slithered over the footboard, snapping his broken teeth inches from my nose. The stench gagged me.

A rigid hand seized my shoulder, and I struggled against the monster's iron grip.

"Calm yourself!"

Familiar eyes peered into mine. I cried, grasping Tsura's forearm as she settled onto the seat beside me. Hugging her stiff frame, I peered over her shoulder, but the creature was gone.

"I thought you were the mullo," I said, my face wet with tears. "What took so long?"

Tsura took my face in her rough hands. She dabbed my eyes and nose with the edge of her skirt, then produced a black wooden box. Under the squeaky lid, a glass vial lay nestled in a bed of velvet. The liquid inside was far darker than any potion I'd ever seen, and too viscous to be perfume.

"What's that?" I stuttered, my voice thick.

"Our weapon," Tsura said, tucking it back into the box. "I consulted with another shuvani who had the ingredients I needed. Though, she needed convincing of the value of your watch."

"He's getting stronger." The hair rose on the back of my neck as shivers crawled down my spine. "Can you get rid of him?"

"Only a creature who fears nothing can kill the mullo; a werewolf."

* * *

The nearest gadjo cemetary was three towns over, far enough to be at the edge of the rainstorm. Dark clouds still blotted out the sun, and a cold drizzle fell here too. I picked my way through seven rows of headstones, on the lookout for the freshest graves. Careful to keep my silk skirts lifted above the mud, I followed Tsura until she stopped at the tombstone of Clarence Henry Ernest, who'd died no less than a week ago, judging by the freshly tilled dirt over his final resting place. Tsura closed her eyes and breathed deep, then held out her hands, moving them slowly over the grave.

"What are you doing?" I asked, patting the equalizer in my right pocket then shifting the VersiTyle's Rod into my other hand. "The mullo might appear any moment now."

"This man." Tsura opened her eyes. "Dig here."

"Why?" I turned the dial twice then pushed the button at the base of the rod.

"Evil begets evil," Tsura said, stepping away from my device with disapproval. "A pious man will not take to the curse."

The apparatus hummed then clicked, shifting a series of steel plates. I gripped the handle as it assembled into a dousing rod, pick, scythe, and finally, a shovel.

"Are we exhuming the body of a killer?" I shivered as I buried the blade into the grave.

"No." Tsura's eyes glittered. "You till the earth of this child predator while I prepare the curse."

I nodded, digging deeper. Tsura opened her bag and withdrew a stone mortar, pestle, and a roll of leather. She unfolded the worn material, revealing a sprig of wolfsbane, the purple petals still fresh with dew, a tarnished silver dagger I recognized as my grandmother's, the glistening vial of werewolf blood, ten red candles, and a glass bottle of black powder.

Tsura lit the half-melted beeswax with a whispered word and set them around the grave.

"Whatever you do, don't leave the circle," She said noting my alarm. "He will not harm you."

She stripped the plant into the bowl and sprinkled black powder before crushing them together. Calmness settled over her shoulders as she murmured under her breath and added more dust to the mixture.

"Stay focused," Tsura said.

Exhaling, I continued digging, groaning as pale worms and beetles squirmed to the surface. Civilized society would scoff if they saw me ankle deep in filth and laboring in conditions no more sanitary than that of industrial workers. My arms wobbled with exertion as Tsura methodically thickened the potion.

Finally, Tsura uncorked the werewolf blood and dribbled it into the mixture. The draft steamed and spit, but she continued grinding until green fumes kissed the surface. Satisfied, she held out the bowl and blade to me.

"Take them," she said. "You need to add three drops of your own blood and say your deceased husband's name."

Dropping the shovel, I accepted the draught and knife. The tool pricked my thumb deeper than anticipated and I hissed as blood dripped into the potion. The liquid boiled black and bubbled over my fingers, drenching my lacy cuff before spilling onto the grave.

"Suffering from his hands, she names her abuser," Tsura chanted.

"Niko," I whispered, the sound sickeningly familiar on my tongue.

The air became heavy and charged.

"Dead by her hands, she names her victim."

"Niko," I repeated, tipping the bowl's remaining contents onto the grave.

Tsura's hair rose with static, and my skirts zapped as they clung to my legs.

"Though this soul departed, the vessel remains tainted with evil. Rise, foul beast, from the grave and hear your enemy's name. Hear the name of the mullo."

"Niko Burch," I rasped. "Kill him once and for all."

Ten candles flared bright then snuffed out one by one. The ground rolled beneath me, and I dropped the mortar and dagger. A clawed hand shot through the overturned dirt, spraying me with blood and mud. Another followed, grasping my polished leather boot.

"Birth your werewolf," Tsura spat. "Give him life with your vice and your blood."

I grasped the beast's muscled wrists and pulled him from his grave.

The werewolf keened, shaking dirt and centipedes off his matted grey fur. Barbed incisors, coated in blood and slime, glowed in the moonlight as he panted. He glared at me, his creator, with yellow eyes. In those glinting depths burned coals of hatred, and I cursed myself and Tsura for the evil we'd brought into this world.

"He learned the name," Tsura said. "Teach your spawn the scent."

"With what?"

"I tore this from the bastard's shirt that night in my vardo," Tsura said, tossing the scrap of tattered linen at me.

With a trembling hand, I grasped the piece of cloth and held it out to the beast.

"Careful of the teeth," Tsura murmured.

My arm quaked as the towering monster sniffed the cloth with interest. Discovering my bleeding digit, he nosed my palm. I held my breath as a rough tongue licked my thumb, leaving a wake of burning saliva. Then, with an ear-splitting howl, he was off, vaulting through the trees on all fours.

"Follow him," Tsura urged me. "We must ensure that the mullo is killed before we can rest."

With a nod, I lifted my skirts and ran after my creation, branches snagging at my clothes and heart pounding in my chest. I followed for several minutes, listening for the occasional howl to draw me in the right direction. A stitch in my side forced me stop and I doubled over, heaving for breath. Fog blanketed the forest floor, and the trees' gnarled limbs formed twisted creatures of the night. Tsura wasn't behind me like I'd thought. Had she stayed behind at the grave? I couldn't remember if she said she would follow.

As the pain in my side abated, I quickened my pace once more, noting the ground's sudden, steep shift beneath me. Neither my dress nor my shoes were made for more than a stroll through untended woods, and as I lifted my heavy skirts I lost my balance, sliding down the hillside. I cursed, knowing the silks were torn and soiled beyond repair, and my top hat now lost to the forest floor. The inhuman cry that echoed through the forest stopped my heart.

I hurried towards the sound.

At the bottom of the hill, my werewolf charged the mullo with bared teeth and raised claws. He stood a good two feet taller than my ex-husband's corpse, the corded muscles of his legs springing him into the air.

I hid behind an ash tree and peered around the trunk.

Niko evaded the onslaught by leaping over the beast's broad shoulders, twisting to face his opponent upon landing. A gasp escaped me. The mullo was too fast for the creature. Just as he was too fast for my bullets and laser beams.

Niko spun around. Those empty sockets locked onto me, and a smile crept onto his face.

The werewolf charged. This time Niko misjudged the distance. The werewolf grasped him by the throat as he jumped, and he hung from the monster's claw like a ragdoll, kicking his legs in vain. With his other paw, the werewolf tore into the mullo's chest, pulling out his shriveled heart and stuffing it into his mouth. He chewed the organ, blood squirting over his snout as the mullo's body spasmed once, twice, and then ceased moving.

With a triumphant howl, the werewolf tossed the mullo's body then ran towards me. I pressed myself against the bark, praying Tsura had a plan for ridding us of the werewolf. Crashing through the brush, the monster bounded past me and disappeared into the fog.

I sighed. It was over. Best get back to Tsura and leave this cursed place. But, curiosity got the better of me.

"Be a good boy this time and stay dead." I entered the clearing with hesitant steps, watching Niko's twice dead corpse for the smallest sign of movement.

He lay with his back to me in a pool of black blood. I gagged as the stench of rotting flesh assaulted my nostrils, so I pulled out my handkerchief to cover my nose and mouth. Circling the body, I gasped. The advanced decay of Niko's body suggested he'd been lying in this spot for weeks. Nudging his head with the toe of my boot, I was relieved when he didn't move. A smile still pulled at his gaunt cheeks, and anger gripped me. I stepped on his jaw until the ligaments snapped and bone crumbled beneath my sole.

He was good and dead this time.

"It's over." I grinned and left the clearing.

The hike back up the hillside was slower and more laborious, and I stopped several times to rest. My ribs felt bruised under the whalebone corset, and I considered tearing it out during one of my rests. The dress was shot to hell anyway. In the end, I couldn't bear to cause any more harm to the blue silk. I could still salvage the corset and employ a tailor to fix it once I returned to civilized company. Tsura was probably wondering what took so long. Only fifty yards to go, I told myself as my aching legs protested yet another step.

A guttural, human scream ripped through the chill night air. Shrouded by mist, the shadows of headstones loomed ahead; the cemetery!

"Tsura!" I shouted, no longer mindful of my exhausted body.

I staggered between the tombs discovering my sister packing her magic ingredients into the leather roll. New dirt covered the illicit spell performed on this gravesite and my VersiTyle's Rod remained propped against the tombstone, once again a compressed metal stick.

"I heard a scream." I panted.

Tsura took in the state of my torn clothes and my flyaway hair. Shame coursed through me as I smoothed curly locks behind my ear and straightened a torn sleeve. Of course, I was being ridiculous. There was no need for me to charge up here like a savage and assume the worst. I was still in shock from witnessing my ex-husband's second death.

"The mullo's gone?" Tsura whispered.

"Yes, there is no—"

"—Are you sure? Tell me you saw it with your own eyes."

"The bastard's dead," I snapped. "The werewolf destroyed him. We can leave now, and I can return to my home and accept a certain gentleman's proposal."

"Good, good." She sighed and clutched her amulet until her knuckles turned white.. "Help me pack."

Tsura hunched over and collected the remaining candles, while I picked up my grandmother's ritual knife. The silver blade felt lighter than I remembered, and if there was magic infused into the metal, I couldn't tell.

"Keep it."

"Are you sure?" I tried to meet Tsura's eyes, but she kept her face hidden beneath her bushy hair. She nodded, securing the wooden box under her arm and gesturing that we walk. I grabbed the metal rod and once again picked my way over the graves back to my carriage. Tsura lagged behind grumbling about steam inventions.

"How did you get rid of the werewolf?" I asked. "I'm sure there is some ritual to put it back to rest."

"With silver," Tsura said, her voice cracking. "You kill a werewolf with silver. Do you remember the story of the two birds, Miri?"

I frowned. The two birds was a story Romani women told around the campfire. The tale was long lost to childhood memory, but I remembered screaming when the one killed the other in penance for the evil it wrought, and later Tsura calming my night terrors.

"Magic is an unpredictable seductress." Tsura said. "She thirsts for sacrifice. Yet, she's never sated."

Dread crept over my skin. "What are you saying?"

"Great-grandmother always told me the one rule of magic is to never use it to kill. She said murder is like a wheel, and once you've set it to spinning, it will never stop." Tsura's voice sounded scratchier than before, and she clutched at her throat.

A low growl vibrated from my sister's chest. I dropped my rod and my breathing quickened. Fur sprouted on Tsura's arms and she howled as her bones cracked, her body contorting. A monster formed before me, dressed in Tsura's clothes. Towering over me, her yellow eyes glowed with anger as she licked her chops.

"Tsura?"

The werewolf growled, dropping to all fours.

I don't remember grasping my grandmother's silver knife, but now I clenched it tightly in my right hand.

She lunged.

About the Authors

Kara Seal holds a B.A. in Creative Writing from Colorado State University. By day, she's a Programming Assistant at a public library district. By night, she's a writer of young adult and middle grade fiction, and an active member of Rocky Mountain Fiction Writers and Pikes Peak Writers. Kara was a finalist in the 2013 Colorado Gold writing contest. She lives in Colorado with her husband, Allen, and two high energy dogs. Follow her on Twitter @KRwriter.

A former teen librarian, L.H. Parker is a marketing professional at MSU Denver's Center for Innovation and senior writer for Colorado Music Buzz Magazine. She holds a B.A. in Journalism and Psychology from the University of Northern Colorado and is a member of the Rocky Mountain Fiction Writers and Pikes Peak Writers. L.H. Parker writes YA, new adult, and adult speculative fiction. Visit her online at:

www.lhparkerbooks.com

THE NOONDAY SUN

Vivian Caethe

T he noonday sun shimmered across the black land as mirages smudged the border between earth and sky. Places like this in the New Mexico Territory bred ancient stories and whispered dark secrets. Hazel could imagine obscure tales hidden in the sharp-edged volcanic rock and the winding tunnels that yawned like open mouths to swallow the sky.

She rode into Cibola on the day after her twentieth birthday, getting fewer stares than she had anticipated. The rumors about the town—that it was cursed with a plague, with monsters, with witches—had drawn her to it. There had been rumors of "lloronas," vampire-like creatures endemic to the area. As a monster hunter, it was her trade to seek out such places.

The streets were empty, and only a few women watched from their windows as she rode down the empty main street. The only motion came from the dust that puffed around Rociante's hooves as they came up in front of the saloon. She searched each of their faces, hoping she would see Dulcinea's.

The heavy sound of Rociante's hooves on the packed dirt echoed through the empty streets. If a curse hung over this town, there might not be that many folks left to wander around during the day. The silence stretched as the afternoon faded the wooden storefronts to silver, the adobe walls to gold.

Reaching the center of town, she dismounted from her Belgium draft horse and stretched. Rociante was the biggest horse she'd ever seen and stood close to seventeen hands His gave her room to hide behind as she checked her powered armor's fittings, ensuring the long ride hadn't jostled anything out of place. Rociante permitted her to pat him affectionately as she tied him in the shade.

Looking up, she read the sign above the door, "Small Comfort Saloon," she snorted. If lloronas owned it, the comfort would be solely theirs. She loosened her guns in their holsters and pushed open the swinging doors.

The brothel's interior cooled Hazel's sunbaked eyes as she glanced around, her hands resting casually on the butts of her Schofields. What sort of saloon in the Territories was empty at noon?

The short, mustached bartender looked up when she entered. "Something to drink, miss?"

"Whatever you have." She took off her hat and placed it on the counter next to her. The bartender poured her a shot from an unlabeled bottle.

As she toyed with the shot glass, she dearly wished she could take off her duster, but the sight of her armored exoskeleton in a new town tended to have one of two predictable results: she became a freak show or some trigger happy fool'd decide she needed to be relieved of the exoskeleton on principle. She wished she had a penny for every time she heard, "What's a pretty lady like you doing with all that metal?"

Of course, they didn't ask when they saw her legs. Polio had been her greatest curse and her greatest blessing. Without it, she never would have donned the exoskeleton nor had the courage to become a monster hunter. She had heard of monster hunters growing up, but who hadn't? Tales of Sheriff Pat Garrett had kept her riveted for weeks. She still felt the small twinge of jealousy at the thought of his adventures hunting the werewolf Billy the Kid.

The wilds of the West teemed with monstrous creatures. The string of forts that ran up and down the Rocky Mountains were testament enough to the danger. She had traveled to Arizona to hunt chupacabras attacking ranchers' cows, gone to the rough country of Colorado to look for sasquatches that threatened the mining operations. And now she had come to New Mexico, the land of enchantment, the heart of monster country.

"What brings you to these parts?"

Hazel looked down at the empty shot glass then glanced to the open door to the kitchen where an edge of skirt could be seen. "I'm looking for an old friend, picking up work as I go along."

"Are you a mercenary?"

"Sort of." Hazel allowed a wry smile to crack her face. "I'm more of a bounty hunter, but I don't aim for men."

"I've heard tales of folks like you. You go after the monsters." The man had a strange gleam in his eye. Could that be hope?

"Yeah." Hazel smiled. "You seen any monsters around here?"

"Cibola is too small to be a town." The man looked away. "And the People protect us."

"The Indians?"

"Their mesas surround this area and the land is sacred to them. They wouldn't let monsters live here."

"But you've heard stories, haven't you?"

"Would you like some breakfast? I'm the best cook in Cibola. But I don't get to cook very often. Most of the men drink their dinners."

"You didn't answer my question."

The man's jaw set stubbornly. "The People protect us. There's nothing wrong. It's just a sickness, is all."

"Sickness?" Hazel asked.

He sighed. "There's been stories about witches that attack the men in their sleep. Some of them have gotten sick. The People won't come into town until they've passed or got better. Most of them don't get better."

"And then they die." Hazel said. His story sounded familiar enough to confirm her suspicions. There were lloronas here. Her attention went back to the skirt in the kitchen. It wasn't like such creatures to hide. They were bold, sensual. "Who's hiding in the kitchen?"

The edge of skirt twitched and Hazel exchanged a glance with the bartender. She stood, putting her hand on her right revolver. "I feel compelled to tell you, sir, that I do not much care to be spied upon. Nor do I take chances in my profession."

"Come on out niña." Juan sighed.

The girl that stepped from the kitchen looked like Dulcinea. Hazel hid her reaction. Tere was no use in getting her hopes up.

"You don't look like one of them," Hazel said.

The girl flushed. "Just because I live here doesn't make me one of the employees."

Hazel opened her mouth then realized they were talking about two different sorts of things. She had forgotten this was a brothel as well as a saloon.

The girl recovered her composure. "Who are you looking for? Your old friend?"

"An old friend of mine. We grew up together, but my family … well, it's not a pretty story."

"If you don't mind, I'd like to hear it." The girl seated herself at the bar at a safe distance from Hazel. "It's been awhile since I've heard a story from a stranger."

Hazel took a breath, hurt by the implication that she was a stranger. Perhaps she had been wrong after all. "Well … like I said, I grew up on a ranch in Texas. Our cook had a little girl, only a couple years younger than me, and we used to play together." Hazel took a sip of coffee. "My father, well … he wasn't a very good man when it came to women. My mother shouldn't have been surprised, but he made some overtures at the cook after her husband died. My mother got wind of it and was out for blood. She would have had the woman whipped, you see. The cook wasn't white like my family; she was from south of the border, somewhere in Mexico."

Hazel paused, looking at the girl out of the corner of her eye. She was caught up in the story, but without a flicker of recognition. After a moment, Hazel took a breath and continued. "Well, I warned the girl and her mother. T'wasn't right what my father had done, what my mother was going to do. My friend and her mother escaped in the middle of the night, headed out for the Territories before my mother could get the hands riled up. My mother was as bad as my father. She was just better at hiding it."

"So you've come out here looking for your friend and her mother?" The girl asked.

"I heard she might be out here, might be in trouble with all the monsters here." Hazel said. "Heard about the curse here too, like I said. Figured if nothing else, I'd get a bounty from the railroad. They don't like it when there's interference at their depots."

The girl nodded, "What was your friend's name? Maybe I've seen her around town."

"Dulcinea." Hazel said. "Her name was Dulcinea."

Shocked, the girl's expression turned from curious to bewildered. "If I'm her, I don't remember you at all."

Hazel shrugged, trying for nonchalance, "I figured it was a long shot."

"No, it's not that." The girl shook her head, dark tresses spilling over her shoulder with the motion. "I don't remember anything. I don't ... I don't even remember my mother's face."

"I'm sorry." Hazel said, her throat constricting. She swallowed and spoke again. "If you think ... you might be her. I can tell you about your mother if you'd like."

The girl nodded shyly. Hazel sat on the stool next to her and took her hand, marveling at the softness against her own rough skin. "She had a smile that could light up the night. She had the most beautiful accent; it made everything she said sound like music. I remember sitting in the kitchen with you, listening to her sing as she made empanadas, both of us just happy to be there and hoping to sneak one or two."

Dulcinea laughed softly. Hazel continued. "She was always singing, smiling. She was the most beautiful woman on the ranch, and your father was madly in love with her. They used to walk around the pasture at dusk, holding hands and watching the stars come out."

"Your mother ... you look a lot like her." Hazel took a breath. "You have her hair. It was always so soft and long. She used to let us brush it at night, after your father died."

"Did you miss me?" Dulcinea asked, then blushed. "I'm sorry, I didn't mean ... "

"Of course I did. I wouldn't come looking for you if I didn't." Hazel smiled. She owed the girl a debt, for what her family did to her and her mother. It was more than forcing them to flee, it was forcing them to flee in the middle of monster territory.

"What are you doing here?" A woman's voice intruded.

Hazel looked up to see a pale woman standing in the hallway. She stood, her hand going to her guns. The woman advanced down the stairs. Her skin was deathly pale, and she wore a nightgown even though it was well past noon. "Who are you? Get away from her!"

"Sarah, it's all right. She's my friend." Dulcinea moved so she stood between Hazel and the woman. "We were just catching up."

Another woman came down the stairs behind Sarah. They could have been twins. "Get away from her, Dulcinea. You don't have any friends."

"Rachel, it's all right." Dulcinea's smile wavered.

In these parts, creatures like these women were called lloronas, foul creatures that preyed on the men of the Southwest. She had suspected when she heard of the curse ailing Cibola, but there was nothing like confirmation staring you in the face to get the blood boiling.

She unsnapped her holster and eased one of her Schofields out with her left hand. Juan had disappeared into the kitchen, and Dulcinea should have as well. If she needed to, Hazel could push Dulcinea out of the way and bear down on the two lloronas.

"Dulcinea." Hazel pitched her voice low, even though she knew that the creatures could hear her. "You need to get out of here. Get into the sunlight."

"But, this is Sarah." Dulcinea turned to Hazel. "Sarah and Rachel are my guardians."

"Go!" Hazel shoved Dulcinea out of the way. The girl gasped and stumbled. Sarah lunged down the stairs toward them. Claws grew from the woman's fingers as she slashed at Dulcinea. Hazel blocked and pushed Dulcinea further toward the door. The llorona's claws skittered across Hazel's exoskeleton, tearing gashes in her leather duster.

"Monster hunter!" Rachel spit. Fangs distorted the woman's mouth as she made a grab for Dulcinea. The girl screamed and tried to scramble out of the way. Hazel didn't have a good shot, not with the girl dithering about. Instead, she swung the butt of her Schofield into Rachel's nose with a crunch. The creature snarled and spit again. Black viscous blood spattered across Hazel's duster, sizzling where it struck.

She couldn't take on both of them and keep Dulcinea safe at the same time. Growling in frustration, Hazel holstered her gun and pushed the girl toward the swinging doors. Sunlight would protect them. She could come back for the monsters later.

Stumbling into the blinding sunlight, Hazel pushed Dulcinea forward until they were free of any shadows. Tied by the entrance to the saloon, Rociante stomped dangerously. Hazel pulled her guns and pointed them at the dark entrance of the saloon.

Dulcinea bit back a scream and pointed down the street. Looking, Hazel cursed softly but vehemently.

Dead miners shambled down the street toward them, still clothed in their funeral best.

"Come on." Hazel grabbed the girl's wrist and dragged her to Rocainte. She felt more than saw Dulcinea's gaze on her arm, on the metal of her armor.

Letting go of Dulcinea's hand, Hazel took hold of the reins and murmured to the stallion as he fussed. Reluctantly, Rociante knelt before them. Glancing back down the street, she mounted quickly, flashing metal in the sunlight. Dulcinea stepped back, her eyes on Rociante's hooves.

Hazel held a hand down to her. "Get on and hold tight."

She yanked Hazel off the street as the massive horse stomped, baring his teeth when he saw the creatures. Hazel smiled and murmured, "All right, Rociante. Let's go."

The once-men turned toward them, sniffing the air. Hazel called over her shoulder, "It'll only be a moment before they catch wind of us. We will outrun them for now, but their mistresses will join them at nightfall."

She felt Dulcinea's grip tighten around her waist as Rociante tensed and charged. The immense horse barreled down the main street toward the once-men. The last time Hazel had fought creatures like this, they had swarmed at the slightest motion. Rociante could outrun them, but only if they got through the horde first.

Behind her, Dulcinea hummed a song that tickled the back of Hazel's memory. Rociante seemed to feel something from it, his charge became smoother, his strides longer. He barreled into the once-men, trampling them as Hazel fended off their grasping hands. Fingers turned to talons by death grasped and grabbed, trying to find purchase on Hazel's duster.

Dulcinea shrieked. Hazel glanced back. One of the creatures grabbed her skirt, winding its talons into the folds. Flicking her wrist to extend the knife in her armor, she twisted in the saddle and cut through Dulcinea's skirt. The girl gasped and flinched, but the once-man fell back, the scrap of cloth clutched in its hand.

And then they were through. The once-men shambled after them, but they were too slow to catch Rociante.

Outside of town, the stallion's hooves thudded into the desert, casting up puffs of sand into the late afternoon light. Hazel guided Rociante into the wilderness where she hoped they could find a place to make a stand for the night.

As they rode, a thunderstorm gathered above the mesas. Lightning struck the heights, flashing through the dimness of the clouded afternoon. Within minutes, the clouds opened up and rain drenched them.

* * *

"Where are we going?" Dulcinea asked as Hazel slowed Rocinante to a halt.

"We needed to get away from the town, away from their power base." Hazel dismounted and glanced around. "But now, we need to find a place to hunker down for the night. There has to be somewhere around here where we can make a stand."

Hazel glanced up at the girl and her eyes met Dulcinea's. She found herself blushing, of all things, as she noticed that Dulcinea's wild hair cascaded loose down around her shoulders. She swallowed against the sudden dryness in her throat.

There was no chance that she would remember. ... Hazel shook her head and held her hand up to help the girl down from the horse. It wouldn't be right. Dulcinea had been through so much. It would be too much to ask. ... She glanced around. "There's a cave over there. We can seek shelter for the night and figure out a plan in the morning. "

"Can I help?"

"Not with him." Hazel busied herself with picketing Rocinante at the mouth of the cave. They had just been friends, childhood friends. There was no way that Dulcinea could have the same feelings.

She glanced at Dulcinea and had to quell the sudden urge to take her hand. Instead she rummaged in her saddlebags and pulled out a torch. Dousing it with alcohol, she struck a flint and lit it. Glancing at Dulcinea, she led the way into the cave.

Although it was summer, the cave was freezing, the stalactites covered with the sheen of ice. Hazel shivered, feeling an unusual cold settle into her bones. It had to be at least thirty degrees colder in the cave than it was outside. An uneasy feeling settled into her stomach, and she used her free hand to unsnap her holster. Caves were always the homes of unpleasant things, but she had little choice.

The stalactites glimmered in the torchlight and the silica in the walls reflected the torchlight. She glanced at Dulcinea and wished she had taken the girl's hand. She was pale with fear. "Are you all right?"

"This is one of the sacred places," Dulcinea murmured. "We should tread carefully here."

They built a meager fire with what little wood they could gather and sat on either side of it. Swallowing down her emotions, Hazel watched the girl curiously. What was it about this girl that had interested the lloronas? Why hadn't they taken her already?

"They'll follow me, won't they?" Dulcinea's voice was barely audible over the sound of the crackling fire.

"Maybe an hour until sundown and another while they're on our trail. They can travel as fast as a horse." Hazel undid the latches at her shoulder and began to disassemble her exoskeleton. Drenched by the rainstorm, she needed to make sure that none of the parts had been compromised.

"But what are they?" Dulcinea asked.

"The lloronas? Closer to the Rio Grande they tell the stories in the night." Hazel rolled her shoulders to ease the strain of carrying the exoskeleton all day. "They say the first one was a poor woman who was very beautiful. One day a Spanish lord came to her and began to court her for her beauty. She grew to love him, believing that he loved her in return."

Dulcinea watched, wide-eyed, as she cleaned and inspected her exoskeleton, taking it apart in segments and putting them aside as she determined they were sound.. "When it became public knowledge that he had gotten a child on her, he disavowed her as a witch, claiming that she had seduced him in the night."

Checking the engine that rested on the structure that covered her spine, she was glad to see that the creatures hadn't pierced the protective cover over the batteries. If they were compromised she wouldn't be able to move, much less fight. "After the child was born, he stole it and threw it into the Rio Grande to hide the evidence."

Hazel began reassembling her exoskeleton, latching on the legs first before assembling the rest of the machine over her body. She strove not to be self-conscious about her withered legs. It never bothered her when she was in her armor, when she felt whole and strong. But now, now she was exposed, vulnerable. She kept her eyes down, finishing the story. "The bishop and his priests arrested the woman. They stripped her naked, examined her for marks of Satan and then declared her a witch for the blemish she had on her back. The next day they burnt her at the stake."

She stood and stretched, the pistons hissing slightly as she made sure her legs were settled into the braces. The cold and damp hadn't affected them, but she would probably have to replace the gaskets soon. Dulcinea's voice was hushed as she asked, "But what caused the lloronas?"

"After she died they threw her ashes into the Rio Grande to rid themselves of the stain of witchcraft." Hazel flicked her wrists up to eject the daggers from their sheaths, making sure the mechanisms were clear of grime. Retracting the knives, she checked her revolvers. Releasing the barrel latch, she flicked both open one handed and made sure that they were loaded. Flipping her wrist back up, she closed them and reholstered them with one motion. Perhaps a little showing off was forgivable. "La llorona rose from the river that night, a vengeful creature who wanders the banks of the river crying for her child. The lloronas here, your guardians, are the descendants of that creature. Whether or not that's what actually caused them, they're attracted to places of misery and injustice, preying on the heartsick and the lonely."

"The lloronas...." Dulcinea took a breath. "Why has no one stopped them?"

"It's likely no one knows what the problem is. Or no one has the wherewithal to hunt them as I do." Hazel shrugged, now fully encased in her armor. "I don't suppose the two there were preying on anyone but the mining men. Two are powerless, comparatively harmless in the grand scheme of things. Three is too many for a small town like Cibola. They would leave the town, bringing sickness with them to every place they visited. When there are three, no one can stop them."

"I don't understand. Why did they need me?" Dulcinea rubbed her hands on her skirt. "And why did they wait?"

"Because you are the child of sorrow." Hazel's said. "They couldn't take you until you became a woman, filled with the desires of a woman. I don't know why they waited as long as they did."

"But they never told me. They kept watching me with the men, but they had to know. That ... they had to know I ... " Dulcinea's gaze was riveted on the floor. "If they wanted me to be one of them ... "

Hazel barked a laugh. "You thought they would ask? They run a brothel for a reason. They take what they need from men without permission or consent."

The silence of the desert above was broken by an eerie wail. Hazel watched as Dulcinea shivered. "What is it?"

"I've heard that wail before ... I ... I was so afraid. My mother sang to me." Dulcinea looked up, her eyes moist. "I can remember her face."

Hazel smiled briefly, but before she could say anything, there was another wail, closer this time. She crouched at the mouth of the cave, blinking against the darkness. Of all the monsters she had fought, creatures like lloronas were her least favorite. Most other monsters had the courtesy of at least sometimes attacking during the day.

She heard them coming. The soft sound of footsteps on sand, the crunch of dead men's boots on pumice. She unholstered her revolvers and held them steady at her sides. "They're here."

They'd only have one chance to get the upper hand. She didn't like the odds. Two against two was fair odds. Two against a score or more made things a little more complicated. "Stay here. Keep the fire going. It should keep them at bay."

"All right," Dulcinea said in a small voice. Hazel glanced back and gave her a quick, reassuring smile. Or at least she hoped it was reassuring.

When she exited the cave, she looked around, trying to adjust her eyes quickly to the moonlight. A shape darted across the moonlit desert to her right. Hazel tracked it with her revolvers and fired. The other came from the left and she fired at that one too. A high-pitched shriek split the air, and she smiled in grim satisfaction. It wouldn't stop them for long, but it sure felt good to score a hit.

Then the monsters were on them. The dead men walked forward, as unstoppable as a force of nature. She slashed out at the llorona as it passed, then turned to the men.

Her first shot caught one of the men in the torso, it kept coming and she thinned her lips in irritation. So it was that kind of gunfight. She shot him in the head and dropped him.

Another blur to her right and Hazel holstered her right hand revolver. Twisting her blade free, she struck out. The llorona was faster than it looked and dodged the strike. She spun to follow it and fired with her left revolver, missing by inches. The barrel flash lit the creature's features, teeth sharp and silvered.

The llorona leaped on Hazel, trying to claw and slash through Hazel's exoskeleton. The creature was horribly fast, faster than she had anticipated. But these creatures were after more than just food, driving their desperation.

As the llorona snapped at her, she caught its face with one hand and squeezed, feeling the bones bend under the augmented strength of her exoskeleton. With her left arm, she blocked a claw and fired her revolver, once, twice. She had one bullet remaining in that revolver, five in the other.

The llorona's body buckled with each shot and Hazel could smell the rotten stench of its blood. Shrieking again, the creature tore itself free from Hazel and tried to dash to the cave mouth.

"Oh no you don't." Hazel leapt after her, her armor providing the burst of speed she needed to grab it by the hair and yank it back. She fell on top of the creature and plunged her knife into its throat.

The llorona writhed and knocked her off with inhuman strength. Wrenching its head, it tore free, leaving most of its hair in her grip. Dropping it, Hazel pulled her other revolver, firing the last shot from her left-hand revolver into the creature.

In the moonlight, the llorona looked nothing like the beautiful women in the saloon. Bleeding from her wounds and missing most of her hair, she was a bedraggled, skeletal creature. Feinting right, she dashed left, making for the cave entrance. Hazel shot the few remaining bullets in her right revolver and holstered it to give chase.

Hazel skidded down the loose sand to the cave's mouth. Even in their damaged state, the lloronas were swifter than she was in her exoskeleton. She pushed herself to go faster. Dulcinea was down there. She should have left the girl a revolver.

Down in the cave, the creatures circled the fire, their features lurid in the firelight. Hazel reloaded as fast as she could, trying not to think of everything that had gone wrong. As she slid the special silver bullets into the Schofields, she exhaled, calming herself.

Dulcinea stood transfixed as the creatures neared her. She walked forward, reaching out to them. To the girl, they weren't monsters, they were the women who raised her.

"No!" she shouted. "Leave her alone."

"No." Dulcinea echoed, more softly. The lloronas eyes shone and they held out their hands to the girl.

"Come with us, Dulcinea." They spoke in unison, their voices echoing in an eerie harmony. "You belong with us. We are your mothers. We are your sisters."

Dulcinea stopped walking forward. She shook her head. Hazel tried to get a good angle on them, but they kept circling the fire, moving closer to Dulcinea with every step.

Frustrated, she holstered her gun and ran forward, grabbing the closest one. The least damaged of the two, vaguely recognizable as Rachel, snarled and turned. Its fingers elongated into claws that raked across Hazel's face. Despite the pain, Hazel kept her grip on the llorona and snicked out her blade, ramming the blade up and into the creature's heart.

Sarah dashed around the fire to Dulcinea, its movements impossibly fast. If she hurt one, the other became more powerful. Hazel slashed at the llorona through the fire, drawing blood black as ichor.

Grabbing and pulling Dulcinea's hair roughly, Sarah snarled. "None of that now."

A weight landed on Hazel's back. She stumbled and turned. Rachel scrabbled through her thick duster, tearing large rents in the leather. So close, the llorona's stench made Hazel gag and cough. The cloying smell of decay insinuated into her lungs as she tried to shake the creature off.

With a horrible snapping noise, she overbalanced and fell backwards. Rachel jumped clear as she landed. Her head fell back and hit the ground with a sharp crack.

Out of the corner of her eye, she saw Rachel throw something metal to the floor of the cave. Her battery pack.

Sneering, the llorona returned to its sister. "Enough of this."

Hazel cursed and rolled over, her head throbbing. Dulcinea stood with the two creatures. One of the creature's mouths opened more than was humanly possible, rows of teeth ready to latch onto Dulcinea. The girl's eyes were wide, unseeing as the creature opened its mouth wider.

Hazel raised her heavy arm and tried to grab for her guns. Without the battery's power, her limbs were weak under the weight of her armor. Thinking furiously, she tried to come up with a plan. Whatever she did, she needed to do it fast and without power.

The llorona's thralls would be coming after them soon enough. One thing to try then.

Hazel raised her revolver, heavy without the support of the pistons. Her arms shook as the creatures leaned in toward Dulcinea; the humming sound they emitted grew louder and louder. They had paused, as if caught in honey, the tableau before her apt to break at any moment.

The gun was heavy, her arm was heavy. Her heart was heavy. If she died here today, it would all be for nothing. Dulcinea would still be dead, the monsters would have won. If only … She raised her gun, aiming as best she could.

Before she could fire, the creatures' voices sneered in her head. "You would kill us when the men of this land would do the same to you? You think we wouldn't notice? The way you protected her? The way you looked at her?"

"No." Hazel whispered, the sound jerked from her lips. "No. She's my friend."

"She'll think you're a monster like me, once she learns of your desires. She'll run from you like she ran from me."

"No." But what if it was true? What if Dulcinea despised her?

"You think you hunt monsters? You are a monster." The sibilant hiss of the words tore through her lassitude, giving her strength. She might be a monster, but she fought monsters for a living.

"I don't eat people." Hazel fired, once, twice. The recoil nearly dislocated her shoulder without the power of her armor to dampen it. The muzzle flared as she fired again. The creatures turned toward her, their distended jaws open, their shrieking laughter cutting through her like knives.

"She'll think you're a monster." The creatures laughed, a gurgling, bubbling sound through the holes in their chests.

She aimed one last time. Two more shots.

Blood black as sin spurted from the creatures' heads, the impact of the bullets tearing their skulls apart. Dulcinea screamed and tore her hands from theirs. Mutilated, half of their faces missing, they still clawed at her. Hazel slumped to the ground, worn out. They wouldn't stop until their corpses were burnt and their ashes scattered to the winds.

With wide eyes, Dulcinea looked at the creatures before her, her eyes wide with memory. Hazel forced the words free. "Remember, Dulcinea. Remember your mother's songs."

Haunted, the girl looked at her for a moment, before turning her gaze to the creatures that fought against death, slowly rejuvenating before her. She folded her hands in front of her and closed her eyes.

"Duérmete mi niña, duérmete mi sol, duérmete cariña, de mi corazón." Dulcinea's voice was high and sweet, soothing the lloronas' gurgling shrieks. "Esta niña linda, que nació de día, quiere que la iglesia, por la Virgen María."

The creatures screeched louder as she completed the simple round. After the last words echoed through the cave, one of them, Hazel thought it might have been Sarah, fell to its knees and keened.

"Duérmete mi niña," Dulcinea walked around to the other side of the fire, continuing the round, "duérmete mi sol, duérmete cariña," she held out her hands to the monsters, "de mi corazón."

Both of the creatures turned to her like hounds on a scent. Slowly, as she continued singing, they inched towards her, ignoring the fire. "Esta niña linda, que nació de día ... "

The creatures followed Dulcinea's voice, crawling and scraping into the fire. The flames licked up their bodies, burning blue when it touched their blood. Kneeling, Dulcinea lowered her voice, almost murmuring the words, "... quiere que la iglesia, por la Virgen María."

The fire consumed the lloronas, burning them until they could no longer make a sound. The flames burned blue, and then green, dying out as they ate the final scraps of bone and ash. When there was only dust left, Dulcinea stopped singing. In the absence of the comforting sound, Hazel felt like crying.

With an effort, Hazel rolled up to a sitting position and looked around. The creature had torn the battery pack off, but if the safety detachment had worked, it might still be undamaged. If she could get to it, she could repair it. Then she could leave. The creatures were right. There was no point. Compared to Dulcinea, she was a monster.

* * *

With Dulcinea's help, she was able to get her exoskeleton back together. She avoided the girl's gaze. She had heard what the creatures had said. She had to know. Hazel was surprised that she hadn't left already.

Then she remembered the once-men. They would still be outside, and without the control of their mistresses, they would fall apart, but it could take days, if not a week. They needed to be dealt with.

Hazel shrugged her shoulders to settle the battery pack in its place. She would have to take it all apart later to repair it, but for now it would serve. Reloading her Schofields, she glanced at Dulcinea. "We'll need to take care of the once-men. Do you have a song for that?"

"I think ... I think so." Dulcinea smiled tentatively. "You'll be with me?"

"Always." The word left Hazel's lips before she could stop it. Wasn't this what she had wanted all these years? To find the friend her family had wronged? It was just. ... She firmed her lips. "Let's go."

They slowly walked up the short ascent to the mouth of the cave. Night had fallen further, deepening toward midnight. The moon still illuminated the desert floor where the once-men shambled between the scrubby plants.

Hazel unholstered her Schofields and waited. After a moment, she turned to Dulcinea. "If you're going to do something, I would suggest you start now, before they smell us."

Dulcinea swallowed and nodded. She folded her hands in front of her and closed her eyes, taking her time. Hazel shook her head slightly as she watched the once men sniff the air. There wasn't time, but Hazel knew she couldn't force the girl to remember. Cocking the hammers back on her revolvers, she interposed herself between the creatures and the girl. She would have to reload at least twice, three times if she wasn't lucky.

"A ... a los niños que duermen, Dios los bendice, a las madres que velan, Dios las asiste." Dulcinea's voice, hesitant at first, grew and resonated through the desert. "Duérmete niño, duérmete niño, duérmete niño, arrú arrú ... "

The last turned into a lonely sound that echoed like a coyote howl off the mesas in the distance. The topography of the desert bowl conspired to amplify the girl's soprano. She opened her arms, holding them out to the once-men who turned toward them.

"A ... a los niños que duermen,.." Hazel fired, once. "Dios los bendice ... " twice. "A las madres que velan," headshot. "Dios las asiste," headshot.

"Duérmete niño, duérmete niño, duérmete niño, arrú arrú ... " Hazel emptied her revolvers into the crowd of once-men. As she reloaded, she glanced up and saw the creatures falling, one by one. The lullaby, cascading from Dulcinea's lips, sent them to their final rest. Even the ones nearest to them collapsed, their drive for human flesh quelled by the song.

The song was over. The once-men littered the desert, their arms flung toward Dulcinea and Hazel. They would not stir again. Hazel holstered her revolvers. "Come on."

* * *

The hour passed beyond midnight and into the earliest morning as they rode back to Cibola. Dulcinea held onto Hazel, shivering in the cold desert wind. Sensing Hazel's mood, Rociante didn't tarry but rather allowed himself to be encouraged to a canter that ate up the desert sands beneath his hooves.

Silent, the empty windows of the town watched them reproachfully as they returned to the Saloon. A light in the window greeted them, and Hazel glanced at Dulcinea warily. Who would be waiting for them?

She dismounted and helped Dulcinea down from Rociante's broad back. Dulcinea took her hand, shaking her head as Hazel flipped the snaps off her holsters. "Juan."

Hazel nodded, remembering, but she didn't let her hand off her gun. "We don't know if they got to him too. We have to make sure that the curse has been lifted."

Pushing the doors aside, Hazel led the way into the saloon. Dulcinea refused to let go of her hand, so she used the contact to keep the girl behind her. With her other hand, she pulled one of her revolvers, holding it close to her chest, half hidden behind her tattered duster. "Juan?"

The bartender stepped out from the kitchen, a shotgun in his hands. He trained it at Hazel, his eyes dark. "Did you kill them?"

"I did." Hazel met his gaze.

"Did you burn their corpses?"

"Yes."

After a moment, Juan lowered the shotgun. "I thought that no one would come, that no one would be able to save us from them. And the niña?"

"I'm safe, Juan." Dulcinea stepped out from behind Hazel. "She saved me."

Juan put down his shotgun and walked to embrace the girl. "Mi corazón. Your mother would be so proud of you."

"I think she would be." Dulcinea's smile lit up her face. She turned to Hazel. "Please, accept my thanks and what hospitality I can provide."

"I ..." Seeing Dulcinea's hopeful expression, Hazel discarded half-formed thoughts of leaving in the night, of riding away, as far away as she could. There would be time to run away later, once she was sure her armor was intact.

Dulcinea led her up to one of the rooms and leaned against the doorway. "What you did to save my mother and I ... I owe you for tonight as well."

"I did what I had to." Hazel said, taking off her exoskeleton piece by piece. She didn't care if Dulcinea saw any more. She couldn't be any more of a monster than she already was.

"You think I listened to them, don't you."

"Of course you did." Hazel placed each part of her armor on the bed next to her, as neat as a skeleton.

"I don't ... you're not a monster."

Hazel shrugged out of the harness that supported the battery and swung it around to examine it. "Look at me and tell me that."

"You're not a monster." Dulcinea came and knelt next to Hazel, forcing her to meet her eyes. "Not for your armor, not for your legs, not for your heart."

"Do you remember?" Hazel looked away, her hands tightening on the straps. "Do you remember anything?"

Dulcinea helped her place the harness to the side and took her hands. Looking up into her face, she smiled hesitantly. "No. But if you'd like ... if you would like to tell me about it, I would ... would you stay and tell me the stories?"

"Stay here?" Hazel looked at her. "You would want me to stay?"

Hazel could feel Dulcinea's heart thumping through the pulse in her palms. "There are still stories to tell. And I think I'd like to make this an inn. With the town growing...."

Hazel's heart pounded in the silence as she trailed off. She dared not interrupt.

After a moment, Dulcinea continued, looking down. "We could ... we might have use of a marshal. You haven't claimed the bounty yet. And I would hope ... maybe we can make some more stories." Dulcinea hesitantly reached forward and brushed a strand of hair out of Hazel's eyes. Her fingers brushed lightly against Hazel's cheek.

Hazel took her hand and met her eyes. She had not expected this. Not here. She had expected to find her friend at some point, maybe. But she would be happy to merely know that she was alive and well. And now ... She smiled, vulnerable yet hopeful. "I would love to."

About the Author

Cross-genre author, and avid tea connoisseur, Ms. Caethe writes and edits in the wee hours of the morning while working a night job. That clicking noise you hear? Probably the sound of her keyboard. Probably. Unless you have spiders in your house. Large, scary spiders that stare at you while you sleep.

Ms. Caethe was introduced to speculative fiction at an early age by growing up in the Land of Enchantment. She knits and cross stitches in her spare time.

The author of multiple short stories and novellas, her work has appeared in various magazines and anthologies. Her post-post-apocalyptic proto-Victorian gay adventure series, The Adventures of Vernon Auldswell, Gentleman Explorer, is available through Bold Strokes Books. She is currently working on a novel in which demons roam the earth and the lunatic wind removes the last ounce of sanity from a post-apocalyptic world.

THE
DEMON TRAIN

Quincy J. Allen

Anita sat motionless in the pale glow of a gaslight above her head. She'd run out of tears, a river of them spent in the hours after some nameless, golden-haired boy delivered the telegram now clenched in her fist. The SANTE FE STATION sign swayed gently in a light breeze, a rhythmic squeak of rusty chains giving a solitary voice to the night.

Her sisters were dead. *Murdered.*

The words were burned into her memory.

```
TO: Anita Escamilla

Regret to inform: sisters Carmen and Mariana
shot and killed in The Copper Load Saloon,
Helvetia, Arizona. Sheriff unwilling to press
charges.

Apologies.
```

Such was the justice for working girls in Arizona, particularly if they were Mexican. Horses were valued more than she and her sisters.

She pulled a worn pocket watch, given to her by a lonely miner years before, and peered at faded numbers exposed to the air. The glass had long-since broken, but it was the only timepiece she possessed. Ten-forty, and the freight train was due in at eleven o'clock.

Placing the pocket watch back in her purse, she checked her ticket again. She'd had to beg the clerk for one round trip seat and space for two coffins in a cargo car, and that had cost her half of what she'd squirreled away over the years.

A train whistle blew in the distance, a long, mournful sound that seemed distorted somehow, sending a shiver inexplicably down her spine. She looked down the tracks and picked out the glow of a distant light cutting through the darkness. She could just make out the engine, and some trick of the night gave it an almost ruddy glow, the plume of smoke rising from its stack a hazy orange drifting up to fade into a black sky.

She rose, picked up a small carpetbag beside her, and stepped to the edge of the platform. She heard the chugging clack of the train as it approached the station. It didn't take long before she was awash in the bright glow of the headlamp. The engine slid by, but no one appeared in the engineer's window. Finally, as the coal car passed, a single passenger car came to a standstill before her, the train gasping out one last breath of steam and giving off a clank of metal on metal. A single boxcar lay behind the passenger car.

She walked up the steps and into the car, surprised to find its dimly lit interior, row upon row of benches, completely empty save for one black-cloaked figure at the back of the car. His features were hidden beneath a hood, and she could just make out a long pointed nose peeking out from the shadow. At first she thought he was a priest of some kind, but his bent, crippled form and the black fabric spoke of something far less than Godly. With a shiver, she slipped her bag under the seat.

"Ticket please," a gravelly voice said from behind her.

Anita nearly jumped out of her shoes, turning in surprise. She'd never heard anyone enter the car.

He was a small man, his ancient, gray skin a crisscross of jagged wrinkles. Bright, beady eyes as green as emeralds stared out from beneath bushy gray eyebrows, and an engineer's hat perched atop his head seemed to be the only thing preventing wild, wiry gray hair from flying away in all directions. Dingy dungarees covered his skeletal form, and he held out a grizzled, hairy appendage—more claw than hand—expectantly.

"You startled me," Anita said in a slight Spanish accent, reaching for her purse.

"Yes," he said, his tone unapologetic. He narrowed his eyes. "Ticket, please."

She placed the ticket to Helvetia in his open palm. The return ticket and papers for her cargo space remained in her purse.

Without looking, he closed his hand slowly around the paper and lowered his arm.

"Take your seat," he said, turning towards the door to the coal car. "We're leaving immediately"

Anita had been told the train would depart at eleven-thirty. She said, "But I thought—"

"*Immediately*," he injected, opening the door.

"Why was the train early?" she blurted out.

The ticket man paused in the doorway, his head tilted to the side a fraction of an inch. Several heartbeats went by, and she began to wonder if he'd heard her.

"It wasn't," he said and closed the door.

A dry, brittle chuckle like the twisting of dry reeds drifted up from the back of the car. Anita turned in her seat and almost gasped. The man in black had pulled down his hood.

"Not much on manners," he said in a raspy, file-on-steel voice. His skin was as white as paper, and where the ticket master's flesh had been thick and wrinkled, his was taught, stretched thin over angular features. His face looked as lifeless as a corpse ... all but the eyes. His bright, blue eyes held an almost impish delight as he stared at her. "Helvetia, eh?" he asked.

"Yes," Anita replied. "How did you—?"

"I'm the master of this train," he interrupted. "And there are no stops scheduled between here and Helvetia."

"Do you own it?"

He raised an eyebrow and smiled, barring a mouthful of long, bone-white teeth. "Own it?" Another chuckle escaped his lips. "No. I'm not the owner. I just run it for the one who does."

There was something about how he said it that filled Anita with unease. The words had been loaded with something dark and ominous.

A silence stretched between them, and his eyes never left hers.

The whistle blew twice, and then the train lurched with a mighty chug of steam. It's pace increased in tempo, and still his eyes were fixed upon her.

Quincy J. Allen

Finally, she asked, "When do we arrive?" She couldn't wait to get off the train. Between the ticket man and the train master, Anita felt as if she was in unwholesome company.

His smile disappeared. "In the morning." He raised a bony hand, pointing a finger that seemed to barely have any flesh upon it. "You should get some sleep. I'm certain tomorrow will be a long day."

He said it as if he knew what lay ahead of her. *Impossible*, she thought.

"Perhaps I will at that," she said, and faced forward. She slid her hand into her purse and gripped the Derringer tucked inside. She might sleep, but if he or anyone else came at her, she was prepared to defend herself.

"Sweet dreams," he rasped, and it seemed as if he really meant it.

* * *

Anita woke with a start as the train whistle shrieked out three short bursts. Rubbing her eyes, she looked out the window and saw what she assumed was the Helvetia platform sliding towards her. There was no building, no benches, not even a sign, just an empty platform of weather-scored planks. Turning in her seat, she saw that the train master was gone.

She stood, grabbed her bag, and quickly left the train, pausing upon the platform to take in the town of Helvetia. A single, dusty street lined by mostly one-story buildings of whitewashed pine stretched off to her right. Halfway down the street she spotted the Copper Load Saloon, one of the few two-story structures, and the only one painted bright red.

A two-story hotel, directly across from the platform, beckoned to what few travelers might visit the town. The arid, copper-rich hills of the region rose and tumbled in every direction, the landscape covered in sage, cactus, and yucca.

She stepped down off the platform and made her way to the hotel. The interior looked like every other small town hotel, with a handful of rough tables and rickety chairs. A thin, tall man with dark hair swept over a balding head rose behind the front desk, placing a penny dreadful upon its worn surface. He wore a threadbare brown suit covered by a stained apron.

"Can I help you?" he asked in a pinched voice that seemed to run entirely through an oversized nose. "We don't' get many folks comin' in on Sundays."

"I'd like a room for the night," Anita said.

He stared at her for a second, a curious look upon his face, and said, "Eight bits, and that'll include tomorrow's breakfast." He was thoughtful for a moment longer. "You look familiar. Been to Helvetia before?"

Anita's stomach churned and her heart ached. She didn't want to talk to every person in town about what happened. "No, sir."

"I swear I've seen you before." He scratched behind his head, dislodging a few strands of his hair and sending them dangling down past his ear.

She sighed and swallowed hard. "I'm here for my sisters."

His eyes went wide, and a look of shame crossed his features. "Oh," he said, looking at the floor. He reached behind the desk and placed a key in front of her. "Room six. Top of the stairs. Last door on the right."

Without a word, Anita picked up the key and headed up the stairs. Halfway up, the clerk's voice stopped her.

"Miss?"

She turned and faced him.

"Stay away from Broden Grady. He's bad news. And don't go near the Copper Load Saloon." Then he picked up the penny dreadful and sat down, his eyes quickly going to the print before him.

Anita nodded. The man clearly didn't want to say more, but she wondered who Broden Grady was and whether he was the man who killed her sisters. She turned and went to her room.

Thirty minutes later, Anita walked past a still silent clerk and stepped back out into the sunlight. She turned and made her way along the creaking boards that stretched along both sides the street. The sun burned down, raising perspiration upon her brow. Most of the buildings didn't have an awning, so the sun beat down upon her with a vengeance. She spotted a church at the far end of town. The double-doors to the house of God opened, and a small group of people shuffled out, some in silence, a few speaking quietly as they ambled away.

Two men broke away from the group and headed towards the small, one-window jail two doors down from the church. The one in the lead was tall and ample around the middle. He wore a red shirt, faded jeans and a large gray cowboy hat that might have once belonged to the Confederacy. She spotted the glint of a silver star beneath a black vest that opened wide across his belly. A shorter, skinny fellow a tan suit and brown bowler followed in his wake. They disappeared into the jail, and Anita saw several people speaking in hushed whispers as they watched the men disappear into the jail.

Part of her wanted to follow the men in and confront them about what happened to her sisters, but something about the telegram led her further down the same side of the street. She had to find out whatever happened on her own first. The place to start—despite the hotel clerk's warning—was the Copper Load Saloon.

The front doors were propped open, and she could hear several men speaking within.

"Ha!" a man's voice shouted. "That's three in a row. You cusses don't' stand a chance!"

Anita stepped in and saw a red-headed bartender pouring beer from the tap. In the far corner sat three cowboys playing cards, and of the three, only one stood out. The man raking in a pile of money, his back to the far wall, was like no cowboy she'd ever seen.

A third of his face was covered in dull brass, the metal stretching from his left cheek up to his forehead to disappear beneath a wide-brimmed black hat. His left eye was covered by a triangular plate of dark metal with a milky-white lens set in the middle. At first she though both of his hands were covered in brass gloves, but then she realized that they were actually his hands, the metal disappearing up under the cuffs of a grungy, blue shirt. She noticed bulges at his shoulders, making it appear as if the metal went all the way up.

The right side of his face was alight with four, deep scratches where someone had clawed him with long fingernails.

"I think I've had enough, Grady," one of the cowboys said, scooting his chair back from the table.

Grady's smile disappeared in a flash, replaced by a snarl. His good eye narrowed to a slit, and the milky lens turned blood red.

"Sit your ass back down, Phelps!" Grady growled. "I ain't nearly done with you … not while there's money in front of you."

Phelps paused, half out of his chair, and then slowly sat back down. "Well, I reckon I can play a few more hands," he said weakly.

Anita caught the bartender shaking his head slowly. She immediately understood the hotel clerk's warning about Grady. She'd seen men like that before back in Santa Fe, although, back home, the town marshal would run them out fast. The marshal was a good man in Anita's eyes, treating justice like it was supposed to be … fairly and for everyone.

Grady's gaze drifted from Phelps to lock onto Anita, taking in her long dark hair, tanned skin, and curves.

"Well would you look at that," he said with a sickening hunger.

The two cowboys turned to ogle her as she walked towards the bar, ignoring them. The bartender set down a third mug of beer and nodded to her. Slowly, his face took on the same thoughtful look of recognition the hotel clerk had given her.

"Can I help you?" he asked as she stepped up to the bar.

She smiled weakly and nodded towards the far end of the bar, away from the men at the table.

"I'll be right with you," he said and picked up the three mugs.

Anita slid down the bar.

"About damn time!" Grady shouted. "Jee-sus, O'Connell, you get slower with them beers every god damn day."

"Didn't mean to keep you waiting, Mr. Grady," the bartender said quietly.

"Who's your friend?" Grady asked.

Anita felt their eyes upon her.

"Don't know yet. Fixin' to find out, I s'pose."

Grady raised his voice to make sure she heard him. "Well, if she's a workin' girl, tell her I got two fresh openings ... if she's a whore that can mind her place, that is." Grady guffawed and slammed his hand down on the table. She heard the other two men chuckling right along with him.

Anita's insides turned sour, a wellspring of heartache and rage. She sat at the bar wringing her knuckles till they turned white. Finally, O'Connell stepped up in front of her.

"You're her," he said in a whisper. "You're Anita."

She nodded slowly, and she could feel tears welling up in her eyes.

His face paled. "I'm sorry for what happened to your sisters," he said, and he looked both remorseful and ashamed. "Grady's got three more workin' girls upstairs. He runs this place. And them." O'Connell's eyes dropped down to the bar. "And me."

Realization struck Anita. "*You* sent the telegram," she whispered.

His eyes went wide with fear and darted briefly to Grady then back again. He shook his head almost imperceptibly. "Please don't mention that to anyone," he said, and she could barely hear him. "I figured you had a right to know, but he'd kill me if he ever found out."

"Can you at least tell me what happened?" she asked.

"Nobody 'cept Grady really knows." O'Connell looked down at the bar, obviously reliving what had happened. "Some of the miners were down here, drinking it up as usual. The upstairs was full, and Grady had ... gone up with both of your sisters." O'Connell took a deep breath. "He took one or more up every night." He closed his eyes, and she could see the disgust on his face.

Anita felt a wave of nausea fill her. "Go on," she finally said.

"There was a scream upstairs, and then another. The bar went quiet, and then somethin' heavy hit the floor. We all heard one of your sisters shoutin' in Spanish. There was a struggle, and then Grady hollered, like he was in pain. I figure that's when he got those marks on his face...." O'Connell swallowed hard. His eyes flickered up to hers, full of pain. "Then we heard the gunshots. Four of them."

He stopped then, just shaking his head.

"And nobody went up to see what happened?" She was appalled.

"Folks just looked at one another ... including me, I'm sorry to say. It was *Grady*. It was his whor—" O'Connell caught himself. "It was his working girls." He rubbed the back of his neck, as if he was trying to rub away an ache that just wouldn't go away. "Finally, Sheriff Turn came in and went upstairs. There was some talking, but nobody heard what Turn and Grady said. Then Turn came back down ... said it was self-defense. He got old man Wilson—he makes the coffins, you see—to box 'em up."

Silence stretched out between them, and the ocean of pain within Anita slowly turned to rage ... like so much blood into wine.

"Damn all of you," she whispered, and she meant it from the bottom of her soul.

The words seemed to make O'Connell shrink before her eyes.

"There's more," he whispered, and Anita suddenly felt like his confessor. "This ain't the first time."

Her eyes went wide, horrified.

"Every six ... eight months or so...." He stared down at the bar, wiping it absentmindedly with a dirty rag. "They carry another one out. Always self-defense."

"And the sheriff goes along with this?" she asked. There was no hiding her disgust.

"Self-defense," O'Connell repeated.

"The whole town knows," she said. She knew it had to be the case.

"One way or the other." He sighed. "Folks on this side of the Bible, them that drink and carouse and take to callin' on workin' girls. They—*we* just let it slide. You hear 'self-defense' enough times, you just sort of swallow it. And them folks on the other side of the Bible, the ones who go to church every Sunday. They just figure workin' girls who turn up dead get what God meant for 'em. Payin' for their sins, you know? I've heard 'em talk about it."

"God damn this whole God-forsaken town…. Damn you all to Hell."

"I reckon you're right about that," O'Connell said.

Anita shook her head.

Starve or sin—those were the choices for women like her. Either that or marry some drunkard with a habit of nightly beatings. She'd seen far too much of all three.

"Where are my sisters?" she finally asked.

"In the cemetery, up the hill on the other side of the train platform. Old man Wilson took care of it. I helped him dig." He took a deep breath and let it out slowly. "I'm so sorry," he added.

"What are you two whispering about?" Grady called out. "I'm startin' to feel left out!"

"Nothin', Mr. Grady," O'Connell said. "She was just asking about someone who might have passed through town. I told her I ain't seen him and that she should move on down the line." He locked eyes with Anita. "Ain't that right, Miss?"

Anita hesitated for a moment. She placed her hand on her purse and felt the hard lump of her Derringer. The thought of shooting Grady where he sat and taking the consequences passed through her mind. Finally, she discarded it, thinking that killing Grady, assuming she could, wouldn't be enough. She wanted the whole town to pay.

With a deadpan face she said, "That's right. I just need to go check with the sheriff and then I'll be on my way."

"Too bad, missy," Grady said. "I could put you to good, honest work. You let me know if you decide to stick around Helvetia. I damn near own this town. You wouldn't regret it!"

"I'm sure I wouldn't," Anita replied, never taking her eyes of O'Connell's. "I guess I'll be on my way, then. Thank you for your help."

She grabbed her purse, turned her back on them all, and walked out into the sunlight. She crossed the street, making a bee-line for the jail. There were still quite a few people in front of the church. Every pale face turned towards her, and the whispering went silent. She ignored them, her head held high. Lifting her skirts, she marched up the steps of the jail, opened the door, and walked in.

The place smelled of dust and whisky. Turning, she saw the sheriff sitting behind a battered desk, a bottle of Old Grand-Dad whiskey in his hand poised above a short tumbler. She heard sweeping beyond a door at the back of the room.

Quincy J. Allen

He looked up at her, and his eyes narrowed, darting back and forth for a heartbeat as he calculated who she might be. He slowly placed the bottle on the desk and stuck the cork back in.

He licked his lips and asked, "You need something?" His voice was gruff and mean, like he'd been surly since the day he was born.

She stared at him for a few seconds, a disgusted look on her face. And then the words just tumbled out of her mouth. She could feel the anger burning within her.

"Not much of a sheriff, are you?" she asked, not caring what happened.

"Excuse me?" Sheriff Turn blurted, rising quickly out of his chair as his face turned red. The sweeping in the back room stopped.

"How many?" Anita asked. "How many women have been murdered in this town while you turned a blind eye?"

She never saw the hand that came across her face with a *SMACK!*. Her head jerked to the side. She turned back to him, her cheek burning. She could already feel the welt rising.

"We ain't even human to men like you and Grady, are we?" It wasn't an accusation. It was a statement of fact, like telling him there was sunshine and rain. "Does he pay you off, Sheriff? Or did you let him murder those women for free?"

Turn's face went purple and he raised his hand again.

Anita didn't move ... didn't even flinch. She stared him right in the eyes. Defiant. Waiting for it. Her eyes told him there was nothing he could do that he hadn't already done to her sisters.

The door to the back room opened, and the small man with the bowler stood there, a broom held in his hand and a stern look on his face. "Them whores was ungodly," the man cried, a self-righteous look on his face.

"Get back to work, Smiley!" the sheriff growled.

The small man, cowed by the sheriff's tone, quickly shut the door, but the sweeping didn't start up again.

"I'm leaving, Sheriff," Anita said. "But I wanted you to know what I thought of you before I got out of this God damned down."

"I think you better do just that," he said through clenched teeth.

Anita spun on her heel and walked to the door. She swung it open and stopped in her tracks. The people in front of the church all turned and stared at her as she stood motionless in the doorway. She gave them a disgusted look and then spoke over her shoulder loud enough for them to hear.

"You know, *Sheriff*, you're a hell of a lot worse than Grady is. At least he doesn't pretend to be something he's not. You, on the other hand are a living lie. You're supposed to *uphold* the law." Stepping down onto the dusty street, she stared at the townsfolk gathered there. "Someday this town is going to pay for what you *all* did to those women. You're *all* gonna pay!"

"Get out of my town, you *whore!*" Turn yelled from the doorway. "Either that or go work for Grady and get what's coming to you!"

Anita stepped out into the street and marched back towards the train platform. She heard the sheriff stomp down the steps.

"And if you want your sisters," he shouted, "you're welcome to take them with you, but you'll have to dig them up yourself!"

Without even looking back, she marched up the center of the street and angled towards the platform, heading for the cemetery. Faces in the windows stared at her through pulled back curtains as she walked by. The train she'd arrived on was still parked at the platform.

She walked around the front of the engine, but something caught her eye and she stopped. On the nose of the engine, where she'd normally seen blocky numbers, there was a strange symbol. She stared at it for a few seconds, trying to figure out what it was. It finally occurred to her that it was three nines, arranged with their backs to each other. She'd never seen anything like it and wondered why they'd arranged it in such an odd fashion.

She finally tore her eyes away from the symbol and walked up the hill beyond the train. The cemetery was there, right where O'Connell had said it would be. At the back, separated from the headstones and crosses in the main part of the cemetery, lay a row of unmarked graves. Two of them were freshly dug, while the others had increasing amounts of vegetation growing upon them.

Six. She counted six graves. *Six murders*, she thought.

She stepped up before the two fresh graves and dropped to her knees, grabbing a handful of dirt from each. She felt tears trace their way down her cheeks. "… ashes to ashes," she said, letting the dirt slip from her fingers. "… dust to dust."

She wept until the tears, once again, wouldn't come. She lost track of time, awash in grief and a deep sense of helplessness. *Is this all there is for us?* she asked the heavens. *To be used and cast aside with such indifference?* She stayed there until the sun dipped low above the hills and dark clouds rolled out of the southwest, promising rain and thunder.

"It doesn't have to end like this," a familiar file-on-steel voice said from behind her. "With you ... down there ... weeping in the dirt."

A chill ran down her spine. Kneeling over the graves of her sisters, the soil damp with tears of anguish, she realized that perhaps destiny had brought her to Helvetia for some deeper, darker purpose. She rose slowly and turned to see the train master standing before her.

His cloak was once again pulled back, and his blue eyes gleamed like stars, even against his pale skin. His body, now that he stood before her, seemed crippled and bent, as if his long black robes hid a litany of horrific deformities.

"Who are you?" Anita asked. The man scared her, as if she gazed upon something not quite human ... something dark and dangerous.

"I told you. I'm the Train Master. My name is Raspa. And I get the sense that you have unfinished business with the town of Helvetia."

"I do," she replied. She felt the rage welling up within her. Impotent rage that had no outlet. "But what can I do?" She clenched her fists. "I'm alone, and there's a whole town."

"Let's just say that I can even the scales." He raised an eyebrow and a single, spindly digit. "But there is a price, my sweet. A heavy one."

"I don't care," she said with utter finality. A glimmer of hope rose within her. "If it will make this town pay for what happened to my sisters ... to all of them ... it will be worth it!" She shut her eyes tightly against the pain.

"Then we have an agreement?" he asked, and his face pulled back into a rictus of a smile.

"Anything," she said.

"*Agreed,*" he said.

* * *

Thunder rolled across the sky, reverberating inside the boxcar where Anita stood. She stared down at the black-cloaked tangle of limbs that was Raspa. He knelt upon the dusty, dull floor, a calligraphy brush in one hand, an ink-well filled with her blood in the other. He busied himself with the creation of a grand pattern, muttering in a strange tongue as he worked.

"I've made a deal with the Devil, haven't I?" Anita asked. She'd resigned herself to it.

"Who says I work for the Devil?" Raspa replied, quiet laughter slipping past his lips. "And even if I did, who says the Devil doesn't work for the Lord, eh? The Devil is just another angel, is he not?"

The statement shook Anita. "I guess I never thought of it that way."

"Not many do," Raspa said, chuckling. He clucked his tongue occasionally as he continued painting the pattern before him. "It's justice you seek, my dear. And Justice is the purview of the Almighty, is it not?" Another laugh. "Pillars of salt. Burning cities. Plagues. Pestilence. Rains of fire. All of those ... all of that vengeance ... that *retribution* ... it didn't come from the Devil, did it?"

"No," she said.

He continued his work for some time.

"There!" Raspa said finally. He rose slowly, almost painfully, and stepped back from the two-meter summoning circle traced upon the floor. The perimeter comprised two circles containing runes of a language Anita didn't recognize. A bold pentagram lay inscribed within, and at its center another double-circle encased more runes. The central ring of blood was just big enough for a her to stand in. "Do you remember the incantation, the words to bring forth your vengeance into this world?" Raspa hissed. He'd had her repeat the words before he started painting the circle.

"Yes."

A momentary flash of fear coursed through her at what she was about to do. Her resolve wavered, but her desire for a reckoning quickly swept away any trepidation. She stepped past Raspa and placed both feet into the center of the pentagram. She spread her arms just as he had shown her. Taking a deep breath, she uttered the bargain. *Abaddon, Chapthan thal-Fozza. Imla dan il-basthiment bil-qawwa thieghech. I mifthuha ruhi li gircievu inthi!*"

The pattern at her feet glowed brightly red then turned obsidian, traced with deep green lines of electricity. She felt a throb pound through her body, matching her quickening heartbeat. Black, smoky coils surrounded her, obscuring her sight, and the electricity seething through the pattern jumped up to writhe around her. Energy coursed through her body, and she screamed with the magnificent pain of it. The black tendrils coiling around her grew, became a swirling cocoon that thundered with energy.

She felt her flesh stripping way, and something dark and hungry passed through the gateway beneath her feet and slid into her soul. It was a manifestation of her rage, and it filled her to brimming … consumed every shred of fear and doubt within her.

The swirl of energy dissipated, the roar fading to a hiss and then nothingness. She stared down at Raspa, and at first she thought he had shrunk. Suddenly she realized that her head nearly touched the ceiling.

She looked down at her arms and then her body. She gasped, and the sound that came forth was not her voice at all, but a hissing, screeching sound, like that of some beast.

Her flesh and bone body was gone, replaced by a ghostly green form that she could almost see through. Her torso remained, and she could see long strands of wispy hair draped down her chest and swirling around her head almost like snakes. Her arms and grown long sinewy, stretching away from her almost twice as long as they had been, and they ended in hands with extended digits that ended in black talons as long as daggers. Her legs were gone, replaced by a long, snaking tail that coiled beneath her.

"You are vengeance incarnate," Raspa said solemnly.

"What you do now is entirely up to you … and your *sisters.*"

Anita felt something outside the boxcar … a presence … two of them, in fact. She turned away from Raspa and slithered up to the door. Sliding it open, she watched a dark-haired, green apparition glide in from her right. Another slithered over the roof of the boxcar. Both of them came to a standstill on the ground before her.

She smiled, exposing a ghostly mouth full of spine-like teeth. Carmen and Mariana's apparitions smiled back, their full heads of black hair floating in the air around them.

The three ghostly forms rose into the air before Raspa and swirled together, a familial embrace that lasted long seconds. No words were needed between the sisters. They stared at one another and then all three darted off into the darkness. One faded through the wall of the hotel, another through the nearest building. Anita headed straight for the jail. As she passed by the engine, she saw the ticket master staring at her through the window. His face dissolved and his body faded, replaced with a small, ghostly-green apparition that stared at her as she passed by.

* * *

"O'Connell! Bring me another beer, you curr!" Grady shouted. He leaned back in his chair, his head resting against the wall as he surveyed his domain like an emperor upon a throne.

A few miners stood at the bar, drinking quietly, and Grady's two friends stood beside the piano listening one of Grady's working girls, a buxom redhead, as she played a lively tune. Sheriff Turn and his deputy sat in a corner, talking quietly as they nursed their drinks. The other two working girls sat upon the laps of would-be customers at a table near the door.

A scream, heard distantly and muffled by walls, silenced the bar. Everyone turned towards the front doors. More screams filled the night, and then there were gunshots.

"What the hell was that?" Grady asked the room.

A litany of human screams—men and women alike, dotted by the occasional report of gunfire—became a cacophony of sound that pressed down upon those in the saloon. The screams started from the train platform, moving closer with each passing second.

Most of them moved away from the doors, hedging closer to both Grady and Turn. Their eyes were wide with fear. Those with pistols drew them.

Grady stood and looked at Turn. "You best go see what going on, *Sheriff,*" he said with a sneer.

Turn licked his lips nervously as everyone in the saloon stared at him.

"Come on, Smiley," Turn said, getting slowly out of his chair. He drew his own pistol and walked across the saloon with his deputy a few steps behind.

Turn made it to the open doors and scanned the street. Out of the corner of his eye he thought he saw a flash of green disappear through the front door of the jail. The screaming in the town drew closer, horrible cries of pain and terror filled him with dread. He looked down the street towards the train platform but saw nothing.

Turning back towards the jail, he saw it.

A God-awful, ghostly form raced towards him from the jail, it's black hair streaming behind it and long, black talons stretched out towards him. Smiley screamed in terror as Turn raised his pistol and fired.

The thing didn't even slow down. It came straight for him, and then he felt its talons slashing across his body as it swirled around him in a whirlwind of green and black.

Turn's screams of agony filled the saloon.

Everyone inside watched in horror as Turn's body flew apart in small pieces. Blood sprayed in a storm of crimson that covered the boards and doors.

It was over in seconds, and then the thing turned towards Smiley. He raised his own pistol and fired. The apparition's face, its eyes two burning stars, drew back into a wide, hungry grimace. It leapt upon Smiley and swirled around his body. His high-pitched screams were deafening as he came apart.

"Kill that thing!" Grady shouted from the back of the bar.

Every man with a pistol opened fire.

The green form darted to one of the men with a working girl and took off his head a slash of black talons. Then the next man's head went tumbling as both working girls screamed in horror. Gouts of blood sprayed into the air and covered them.

Bullets ricocheted and splinters flew in all directions and the deafening roar of gunfire filled the saloon.

The thing turned and swirled towards the piano. It slashed the throats of Grady's friends, covering the terrified face of the working girl with blood.

The room filled with smoke and blood and screams.

Grady, terrified to his bones, clambered over the staircase and ran up the stairs. He raced down the hall, tore open the door to his room, and slammed it shut behind him. He leapt over his bed and grabbed the Winchester rifle leaning against the wall.

"Oh Jesus …! Oh God …!" Grady kept repeating as the town died around him. The screaming below seemed to go on forever as he shoved shells into the rifle with shaking hands.

Finally, the screams downstairs went silent, although those outside continued, now coming from the buildings closer to the church.

He waited, aiming the rifle at the door. His heart pounded, and sweat dripped into his eyes.

"Oh Jesus …! Oh God …!" he said again, his voice hoarse.

With a sudden *THUD*, black talons pierced the door. The room filled with the sound of shattering wood as the door was torn from its hinges and thrown aside.

The thing beyond stared at Grady with eyes like green stars. They pierced his very soul, and he could feel the devil nipping at his heels.

"Oh JESUS …! Oh GOD …!" he cried. He pulled the trigger, sending a round straight through the heart of the thing slithering towards him. His ears rang with the gunshot. He levered another round into the chamber and fired again, aiming for its face. Again and again, he fired, until the hammer fell with an empty click.

The thing smiled at him, and as its mouth widened, its teeth seemed to stretch out.

Its hand darted out, talons piercing the metal and flesh of his shoulder. He screamed in agony as it lifted him off the ground. He struggled, his legs flailing as he beat against the thing with his metal fists.

It seemed to laugh at him, a grating, bestial sound that tore at Grady's mind. It raised its free hand and slashed across his belly. Again he screamed as his guts spilled out onto the floor in a splatter of blood, meat and shit.

It's mouth grew wider, and Grady looked into a blacked maw that disappeared into an abyss.

His last, terrified scream was cut off as it clamped down, biting his head off completely.

His legs shuddered once, and then the apparition dropped his headless body to the floor. What was left of Broden Grady crumpled in the corner, his left leg twitching with an irregular rhythm.

* * *

O'Connell stood frozen behind the bar. He—the entire room, in fact—was covered with blood. Bodies and what was left of them lay strewn everywhere. The three working girls crouched at his feet, shivering with shock. He couldn't understand why whatever had attacked the town had left the four of them alive. He held someone's pistol in a shaking hand, determined to protect the three women if he could.

The screaming outside stopped, and he wondered if he and the girls had been saved for last, some sort of ungodly dessert in a feeding frenzy. And then he saw it at the top of the stairs, a shimmering green shape glowing through the haze of gun smoke. Out of the corner of his eye he saw two more of the things slip through the front doors.

"God help us," he whispered.

The three apparitions slid towards the bar, the one from upstairs taking the lead. They stopped in front of him, all three staring at him with starry-bright eyes.

O'Connell held the pistol out, the barrel shaking as he pointed it at the nearest apparition. His eyes were wide with terror, but some shred of strength kept him from cowering.

The apparition pointed to the three women on the floor and raised a talon, indicating she wanted them to rise. "Stand," it hissed in an inhuman, screeching voice as it stared at them.

"I think it wants you to get up," O'Connell said, his voice wavering.

The three women looked up and slowly rose to their feet, hiding behind O'Connell as best they could.

"Free," it screeched as it pointed at the women. It raised its other hand and motioned for the women to spread out from behind O'Connell.

The women, shaking with fear, stepped out and faced the thing.

It nodded its head and then stared into O'Connell's eyes, those pinpoints of light boring into his soul.

"Help," it said.

Suddenly it occurred to him what ... *who* was standing before him. O'Connell nodded slowly, a promise to do as she willed.

"Anita?" he asked, wonder and fear filling his voice.

The apparition formed a grim smile, and then the two behind her did as well.

"*Free,*" it said once again.

Slowly, the three ghostly-green shapes turned and drifted out through the front doors. They turned to the right, passed the front window, and disappeared from view.

O'Connell moved around the bar and followed them. He stepped out into a silent night. Somewhere, a coyote howled once and then all was silent again.

The three apparitions made their way towards the train platform, with O'Connell thirty yards behind. They made it to the train engine and slithered up over its metal boiler, coiling and gliding around its surface. The whole train took on an unearthly, red glow.

O'Connell spotted a squat, green shape in the engine compartment, and then he heard the train whistle shriek into the night three times. A blast of steam engulfed the engine, and with a chug the train lurched forward. It slowly pulled away from the platform, and as the boxcar slid past him, he saw a short, spindly man with a ghostly-white face and impossibly long nose standing in the doorway.

The man waved in a friendly fashion as he went by, and then the train seemed to fade into the darkness. The sound of its engine faded as well, and O'Connell watched in awe as it simply disappeared from the tracks.

He stood there for a long time, staring into the darkness. Finally, he turned and returned to the saloon, determined to keep his promise.

About the Author

Quincy Allen, is a self-proclaimed cross-genre author. What that really means is that he's got enough ADHD to not stick with any single genre and, like his cooking, prefers to mix and match to suit his tastes of the day.

He has been published in multiple anthologies, online and print magazines as well as one omnibus. He's written for the Internet radio show *RadioSteam*. His novel *Chemical Burn*—a finalist in the Rocky Mountain Writers Association Colorado Gold Writing Contest—was first published in June of 2012 and is due out in 2014 in a newly revamped edition from Word Fire Press, which will be carrying the *Justin Case* series. His new novel *Jake Lasater: Blood Curse*, is also due out this year as well as a military sci-fi novel from Twisted Core Press. He works part-time as a tech-writer to pay his bills, does book design and eBook conversions for Word Fire Press by night, and lives in a lovely house that he considers his very own sanctuary.

A New Fuel

Ming Drake

Wisps of steam escaped the machine's pressure valves and mixed with the cloud of black smoke that continuously rose from its coal stacks. The pressure of the boiling steam drove pistons on either side of the contraption, pistons that where attached to a heavy steel wheel. Spikes protruding from the wheel's exterior provided traction and drove it forward.

A man sat astride the mechanical beast, the steam engine that powered the motorized bike at his back. The raging inferno of the coal stove in the engine sent waves of heat through the driver as he dropped another chunk of coal, obtained from a leather sack affixed to the machine just in front of his left knee, into a shoot that siphoned it into the stove.

More smoke billowed from the bike as he pulled a lever on the console in front of him and the contraption shot forward under a surge of released power. Leather gloved hands held handle bars that directed the howling beast down dirty roads.

* * *

Ripper yawned as he shoved the power level of his steam bike into the off position and locked the controls. Taking a moment to stoke the coal fire in case he needed to leave in a hurry, he closed the coal bag and set the lock on that as well. Smoke continued to billow out of the large creation as Ripper stood up and stretched, another yawn creeping around the edges of his lips.

Soot and smoke stained the worn exterior of the bar, an obvious den of thugs and cutthroats. Steel I-beams were welded onto the outside of the place in an attempt to strengthen the sagging bricks. Just the sort of place a man like him could blend in. The tall windows of the place were segmented into small six inch square sections, more of which were covered by pieces of wood or metal than still contained glass. A sign hanging from rusted chains above the door proclaimed the dismal place as the "Rutting Boar." Shaking his head, Ripper pushed open the door and wandered into the din of a bar room brawl in progress.

The rough patrons of the place paused in their combat as the stranger walked into their turf. The stranger was a vision of violence and menace as he calmly strode into the middle of the brawl on his way towards the bar. Thick black leather boots shod his feet, the toes covered over in rusting steel. Inch long spikes protruded in a row from the ankle of the boots to their sole on the back. Vambraces adorned his wrists and boasted additional rows of spikes along them, from the wrist up the entire arm. Brown leather pants hugged the stranger's legs, rips and holes roughly patched over with more worn leather. A heavy leather jacket covered the figure's upper frame, dripping dripped with chains and studded profusely with spikes. A heavy 2-inch diameter chain draped between the pockets of Ripper's dirt caked vest. His face was covered in soot except for around his eyes where the outline of his goggles kept them clean. The goggles were tinted glass contraptions that now were set on his forehead, resting on the bandana he wore.

The unnatural calm of the bar room broke into frenzied violence as Ripper continued his trek to the bar. A man built like a warhorse surged at Ripper, rage at an intruder twisting his face into a bestial snarl. Ripper raised his left hand and slammed it into the exposed stomach of the charging bull. Two blinks of astonishment were all the man could muster before he collapsed onto the alcohol smeared wooden floor of the establishment, groans of pain escaping his lips as he writhed in the muck. An area cleared around Ripper as he finished his walk across the bar, the locals giving him weary looks as they went back to pummeling each other, a far safer prospect than trying for the new guy.

"I'll take a glass of whatever you got that has some kick to it, lass." Ripper called as he set himself onto one of the stools at the bar.

Stretching again, Ripper pulled the bandana and goggles off his head and tossed them on the bar. The serving girl took a second glance at the man as he took off his head gear. All the hair on his head had been shaved off except for a stripe that ran from his forehead, down the center of his head, ending at the base of his skull. It was a style that she had seen in the pictures taken of the natives in the new world.

"Looks like you got enough kick of your own there stranger." The barmaid replied as she spilled bright blue liquid into a glass that had once heard of a state called clean. Sliding the drink down the bar, she gave Ripper a nod before continuing her rounds around the bar, refilling glasses and breaking questing fingers as need arose.

The din of the bar became a constant background noise as Ripper sat and studied the odd liquid in front of him. Yes he had asked for something with kick, but he was really expecting something that was either a dark brown in color or clear. This phosphorescent drink gave him pause. Shaking his head, he brought the glass to his lips and was about to take his first sip when the din of the fighting went silent.

Remembering his own welcome when he strode in, Ripper looked over his shoulder to see who the new unlucky victim was. Leaning against the door frame was a tall woman with shockingly white hair, all except a streak of red like a forelock. Pain twisted the pretty face beneath that forelock as she pushed herself away from the door frame and moved into the room. A long leather coat swayed around her accentuating the shapely, skin tight leather clad figure underneath. Pants split up the sides and held together with leather lacing dwelt under a bare midriff and burgundy corset, creating an impressive décolletage.

Like a pack of hungry sharks, the locals moved in on the obviously weakened woman, their eyes gleaming with the thrill of easy prey. The sight sickened Ripper. He put down his drink, untouched, and pulled a chain from his vest—a large and beaten pocket watch, about the size of his own fist, dangling from the end of the chain. With a sad smile on his face, he moved towards the crowd gathering around the lovely woman.

"Looks like we be getting a pretty one tonight boys!" one of the leering locals crowed as he reached out to take rough hold of the girl. The hand never made it to the lady's leather clad arm. Instead, the sickening sound of crushing bone and a howl of pain filled the space as the heavy weight of Ripper's watch pulverized the man's reaching hand.

"Don't you know that it's polite to offer a lady a drink before you go grabbing at her lad?" Ripper called, the buzz of displaced air accenting his words as the slightly bloodied watch spun like a morning star at the end of its thick chain.

With an inarticulate bellow of rage, the small mob of locals surged at Ripper like a many-limbed beast, some ghastly human imitation of a kraken from the deep. Shrugging his shoulders, Ripper waded into the beast, the watch cutting a path of pain through anyone stupid enough to get near it. Yet the carnage the flail inflicted seemed minor compared to what the wielder was doing. The spikes on Rippers vambraces, his boots, and even the ones on his jacket were being put to dangerous use as he punched, kicked and generally brawled his way through the crowd. Every swing of his hand or foot saw another man groaning and leaving the fight, nursing some painful wound or as they met the ground, walls, windows, bar, and anything else in their path as they dropped into the black sea of unconsciousness, some never to swim their way to the surface again.

Within moments the mayhem was over and Ripper stood in the center of a pile of locals. Blood dripped heavily from the watch turned flail and the spikes decorating the stranger. Some dripped from Ripper's nose, the result of an impact with a local's knee, and a cut had appeared above his left eye. Gingerly, he felt the cut as he turned towards the woman he had waded in to rescue. With a sweet smile of thanks, the woman collapsed.

Dropping his weapon, Ripper caught the woman before she managed to bounce off the floor. Worry etched itself on his face as he realized that his hands on her back were becoming even slicker with liquid than they had been after the fight.

"I think you are in need of a doctor lass," he whispered, concern filling his face and words.

"Too late for that love. Pretty sure the bullet shattered when it hit a rib and tore the living hell out of my insides. Good thing you came to my rescue though, I might have been a goner." She chuckled, fresh blood flecking to her lips to replace the dried blood that already stained them. "Now that you have valiantly defended my honor, can I get you to fulfill a dying woman's wish?"

"Quite now lass, I'll do what you ask of me, but I am still getting you to a doctor. I have seen many come back from worse then you have taken."

"Wonderful." She wheezed the word, almost getting it caught in her throat. Mustering her strength, she reached into a pocket on the inside of the long coat and pulled out a vial of glowing purple liquid. She slipped the vial into the inside pocket of Ripper's own jacket. "Good, now get that to … " a fit of coughing cut off her words as her body finally rebelled against the abuse it had suffered. Wheezing from the strain, she again tried to instruct Ripper, but her voice had fled with the coughing fit. With a shake of her head and a sad smile, the light fled from her eyes and her body went limp in Ripper's arms.

"Ah bloody hell, when I said I wanted a stone fox to drop dead in my arms, I didn't mean literally." Ripper cursed as he gently laid her body on the ground. "Didn't get a name … any name. Not her's, not the person this thing is supposed to go to, nothing." Cocking his head, Ripper listened to the silence in the suddenly empty bar and the faint sounds of sirens floating in on the breeze. "Great, and the local authorities are already on their way. How does this shit keep happening to me?"

Sighing, Ripper set the woman gently on the floor before standing up and wiping the blood from his hands onto his coat. Looking around he noticed that only one soul remained in the dingy tavern, the bar maid that he had talked to earlier. Her face was a mask of apathy as Ripper moved towards her, the sounds of the sirens in the distance beginning to close.

"Hey there lass, this woman came to a place like this even gravely injured. Any idea why she might do that?"

"How would I know what goes on in the minds of these people. Most of 'em are crazy anyhow." She replied, a subtle tremor to her voice.

"Look lass, I haven't time for games as those sirens are getting close, fast. This woman came here with a purpose, and given that you are the only person left in this dismal joint, I'm guessing you know what that might be," Ripper replied, closing the distance between the two with long strides and moving around the end of the counter that the woman was hiding behind. "Not like anything you tell me now is going to matter after all, the lady there is stone dead."

Looking from the dead body to the suddenly intimidating form of the man coming closer, the woman gulped and began to stammer. "Look, I don't know anything 'bout what's going on. All I know is that I was given a letter to give to someone who came in asking for the right thing. Was told it would be a striking woman that was doing the asking. That is all I know!" she blurted out, the fear she had kept firmly masked spilling from her as she confessed.

"No worries lass, that is commonly how things like this are done. I am guessing you got some small benefit in the doing of your part too. It seems that the task this lady had has fallen to me now, so if you wouldn't mind handing over that letter, I will be on my way," Ripper replied, a gentleness in his voice that worked to calm the frayed nerves of the barmaid.

"Fine, fine. I don't be wanting any more to do with all this. I'll have enough to handle explaining this to the authorities anyhow." With a newly resolute nod of her head, she reached into an inner pocket concealed in the pleats of her skirt and withdrew a sealed envelope. Setting it on the counter, she pushed it towards Ripper.

He caught the envelope and stuffed it in an inner pocket of his long coat. He retrieved his bandana and goggles before turning on his heel and briskly walking out of the dirty tavern,. Taking the few steps out front of the tavern in one leap, Ripper straddled his steam bike and slipped the lever out that had held the system in suspension while he was in the bar. The sirens were very close now, and Ripper could hear the sounds of steel wheels clattering on the cobbled streets as they came closer. Replacing the bandana and goggles on his head, Ripper turned his bike away from the siren and let the throttle lever out. The bike bucked as power surged through the system and sent the bike hurtling down the street, away from the looming authorities.

The steam powered bike tore down the cobbled streets, kicking up a plume of dirt as it sped away from the encroaching sirens. Ripper had only gone a few blocks when the distinctive sound of a motorized monstrosity came from the next street up ahead. Shaking his head and wondering why one of the authority groups had seen fit to circle around and approach the tavern from the opposite direction, Ripper let the throttle out on his bike. The steel wheels churned even faster as he sped towards the intersection just as the horseless carriage emerged from the side street. The creation looked a lot like a normal horse drawn carriage, if the thing had collided with a steam plant and somehow continued to operate.

A huge steam stack rose from the roof of the thing, and a platform was securely welded to the back of the carriage. On the platform was a large steel box with its top open and a man with a shovel standing in the center of the platform. A thick leather belt with rings on it encircled the man, and long chains ran from the two rings, securing him. The man steadily dipped his shovel into the steel box and tossed black coal into the roaring furnace at the back of the carriage. Steel plate reinforcements adorned the outside of the carriage, and the steel wheels had been outfitted with spikes to give them traction on any surface, much like the wheels that churned on Ripper's own bike.

The carriage was slow and ponderous as it came around the corner towards the small and agile bike bearing down on it. That seemed to be no matter for the mechanized brute as it moved into the center of the street and put as much of itself in the way as possible.

In front of the large steam stack was an amalgamation of tubes and wires that attached to a small bubble of metal with a long tube extending out of it. The tube swiveled towards the oncoming bike, and Ripper found out what it was as a brilliant flash erupted from the tip ad sent a 12 pound cannon ball at him. Leaning hard to one side, Ripper managed to dodge the incoming projectile as it collided with the street, sending slivers of broken stones into the air that tore through anything not protected. Ripper felt a few of those stone lodge themselves in the heavy leather of his long jacket as he righted his bike and aimed at a small opening around the side of the enemy.

Large gears could clanked in the workings of the cannon, the barrel trying to track Ripper as he came closer. Seconds before Rippers bike slid past the carriage, another round from the cannon soared past him and exploded the wall of a building just behind Ripper. The shock of the explosion was so close and fierce that Ripper almost lost control of the bike. Only quick reflexes saved him as he slipped past and continued his way down the street, stray shots from the cannon falling short as Ripper's machine took him far out of range of the ravaging carriage.

* * *

The roar of Ripper's bike filled the cavernous interior of the abandoned steel works, the sound reverberating off the concrete walls. Wincing at the noise, he pulled the bike to a stop and reduced the power control level to lessen the noise. Even still, it sounded like an angry caged tiger.

The steel works looked to have been abandoned for quite some time, dust lying thick on the floor and the paint on the concrete walls barely visible anymore. Ripper pulled the letter the barmaid had given him from his jacket and verified the address. With a shrug he slipped the letter back into his pocket and dismounted his ride.

No sooner had he moved away from his bike then the area within the abandoned factory began to fill with hardened grunts sporting an array of lethal implements. The crowd had everything from lead pipes to hydraulic powered drills and modified firearms. Shaking his head and laughing on the inside, Ripper raised his hands.

"No need to get ugly lads, just here on an errand. Which one of you might be the leader then?" he called, staring from one angry young face to another.

"That would be me." An older man replied as he made his way from the back of the crowd of youths. He was dressed in working clothes and a lab coat, a fine step up from the rags that the mob was wearing. "How did you know to come here stranger?"

"Had a run in with a vision in leather, but the poor doll was just too overcome with it all and died in my arms. Shoved a vial and promise onto me. That led me here." Ripper supplied, pointing at his pocket with one hand while keeping them raised above his head. "Don't suppose I can lower my arms then eh? I think you have me plenty well covered."

"You may, and why did this lovely doll entrust these things to you in her dying moments?"

"Just a cruel twist of fate. I happened to be the last bloke to offer her kindness as the bullet in her back stole her life. Think she would have trusted a street urchin with this if she had to though, seemed mighty important."

"It is and means a great deal more than you can imagine. If you will hand over the vial, my entourage will escort you away from here … minus your bike and cloths of course, there are proprieties to be fulfilled."

Shit Ripper thought, *Got to stall for an escape then.*

"Can't be doing that old timer. You see, I take promises made to dying lasses very seriously, and I need to be sure that you are the people that she meant this for and not just some street thugs in the right place at the right time." Ripper stalled, edging his way back towards his bike as carefully as he could.

"You can stop moving towards your bike stranger. I think that we might have reason to chat a little more anyways. If you will submit to having your arms bound, I will consider letting you leave with your gear after all is said and done. You will need to shut down your bike of course, though I will leave some guards for it," the older gentleman offered.

"That seems a right bit better of an offer then the last one you made. Think I will refrain from trying my luck here. Deal accepted." He nodded and turned to his bike. A couple of flipped switches and pulled levers and the heat from the coals was directed away from the steam chamber and towards an exhaust port. Satisfying himself that the coal would burn down without putting any stress on the rest of the machine, Ripper turned and brought his hands in front of himself, wrists pressed together.

At a signal from the leader, one of the youths handed his weapon to a compatriot and ran forward with a set of steel manacles that he fastened around Rippers wrists. Moving behind the big man, the boy gave him a shove to get him moving in the right direction.

Giving the thug a dirty look over his shoulder, Ripper followed the leader as he turned and headed away from the warehouse and towards a small building off to the side that looked to be a storage shed. Inside the shed was another door adorned with a clockwork puzzle lock on its face. It only took the leader a second to unlock the door and open it, a second that was much too fast for Ripper to decipher the combination for the lock. Stairs made of rusted steel descended from the door into the dimly lit depths.

After several minutes, the stairs finally ended in a long corridor, which in turn ended in a metal door. This one was not as intricately locked, but looked to be of at least ten inches of steel. It would require a hydraulic mechanism to actually open. The leader turned his face towards the lens of a viewing port set into the wall, and after a minute the sounds of machines could be heard as the door finally opened.

On the other side of the door was a vast underground workshop. There were dozens of people working on every manner of contraption. A set of grease stained men were even taking apart a dented and damaged steam chariot. From the looks of the beast, it had been procured from the authorities without their consent. Ripper smiled at the thought of that combat.

It was only a matter of a few minutes before Ripper was seated in a nice chair in a private office across a large desk from the leader, his hands still bound.

"Now then, what would your name be stranger?" The leader asked.

"I am known as Ripper, and you?"

"I am Randolph Weinheiner and I am a wanted man, though I imagine you could guess that, given my accommodations."

"Yeah, that wasn't hard to figure out, especially since the cops were after your lass when she came into that bar. Only way they ever would have come there and in such force. Unless it was to finally tear the place down, that is."

"Very true, very true. That item you were given is a secret that the government does not want to let out into the world. It is a new kind of power source. From what the mole told us, it is hundreds of times more powerful than coal. A vial the size of the one that Jess stole could power one of those steam chariots for a year. The problem is that the government plans to keep it for themselves to tighten their grip on this land. They are already driving the people into dust with their war, and that won't change in the least if we let them keep this new technology."

"Jess eh? Finally got a name. Anyways, that is all well and good, but as you can see, I am a rover. What has any of this to do with me other than the fact that I have a sweet spot for damsels in distress and a penchant for getting mixed up in other people's shit?"

"Well, that is just it. You are mixed up in this now, and the authorities in this land will want your head on a pike. My organization can offer you sanctuary if you are able to perform a simple task for us. That vial needs to get to a team of scientist we have at a bunker in the badlands outside the city. Given your bike and the fact that you made it away from the cops at the bar, I think you might be able to get this done for us."

"Really, just that? Sounds simple enough."

"It would be if Jess hadn't been caught stealing the vial. Now the powers of order and justice will have the entire city locked down and blockaded in an effort to find that vial and kill anyone they find associated with it. That would be you and me if you hadn't gathered." Randolph chuckled, pouring a thick auburn liquor into a glass on his desk from a bottle he pulled from one of the drawers.

Licking his lips as he watched the liquor pour, Ripper took a moment to think. Finally he rose and set his hands against the desk.

"I'll run this blockade for you, but I have a couple of requirements other than protection if I do it."

"And those would be?"

"I want some of this fuel and some time to adapt my bike to use it. If what you say is true, it will let me run that blockade easier and your scientists shouldn't need the whole vial to get the recipe. Get my bike down here, give me two days and half the vial and we have a deal." The light of inventive mischief sang in Rippers eyes as he laid out his demands.

"That is a mighty high price you are asking. I hope you are worth it. Though to be honest, I want to see that stuff in action anyways. I accept your deal as long as you allow me to assist in the modifications on your bike." The same insane glow began to light Randolf's eyes. Here he had found a man with a spirit akin to his own.

"It is a deal then!" Ripper laughed as he casually broke the large chain between the manacles on his wrists and held out his hand to shake on the agreement.

Shock and wonder passed quickly across Randolph's face before he held out his hand and shook Ripper's outstretched hand. As Ripper turned to head into the shop, Randolph stopped him.

"I will have a work area cleared and your bike brought down. Also, here is a key for your fancy new wrists bands. You know, I would have taken them off after we had agreed to terms."

Ripper looked down in bemusement at the manacles and the short lengths of dangling chains.

"I underestimate the strength of things when I get excited about a project, sorry about that."

* * *

The two days passed in blissful occupation for Ripper as he modified his bike to take the new fuel source. Over the two days he worked and talked with Randolph, he learned a great deal about the movement Randolph was a part of.

For years, the ruling power of the state had constantly been at war with its neighbors. As soon as one war ended, it would turn around and start another with someone else. The balance of power in the area never shifted either, it was as if the ruling powers of all these states were using these wars as nothing more them a means to oppress their citizens. At least, that was Randolph's theory.

The fact of it was that the people were little better than slaves at this point. The wars ensured that the government had the power to force them to work and the leverage to reduce their wages and living conditions because of the hardships of the wartime economy. That might have been accepted if the owners of the factories and the politicians in those owner's pockets did not live like royalty. The movement was an underground group working to bring the whole system crashing down around the fat cat's ears.

"Well, that should do it!" Ripper called as he made a final adjustment on an outlet valve. "I think the modifications are done. I have managed to make it so that the bike can run on either fuel and can switch with nothing but the flip of a lever. I figure that way I can save the new fuel for a boost when I need it."

"That is amazing work Ripper. I would not have expected such a mind to reside in such an imposing package. It was a pleasure to meet you. You leave in the morning then?" Randolph asked.

"Nah, I think I will leave at midnight tonight. That should get me to the blockade at around three in the morning. The guards should be tired and dull-witted at that point. Though I'll need to go catch some sleep before then." He chuckled as he gave his bike a loving pat and headed towards the cot he had rarely used in the last couple of days.

"Sounds good. You know where we need you to get that vial. Also, here is a letter of introduction. I am sure that they will find ample use for you in exchange for your protection should you choose to stick around. It was a pleasure working with you. Rest well." Clapping Ripper on the shoulder, Randolph handed the letter over and moved towards his office. Giant yawns betrayed his calm demeanor as he thought of his own cot in his office. Ripper had worked them both like demons, but the result was a creation of beauty. Randolph was sure that he would dream of starting work on creating his own bike.

* * *

The night air was cool on Ripper's face as he rode away from the abandoned warehouse and his new friend, wondering if he would ever get to work with Randolph again. Shrugging, he let the throttle lever out and gave the beast more power as he entered the straightaways leading away from the factory district.

The moon shown bright in the sky as Ripper pulled his bike away from the cover of the city's building and on to one of the major roads out of the area. Out there in the dark was a blockade that would try to stop him, but the thrill of the night and the roar of the engine assured Ripper that he would make it through. With a flick of his wrist, the door on the lantern attached to the front of the bike fell shut and sealed away the betraying glow. He wanted to be right on top of the enemy before they noticed him. A dream, really, given how loud his engine was, but one that he chose to indulge.

A mile passed under his wheels before he saw the blockade take form in the moonlight. The authorities had placed two of their giant carriages on the road as a barrier and extended a fence from those carriages out into the hard packed sand dunes surrounding the city, fierce shrubs crowning the tops of the dunes.

Ripper thought about options for only a minute as he sped towards the wall of steel. Lights flickered on as the guards at the station heard the oncoming bike. Figures could be seen climbing into the carriages and taking up positions behind cover with long rifles at the ready.

With a howl like a banshee, Ripper flicked the lever that disengaged the steam engine and engaged the systems with the new fuel. His steel wheels spun with insane force as the new system took hold. The bike heaved forward, accelerating at a rate Ripper had never before known. Time seemed to slow as the beast plunged towards the blockade, the massive power from the glowing blue liquid closing the distance between the two with mind numbing rapidity.

A grin of pure adrenaline spread across Ripper's face as he got his bike under control. A quarter of a mile before the blockade, Ripper leaned to the right and sent the bike hurtling off the main road and into the dunes, the sounds of rifle shots heralding his course change. With uncanny skill he wove his way through the dunes and finally lined up with one near the fence. Cackling like a madman, he let even more power into the bike as he hurtled towards the dune.

His theory was sound and proved accurate as the bike left the ground at the top of the dune and sailed over the fence, landing on the other side in an explosion of sand and plants. It took everything Ripper had to keep the bike under control as he landed, even with reducing the power flow to the engine while he was in the air. Sweating under the strain, he brought the bike back on course and aimed it at the road.

As he neared the hard packed road, he saw that the guards had seen enough to know that their prey was past them. With the slowness of a lumbering giant, the carriages where turning away from the city and starting to head down the road in pursuit.

The first cannon ball landed short of where Ripper finally emerged on the road, a shower of dirt obscuring the sight of the carriages from him. Ripper pointed the nose of his bike down the road and smiled once again. Cannonballs descended from the heavens and cratering the roadway as he opened up the throttle, revving the new engine to max and blazing away from the sluggish carriages. A plume of dust rose to the heavens behind him as the glory of this new speed and power filled his soul.

About the author:

Ming Drake is an archaeologist living in Denver CO and working in the four corners states. History and culture have always been a passion of his, and it is through the act of participant observation that he was dragged to his first Steampunk convention. Upon interacting with the people, the costumes, and the general atmosphere, he fell in love and has been avidly writing and creating characters and costumes in the genre ever since.

Ming Drake

This twist of fate is not all together unheard of. Mr. Drake grew up participating in LARPs and helping to build and run local haunted houses where he learned to be creative with props and costumes. Soon after, he began to dabble in writing and spends most of his time in the creation of something interesting and very possibly insane.

You can get in touch with him at mingdrake@gmail.com or find him on FaceBook.

Made in the USA
Charleston, SC
06 June 2014